MAN KILLS WOMAN

MAN
KILLS
WOMAN

D. L. Flusfeder

FARRAR, STRAUS & GIROUX
New York

Library of Congress Cataloging-in-Publication Data

Flusfeder, D. L.
Man kills woman / D. L. Flusfeder.
p.   cm.
1. Man-woman relationships—England—Fiction   2. Biographers—
England—Fiction.   I. Title.
PR6056.L77M3   1993
823'.914—dc20   93-21735   CIP

To Susan

MAN KILLS WOMAN

Y ou know how it started, and where. That afternoon on the Common, picnicking on the slope, looking down at Boston. We'd finished one bottle of wine and were getting to work with another and you still wouldn't tell me why you hated picnics so much and wouldn't allow me that this one was different. You held yourself so close in your blue summer dress. You brushed a wasp away from the curling slices of Italian meat and you looked at me solemnly. You hadn't been looking at me for a while. Then you took that envelope out of your bag. A silver stick of French lipstick had snuck inside and you lifted it out and looked at it as if you didn't know what it was for a moment, and then I think you smiled, dropped the lipstick into the bag, pushed back your brown hair, and held the envelope out to me as if you wanted me to reach for it just so you could yank it away again.

"Why *do* you hate them so much? Picnics."

"It doesn't matter. It's a silly word. I don't know. Have you ever written a biography?"

You knew perfectly well I hadn't.

"Would you like to? I think you'd be good."

You handed me the envelope. Three photographs and a crinkly obituary from an English newspaper dated 1980. I laid the photographs on the grass between us, shifted them slightly away from the focus of the late-afternoon sun.

"Who is he?"

Three photographs in order of age. I still have them. I'm looking at them now. In the first he's a pale solemn boy sitting on a piano stool. His hair is sticky with pomade and flattened down like a junior Jazz Age crooner. It's hard to get a fix on his face, there's no expression to hold you. Instead you look at the skinny wrists protruding from the stiff formal suit, the hands clasped into a cathedral, and, just above the italic imprint of the photographer—*Gerald of Norwich*—at his feet in polished boots hooked around the stem of the stool. I look at his face and maybe it's because there's no sense of anything going on inside, just the slightest suggestion of sickly haughtiness, that I look down at the boots again, the way they're hooked around the stool, because that's the only thing that gives you the sense that this is the photograph of a child.

In the second he's a handsome strong man, no longer quite young, with a grinning mouth beneath a matinee-idol mustache. He looks like a suave man. Behind him, there are sand dunes and a rough ocean and a German shepherd dog waiting with a stick in its mouth. The dog's master raises a cigarette to his grinning mouth and his black hair lifts in the wind.

The third one is blurred. He stands in color, pink-eyed from the flash, looking down at something metallic glinting upon a table. His chest is bare and even though he is getting old, with a gray mustache and a brown-freckled head, his chest is not an old man's chest. A blue ink stain curls around his navel. A mirror on the wall behind him reflects the white flash of the camera and below it, in shadows, the body of the photographer, a young woman, naked.

"Is that you?"

"Don't be tacky. Of course it isn't me. You want to do it? You'd have to go to England."

"Who is he?"

"I'll be coming back in a few months. We could sort of work together. You'd like that, wouldn't you?"

You said it so uncomfortably, unaccustomed to flirting to get what you wanted.

"Who is he?"

You smiled a sweet publisher's smile. "An English gentleman of leisure and letters. An adventurer and a war hero. A father and a husband. A monster."

"That's dumb. Nobody is a monster."

"He was a monster."

Nobody is a monster. People are okay and bad, a mixture. There's no such thing as good or evil anymore. I turned to the second photograph again. A hard sensual face, looked as if it belonged in ancient Rome.

"And what is he to you?"

"A good subject of a biography, that's all. A hero of his time. Biographies sell, didn't you know that? He was big in Japan, did some translations. Mishima, Tanizaki too, I think."

I reached for the obituary but you grabbed it away, replaced it along with the photographs inside the envelope and moved the package back toward your bag. Then you hesitated like a bad actress and looked at me.

"We'll give you a good advance for traveling expenses and the rest of it. Well? Are you going to do it?"

Of course I was going to do it. I needed the money, you knew that. There was someone I was running away from in Boston and you knew that too. A paid trip to England was appealing, and I wanted to see you again, and you'd made me realize this was the only way to make sure of that.

I put the envelope in my jacket pocket and we finished off the second bottle of wine. Your cheeks were flushed and that (and maybe your silence, but I was used to those) was the only sign of the liquor having taken any effect. Your office was being redecorated, so we arranged to meet the next day at a pizza parlor in the North End. I would sign some papers, ask some questions, be given the first third of my advance and receive what contact addresses you had of people who knew William Ivory, monster. I walked you to a tall glass building on Milk Street, received your dutiful red-wine kiss in front of the revolving door, and caught a bus out to Fenway Park. Roger Clemens was pitching. I read the obituary on the way. You know how it started, and where. You also knew why, but that you never told me. I had to work that out for myself.

WILLIAM IVORY

(1925–1980)

It is difficult to imagine a world without Will Ivory. He was a man of many parts: scholar, traveller, musician, therapist, novelist, translator; gifted beyond the ordinary run. He was an interested friend, a generous host, a proud father. A perfectionist in his own life, he was guilty perhaps of impatience with the faults of others; fools he never suffered gladly. But he was always forgiving. Soon you would be invited back to his Norfolk table for another of those splendid meals, always prepared by his own hands, with red wine flowing and brandy to follow. A splendid improviser. We who were lucky enough to be his friends would often toast the dawn to the accompaniment of his witty and fluent piano.

He was born at Hobart Hall near Norwich in 1925, the son of the Ambassador to the USA. The War interrupted his studies and his otherwise inevitable progress to the Royal Academy of Music. Ill-health, which plagued him throughout his life and to which he displayed a brave and stoical fortitude, kept him out of the armed services, but his work in London during the Blitz showed no little courage, and his heroism was rewarded with the George Medal.

After the War, and a "bohemian" episode among the artists and poets of Soho and Fitzrovia, he endured a brief period in business before his roving nature led him away from these shores for travels around Europe. He travelled widely, spending quite some time in France, and Japan in the 1960s; but he always returned to the Norfolk he loved, for which his family had an historic as well as a sentimental attachment.

Because of his many gifts, and his sometimes combative nature, he was not always the easiest of companions, but certainly the wittiest and most entertaining one I ever had the good fortune to encounter. Privileged by birth and of independent means, he never rested on his laurels nor relied upon his social position. Throughout his life, he worked as hard as any young man driven by need, and this perhaps goes some way to explaining the sad fact that neither of his marriages lasted. Sometimes spiky in debate, he was nevertheless an astute judge of the human psyche, famous for his diagnostic abilities.

His name came belatedly to the public notice in 1973 with his *Decadent Pleasures,* a wide-ranging historical and cultural study which was *un succès de scandale et* *d'estime.* It is only now that his novel *Morita* (1976) is gaining the attention it deserves.

A friend of Japan with a particular affinity for that great civilization, he translated many important works into English. His untimely death robs us of his future triumphs and leaves the world a meaner and less gentlemanly place.

A monster? That's what you called him. To me he sounded like a regular guy. I'd stand him a drink in a bar. Listen to his stories, maybe tell him some of mine. A little difficult in company, an opinionated bastard, I'm sure, but I liked the sound of the aristo-bohemian-traveler-therapist, and a war hero to boot. That's the trouble with you British women—you don't have the right respect for heroes. Did I ever tell you about Ted Williams? Luis Tiant? Bill "Spaceman" Lee? Or while we're on the subject, the Antichrist himself, lame Bill Buckner?

I read the obituary on the bus out to Fenway, and I read it over time and again as I spent two weeks in Boston dodging the angry words and sick fading smile of a girl named Mary and the wheedling attentions of a bunch of impoverished band-leaders; and I read it again after meeting you that brief time in the North End pizza parlor where you apologized for the money not being ready and you gave me a date when you promised to send it on, poste restante, American Express. Then you left me with an airplane ticket and a small wad of sterling and an untouched glass of wine in front of the place where you'd been sitting (and you'd blamed the slowness of it all on office politics and I could see that—an untested biographer on an international mission raises some eyebrows I'm sure in corporate buildings). And I read the obit again on the plane over to England; and I read it for probably the hundredth time after I checked into the fancy hotel in the west of London. It didn't reveal any more. I kept it out though, along with copies of the notices I'd faxed into British journals advertising my interest in William Ivory, 1925–1980, and asking for personal testimony from anyone who had known him. I slipped the three photos into the gilt-rimmed wooden frame of the vanity-table mirror.

8

You'd booked me into the kind of place where room service comes on silver plates and you leave your shoes outside your door at night for a guy called Boots to take away and clean. I wanted you there in my fancy room. Sitting flushed with liquor on the leather armchair by the French windows that led out to the balcony. Fixing your hair at the vanity table, the mirror reflecting the oil painting of a racehorse above the wide brass-handled bed. Hanging up your clothes in the walk-in closet. Hunting with me through the TV channels, remembering this isn't America, even though there are two New York cop shows on, dimly remembered from canceled runs a few seasons back, and a football highlights show and a Bugs Bunny extravaganza. Laying out your jars and bottles and tubes along the marbled sink top, a rainbow pattern of conformity and indulgence, Nivea, Floris, Clinique, Chanel, Body Shop, Annick Goutal, Clarins, Helena Rubinstein, Elizabeth Arden, Revlon, Max Factor, Guerlain, Christian Dior, Boots No. 7, Mary Quant, Bourjois, Yardley, Shiseido, Lancôme, Estée Lauder, assorted higgledy-piggledy, refracting the overhead neon into promiscuous lines of broken color. (But that came later, didn't it? I didn't know about them then. Stick to the right order, Tierney, struggle to make this true, otherwise there's no point to it at all.)

I walked out onto the balcony. Fancy whores down in the street in business vampire outfits smoking cigarettes. I joined them in a smoke, invisible three stories up. I flicked the burning butt out into the street when I was done with it and they paid it no heed. And somehow that moment made me realize that I didn't want you there at all, not at all. You'd set us up on the start of something. A fairy tale of sorts: you, me, a quest, and a monster. But not a monster to kill; one, instead, to bring back from the dead.

I went downstairs and drank tiny measures of Irish whiskey in a bar the color of mud, sitting in my creased linen suit feeling like a bruiser. I leered at women with the confident zaniness that jet lag brings, and exchanged discreet confidences about the weather either side of the Atlantic with a bartender whose shiny wig was made of the same stuff as his dicky-bow.

I went back up to my room when one of the fashion harpies at the bar started to show interest. You would laugh at this if you could, but I was keeping myself pure, for you.

Two messages had been slipped under my door, *While You Were Out* on hotel stationery, printed copperplate italic. Both were responses to my advertisements. Julian Brougham Calder and Nicholas Wheel. Brougham Calder (two words, no hyphen, the message commanded, a strict prescription written in brackets beside his name) left a home telephone number. No number for Wheel, just the address of a bar in Chelsea, and a time and a word. Tomorrow.

But first, Helen Ivory. One of two meetings that I'd managed to set up before leaving the States—the other, in several days' time, down in Brighton, was with Roland Gibbs, Ivory's generous obituarist. But first, Helen Ivory. Tea at Fortnum & Mason. The Fountain Room.

Like a woman wrapped skin-tight in clinging plastic, her look was of a preserved dead thing, flesh smoothly lined, sickly to behold (hear this? I'm learning to talk like him!), eyes dull and black, a string of pearls harsh against her dead, scrawny throat. She'd described herself in different words, but equally cruel and dispassionate ones, and she wasn't hard to find, white-haired, black-dressed, shaking as she smoked a cigarette that was flattened on one side. The shaking was the real giveaway. A diseased friend of Parkinson's, she'd said over the long-distance line, a woman who'd got too old and didn't know how to stop.

She offered me a hand and I didn't know whether to kiss it, shake it, or find a specimen jar to pack it in. I held it very carefully, looked at the veins and liver spots which together formed an illegible map to the land of the old, and then, when I started to think I'd been looking at it too long, I told her how much I admired her rings.

"Paste. Sit down. You make me dizzy."

The shakes seemed the only alive thing about her. She ordered cheese on toast by some fancy name for the two of us and a pot of Lapsang tea to go with it. She was very grand.

"This was once a rather beautiful place. They ruined it. A few years ago. By lowering the ceiling. Don't you prefer high ceilings? I still come here. Out of habit. Some people despise habit. I cleave to it. And the service is good too. They don't rush you and they don't seem to mind you if you're ugly."

I tried to say something flattering.

"Thank you. You're very gallant. What is your view on habit? My late husband despised habit. Do you know Prince Boothby? He was a Regency fop so refined that he. Ended his life because it was such an awful bore dressing. And undressing every day. Sometimes I know. How he must have felt. Does my Parkinsonianism put you off? I rather think it might."

The food arrived and I was surprised at the way she shoveled it home. For a half-dead thing she could sure put it away. Only a little of it spilled before it got to her mouth.

"You are interested in my late husband? He was a very interesting man. He interested me. It would probably be accurate to say he fascinated me. Like a snake. With a rabbit. Maybe that's a little too bald. After all. I was a very knowing· rabbit. And I wasn't a spring chicken. I was older than he. I was quite a rich rabbit too. But that was a long time ago. Are you aware. Of the plight of the Albanians?"

She kept talking. She wouldn't stop. I wish this could make you cry. She was like someone who hadn't spoken to anyone but shopgirls and waitresses for at least a decade. She talked on about the Albanians in her fragile staccato for as long as it took us to get rid of two pots of tea. She was on a church committee which organized packages of clothes and medicines to ship out to Tirana. She touched me for a donation and I slipped her a traveler's check from the pile you had bought for me.

"Thank you. It's very pretty. Is it currency?"

I assured her it was.

"American, isn't it? I rather thought. You were an American."

"I'm from Boston."

"That's a pretty little town. I've been there. Isn't that where Henry James originated?"

"Maybe. I always thought he was from New York."

"I'm afraid I've always found his books. Somewhat repugnant."

"You prefer something a little racier?"

"I used often to go to New York. On family business. I would have papers to sign. Decisions to pretend to make. Fortunately.

My late husband learned how to protect me. From all of that. Would you mind terribly looking the other way? I have some pills to take. It's a vanity of mine. Not to like being observed. When I take medicines."

She hid the lower half of her nodding face behind a napkin and made several passes at her handbag before her fingers managed to find their way inside. I turned my chair away. The restaurant had been crowded when I arrived; it was now almost empty. Just a few clutches of mother and daughter combination shoppers, and at the soda fountain, one fat man in a pinstriped suit who was delicately spooning marshmallow clouds of ice cream to his face.

"Thank you. You're very kind. Gallant. I'm afraid I must make. Rather grisly company. What is your interest in my late husband?"

I told her about the biography. "I have to admit," I said, "that you're the first person I've seen. I'm trying to meet people who knew him, start from there. To make sense of a person's life, I've not done this kind of thing before, I'm a journalist mostly, this is all very confusing to me."

"Quite. And I'm the first person you've seen. Who was it that commissioned this. Biography?"

"A woman named Dorothy Burton. In Boston. An English-woman."

"She knew him? A contemporary of his, perhaps?"

"No, she didn't know him. I don't think she did. She's a young woman. She didn't say she knew him. I don't think she did."

"And what manner of book is this to be? I hear of a rather personal trend in biographies nowadays. I'm afraid I don't think. I can approve of that. The betrayal of past intimacies."

"It depends what I'm told. As it stands, all I have is a newspaper obituary. That's all I know so far."

"He was a very remarkable man."

"So I gather. How long were you married?"

"We were married in nineteen fifty-six. He was thirty-one. I was older. He was remarried in nineteen sixty-nine I believe."

"You remarried too?"

"I was born a Roman Catholic. I remain a Roman Catholic. I was only married once."

"I notice you still wear a wedding ring."

"Conventional religion did not mean. That much. To my late husband."

"Are you saying you don't believe in divorce?"

"I believe in a lot of things. I am perfectly capable of belief in impossible things. That is the blessing of faith. I follow the teachings of the Church on all matters."

This was already getting murky.

"Can I interpret that as meaning you were never divorced?"

She nodded her head and shook her head, but she was doing that already. She put another of her funnily shaped cigarettes into her mouth and I followed it around with a match until it was lit.

"Was it a happy marriage?"

"I cannot answer that question. I cannot begin to. It is an impossible question."

"You had children?"

"Two. One of each."

"Names of?"

"Matthew and Deborah."

"How old are they?"

"Matthew was born in nineteen sixty. Deborah in nineteen sixty-two."

"You see them much?"

"We were seldom. A close family. Deborah sends me. Two cards each year. One on my birthday. The last was from Montreal. The other on the anniversary of my marriage. Matthew lives in a mews house in Chelsea. He sends me money through a solicitor. Which is. As much. Contact. As he can bear. Does this sound too sad?"

"They were closer to their father?"

"He was a powerful man. He had a powerful effect on everybody. His children included. He was a strong man. Not an especially demonstrative. Man. I am finding this difficult. Perhaps we could stop."

"I would like to continue this another time, if you could do that."

"You have my telephone number. Please call me in two or three. Days. And we will arrange. Something. How did you come by my telephone number?"

"Dorothy Burton. The woman who commissioned the book. She gave it to me."

"I do not know a Dorothy Burton. Whom else did she arrange for you to call?"

"Just you, and Roland Gibbs. He wrote your husband's obituary. And I'm arranging to meet someone called Julian Brougham Calder and someone called Nicholas Wheel."

She colored slightly. "Forgive me for correcting you. English names can be hazardous. To the outsider. It has actually no *f* sound. Whatsoever. It is pronounced '*Broom* Calder.' Like the sweeping device. You will enjoy his company. The others I'm afraid. I don't know. And now I really do have to go. Perhaps you will walk me. To my bus stop?"

She shook herself inside an astrakhan coat, the kind that girls I knew at school would pounce upon in neighborhood thrift stores, and leaned lightly on my arm. We walked out through the food hall and onto Piccadilly, which was a riot of road maintenance and buses and cabs and tourists in Burberrys and English kids dressed for some reason maybe a sociologist would understand, or a witch doctor, in the suburban uniforms of 1960s America. Helen Ivory pulled more nervously on my arm when we were outside, as if the world was too loud and bright a place for her.

I tried to persuade her to catch a cab home but she wouldn't hear of it. "I have a free. Bus pass," she told me, in a tone that seemed to approach pride. After a couple of false turns we found her stop and I waited silently along with her until the bus had come. I helped her onto the platform and watched her through the glass as she permitted herself to fall into a seat. She gave me a wave and pulled her face into something like a smile. I wandered around until I came to a pub where I dove inside and drank two quick tiny whiskeys. She'd looked sadder when we left than when I'd arrived and that made me feel bad. The whiskeys lifted away some of the strain of English politeness and I ordered another and that made me feel better, and then I had another.

When I got back to the room I pulled out the tape machine hidden in my suit pocket. I transcribed her sounds onto a yellow legal pad and when that was done I contemplated the words written there and tried to decipher what I'd learned about William Ivory beyond the legal fact that he had never divorced the first of his widows and the emotional fact that she still loved him.

A shrieking clarinet solo missing out the difficult notes, an old man's rhythm on a plodding bass plucked out by a pizza-faced boy hiding his complexion behind a goatee and beret, an avalanche of percussion from a long-haired boy in shorts and faded tour T-shirt whose eyes kept fixing on the very few girls in the audience, a sax and trumpet duo in ill-fitting dead-men's clothes squeaking and farting accidental sounds, and throughout it all a frantic procession of pretty half-melodies lightly coaxed out of the piano by a small man with balding shaggy hair roughly peroxided; he muttered to himself as he played, like an amnesiac searching for a familiar tune.

Nick Wheel was on the bandstand, that's what the man at the door had told me, so I took a table in that basement bar. A free table wasn't hard to find. I munched on a burger that halfheartedly claimed to be beef and tried to guess which one was my man. I figured the pianist. I had nothing to go on, but Ivory had played the piano, I knew that, and the pianist seemed marginally the most interesting one of the band. Each time they managed to get to the end of a number, a hopeful murmur rose up from the thin crowd, only to die down again when they lurched into another.

I was joined at my table by a flipper, there used to be a whole school of them, those birth-drug victims, out near Cambridge, Mass. It was across the way from a restricted-membership golf club where we used to go hunt for lost balls to sell back to the club pro. We'd see them sometimes, near the rough on the seventeenth hole, sprinting apologetically in the school grounds. This one was dressed in black jeans with a heavy studded belt, kung fu shoes, a blue denim shirt cut off at the sleeves, and a red bandanna. Razored hair above a bruised scarred face. His short arm flaps were clapping a pint of beer.

"Sit here?" he asked when he already was.

"Sure. Help yourself."

"You're a Yank." He sluiced some beer around his mouth, gulped it down, and wiped off the foam by nimbly stroking his knee across his face. His observation didn't seem to require much of an answer so I didn't give him one.

"I said you're a Yank."

"I heard you."

The clarinetist was getting into his stride again so the flipper had to shout to make himself heard. He had a thin aggressive voice.

"My name's Butcher Bob. I'm a killer. I'm a Yank-killer."

"Groovy. Get a lot of work?"

The music died right down, so Butcher Bob settled into his favorite voice, a soft braggartly whine.

"Do you know what the most common dream is in this country?"

"Tell me."

"Do you know? DO YOU KNOW? The most common dream in this country is having tea with the Queen. I think that's fucking pathetic." He spat into his beer, started to look pleased with himself, and leaned forward. "And do you know what most men's worst nightmare is? Their very biggest fear?"

"Tell me."

"You don't know do you. You're a fucking Yank. You don't know anything. I'm a political radical. Do you know what the most macho fucking man's very biggest fear is?"

"Surprise me."

"I'll tell you. The most macho fucking medallion fucking man's biggest fear is getting beaten up by a midget. Did you know that? Surveys prove it."

The musicians had left the bandstand. The drummer joined a table of long-haired girls. The piano player was already standing by the bar. The others had taken a table together and were silently drinking beers from the bottle.

"And I'll tell you something else. Do you know what is much much worse than getting done over by a midget? Much more PSYCHO-logi-cal-ly damaging than that? It's being done over by a fucking thalidomide. Do you want to step outside? I'll show you."

"Another time maybe. I'm meeting somebody here."

"Who are you meeting? I probably know her. I know everybody. But listen to me, I'm offering you a genuine cultural cross-reference experience. And if you don't come outside and I mean RIGHT NOW! then you know what I'll do. I'll go there by myself and I'll fucking wait for you. You calling me a liar?"

"I'm meeting someone called Nicholas Wheel. You know him?"

"Nick Wheel. I fucking know Nick Wheel. He plays the piano. You a friend of his? I don't care if you're a friend of his or not. I'm going to finish my pint and go outside and start waiting. A-a-a-and I'm going to count the minutes and every minute you're not there you're going to get it even worse, you know what I'm saying? I carry kung fu death stars, you want to see them? Oi, Nicky, this Yankee cunt says he's a friend of yours. You want me to bring him back after I'm done with him? Come on you, we're going outside."

He dropped his beer glass to the floor and started to flap at me with his right arm. Stinging slaps to the side of the face. I swatted them away and he coiled down into a karate crouch. The piano player had appeared behind him. He was grinning, showing off bad English teeth. I got up and the flipper aimed a kick at my head which caught me on the shoulder. I managed not to stagger back and pretended not to notice it.

"You Nicholas Wheel? My name's Richard Tierney. I got your message."

"Ye-e-e-ah." He drawled the word out and finished it off with a giggle.

"He says he knows you. He says he's meeting you here. I say I'm going to fucking do him."

"You called me at my hotel. I put an ad in. About William Ivory."

"I did? Yeah I did. You enjoy the set?"

The flipper made another sortie at me, this time with his head into my belly. I got him by the shoulders and pushed him away but not before he'd winded me a little.

"You going to call this creep off?"

"Let's sit down. I want to talk to this man, Butch. Leave it out a moment, yeah?"

The flipper sat down, lifted his beer glass up off the floor with his feet, and poured the dregs over his head. "Did you spill my pint? Yeah? All right, Nicky, I'm going. But you, cunt, you're a dead man, son."

Our aggressive sport swaggered away through double doors and up a fire-escape exit. I sat down again. Nick Wheel took the flipper's chair. Someone put a record on and music started up again, loud and ugly.

"Did you enjoy the set?!" he shouted.

"No!" I shouted back. "You were okay but the rest were shit!"

The music was abruptly lowered and we could talk like we meant it.

"How did you know William Ivory?" I asked.

"He was my father."

"What?"

"He was my brother. My friend. My end. My sister. My blister. My next-door neighbor. My baby. My maybe."

"All these things."

"Me bruvver. Me lover."

He grinned at me like a schoolboy showing a teacher his special thing. "He raped me. The rapist."

"Raped you?"

"The rapist."

He repeated the same two words over and over with different intonations and in different voices until the penny dropped. "He was your therapist?"

"The rapist. Yes."

He was like a boy, silly teasing manner. But he was older than a boy. His peroxided hair was already thinned out. There were lines around his dark eyes and lines beginning to pucker around his mouth.

"How old are you?"

"How old are you? Do you fancy me? I bet my dad's bigger than your dad. My dad's a policeman."

"My dad's a soldier."

"My dad's a general."

"You win."

"My dad's a field marshal, and he's a woman. To boot. Do you think I've got problems? Acne? Learn to live with it. Male pattern baldness—it's the scourge of the species."

"I think your friend's got problems."

"Butch? You know why he's called Butcher Bob?"

"I can guess."

"I bet you can't."

"Because he likes to butcher people?"

"Because his name is Bob." He looked at me proudly.

"I should have guessed."

"He used to be called Kentish Town Bob. But then he moved in above a butcher's shop."

"William Ivory."

"Butcher Bill."

"Can we talk about him? Isn't that what we're here for?"

"I'd love to. Honest Injun. But my public is waiting."

In the brighter second-set light, you could see the acne on the faces of the band. Only the romantic drummer and the obstreperous piano player had clean faces. The music they played was as bad as ever and I left before the end of the first number. The flipper was waiting for me outside. He was shivering and wet and hungry for a fight. I put my hand out to hail a cab and held him off until one arrived. I left him furious and cursing and headed back to my hotel.

T he knock on the door came at around 3:30. Nick Wheel was there in the corridor, standing casually on top of a pair of shoes which I'd left out for Boots.

"You really did for Bob. Nice dressing gown. Can I come in? I've got stuff to tell you. Anything to drink? I love drinking. I love being drunk. That's the best."

We cracked open miniatures of Scotch whisky from the mini-bar. He sat on the bed. I took an armchair.

"Butch wanted to come with me. He thinks you look just like Lee Marvin. He wants to kill you. Doesn't think you take him seriously."

"He gets a little tiresome after a while."

"Nice dressing gown. Suits you. Have you got one for me? People ought to dress the same, don't you think? Eradicate class differences. If you got one for me I could wear it and someone wouldn't be able to tell us apart. If Butch followed me here. I don't think he did, but he might of, you never know, then it would be safer for you, wouldn't it? he wouldn't be able to tell us apart. What do you think? Strategy."

"It's the only one I've got. Skinflint hotel."

"Yeah. Skinflint. Skinful. Skinhead, that's what Butch used to be. What are you fiddling about with in your jacket? Have you got a gun in there or are you just pleased to—"

"You said you had things to tell me."

"These go down a bit quick. I've finished mine. Have you finished yours?"

"Have another. Have three. The rapist?"

"You only rape what you sow . . . Mom! Uncle Jack, he, he he raped me! The shame, and me a vegan . . . Do you like London?"

Did I like London? London was a chore, a dull setting, dull

as Wheel's puns and homonyms, for an impossible task, a gray infirm place where everything was fake. But not American fake, not Las Vegas fake, just solemn-bad-sham-amateur fake like the acne boys in a basement club who played feelingless bebop with the wrong kinds of sounds and the right cuts of suits; not cruel-big-hungry-Caesar fake like the Kennedys or stop-your-heart-this-could-be-our-year fake like the Red Sox, but lying fake, ugly fake, a-flipper-pretending-to-be-a-thug fake, a-city-broken-into-a-thousand-pieces-and-glued-randomly-shabbily-together fake, David Niven fake instead of John Wayne fake: the-past-was-too-long-ago fake instead of there's-something-we're-missing fake, I-know-we-had-it-yesterday fake.

So far, I'd got stuck on you; I'd nearly beat up a man with no arms; exchanged courtly meaningless chat with a widow who seemed deader than her husband; and listened to bad jazz and worse puns. And under all this, a dead man to find, without a map to the cemetery.

"I'm tired. Tell me about William Ivory. I haven't got the patience."

"Like an unsuccessful doctor, yeah? You heard of schizophrenia?"

"Sure. Sure I've heard of schizophrenia."

"What about hebephrenia? Paranoia? Tourette's syndrome? Manic depression? Epilepsy, petit mal and grand? Hysteria? Neurosis, psychosis, regular or amphetamine, alcoholic poisoning, adolescent angst, normality?"

"Most of those too."

"Diagnosis? You heard of diagnosis? And the plural. You know—diagnoses. All those are diagnoses. Of me. Yours truly."

"By Ivory?"

"No. By psychiatrists. By analysts. By doctors. Thin doctors, fat doctors, doctors with beards, biblical like Moses, doctors with little hepcat goatees, woman doctors, androgynous doctors, doctors in clinics, in offices, in converted rooms of West Hampstead houses, doctors with couches and signed photographs of Herr Meister Fraud, doctors who play music and hug you, doctors who shout at you, doctors who want you to take all your clothes off and call them Daddy, doctors with Reichian fucking orgone machines, Jungian doctors, Kleinian doctors, Lacanian doctors, Laingian doctors, Zen doctors, state doctors, private doctors, doctors who aren't doctors really but call themselves doctors, and doctors who are doctors but don't like to call themselves doctor because it's distancing, and you're not a patient you're an analysand, or because it's a reification of state power, and want you to call them Larry or Ronnie or Leon, or Julia."

"Or William?"

"No. Not William. Mister Ivory. Always. I only found out his first name when . . ."

"When what?"

"Don't push me. I'll fall over."

"What did he call you?"

"Nicky. Sometimes Nicholas."

"And what was his diagnosis?"

Wheel finished his third miniature and held out his hand for another. "That's private. That's between me and my doctor."

"You're wasting my fucking time."

"That's what he told me. Not in so many words. He didn't use vulgar language. He told me I was a professional patient. Said my family was fucking me up. Families do that. Families kill you. You know that line of David Cooper—'There's no such thing as natural death: all deaths are either suicide or murder'?"

"Which was he? Ivory."

"I don't know, I never thought of it like that. That's clever."

"So what happened? When he told you you were wasting his time."

"I fucked his daughter. Up the bum."

"Why?"

"That's the way she liked it."

"What did he do?"

"He sold tickets so people could watch. Hey, only joshing. It impressed him. My desire for change, he said. It worked. He took me back into treatment."

"And what was his treatment?"

"I talked. He listened. Then he talked and I listened. We

took turns. Sometimes we talked both at the same time and sometimes neither of us said anything for the whole session. Sometimes we played the piano together. He knew his Ravel and Debussy. I showed him jazz. He knew it already. I think he saved my life."

"You liked him?"

"I hated him. He was horrible to me. I never knew what was in his mind. I miss him."

"What about his daughter?"

"I don't know. She liked me to play the piano for her. She was probably more fucked up than I was. Give me another drink. I want to get drunk. Who are you anyway? Why do you care about Ivory?"

"What I said in the ad. I'm writing a biography of the man for an American publisher. What was he like as a therapist?"

"He used to say that almost nothing can change a person after they're about seven, only something really mind-shattering, something really big, like war. Sometimes he called it the apocalypse and sometimes he just called it the Big Thing. Capital B, capital T. He aimed to be the Big Thing to his patients. I think it usually worked." Wheel stretched out on the bed. "Gosh. It's hot in here, Mister Tierney. I declare." A ghastly impression of a flirtatious Southern belle as he loosened the top button of his shirt to reveal pale hairless skin. "Do you want to sleep with me? Where are you from?"

"Boston. No. I don't want to sleep with you."

He flashed me a broken-toothed winning smile. "That's okay. Just asking. I better be off. Find Butch. Make him feel better. Do you want help? I'll work for you."

"Why?"

"Because you're an American. You'll pay me Yankee dollars. I like getting drunk. You need money to get drunk with. I can drive cars. I can ask people personal questions. I miss him."

He climbed off the bed, went to the vanity-table mirror and looked at the photographs of Ivory. He pulled them out to have a closer look. "Ugly solemn boy. Dirty old man. Handsome." He turned them over and read out the inscriptions on the backs. " 'To Mattie.' Who's Mattie? To my own little girl.'

'My darling wife' . . . You look like you haven't noticed those.
I thought a biographer was like a detective. Makes you defec-
tive. Have I got the job? Am I your boy?"

"You're too old." I shooed him out of my room. I didn't think
I'd ever see him again. I didn't think anything he'd said would
ever be of help but I had my professionalism to maintain. I
took the machine out of my jacket and wrote down his skewed
words as quickly as I could.

I woke up late. Disorientated. Old baseball pains in my knees and hips. The red digital clock on the TV set announced the time as 13:13 and I kept on staring at it until it said 13:14 and that made me feel a little safer. Dialed room service to send up a stack of toasted bagels with cream cheese and onions and lox, and they negotiated me down to a BLT on toasted white. Our kitchen prepares its own mayonnaise, the girl said, in an offhand sinister way.

The sandwich was bad. The mayo was tart with too much lemon. The bread was thin. Not enough bacon inside. I picked away the bacon and tomato and threw the rest out of the window for the birds to peck at. I padded around the room. Stared at the photos and examined the dedications on the backs. Formal pomaded boy on a piano stool, *To Mattie*. Who was Mattie? His son Matthew? But the handwriting looked too long ago for that. A child's gothic, faded by time. The next one. Smoking a cigarette, handsome on the coast, *To my own little girl*. His daughter? His wife? A floozy? And the final one, *My darling wife*. He was balding on that one. That couldn't be to Helen. They would have been long separated by then. And anyway you don't send ex-wives photographs of yourself taken by a naked woman. Must have been his second wife. No one had told me anything about her yet. Where was she?

Endured a shower—twin jets of hot and cold spurting out side by side. Then I climbed into my second-best linen suit and wandered out. Uniformed Guy at the desk (with name badge, Guy) gave me a clenched-teeth smile and directed me to the nearest bookstore.

I remember my mood as I walked along a sunny market street where they were selling vegetables and fish and bathroom utensils and gift boxes of European candies, through a resi-

dential square where bare-chested toddlers of every available
color ran in shrieking circles while their parents lounged on
the window ledges of their apartments smoking cigarettes and
reefers as music blasted out of their rooms to collide in a
pleasant cacophony in the center of the square, past a street
of fancy restaurants, Italian, French, fake-American, all full of
expensive people looking happy at what their money was
bringing them. And I felt happy for them too. I'd escaped from
Boston, it had needed escaping from, and even if I'd done a
cowardly cruel thing there was no past anymore, only mystery,
and I looked like Lee Marvin when he was young, and my only
responsibility was to the truth.

I returned to my hotel, which was looking grand and old
on its own residential square, and went up to my room (#244,
but you know that, you chose it for me) with my booty, *Decadent Pleasures* ("lavishly illustrated . . . a scholarly and thought-
provoking survey of history's excesses") and *Morita* ("disturbing
first-person narrative by Yukio Mishima's first lieutenant and
chosen assassin . . . with a grisly coda . . . stylish exploration
of darkness"). I browsed through the coffee-table book, taking
in pics of Ancient Rome, Ben Franklin at the Hellfire Club, the
fairy-tale castles of mad King Ludwig of Bavaria, Aleister Crowley, Gilles de Rais. Looked for a long while at the portrait of
the author, a delicate line drawing by Philippe Jullian of a
mustachioed dandy in a green suit leaning against a balcony
wall, and I remember then thinking about my own book. My
scholarly, thought-provoking, stylish exploration of William
Ivory (1925–1980). The black-and-white pic on the back-cover
flap of moody me; the photographs of the man himself dis-
tributed throughout the text, not cheaply bundled together in
the middle; the cover? I wasn't sure about the cover, just a
simple photograph maybe, the one of Ivory in front of the
ocean with his German shepherd dog behind him (*To my own
little girl*), or maybe just his grim handsome face superimposed
over images of glamorous decadence with his name coupled
with my name, and a startling phrase as the title, probably a
quote of some kind taken from his own work; a thorough index
at the back, maybe a bibliography too; maybe a couple of

quotes on the flyleaf to show the depth of my thought; and a dedication, perhaps, to you.

It's kind of cold in this flat. I never did figure out the heating system and there's no one left to ask. Are you comfortable? Are you listening? Maybe I should get more lyrical or more demanding. Maybe I should teach myself to play the piano in the downstairs drawing room. Maybe I should give this place a clean. Throw away the crap in the fruit bowl. Go crazy with detergents on the kitchenette and bathroom floors. Make some long-distance calls and swallow my pride and take a great big bite out of a humble pie and reestablish my previous life. It's too late for that. I miss Boston. I miss baseball. The season will be all about pennant races by now. There's too much graffiti on the walls. The window is grimy. Rub a hole through the nicotine dirt to look down at the street and see nothing going down there at all. There was a moment when you were interested, wasn't there? When the Little Things all veered into sudden sight: the tired ladies with their supermarket carts, pausing mid-trundle to swipe their hands across perspiring foreheads; and the neighborhood kids striking their attitudes half mad with self-consciousness and all the more dangerous for that; and the office types trickling back from work with the same newspaper under all their arms; and even the cats, sleeking around the corners of houses and laying down to vigilant rest on top of stone fences. Forget about that. Enough. Push that back for now. We have all of time for that. Back. To when things were still confusing, when conflicting stories of Ivory got themselves told by an ancient bohemian with a hidden ax to grind.

D id you ever know a murderer?"

His voice spins out of the tape machine. Aristo drunken vowels. Wartime recollections. Make it louder. Turn up the volume.

"Did you ever know a murderer?" Insistent delight in the old man's voice. "How then would you picture one? Perhaps quiet and punctilious, a dry little mouse of a man with a worm of passion inside him, a Crippen? Or else a sly creeper with something rotten in his eyes like John Christie? Funny, isn't it? how so many of them wear specs. Do you believe myopia to be a function of the killing instinct?"

"I guess most of them look just like anybody else." My voice, clumsy in his company.

Julian Brougham Calder (I remember still finding it hard not to think of him as Bruffham) grabbed some breath. What's that sound? Did it startle you? It's only an old man breathing on magnetic tape. Let me set the scene for you. Woo you with words. Win you over with my powers of description. We were facing each other across a low table in a second-floor walkup club above a Greek taverna on a side street in Soho. It was a comfortable place, I liked it. Old beat-up armchairs which accepted your shape, dim lighting to flatter into invisibility cherry-blossom noses and varicose-veined complexions. A sallow unfriendly man behind the bar. Paintings on the walls, looked like slabs of meat in the perpetual twilight. Dark wood paneling weathered like the skin of a dying elephant.

The final time I would see him he would be dressed like an Elizabethan buffoon, drinking brandy through a straw. But that night, our first meeting, I didn't see him as a buffoon. My host was an elderly graceful man in a white corduroy suit and open-necked yellow shirt. His smooth skin was lightly dappled with alcoholic red. His hair was cut very short, a soft white stubble dotted across his head. He had a noble, bruised face, high cheekbones, brief well-made nose with a bump on the bridge. Start the tape again.

"I could tell you a murder story," he said. He looked down almost bashfully at the champagne in his glass. "If you like."

"Yes," I said. "Is it connected?"

He smiled expansively. "Everything, dear boy, is connected. Shall I begin?"

He took a deep breath and held it and uncrossed his legs and closed his eyes and rubbed his forehead vigorously like he was trying to start a fire, or maybe it was just what he had to do to give his memory the necessary kick-start.

"What do we require for our story? What are the elements? Consider your hard-boiled sorts in their corrupted cities, or even our own tame little drawing-room puzzles. We require a setting, then the careful introductions of our dramatis personae, we must watch them with careful detective eyes at the scene of the crime, will their behavior give us clues to motive?, and finally we shall bear witness to the grisly deed itself. We will begin with atmosphere and end in blood as all the best stories do.

"Our setting is London, the War, so let us remember it, the Blitzkrieg in all of its glory. I wrote about the period of course in my memoirs but there were stories the legal boys cut. I fought, it was a bloody campaign, but the legal boys won as little men often do, and anyway an eagle does not catch flies. The War. The Blitz. London at its best. Wonderful, privileged times. Don't let anyone palm you off with a picture of a smudge-faced cockney sparrow in a tin helmet whistling Vera Lynn while he navigates his bicycle around bomb sites where children and women wave sternly—'Good on ya, Bert,' 'Cheerio, Mabel, that Adolf's got a lesson to learn and I reckon we're the ones wot's gonna teach it . . .' Propaganda! Missis Miniver-ism! Those were shabby sentimental scenarios dreamed up by fat clever boys from the provinces skiving the services.

"The War was liberation! The city was our playground! Everything in flux. Look up to the sky. Bombs dropping like stars around our heads. Those boringly familiar things are suddenly, overnight, gone. You're on leave from your squadron, you're smoking a fag waiting for opening time and beside you a bus passing down an intact street is suddenly, magically, buried high off the ground in the roof of a new beautiful ruin where wildflowers will soon take root. Everything is for sale or the taking, you feel so alive breathing in that dangerous air, everything is possible when everybody is dressed for war." His florid thrilled voice dropped to an elegiac tone. "Like bluebell woods and bottles of whiskey good things never last for long. Even war grows weary. Later on, Londoners become a shabby anemic breed in tattered clothes, the aroma of rotting fish and open sewers and burning plaster fills the heavy brick-dust air, the Blitz is over and people need sleeping pills at night to stand the quiet. But this is 'forty-one, the grand debauch, things are fluid, up for grabs, chance and desire and violence are the currency of adventure, the pounds, the shillings, and the pence. Am I making myself clear?"

"Would you like me to refill your glass?"

"Don't bugger me with interruptions!" He clamped his mouth shut like he was denying me treasures contained there and he looked at his empty glass. After I'd refilled it, he started up again as if there had never been any bad feeling at all.

"We're toddling over to Fitzrovia. A charmed country where the word is king and beer prime minister. We're going to a small flat on Percy Street. The facade needs a paint job. Downstairs is the ironmonger's shop, over on the corner the Wheatsheaf where the boys are getting tight and the girls know what they're after. No bombs today, quiet alcoholic-haze days in the Fitzroy, the Marquis of Granby, the Burglars Rest. The pubs are calling but we're drifting off, not time for that yet, let's back to Percy Street, the flat above the ironmonger's, lace curtains, stillness, a patina of dirt over dark windows, move inside like a camera, three small rooms, mustard-painted walls decorated, if that's not too elegant a word, with dreary watercolors in the pastoral mode. In the largest room, once a dining room, there hangs from a hook a gilt birdcage that once held an albino macaw and still retains some of its desiccated droppings, odorless, in memoriam. Crumpled atop a paisley sofa is a tiny thin dame in a white dress crispy with dried wine stains. A candy-floss puff of yellow hair, yellow liverish skin, her hooked Levantine nose emitting a roaring oceanic elemental snore. It's the Countess F——, mad Eileen, la dame aux Benzedrines.

"Tread soft, you'll harm her to wake her, she's been up for four days, sleepless, not blinking, this amphetamine lush with an amphetamine flush in her cracked cheeks once albino, performing strange lurid dances on accidental streets, haunting the pubs and the clubs and the drinking dens and gambling parlors, squawking without words, she's gone beyond words, harsh calls like a bird cawing her enormous appetite for Benzedrine pills and cream puffs, that's all anybody has ever seen her eat, and now the pills have worn off, her body is in crumpled repose, and she will sleep for a day, maybe two, then the binge will begin anew.

"Young Will Ivory is in his room, a tidy oasis in that flat of desert dirt, a Debussy étude will be quietly playing upon his gramophone, he was no mean shakes as a piano player himself, you know, I'll admit that, derivative, but good. He's just returned from his shift at Westminster A.F.S. and he's removing his uniform, his smart blue fireman's uniform with its brass buttons and white sash for his ax. They're an odd breed the A.F.S., few of them are real firemen, a mixture of men with mild disability, some who were too old for the services, conshies, and—"

"Conshies?"

"For God's sake don't interrupt me. You want me to stop? I could stop, you know, just like that. Click my fingers and finish. More vino, Cunty! At least you're listening. People have lost the gift of listening. Cicero today would be derided as a bore and reduced to buttonholing old ladies at bus stops. You know why no one can listen? There's too much din, motorcars with pop pop parp fart engines, novelists screaming like politicians, everyone's a weatherman nowadays, belching hysterical bluster. There are no adagios anymore. You know what Trotsky said to Mayakovsky? 'You shout too much, who will hear you when you whisper?' Conscientious Objector, that's what a conshie is. But let me tell you this, there were men of greater distinction than our little Ivory in the A.F.S., Stephen Spender, William Sansom, not one of his colleagues knew that the modest Henry Yorke was an aristocrat and under the name Henry Green wrote the greatest novels of our generation, oh no, but Ivory, this our beardless youth, there's no hair on young Willy's handsome lip, and you know what they called him? 'The Honorable.' Don't get me wrong, it was not out of respect, it was a jeery remark. Let me tell you this, he was an oik."

"I thought he was an aristocrat? The ambassador's son?"

"You're interrupting again. Thank you, Cunty, have one for yourself, the Yank's paying. More wine, Rupert? Champagne to your real friends and real pain to your sham friends. Cheery ho."

I let him refill my glass. I didn't bother to correct him on my name.

"The Countess F——, some just call her Eileen, she's a generous-spirited, amphetamine-addicted, drink-dazzled, life-wasted, hopeless, silly creature. She's a hollow woman who does the occasional stint of washing-up at Claridges to supplement her inheritance, and she takes in lodgers who need a little succor and took in Ivory when his fortunes were low. They make a strange couple, the aristocrat and the arriviste. What brings them together? Money, possibly. Company, certainly, the Countess F—— cannot bear to be alone. Sex? I rather think not. Our teenaged Willy is an adolescent of fastidious taste. A harmony of temperaments? Seems unlikely." His voice got suddenly harsh like a bird's. "I'll tell you. Bloody social climbing, that's all. And on her part, a twisted motherly urge."

"Ivory had come to London from Norfolk?"

"So the story goes. He was a boy, perhaps fifteen? But he was old for his age and soon he was led to discover"— Brougham Calder rolled his eyes and lifted his arms out wide like a pantomime drug fiend reaching to catch the corruptible flower of youth in his embrace—"the joys and vices of bohemia! Fitzrovia!" He leaned forward, winked at me, his fingers pressed together. "The Blitz made a man of many."

"How well did you know him?"

"Knob off! I couldn't stand the man."

I didn't know what I'd said to outrage him. I didn't know how to unsay it. He withdrew into a sullen silence, sat back in his chair with his champagne flute bubbling in his hand, a fixed hurt look in his eyes. I started to say something peaceable and he sat up rigid like a soldier and interrupted.

"We're dawdling. Let's not lose our narrative thread. A murder story cannot bear too many longueurs. It's time for some introductions. Where shall we find the rest of our cast? Our dramatis personae, Matthew Glaven, Martin Poulsen, the Sniffer, and George, the Silvertown boy. Who will lead us to them? The sleeping countess or the swanky underage fireman? I think the fireman is the likelier bet, don't you? We can leave Eileen and we can return in a day's time and her snores will still be filling the mustard room. Let's follow Master William out into his night.

"First port of call is the Wheatsheaf. Push open the door, turn down your collar, it's cozy inside. Tambi in a shabby suit is looking like a disguised fairy-tale prince, with girls and pansies fluttering around him and mediocre colonials taking it by turns to buy him drinks in the hopeful exchange for a page or two of their mediocre verse in the next issue of *Poetry London*. Aleister Crowley is there, his eyebrows teased into Mephistophelian cuckold horns, his horny magus fists beating a voodoo stick in a gamelan rhythm against the scarlet lino floor. He's trying to interest Dylan Thomas in the joys of heroin, maybe buggery too. You know how Dylan skived the services? Drank himself half to death the night before his Board so he came out in frightful shirker's spots. Or Francis Bacon?—those are his paintings on the walls, he thought they'd been burnt, didn't come here after the War, had a little contretemps with Cunty's dad, Big Cunty—Bacon hired an Alsatian dog from Harrods the day before his Board, slept with it all night, allergic to the hound, it brought out his asthma something rotten, he saw out the War painting horrors and drinking champagne and dipping his wick into boys and dicing at cards and filling his face with oysters, and that's all by the by . . .

"Ivory sips his pint of bitter at the bar. Falls into conversation with me, I'm on leave from my R.A.F. squadron, we know each other from Percy Street days, I was living there when he arrived, the damned bloody schemer got me kicked out of my room and onto the sofa, but I got my revenge, oh yes, revenge is a dish best served cold, later I displaced him, when things got a little too hot for him in town, then the boy went running back to his Norfolk home and I reclaimed my room for good. But we were on terms back then and we chat of this and that, literary subjects mostly, and I show him the copy of *Penguin New Writing* that includes my first published poem and we close our ears to the piss-awful slogans of the so-called wits of the place, and I'm returning the poetry book to the pocket of my officer's dress jacket when the Sniffer arrives.

"The Sniffer—da da da *da!*—a swell of brass music, a beating of drums, a shadow emerges from dark deep ruins. The War rewarded some sinister talents and the Sniffer's was the most sinister of all. A tall figure, looked like Death, hunched inside a black long overcoat, walking carelessly through the smoking ruins of buildings, a skinny man with a brick-dust halo, behind him his retinue from the Heavy Rescue Squad. We never knew his name, just called him the Sniffer, and that was what he was, that long talented nose sniffing out hidden blood beneath the ruins. 'Move on. It's a stiff.' 'Dig down there, it's a live one. Fresh blood and still flowing!' He had a nose for blood, and his particular gift, no one knew how he did it, he was able to smell whether the blood was seeping away from a living body or a broken corpse.

"You shudder, yes? This is the singular stuff of horror pictures. No one knew what he had done before the War or where his dark gifts led him afterwards. But in wartime, in Blitzkrieg time, he saves lives, his skill means that unnecessary labors can be avoided. There was quite a vogue for him at smart parties. You'd see him at soirées, at nightclubs, in the Wheatsheaf in his regular place, on the sofa at the bottom of the bar below the bow window where a china swan sits in a puddle of discarded beer and cigarette ends. The Sniffer dressed in his overcoat, smiling, always a retinue around him, being pushed for ghoulish anecdotes and sometimes giving them, thin voice, common like a maths teacher's. Had he been less horrible in appearance he would have been a hero. Because heroism depends on looks just as much as on deeds, don't you think?

"Photogenic William Ivory, always a one for the ladies, he looks so dashing in his evening dress. Are you there? Are you with me? We finish our pints and I fill my hip flask with Red's cheapest brandy, and we decide against the Gargoyle in Meard Street—we called it Merde Street, Attic wit isn't quite the thing in wartime—instead we elect to go dancing. Have I told you the date of this particular day? It's March the eighth, nineteen forty-one.

"We walk through the blackout over to Leicester Square, the Café de Paris. Go through the street-level door, pass underneath the Rialto Cinema, and there we are, a wonderful place, billed as the safest nightspot in town and modeled on the ballroom of the *Titanic*—talk about choosing your destiny! There's a band there tonight, Snakehips Johnson and his West Indian Dance Orchestra, they were good, the Snakehips and his boys, black boys in white tails, played swing but not white man's swing, the trombonist was the only white man in the band and they blacked him up to preserve authenticity, but most people knew . . ."

He opened his eyes and blinked them a few times. Stared at me in a hard way.

"You are listening? Because otherwise . . ."

"Go on. Please. I'm listening."

He rewarded me with a smile and closed his eyes again.

"Snakehips Johnson and his band are playing there tonight, and Martin Poulsen, a sleek snappy man in civvies, is there, he's chatting up the ladies and Ivory has come here expressly to talk to him, he's after a job playing the piano. Poulsen owns the club and has made a fortune cornering the West End market in champagne—shall we order another bottle? For the sake of their memory? For the sake of atmosphere? No? Snide boy— and Ivory is about to leg it over to Poulsen but something brings him up short and that's the sight of Mattie.

"You start, you're a sly one, do you know that secret history? Maybe a little. Yes? Mattie, Matthew Glaven, his cousin, the two of them desperado runaway renegades, two boys with a sickly sense of purity and a talent for the grotesque. They arrived in town together, pawky provincials on the run. Mattie's a pale one, he's queer as Dick's hatband with a passion for rough trade and a penchant for uniforms. Nights will find him out on the towpath by Putney Bridge dressed like a Confederate general or on the Heath at Hampstead in Napoleonic gear, or propositioning stern young men in tube carriages, or, most often, down in Silvertown, where potato-faced urchins will do most anything for half a crown. The two of them, thick as thieves, ran down to London together when the first bombs landed. It was a funfair for those two, looting in the ruins—and they weren't alone in that—dressing for war.

"Mattie and Ivory haven't been speaking for a while, they had a falling out, these two boys with their sickly secrets. Ivory is surprised to see his cousin there, fine blond hair over a prematurely lined face, thin boy, dressed as an officer in the Free French because that is how he feels tonight. He stands, this anemic faux Frenchy alone on the gallery, looking down at the dance floor, at the bar along the side, at the bandstand where Snakehips Johnson introduces the next number, 'A real killer diller' he calls out in his ersatz Harlem voice, 'Dear Old Southland,' that's its name, a slow swinging number, their signature tune, he stands poised and still for a moment, a red carnation in his white tailcoat, a baton in his right hand, and there's a small group on the stairs beside the bandstand where Cousin William stands respectfully behind Martin Poulsen.

"Mattie's a boy with a destiny and you can smell it on him. Maybe that's why the others along the gallery don't push up too close, the officers and ladies and spivs and even a few Commandos, that's Piccadilly Commandos, whores in slick red two-pieces, sheer silk stockings gallantly donated by the first Yanks in town, their torches in the pockets of their furs in the cloakroom, here you can tell hardly any difference but out on the street, on Piccadilly beside Half Moon Street, they make a grand surrealistic sight, hundreds of them, rows deep, shining their blue air-raid-warden torches silkily up and down their stockinged legs—but seldom at their faces—so the customers can see what they're shopping for in the blackout . . . Hard though to think why anyone should choose to pay for it because danger and death are the greatest aphrodisiacs invented by man, it's everywhere, the smell of sex, like a rutting animal, that's how the city smells, everyone's doing it, wild, abandoned, licentious, a dionysian rite, all sexes, all combinations. Ivory had a way with words. Often, and mark me well, it was just a cheating matter of latching onto someone else's formula and adapting it for himself. He was never an original man. He was a cheat and he was a thief and if the factory girl had looked his way instead of mine and if he hadn't had dangerous things on his mind, then that night might well have been different and one fewer person might have died. But he described it as a tropical flowering of sexuality, that time of the Blitz."

Brougham Calder was getting angry. Resentment was getting in the way of his sneer. He pinched his nose with one hand and rubbed his forehead vigorously with the other.

"Mattie's not alone anymore. He's got a rough boy with him now, probably a Silvertown boy. I take to the dance floor. I'm due back at my squadron the following day and time's a-wasting if I stay with Ivory or ponder over why Mattie's piece of rough is wearing a peculiarly triumphant expression as he looks down on Ivory. Where were we? Don't speak. Don't say anything. I'm in charge of this one."

We looked at each other. He nodded, encouragingly. I nodded back. He closed his eyes and sat back. I stayed where I was, looking at the red lizard skin on his eyelids.

"March the eighth, nineteen forty-one. A very favorite and very deadly night. Let's break for a romantic interlude. There was a girl. She was twenty-one. An R.A.F. officer who wrote a little poetry spooned and wooed her on the dance floor of the Café de Paris. A boy with blond curls, he had a volume of poetry spoiling the line of his officer's dress jacket, and she was a pretty thing, flushed with youth and danger and champagne. It's a typical story, wartime, boy and girl, drink, danger, dancing. The obvious equation with the obvious solution. There were no virgins then. Snakehips announces the next number, 'Dear Old Southland.' 'A real killer diller,' he calls, and the band plays its signature tune but our boy and our girl are not going to stay. It's done without words, for this boy and this girl. She took to his curls and he took to her charms and as 'Dear Old Southland' gave way to 'Oh Johnny' they took themselves off into the blacked-out night and he took her to a hotel that was near to the British Museum where they signed the guest book as Lieutenant and Mrs. C. Chaplin. Vous comprenez?

"Sshh. Please. Hush. I can hear you thinking. You'll spoil it. Listen, only listen. It was a night like many others and there were many others having an equal kind of night and that made it queerly intimate. And they took off their underclothes, hers with a silky rustle, and they spent a night a lot like any other, and either of them could have been with anybody else and that made it more perfect than can be. And after they were finished they smoked French cigarettes, Caporals, and they drank cheap brandy from the hip flask he had brought and they curled up together and for a while they slept. And there could have been bombs around them but they didn't hear them and even if they had, even if one of them was awake all night straight-backed with fear, then at least the sight of the girl asleep in her silk slip, curled like a girl, restful like a child, with hair to stroke back away from her brow, and I'm not saying that he was awake, but if he was, then everything would be strangely calmly all right.

"They each would have duties in the new day, so they woke in the dawn morning and they remembered each other's names and they kissed like strangers because strangers they were, and when she got dressed he turned over on his side and he saw the thanking look she gave him in the mirror beside. They strolled out together down creaking carpeted stairs and she entwined her arm through his and he felt proud at the flush on her face and as they were passing the desk she stopped to give him a kiss, a lover's kiss not a stranger's kiss, and she whispered loud enough for the night manager to hear, 'Who cares if Hitler comes so long as we can have fun like this.' "

Brougham Calder was smiling. He opened one eye and closed it again when he saw he still had my attention. The smile was replaced by a baffled frown.

"Night managers don't have the best of lives. They guard other people's valuables and listen to other people's rattling bedsprings and they have books to balance and cooks to pacify and chambermaids to make passes at and sack, and all these things and more can produce a sour vinegar blood and a bitter lemon heart. He would regard himself a patriot, this sour bitter night manager man, with his tatty gray cardigan and his metal-rimmed spectacles. He called to them from behind his night manager desk and asked them if they would mind waiting a moment. And they did, because he had asked them to, and out he stepped into a cold London morning, the sky was gray over the blacked-out ruins of London, and he fetched back a policeman from out of the gray and stood him in front of the nighttime couple and he told the policeman the words he had heard the pretty girl say."

"Why?"

"Isn't it obvious? Envy and bitterness and hatred of youth and pleasures. The feelings that drive a man to suicide or pettifogging tiny vengeances. Misery loves company. They were taken away, our loving-cup couple. The poetic R.A.F. officer was sent bashfully back to his squadron, and the girl, she was only a factory girl, not even a munitions worker, and therefore ripe to waste and make hard, she was tried for entering a false name in a hotel register and sentenced to one cruel heartless month in Holloway women's nick."

I risked another question. "Why?"

"To be made an example of. We were living in a military dictatorship, there was a law against spreading what they called 'alarm and despondency,' loose lips got you in the shit."

"How long were you in the R.A.F.?"

"I was invalided out in nineteen forty-three." Brougham Calder opened his eyes. He leaned forward to refill his glass, and he poured the wine down his throat in one long swallow. He lit up a cigarette. It was an English brand, I was disappointed by that.

I signaled over to Cunty to bring us more wine (now that I knew I was settling the account, I'd put a stop to champagne. B.C. didn't seem to mind, I think he was pleased he'd got away with an evening's worth). He was looking at me, moving his lips silently, a gloss of wine upon them. I figured he was practicing his words, those accidental rhymes don't come cheap. There were some questions already forming in my mind, but I was hesitant to intervene.

"I got waylaid. Forgive me. A romantic interlude. Our murder story is moving towards its consummation. Where were we? Don't say. Mattie's on the gallery, his hair when he shakes it comes down to his collar. His body sways to Snakehips's swing. Ivory's on the dance floor now, elegantly traipsing after Poulsen. Mattie's watching his cousin and standing next to his piece of rough, bodies close together, rubbing together on that libidinous gallery. Ivory spins away from Poulsen. He watches his cousin, meets him in the eyes, and his cousin comes slowly down the stairs beside the bandstand, his rough beside him, the band's playing 'Oh Johnny' now, a quickstep number and there's plenty dancing to it, and if you look quickly over at the exit you'll see a curly-haired R.A.F. man with a paperback of poetry in his pocket leaving with a pretty dancing girl . . .

"They're on to the second chorus of 'Oh Johnny' and Snakehips is doing his snakehips dance, and Mattie has reached the foot of the stairs and Ivory has his eyes on him and the crowd are clapping and dancing and spooning and that's when— crash!—the bombs hit. Two bombs, fifty kilograms of high explosives a blessing down from the sky, smashing through the glass roof of the Rialto, breaking the cinema floor and down through the nightclub ceiling, and the first with a blue flash explodes right next to the bandstand.

"Snakehips is killed instantly, but immaculately, like everything he did, he's lying there, full length on the remains of the bandstand stage, seeming untouched, no blood, his unspoilt carnation the only splash of red on his handsome long body. The bandstand is a wreckage, dead bodies on the dance floor. And when the second bomb goes off, scattering masonry and plaster and clothes and roof beams over the wreckage, it's bedlam. A charnel house. All in all, there're thirty-four people dead, many more trapped in the wreckage.

"It's crazy in there. Bedlam. Screams for help, screams of pain. One girl who's had her clothes rushed off her by the blast of the bomb stands shock still, trying to cover herself like an allegorical statue of Reluctant Modesty. Poulsen is dead, leveled, the champagne nightclub king. Ivory brings his fireman training into the fray, he's bleeding from a shrapnel splinter in his leg but he organizes a work party of survivors to pull away the wreckage from others. Brave Ivory. Heroic Ivory. George Medal-adorned Ivory.

"The A.F.S. comes, puts out the remaining fires. The Pioneers come, that raggle-taggle band of convicts and deserters, waiting smoking cigarettes by the side of the hall, knowing that by the time they're called into action there'll be little looting left for them. The Heavy Rescue Squad comes, and with them, the Sniffer.

"Ivory's been working like a demon. Shifting wreckage from around the bandstand, kicking away rubble, throwing off to the side the battered shattered instruments of the West Indian Dance Orchestra, grappling with wounded dancers and fragments from the smashed bandstand, absentmindedly pulling survivors up from the ruined floor, working in on his target, barking orders in his young man's voice. The Sniffer in his wake strolls into action, his long sinister nose close to the ground, his body hunched inside his coat, his retinue behind him of cowed awed strongmen.

"Now Ivory, smooth Ivory, grudge-bearing secretive Ivory, finally reaches the point he's been working towards. It's between the bandstand and the gallery staircase, the spot where he'd seen Mattie and his bit of rough fall. He looks around, cautious in the mayhem. The Sniffer is sniffing, nose down to the ground. The nightclub manager is scratching his head with his missing fingertips. Parts of bodies, alive or dead only the Sniffer knows, peep out between lumps of masonry and broken roof beams—a naked foot, a uniformed arm at a sickening angle, a charred girl's face, disembodied, praying for God's help.

"Ivory has his eye on other game. The two unconscious blond boys beneath him, only loosely buried. He's dragged over Poulsen's body, the convenient camouflage corpse. Ivory very carefully, oh so deliberately, covers what he thinks is his cousin with the dried-blood body of Martin Poulsen. And over the corpse that is and over the corpse to be he builds a tomb of bandstand wood to cover the deed. Strong Ivory. Vengeful Ivory. Mistaken Ivory. It was dark in there and there was powder and dust all around, and no matter how much of a demon you are you can still make mistakes. In a bomb-shattered place one blond boy can look much like another. And when the Sniffer got to this spot beside the bandstand by the gallery staircase, he was indeed fooled by Ivory's endeavors, but not quite in the way our brave hero had supposed. His men behind him, poised with shovels and crowbars and sticks, waited for his orders. 'Dead blood down there. It's a stiff!' and next to it, 'Fresh blood down there and still flowing!' And the men of the Heavy Rescue Squad dug and removed shocked damaged alive Mattie and pulled him out in his tattered Free French uniform and one of them spoke to him in pidgin French, to which Mattie replied with a spray of English, repeating over and over again, 'You have to rescue George!' but they paid him no heed, the Sniffer had spoken, dead blood down there, it's a stiff, and they moved on, leaving Mattie to dig alone with impotent hands to try to rescue, and fail to rescue, his casual rough chum.

"And Ivory had gone, back to Percy Street. And the Sniffer had gone, fresh jewelry and money in his pocket, and the boys of the Heavy Rescue Squad had gone, loaded with the stuff the Sniffer had left behind for them, and by the time the Pioneers had managed to bundle out the kitchen woman, who was calmly stirring a stewpot full of bricks and rubble, by the time they got to where Mattie was still weakly digging, they finally hoisted up the body of Martin Poulsen, and then, beneath, the corpse of suffocated George."

Brougham Calder licked his lips. He finished off the last of the wine and ordered some more. He looked proud and he looked content. I asked him a question and I knew it was going to offend him.

"But you admitted you'd gone by that time. How do you know he was trying to kill his cousin?"

He smiled placidly. He rubbed his finger along the rim of his glass.

"It's got to be hearsay. You were in some hotel fucking a factory girl and lying awake scared shitless all night at the air-raid warnings in the street. You don't know. What proof do you have?"

He smiled. He had me. "Mattie's oldest sister, Sophie, was sent by her family to find their errant child. Night errant child. She was there. That night at the club. Ivory didn't recognize her but he inadvertently rescued her too. Do have a George Medal, Mister Ivory. She saw what he did. She told me . . . Did you ever know a murderer? I did. His name was William Ivory. A little more wine?"

I don't know how this makes you feel. Maybe not anything. I nodded my head and drank some more wine and Brougham Calder's head got hazy in my vision. He had a strong head for liquor, that dissolute author. He started to tell me about some of the books he'd written. I don't remember which titles he gave. He saw my lack of attention. I don't think it bothered him.

It was late in the night and everyone else had left for their bedtime lives except the two of us and the sallow man behind the bar. Brougham Calder shouted over to him.

"Hey, Cunty! Another bouteille of your best piss water!"

"Fuck off. We're shut."

"Just one more. I'm entertaining a foreign friend."

"He can bugger off too. I'm closing up."

"I'm resigning my membership."

"You never paid it. Go home."

Brougham Calder looked on the point of tears. "He's an awful cunt," he confided. Then he cheered up. "Where are you staying? We can continue this there. I know a cab firm where we can buy more bottles."

"I'm kind of sleepy myself. Maybe we should reconvene another time."

He nodded, distraught. "Yes, yes, of course. We can do that. It's just that I'm rather in my flow, you know. I hate to break up an evening. Let me walk you to your place. Don't worry about the bill, you can settle up tomorrow. I have many more stories about our William Ivory. The things I can tell you about *him*. You'll like them, I know you will. You will be back to-morrow, won't you?"

"Tomorrow I have to go to Brighton. I'm seeing Ivory's obituarist."

His face got worried. He needed his audience. "Then you'll be back the following night. I'll be here. I'm always here. You will be back, won't you? Please."

"Whatever you say. I'll be back."

He relaxed. He'd been holding his breath, waiting for my promise. "I suppose you had better pay the bill now anyway. Cunty doesn't approve of tick."

When I returned to my hotel (your promise of funds encouraged me to settle extravagant champagne bills and take cabs everywhere) there were messages from Nick Wheel placed under the door. I threw them in the trash can. I climbed into bed. I was tired, too tired to read any of *Decadent Pleasures* or even the grisly coda to *Morita*. I was tired of tales of seedy antiheroism. Oh Brougham Calder, one day a rebuttal will be issued.

I was expecting part of my advance the following morning. It didn't arrive. I went to the American Express office on Haymarket, whispered the magic words "poste restante," spelled out my name three separate times to three separate clerks, and walked back out onto the street with the same amount of money I'd come in with. I felt neglected and I felt poor. I began to resent Brougham Calder's alcohol consumption. I was worried how I was going to pay for my hotel. I imagined you back in Boston with bigger fish to fry, forgetting about your biographer in your office which I'd never seen.

I wandered up past Eros in Piccadilly Circus, the statue covered in scaffolding, around its steps tight bunches of Scandinavian children taking photographs of each other, and a little raggle-taggle battalion of elderly punk rockers, tattooed arms holding cans of beer or bottles of cider or lengths of string attached to the necks of amiable three-legged pooches. I walked along Piccadilly and stood on the corner of Half Moon Street and tried to imagine it when there were rows deep of prostitutes in red two-pieces, sheer black stockings given by their American friends, shining the dim blue light of their wardens' torches up and down their bodies but seldom at their faces. I tried to imagine the street Ivory would have seen, the street he'd have walked along, the smell of brick dust and rotting fish and open sewers and burning plaster in his auxiliary fireman's nostrils, the feel of his blue trousers flapping against his underage legs, I tried to conjure up the spirit of Mattie, a cousin with a destiny, I tried to imagine the sinister Sniffer there, smelling blood beneath disaster. And none of it held. An old street on a dull day, no roar of grandeur, no flash of truth, no sense of Ivory or Mattie in the smug rush of girls with ski-resort complexions, young men dressed like old men with the faces of babies.

You wouldn't be interested in the drive from London to Brighton, the weekend-deal rental car that took me there, my overnight bag in the back of it, the hitchhiker with his tale of being on the run because he knew where magic mushrooms came from, the sudden reassuring sight of the sea, the circus trailer we got stuck behind and the stones the hitchhiker threw at it. I don't even know how interested you are in Roland Gibbs, a mild fraud with a foolish manner who blinked a lot and puffed on a pipe while presiding over a violent game of croquet on the back lawn of his house.

I dropped my hitchhiker off and called Gibbs from a pay phone by the seafront. (How do the British tolerate resort towns with stony beaches?) I started to remind him of my mission but he interrupted, wanted to know where I was from. I told him Boston and he asked me if that meant Harvard, and I told him no, just Boston. That took him aback slightly but before I could say anything more, he gave me directions to his house in Little Milton. I hit Great Milton three times along the way before I pulled up at an ugly pile in a timid village.

A lumpy woman in a floral sack dress pulled me along a cluttered hall through a kitchen that smelled of bacon and dogs and out to a lawn dotted with different-colored balls and studded with silver-colored hoops. Youngish people of different colors and shapes were standing there in varying degrees of despondency. A lot of them were balancing sadly on one leg. Everyone was holding a mallet.

"Darling? We have an American."

"Oh good." Gibbs came blinking toward me, a gray-haired man in English-gent tweeds, a croquet mallet in one hand, a pipe in the other. "Harvard?"

"Boston. I think we might have done this one."

He cocked his head to one side and opened his mouth to show me long yellow teeth. "Name of?"

"Tierney. Richard Tierney."

"Tierney Richard Tierney." He opened his mouth wider and

snuffled briefly through his nose. I took that as signifying laughter. "We were expecting a Wilson William Wilson. From Harvard. Ha ha. Not a Tierney Richard Tierney from Boston." He snuffled a little more and looked at me hopefully.

"We spoke by telephone a few days ago. I don't want to use up too much of your time . . . I'm writing a—"

"Intriguing. Marvelous. Would you like to join us? We're playing a game. Norfolk crokey. It's crokey. With wrinkles."

He bounded ahead of me to the far corner of the lawn, where a Japanese girl with short bobbed hair balanced disconsolately on one leg. "Meet Masako. Tokyo University. Your partner."

Gibbs scampered back to the center of the lawn to examine the lie of his ball. He went through with a couple of practice swings aimed toward a miserable white-haired boy standing with his left foot against his right knee like a depressed flautist contemplating the loss of his instrument. Gibbs gathered his concentration. He stood behind his ball, legs straight and close together, mallet motionless between them, back arched forward a little, pipe clenched in his mouth. His eyes were keen, his nose was dribbling out a delicate globe of mucus. Gibbs shot, and the ball scuttled across the grass and ricocheted off the boy's ankle. The ball rolled perfectly to a stop in front of the next hoop and the boy fell over, silently clutching his ankle. Gibbs ran after his ball and prepared to hit it through the hoop.

"You're not a flamingo anymore, Thoralf! It'll be your shot next."

Gibbs sent his ball expertly through the hoop, and turned to face us. He sized up the distance between himself and Masako, seemed to decide it was too far, and settled instead for aiming at a blue ball which belonged to a pair of African women. Masako sighed. "This is most unhappy time," she said.

Gibbs was quite the virtuoso at Norfolk croquet. Amid sharp cries of pain and quick grassy tumbles and curses muttered in many different languages, it took about half an hour for him and his partner, a pimply English boy called Ray, to win the game. I muffed my first and only shot and a flamingo I became and a flamingo I remained. We were too far out of the action for anyone to release us, so Masako and I tottered side by side, she in a white silk shirt and baggy black shorts, me in my creased burnt-out-case linen suit, confused flamingoes watching Gibbs.

"What's the occasion? Why are you all here?"

"I think he is sadist," Masako said, as Gibbs ignored a waiting hoop to hit Thoralf on the ankle for the third time. "We are newly postgraduate students in Professor Gibbs's pastoral care. This is called Getting Acquainted Party."

When no one, not even Ray, could be cajoled into another game, our party limped back into the living room of the house where Mrs. Gibbs had laid out glasses of white wine and cubes of cheese and tiny sausages impaled on cocktail sticks. William Wilson of Harvard had arrived, a fat balding boy in a Brooks Brothers suit. Mrs. Gibbs introduced us and I adopted a ludicrous Irish accent to avoid being sucked into an Americans-abroad solidarity.

I lost Masako before I had a chance to get her to tell me about William Ivory, big in Japan. Found myself caught by turns in a group of Italians and Africans discussing the great Ghanaian satirists, in a corner with an anorexic girl who harried me for my opinions on Katherine Mansfield, by the window listening to Thoralf relate to Mrs. Gibbs in great earnest detail the plot of a Norwegian pornographic movie.

That's when I went exploring for my host. I finally cornered Gibbs in the study, where he was proudly showing Masako his collection of Japanese first editions. He seemed a little put out by my arrival, even more so when Masako excused herself and we were left alone.

"Some game, Norfolk croquet," I observed.

That lifted him. He brightened, looked on me as a sympathetic spirit. He relit his pipe, showed me his teeth, clicked his tongue behind them. "You were unlucky. Got here late. Otherwise you might have had a decent run."

"A traditional game in these parts?"

"Not as such. If it were I expect it should be called Sussex crokey."

He wasn't eager for my company. I'd seen the way he looked at Masako. Rather different from the way he looked at his wife.

"Your own invention?"

"Wish I could take credit for it. Devised by a friend of mine. A maestro at the sport."

"You seemed pretty good at it yourself."

"Well yes, but you should have seen *him* play. I still have the bruises."

"Couldn't make it today, huh?"

"Yes. Quite. You could say that."

"His name didn't happen to be William Ivory, by some chance?"

We looked at each other. He puffed on his pipe and I took my hands out of my pockets and put them back in again.

"No actually it didn't. Why do you mention him?"

"I called you, remember? I'm researching his life. I read his obituary. I read what you wrote."

"It wasn't signed. It was a long time ago."

Gibbs yawned. Challenging me to come up with something concrete.

"There was another obit later on—in the *Dictionary of National Biography*—almost identical to the one in *The Times*. You signed that one. I couldn't find any others though. I've checked all the papers of the time. I guess I must have missed something."

He seemed to admit defeat. He rubbed his leg.

"What do you want to know?"

Everything. Wasn't that it? Some kind of truth illustrated through detail. Isn't that what you asked for? How he died. How he lived. What manner of man he was.

"How well did you know him?"

He blinked at me, then looked down to his pipe, cupped his hand around it to protect the embers. Mrs. Gibbs stuck her large pretty face around the study door.

"Darling! We were beginning to wonder . . ."

"Yes. Temporary change of plan. I'm showing this young Harvard man my Japanese collection." He opened his mouth and snuffled politely until she was gone. "He was my friend. I admired him . . . Perhaps you would like a Bloody Mary? It's a Sunday habit of mine I picked up round your neck of the woods."

He opened a refrigerator door cunningly concealed behind

a strictly ornamental set of Boswell's *Life of Johnson*. He fetched out a pitcher of Bloody Marys, a couple of iced glasses, and two sticks of celery. He constructed the drinks.

"Let's sit in the big chairs."

We sat in the big chairs. Companion armchairs half facing each other with a table for our drinks in between.

"I make them extra spicy, I hope you like it that way too."

"Extra spicy is good."

He was waiting for me to take the first taste. I did and pronounced it good. Gibbs stirred his drink round with his celery. He wasn't going to offer any unsolicited information. I felt uncomfortable. I was still new to this game. Then I remembered something Wheel had said, a slice of potential wisdom amid all the silliness.

"Let's start at the end, work back from there. It's nineteen eighty. Ivory dies. Was it murder or suicide?"

It might have been the extra spice that made him come close to sputtering his drink. He jerked up his head and his offended mouth was surrounded by tomatoey red.

"That's an extraordinary question. It's a ridiculous question. If you're looking for Grand Guignol you've come, I'm glad to say, to the wrong place. I have a party of young foreign students waiting for me in the next room. It's not my time I'm giving you, it's theirs. Please have some respect for that."

"I'm sorry. I appreciate your taking the trouble and the time. It's just that in your obituary you never said how Ivory died."

He adopted his pompous tone, which I was going to hear a few more times.

"It is not customary, I believe, for obituaries to be medical forensic reports. The point of an obituary, to my mind, is to be a celebration of a man's, or woman's, life."

"You said he met an untimely death—"

"That is not code for anything. He was not an old man and he died. Untimely is the word. Look. Are you asking, What did William Ivory die of? If that's your question I can't tell you the specific thing that killed him. I can tell you that he was often very ill. Throughout his life. Suffered from rheumatic fever as a boy. That weakens the heart, I believe. He always had a rather serious asthmatic condition. He looked strong. Possessed a notable physique. Acted strong. So people believed he was. He wasn't. There's nothing secret hidden there. No dirt."

"All I'm trying to do is to get a sense of the man. Just find out what I can about him. I didn't mean any offense."

"And none taken. Absolutely not. You have a difficult job ahead of you. I'm delighted to be able to help."

"You met him where?"

"At the university. I invited him actually. To give a reading in the Gardiner Centre from his book *Decadent Pleasures*. You've read it of course? Marvelous work. Gives a flavor of the man, I think. We sort of fell into a friendship. Shared some interests. Japanese literature for one. It's not strictly my field, call me an interested amateur. He was a wonderful translator. If you hold on a moment I'll show you some of his books."

Gibbs sprung out of his big chair and knelt on the floor. He ran his finger along a shelf of books. I tried to get him unawares.

"There seem to be some doubts over his war record."

Gibbs kept on looking at the spines of books. He answered absentmindedly. "I couldn't say. I met him long after all that. Dazai, Endo, Kawabata . . . no. I understand he had a good war and was awarded the George Medal. Mishima, yes, Oe, no, here's one from Tanizaki, these will do for the moment . . . I don't know any more than that, quite honestly."

Gibbs settled himself back in his chair, handed me the two books he'd found. Both collections of short stories. *Patriotism and Other Stories* by Mishima Yukio, *Seven Japanese Tales* by Tanizaki Junichirō. Translator W. S. Ivory. I flicked the pages of each in turn, didn't know if there was something I ought to have been looking for.

"I went up to his house a number of times. Lovely place. Cottagey feel. Very isolated. Fields all around. Very flat with a large sky. And not far from the house, the sea. Miles upon miles of sand dunes, bird sanctuaries. Tremendous smoked kippers you can get round there. His dog, he loved his dog, he used to walk him along the dunes of Holkham Bay."

"That's Norfolk, right?"

"Yes of course. North Norfolk."

"He was born there?"

"I think he was born in Norwich itself. He traveled a lot but always returned to that county. This is something you must appreciate about the English. Rooted in the land. If you are serious about understanding William Ivory, then you must go up and spend some time in the place he loved. We all become a function of our landscape, don't you think? That's a general rule, applies everywhere, but particularly so in the case of the English."

"And you visited him often? In North Norfolk."

"Oh certainly a number of times. He used to give the most amazing dinner parties; he was a tremendous cook and a splendid host and I would try never to miss one of those. At other times he would be there alone or else having, shall I say? private company."

"Women."

"Indeed. Women. Yes. Quite the Don Juan. But he would keep that part of his life ever so discreetly separate. And of course, sometimes his children would be up to stay with him."

"You met them?"

"No. Never. He had a son, and a daughter too, I believe, but no, I never met them."

"How about his wives?"

"Can't say I met either of them either. I'm sorry. I'm not being much help, am I?" He snuffled merrily and drew shapes on the side of his empty glass.

"I don't expect you met any of his women?"

"Only once and that was in London. She was a librarian and when he spotted me he cut me dead, pretended not to know me . . ."

Gibbs shook his head. He poured us each another Bloody Mary. He offered me a fresh stick of celery to munch along with it.

"I was an admirer of his mind, and I liked his books very much, and I loved going up to Binham to stay with him. Lovely atmosphere in that odd old house. Will tinkling on the piano, he was a wonderful interpreter of Debussy and Ravel, or rattling out corny wartime melodies for the rest of us to invent the words to. And his cooking. Lord, how I miss those feasts. Truly marvelous chef. Elaborate meals, sometimes only one color, exotic like orange. Turmeric flaming the wildest curry and paprika in an intense Hungarian crêpe. Everything orange from the starter to the pudding wine. And always such an interesting company."

"*Were* there other obituaries of him? In other papers?"

"Not as far as I know. I couldn't tell you that though with absolute authority. What you have to realize about Will is that he was a coterie pleasure. *Decadent Pleasures* was a tremendous success but Will's mind went too deep for our age. He should have been a Petronius or a Baudelaire, the siren call announcing the death of the age. He was reputed to be writing something very special at the end, but it disappeared when he died. I think it was called *Final Things* or was it *Last Things*? Do you happen to know?"

"I'm sorry. I didn't realize there was another book. It's news to me."

He paused mid-celery crunch. Seemed to be deciding whether I was telling the truth or not.

"Listen. Let me tell you about an evening at Ivory's table. Then maybe we should call it a day. Yes? You know what he looked like of course. Always impeccably dressed like an aristocrat. Mustache. Slightly heavy features. Balding a little and —surprising vanity—tried to hide it with an artful arrangement of the hair. Those penetrating eyes. Teeth that may have been false. His pianist's fingers. So. Let me tell you about a typical dinner party and then I shan't keep you any longer. I'm sure you have a lot of interesting things to do.

"There's a crowd of us there, his literary agent up from London, an academic from the local university, some other bods, a novelist, a brace of scientists, I couldn't tell you the names now, a red-faced fellow named Harkin, what was his first name? Jeremy Harkin I think, that was it. We're drinking cocktails, making small talk, Ivory's rattling out some mood music on the piano."

"When was this?"

"Mid-'seventies. I couldn't tell you the precise year. Must have been after *Decadent Pleasures* and before *Morita*. Nineteen seventy-five? Nineteen seventy-eight? Something like that. It was wintertime, definitely. I remember a strong wood fire burning in the grate and I remember that the roads going towards the house were quite precarious at times. I'm not going to take you through all the courses. I have a lot of students waiting for me outside, it's not fair on them, you do understand of course. Suffice it to say the meal was entirely delicious. For the main course we had one of those French meat stews, some splendid wines from the cellar. Anyway, we're drinking our cognac afterwards, smoking tobacco, chatting, letting it all hang out as we used to say in those days."

"There were no women there?"

"No women. As I say, Will was something of a Don Juan. But he was accustomed to keeping aspects of his life very separate. Anyway, we're all having the jolliest of times. Intellectual gossip, a drunken confession or two, the usual kind of chat. And then Harkin, nervous manner, sort of clumsy in company, apropos of not much of anything at all, or maybe it was, I don't remember exactly, it was a long time ago, perhaps someone asked him a question? I don't know. But anyway Harkin starts to relate an anecdote about Japan in the nineteen fifties. And that's when Ivory makes his intervention.

"Ivory has been taking a back seat up till now. Gently steering the conversation. Allowing different people the opportunity to shine. But you get the impression that Ivory is bored and when Ivory gets bored he can get a little dangerous. He starts to amuse himself with people."

"In what kind of way?"

"Can take a number of forms. Making people who act as if they're clever show themselves up to be fools. Using wine and subtle questioning to get people to give up secrets. Using the tactics of his therapeutic profession to profoundly embarrass. And that's what he did to Jeremy Harkin—No, Jim, that's his name, *Jim* Harkin. Large red-faced nervous fellow. Had just launched clumsily into some story about working in Japan in the nineteen fifties when Ivory leans forwards, smoking a cigar, head resting on his hands, and so innocently asks, 'Do tell us, Jim, that funny story of what happened to you in Bangkok.'

"Now. Harkin blushes. He's quick to blush at the best of times, anything funny or personal will turn his face beetroot red. So he blushes, of course. He shakes his head. He stutters a little. Ivory smiles supportively. Grins that shark grin of his. 'Oh come on, Jim. It's a hilarious story, you can't have forgotten it. That night in Bangkok, remember? You were having trouble sleeping at your hotel and you went downstairs to the American Bar . . .'

"Harkin is in an awful state. His face is as red as red can be. He giggles in a horrible nervous way. None of us is looking at him anymore, all just hoping Ivory is going to drop it. He doesn't drop it. 'I'd tell the story but I don't remember all the details and I'm sure I wouldn't be able to tell it as well as you. Shall I tell it?' Jim doesn't say anything so Ivory starts the story off for him, pretending that he's trying to jog Harkin's memory. Harkin is desperate with shame but he takes over the story anyway just like Ivory means him to.

"It's not the greatest story I've ever heard but that's not the point. It's a slightly shabby, very embarrassing tale that Jim keeps faltering over but keeps going with some prompting from Ivory. So he tells his story—and you have to remember this is a man who blushes if you ask him a question about the weather—about picking up a girl in the bar of his hotel in Bangkok, and you get the impression it's more that he was picked up by her. But he takes her back up to his room, and to cut a long story short—something which Harkin is not able to do, it goes on and on, desperate embarrassment for him, and for us too, mixed in with a kind of horrid fascination and, it's dreadful to admit this but it's true, the whole thing is quite genuinely entertaining even though it's thoroughly base and you're just thoroughly glad it's not you under the spotlight. The punchline of the story, which gets told in a horrified nervous whisper that Ivory gets him to repeat so that we can all hear it for a second time, is that the girl is in fact a boy, a transvestite, and of course Harkin didn't want to carry through with the business that they were up there to do, although some of his answers to Ivory's awfully acute questions imply that perhaps he did want to carry through with it and perhaps even that he did actually carry through with it, but anyway, it all ends up with the boy scooting off with all of Harkin's money and his passport as well and leaving Harkin adrift and penniless in Bangkok and taking several days to pluck up the courage to go for assistance to the British Consulate there."

Gibbs grinned maliciously. He refilled his own glass and apologized that the pitcher was empty. "Of course the evening doesn't have anywhere to go after that, and poor Harkin doesn't say another word and is much too embarrassed to attempt to leave because he knows that we'll all construe it as embarrassment so he stays and doesn't say another word. Just sits in a corner and pretends to read a book. And never turns a page of it all night, face crimson red. And Ivory takes to the piano and plays some lovely delicate French music and the party doesn't finally break up until the early hours. How did I get onto this? The point was meant to be that Will threw some marvelous dinner parties."

"He knew Harkin from where? His own days in Japan?"

"We expect so. That's what we thought. I can't remember how I got onto the subject of Harkin. Never heard from him again. Never mind. And now I really must get back to my postgrads."

Gibbs smiled in that end-of-party way that all bad bartenders use when they're closing up.

"I appreciate all the time you've given me. If I could just ask one or two very quick questions . . . ?"

He looked at his watch. Gave me the coldest of looks.

"Just make sure they are very quick."

"Something I don't understand. You said he was born in Norwich, yes?"

He nodded. I went on.

"In your obituary you say it was at Hobart Hall. That's not in Norwich."

"Of course. It was a figure of speech. He was probably born in a Norwich hospital. That's all I meant."

"He did live at Hobart Hall? His father the ambassador?"

"Quite so."

"How much do you know that you're not telling?"

He blinked, looked at me. "Probably quite a lot. Isn't that what you want to think? Now I really must be showing you the way out. I've been very rude keeping you all this time. I'm sure you've got many important things to do."

"Did he ever have an affair with your wife?"

I expected rage or pomposity for an answer. And I got them both in very strong measure. But also, when he had wound down and was still clenching my arm as he moved me through the foyer on our way to the door, he added, thoughtfully, "And anyway she didn't qualify."

"What does that mean?"

"A pleasure meeting you, Mister Boston. Do drop in again."

And that was it. He wasn't going to be saying any more, that much was clear. He let go of me once we were out on the drive. I climbed into my car. I thanked him, most politely, and asked him where I could go, places that William Ivory belonged to.

"I don't know if he belonged anywhere. You might try Hobart Hall. It's National Trust now." He shut the car door for me, grinned. "He might have, ah, indulged himself in a little self-mythology." Gibbs blinked at me, offered this out, checked to see my reaction, and wished me a safe trip back to Harvard.

When I got back into London I headed straight off to Soho, to Cunty's place, to hear the next installment of the William Ivory story, in the Brougham Calder unauthorized version.

H

ave you read Ivory's books? Were you able to? Do you remember this, from his introduction to *Decadent Pleasures*?

Decadence is the human desire for perfection given a cruel humorous twist by the melancholy condition of dying empires. It is Ludwig of Bavaria's fairy-tale castles and his requirement that ugly servants wear masks in his presence; it is Gilles de Rais, his mad occult excesses, and the city of Orléans which he turned into a giant theatre for a season to celebrate the marvellous martyrdom of Jeanne d'Arc; and it is Mishima's sad awkward death.

Images of decadence glow from the death and love beds of history: Aleister Crowley and his Scarlet Woman failing to arouse a goat for the sexual invocation of pagan gods; the patched-up imitation virgins surgically produced for the tired lusts of the Hellfire Club; the courtesan Mme de Pompadour waiting in the park of Versailles, dressed in the costume of a shepherdess or a nun or a cowherd offering milk still warm, hoping to waylay and arouse Louis XV, her King so eaten with melancholy. Decadence is Prince Boothby murdering himself because it had become such a bore dressing and undressing each day; it is Robert de Montesquiou and his day-long vomiting jag after he experienced his one carnal moment, with the actress Sarah Bernhardt; it is the inoffensive poultry-loving emperor Honorius when messengers brought him the news that Rome had fallen to the Goth Alaric and his relief to discover that the message referred to the city-empire and not to his favourite chicken of the same name; it is the feeling described by the Russian Ivanov, "at once oppressive and exalting, of being the last of a series"; and it is a feeling I first became aware of one fire-filled morning when I breakfasted off silver plates in the ruins of the London Blitz.

The dive was nearly empty and Brougham Calder wasn't there. The damp murmur of a few old men sleeping in armchairs along the side of the room. A couple of beat-up gents drinking whiskeys by the bar. Cunty sneered at me and asked if I was a member. I told him I was looking for Julian Brougham Calder and Cunty looked almost human.

"First day I haven't seen the old bastard since he got kicked out of hospital. Maybe he's snuffed it. Hope so. Give us a chance to clean that fucking chair."

Something I've learned about the British, you like to disguise fondness with aggression. It's something to do with the celebrated English sense of humor.

"Do you know where else he might be?"

"I don't know anywhere else that would have him. You're not a member are you? So fuck off then. You could try him at home."

"Where's that?"

"I'm warning you." He flounced off to the other end of the bar.

One of the beat-up gents creaked a little toward me. He opened his mouth with a struggle and said, "Percy Street. Above the ironmonger's." And he creaked away from me again.

Chez Countess F——, la dame aux Benzedrines, it had to be. Percy Street, north of Oxford Street, my AmEx map took me there. The Wheatsheaf was still standing. I didn't see the Burglars Rest. The ironmonger's was an old hardware store with some pots and pans in the window surrounding a secondhand toaster. Filthy windows above, no need for lace curtains. A green wooden door, no bell or knocker. I beat on the door. And kept on beating. Finally the letter flap opened and an ancient blue eye peeped up at me.

He shrieked out an awful falsetto, "Go away. I'm an old woman. I have a dog, you know."

"Julian. Mister Brougham Calder. It's Rick Tierney. I was expecting you at the club."

"I'm an old woman. Leave me please in peace. If it's money you're after you won't get anything here." He then coughed for a while. The attempt at falsetto was doing terrible things to his larynx.

"I thought you wanted to tell me more stories about Ivory."

Silence. The eye kept on peeping at me, teary now with the effort of his coughing.

"Please let me in."

"If you don't bugger off I'll call the police."

The letter flap closed. I could hear him breathing behind the door.

"I brought you some whiskey."

The flap opened again.

"Let's see it."

I held up the bottle of Irish whiskey, waved it around a little, watched the way the rain hit the glass as I waited. It was getting dark by the time the flap closed. Finally, I heard the sound of security chains being loosened and many bolts being unbolted.

The door pulled open. "Come in. Did anyone see you?" Brougham Calder in a pink bathrobe and black sneakers dragged me in by the arm, kicked the door shut, and twisted himself around me to latch tight two security chains and five bolts.

"Are you absolutely certain no one saw you? Come upstairs."

"I couldn't say for sure. I guess the ironmonger saw me. There was a traffic warden walking around."

"A traffic warden? A traffic warden? I don't think we need to worry about traffic wardens. Come off it."

We went into a room which had a dusty gilt birdcage with a telephone inside it hanging from the ceiling. Faded mustard walls decorated with pastoral scenes. Brougham Calder switched off the overhead light, went to the window, and rubbed a peephole through the dirt to inspect the street.

"It seems safe enough. You were very lucky. Now where's that whiskey? I'll get some glasses. Sit."

I sat. He switched the light back on. I looked at the bookcases around me, didn't see any of his own books inside them. I waited for him to come back and I wondered if his was the kind of sickness of the mind that precedes death.

"You can't stay for long, you do know that, don't you?"

This was the man who had been so desperate for an audience. The storyteller who panicked when it was time to go home. He poured whiskey into dusty tumblers, handed me mine, and sat opposite on an old paisley sofa.

"This must be Eileen's place? Where Ivory used to live? How long have you been here? You haven't done much redecorating."

"Yes yes yes yes yes yes yes. That's not really the point. Why are you here?"

"Cunty said you might be here. I was expecting to see you. I went to the club."

"And who was there? Were there many people there?"

"About five or six, that's all."

"So you might have got away with it."

"Got away with what?"

"I've lived here a very long time, a notably long time. This is good whiskey. I like it."

"You said you were going to tell me more about William Ivory."

"Never heard of him. And who are you? Where do you get off trying to get an old man sozzled?"

He shuffled some saliva from his throat to his mouth and back again. He hugged his pink bathrobe tighter around his narrow body. He leaned forward, crooked a finger to pull me toward him. He whispered, "I'm going to turn the taps on."

I heard him walking around, and I heard jets of water spurting in basins in different rooms of the apartment. When he came back he stretched full length on the sofa, his sneakers dangling off the end. He got me to pull nearer. He talked in his ordinary voice.

"One never knows, does one? I'm glad you brought the whiskey."

"I don't understand."

"I'm sorry to play the Bashful Nashville but the thing is, I'm not really able to talk to you anymore."

"Can you tell me why?"

"That would be telling."

"Would it help if I offered money?"

"Not really, no. You know why? Because others can offer more. Good whiskey."

"Keep the bottle. It's yours."

"I beg your pardon? Even if I don't tell you anything?"

"Even if you don't tell me anything."

"My, you're a good soldier." He had some private discussion or maybe he was just appreciating the power of his belches. "Look. Are you quite sure that no one followed you here?"

"Quite sure."

"Well I don't know, maybe I will. I shouldn't." His expression got kind of teasing. "Maybe just one. I don't know. It's irresponsible. Four walls get awfully tiring. Do you ever get lonely? Do you have any idea how dull life becomes when all your friends are dead? Jack Crew. Dylan Thomas. Paul Potts. Francis Bacon. John Deakin. I've seen them all into the ground. Family is hardly a substitute for friends: Do you know how Bacon skived the services?"

I didn't let on he'd told me the story before. I didn't have the heart. I listened again to the tale of the Alsatian dog rented from Harrods, the painter sleeping with it the night before his medical examination to bring out his asthma. When he was done, I asked him if he knew either Roland Gibbs or a man named Jim Harkin.

"Never heard of Gibbs. I remember Harkin. A man we knew in Fitzrovia and never heard utter a word. Are you writing a book on Harkin now? I expect he's dead too. Have you read my *Necessary Negroes*?"

"I'd love to see a copy."

That animated him. "Would you? Would you really?" He jerked into a sitting position and his robe fell open to show

me a wizened old cock and heavy old-man balls. "I'd love you
to see it. See all my books. Show you I'm not just a talker. My
own copies are in hock, valuable first editions, that's how this
country treats its hommes de lettres. *Teach the Free Man* was my
debut. Nineteen forty-six. George Orwell described it as an
English *Sentimental Education*. Jonathan Cape published it—
lovely, lovely man—price five shillings and sixpence. *Necessary
Negroes*, Allen Lane, nineteen fifty-one, nine shillings. Again
garnered impressive plaudits from the gentlemen of the press.
After the Rain, Martin Secker and Warburg, they offered the
most favorable terms, nineteen fifty-four, priced at thirteen and
six. *Dead Years: An Autobiography of Sorts*, that was published by
Hamish Hamilton, marvelous indulgent man, Cyril Connolly
took him to the cleaners, nineteen sixty-one, thirty shillings.
Lesbians of the Dust: The Collected Poetry of Julian Brougham Calder,
a slim volume but not without merit, Faber and Faber, nineteen
sixty-two, eighteen shillings. *Essays at Twilight*, a lavishly illustrated survey of historical excesses that—"
"Sounds like Ivory's *Decadent Pleasures*."
"Yes it bloody does doesn't it?"
"Is that why you dislike him so much?"
Brougham Calder twisted his mouth up at the corners. A
long time ago when the world was younger and so was he the
expression would have passed for a smile. In the dim light I
admired his false teeth.
"I didn't entirely. He upset my brother more than once and
that made me pleased as Punch and still, even still, he's got
them all on the run, but the point is, he was cruel and beneath
those airs and graces he was common as hell."
"You've said that before—"
"Oh? Now I'm repeating myself am I?"
"I didn't mean to cause any offense. It's just that I was told
he was an aristocrat. The ambassador's son."
"Really?" He laughed and it sounded like choking. "Who
else have you met who knew him?"
"His wife Helen for one. And she didn't describe him as
cruel. Just strong."
"Quite. Omnia vincit amor et nos cedamus amori. Volenti

non fit injuria. There are two benefits of a public-school education—the drawbacks of course are a lifetime of pederasty and flagellation, although some would argue those are benefits also. But to my mind, the first is a competent prose style and the second is the ability to pepper one's conversation with Latin tags. You are sure nobody followed you here? Nunc est bibendum. Which means now is the time to drink. Horace. Your good health."

"What do you mean when you say he's got them all on the run?"

"You're pushing it, chummy. You're sailing very close indeed." He sprung up from the sofa, surprising agility, and went back to the window again. He blew upon it and wiped his breath away with the sleeve of his dressing gown. "Looks clear enough. There's a traffic warden down there. Are their uniforms usually blue? You're not trying to trick me into anything are you? You look innocent enough but that's half the battle. You did show an interest in my work but that could be cover and Americans are like that anyway, you're so compulsive about *things*. If I asked you to describe a woman you'd talk about her clothes wouldn't you? And her shape of course. Nothing interior though. That's probably why I've never sold in America. Look. What did you really come here for?"

"Like I said. To hear more stories about Ivory."

"For your book."

"For my book."

He settled back onto the sofa once more. The annoying thing was, despite his paranoia, or maybe because of it, the old man was enjoying himself. The novelty of being in a place where Ivory once lived was starting to wear off.

"When did Ivory move out of this place? Did he leave things behind? May I see them?"

"You think you're very clever don't you? Mister Sidling Whiskey-Carrying Yank Investigator. Well, Mister Clever, I'll give you a choice. A choice of three tales from the William Ivory catalogue. Which do you want to hear? The truth about Japan, a gambling mystery, or a family saga? You decide."

"I kind of like the sound of a gambling mystery."

"That's your choice is it? Your final answer? Then a gambling mystery it is. Sit tight." He gathered the folds of his dressing gown around himself, took a deep breath of whiskey from the tumbler which he sat upon his chest, closed his eyes, and began.

"The year is nineteen hundred and fifty-one. Imagine a casino in the west of London. Once a house now an illicit gaming club on a melancholy street in North Kensington. There's no name on the door, no brass plaque or Al Caponee speakeasy hatch, just the street number, one hundred and twelve, painted on the right-hand pillar at the head of the drive with a flaring horse's head above. Some people call it the Horse Head Club, some just call it one hundred and twelve, or one-one-two, but the ones who are really in the know call it Jackie's Place. Gambling is big in London in nineteen hundred and fifty-one. The craze started in the War and it's still going strong. Casinos are thoroughly illegal of course but there's always a way round that. At Jackie's Place the big games are chemin de fer and roulette, and blackjack and poker too, Yank influences.

"All righty, Mister Clever. Are you on the street with me? Then straighten your tie and pull off your gloves and let's beat a tattoo on the door. If the bruiser on the door is kind enough to let us pass, and he will, it's all right, you're with me, then it's a queer mix of people we find inside. There are Chinamen and Jamaicans, Jews of course, some doubtful Americans still AWOL from 'forty-five, Spanish and Portuguese who work in local restaurants and blow their earnings twice a week regular as clockwork to keep Jackie in clover. Nobody knows where Jackie himself is from. He's half Portuguese or else half Chinese, or maybe he's Red Indian with a little European missionary Catholic mixed in. I think he might have been Jamaican actually. But it's become the smart place to go, so the debs are there, and the painters are there, and rich homosexuals desperate for a little exotic other to toss off in unseemly locales, and intense young men just down from Oxford fighting respectability, and grammar-school boys who fancy themselves poets, and slum landlords with their prettiest tenants, and middle-class provincial girls set on offering their bodies to anyone who asks, and a whole crowd of us who'd seen off the

War together and all in all rather missed it. That's the kind of crew we see down at Jackie's Place.

"This is nineteen fifty-one remember. The grand adventure of London in wartime is over, even well before V-Day the Paradise Club was having nightly Blitz reunion parties. And Churchill is back in, a depressed old dipso who thinks no one really appreciates him, and there's not enough money going around, and rationing is still on, and everything is all a little piss-colored. So what's the answer? Gambling. Of course.

"Jackie's Place is open every Tuesday and Friday. God knows what went on there the other five days, it was the stuff of many drunken imaginings and there are images of it in all the best novels of the period—you *have* read my *Necessary Negroes*? And for one charmed dangerous period Ivory was there on Fridays.

"He'd become a mystery man. He dropped out of sight after Mattie died. Oh yes, Mattie died, shortly before the end of the War, he had to, it was what he wanted, but I can't go into that, can I, Mister Clever? That comes under family saga and remember I'm only allowing you one. There were rumors of Ivory of course—he was the piano player in a Cairo bordello, he was a diplomat posted to France, he was an astrologer in the Rosicrucian tradition over on the West Coast of America. He was in the merchant navy, in Wormwood Scrubs, he was running guns or operating a slaving ship out in Africa or Asia. I don't know about that, and you'd see him sometimes out in the country at parties. But then he appeared one Friday evening at Jackie's Place in nineteen fifty-one. He'd grown a mustache which made him look a more formidable character, and he'd developed a rather mysterious manner which contrived or not did keep us at arm's length. We didn't know where or how he lived and we could only guess at his adventures and like him or not that did make it all rather intriguing. Sometimes he would join us for a late supper and sometimes for drinks on the following day. But that was it. He never told us about himself. Not in drink or fun.

"He'd acquired a girl. She appeared one night, this awkward unworldly creature in a white sleeveless dress. That's how I remember her at first. Tagging along. It was a very glamorous dress, a sexy French dress, but worn with a granny cardigan over it as if she hadn't quite made up her mind yet which way she was going to go. She was quite a beautiful girl—he always did seem to get them, I never understood how, still don't—but she was a strange girl, with the face of a dark angel and this queer way of walking, brought to mind a mermaid still getting accustomed to human legs. She loved him to play the piano, it did things to her. She'd turn the pages of the score or if he was playing from memory she'd stand just behind him, her body following every touch of his powerful fingers. Like the proudest of mothers standing over her magical prodigy son, any competing noise made her wince. Glasses clinking, gambling chips clicking into stacks, laughter, shrill gossip. She was too much the shy one to demand attention, but you could see how those sounds hurt her. Visible signs of pain.

"Let's go back outside, away from the piano, past the cloakroom, let's nod to the bruiser and hope he remembers our face, let's open the heavy wood door, and let's slip behind the box hedge on the side of the drive and let's allow a week to go by. We're going to wait for Ivory and his girl to arrive. It'll be worth our wait. It's a very special night because Ivory is to take to the gaming table for the very first time.

"Here they come. You can hear their footsteps on the street. Walking with a shy swagger, you'd think him a captain of the Coldstream recently cashiered, with his awkward pretty girl trying to keep step alongside. It's raining tonight and she struggles for the protection of his black umbrella. They turn in past the horse's head and they stop before they get to the door. Her hand is on his arm now. They look around, they don't see us in the hedge. Sshh. Breathe soft now. Don't let them hear you. They're about to do their secret thing.

"Everyone by now has run through generations of wristwatches, but Ivory has kept to a rather exquisite pocket Hunter which he keeps chained to his waistcoat fob, it's a keepsake no doubt from the Blitz. Their love act, their luck fetish, their sacrament, begins this night and it will continue for as long as Ivory gambles and so extravagantly wins. He lifts the watch by its chain and offers it to her. She cups it in one hand, almost as if it is alive and capable of receiving pleasure, and she winds it for him, keeping her eyes on his all the while. When they are done he gives a little tug to the chain so it slides away from her flesh and drops back into the fob. They continue along the path, and he shows his membership card to the bruiser on the door. We follow quickly after.

"She shrugs off her overcoat and Ivory gives it to the cloakroom girl, then they head to the bar at the top of the stairs for a glass each of Jackie's famous rum punch. She's still wearing her cardigan. They return down the stairs, nodding a few times to chaps he knows. Before they go into the Macao Room, which is decorated like a country-house library, they pause in the hall to allow Ivory to beat out a quick melody on the piano for her delight.

"There are two chemmy tables in the Macao Room. Ivory and his girl go to the high-limit table. He's not looking to play just yet. It's not time. They stand tightly together, watching. Let us also watch. We know most of the players. Mike Callaghan is holding the bank. He's a billiard ace from Holloway in a black lounge suit. He's grinning a bad-teeth smile and smoking untipped cigarettes. Next to him sits our old friend Jack Crew from the Wheatsheaf, drinker, composer of sentimental odes to the poor, a shortsighted philanderer and egomaniac who looks as if he doesn't have long to live. Then there's a blond young lawyer with an unfortunate family resemblance to ourself who shortly will be failing his bar exams. Behind him is his highly strung debutante, and next to him a Yank with a very reserved manner who does something of a technical nature in the movies. Beside the Yank is a brutish boy called Freddy who's the heir to a dukedom. The croupier is a tough wiry boy with a very correct manner in a dinner jacket. Short curly hair, dusky mulatto complexion, he sits very straight, sometimes smiling when he scoops away the house's cut of the winnings.

"Ivory and his girl stand behind Callaghan and our friend Jack. Friend Jack is having trouble. He is having a little difficulty telling one card from another. But that doesn't matter a jot to him. He's someone who desires to lose. Already on the front of his faux workingman's trousers are the damp telltale stains. Ivory's girl gives her man a nudge and Ivory lifts out his watch. He shows it to his girl. They remain where they are. Let's watch the game.

"Righty-ho. Banker, that's Callaghan, is hiding a four and a two. Friend Jack goes over the top after having seven with two cards. Not very clever and also entirely illegal to draw to seven, but the man's out of control. Six wins. Jack pulls away from the table to find some more rum punch. Ivory looks at the empty seat and then at his watch. His girl nods her head. The croupier shuffles the decks.

"Ivory slips the Hunter back into its fob, sits at the table straight-backed with his hands clasped together making a cathedral—you know, the thumbs together, the little fingers the steeple—and he calls the word 'banco.' That means he's playing for the banker's entire stack. Callaghan isn't sure about that and greedy little Anthony buys the bank off him. Ivory nods over and smiles ever so slightly. His girl stands behind him with her hands just above his shoulders as if she's ready to catch him should he fall. Ivory looks down at the first card he's ever been dealt. A queen of spades. A nothing card. He turns over the next one. An eight of diamonds. That's it. It's over. He's cleaned out Anthony.

"Let's watch him for a moment. He sits very still and erect at the table, he flicks the cards out of the sabot and he leaves his own where they fall. His hands move just over them, a fraction of air between, his beautifully manicured nails for all to see. He always was a vain man.

"Ivory checks his watch every few hands. People bet to the maximum against him, they're all so eager to take this arrogant tyro to the cleaners. They bet to the maximum and Ivory wins every single hand. Gathers quite a crowd. This sort of thing doesn't happen. After only a half hour he stops. Mark me, a half hour precisely. He raises his palms towards the croupier and leaves the table, with his girl and his winnings. Shortly after, the croupier changes. From a distance we can see the mulatto tough boy talking quite seriously to Jackie.

"Let's walk out with Ivory and his girl. His manner is the

same as ever, cordial and polite and distant, and really rather dull in its perfection, but his skin is reddened like rouge on a Piccadilly tart, and the way he grips his girl's hand to his arm betrays his passion. He does his best to shrug us but he's too correct to do more than drop one or two gentlemanly hints which are easy for us to ignore. We wander around the house, to the bar, where they don't drink but we do—we get a little reckless on Jackie's rum punch—we dawdle by the roulette wheel, we take in the poker game upstairs, and we fire inane observations at him, try to ruffle his feathers: 'Had a good run, Ivory,' 'Why stop when you did?' 'Little lady bring you luck?' 'My brother didn't take too well to you winning,' that kind of thing. The girl is nervous as hell.

"The place breaks up sometime after midnight. It's not one of the wild nights. Some stranger accuses the poker dealer of fixing the deck and gets a poke in the eye from one of Jackie's boys and the bum's rush out of the place from a couple more. Anthony's debutante gets hysterical with rum punch and her boyfriend's lost pride and the tight waistband of her skirt and bursts into tears behind Ivory as he plays some quite wild dance thing on the piano. There are all these tears coming down her face and her hair is wild, and she's pulled off her jacket, and now her blouse, and she's got a bit of an audience but they have to be patient, because girls wore rather a lot of underthings in those days, and the blouse is off and now she's trying to pull the slip out without taking her skirt off first—it's only unhitched at the top—and she can't do it and that makes her cry some more until brother Anthony, the white sheep of the family, he's now a high-court judge incidentally, gives her a jab to the face and pulls her out of there.

"The night moves on to a pub which stays open until dawn, but I return home. I have some writing to do. Fine words *do* butter parsnips. And I remember thinking that really, all in all, I'm getting a little too old for this lark and I'm glad I don't have to go to the office the next day and really, no matter how hard we try we're never going to experience it again, that joy and reverence and discovery of life during wartime. As Ivory said, anything more is just decadence."

Brougham Calder sat back, lifted his tumbler to his face and put it down again when he tasted it was empty. He looked fixed there on the sofa, permanent. But then the telephone rang and he jerked up to his feet and shot baffled worried frowns into each corner of the room. It took him a while to locate the source of the sound. He started, scrupulously, at the jack in the wall, then followed the lead between the fingers of his left hand: along the floor, to the sofa, up and over one embroidered arm, then beneath plump faded cushions and finally up into the birdcage above. He opened the gilt door of the cage and pulled the machine back down into the sofa and fumbled with the receiver. He answered it on the twelfth ring and looked anxiously at me as he spoke with a finger lifted to his mouth.

"No, I haven't . . . Absolutely not . . . just here, all night alone . . . bored . . . yes yes of course . . . I know. Thank you . . . Love to Jane."

He hung up. Focused slowly on me. "It's a matter of money, you know, and those things don't come cheap. Take your bottle and get the hell out of here. Perhaps you could spare me one last glass?"

I refilled his tumbler and set the bottle beside him.

"I said you should keep the bottle and I meant it—"

"Most generous. I'm truly struck by that."

"I just don't understand . . ."

"Ours not to reason why, et cetera et cetera. Perhaps I will be able to return the hospitality at some future date. And now if you would be so good as to find the door . . . ? I do hope it's not raining too heavily."

Contrary passions were moving him. I could see them at work. Fear at whatever message the telephone had brought and his necessary desire to tell stories to me, someone, anyone.

"I had better be going, then."

"Yes you had."

His eyes uselessly scanned the room for microphones or cameras or maybe both hidden behind the yellow-and-green pastoral paintings on the walls. He looked like a boy who's just been denied a bicycle.

"It's a good story. I'm sorry to miss the end of it. Was there much left to tell?"

"Whereabouts was I?"

I had sufficient cunning to get up and head for the door.

"Where was I? Come on. Where was I?"

"The night had ended at Jack Crew's house. You'd watched Ivory playing cards and winning for half an hour."

"Exactly. I went back the next Tuesday, but he wasn't there, he never was on a Tuesday—look, sit down, you make me nervous stamping about like that—but he did return on the Friday, along with his girl. The same thing. Quickly. I'll tell you. I saw her winding up his watch in that silent masturbatory pose and I followed them inside, fortune's little darlings. The usual crowd. Crew was there, and a lesbian, and Callaghan from Holloway, and brutish Freddy, I forget who else. It doesn't matter. A painter, I think. Might have been Lucian Freud. Anthony was around but he wasn't playing. He'd take quite some time to recoup his lost cash and pride. Crew was the big winner for once. His trousers clean of stains. He was sitting there, the Sunday newspapers' image of the poet of the Left in Trotsky cap and self-scuffed workingman's boots, a massive pile of chips in front of him. A signal is given from the girl to the man and Ivory sits down, his back straight like mother's little soldier, his girl behind him, one hand up in the air almost touching her lover's right shoulder.

"Ivory calls banco in his diffident way and reaches behind for his girl to pass him the chips he'd won the week before. Crew smiles, slobbers in anticipation, something is already stirring in his trousers. The croupier is the same mulatto tough of the week before. Shuffles the decks. Everyone lays down their chips to bet on Ivory. His first card is a court card and that doesn't count for anything. His second is a nine. Simple as that. Crew doesn't bother even to look at his own card as the croupier shovels the stack over to Ivory, who arranges them in neat piles as Crew leaves the table, his folded hands covering his groin.

"Ivory's girl is blossoming with his luck. The granny cardigan is gone. She wears a long black dress, Frenchy material layered in perfect creases. It's a moll's dress. A swell's dress. She walks now as if she knows her own power. Her hair is cut more elegantly than before and it's shaped so cleverly that it just falls under its own weight into a perfect shape. What's the name of that film actress, Hepburn?"

"Katharine Hepburn?"

"No no no no no no no. She has a long neck. Nice manners. Simpers a little? Women like her. She's dead, I think."

"Audrey Hepburn?"

"That's the one. That's who Ivory's girl looks like. Delicate. Still otherworldly but poised now. As if she's grown into her body. But typical Ivory, he's less attentive to her than ever. He used to treat her with only slight respect, only occasional attention. But now, apart from their little trick with the Hunter, he acts as if he is either oblivious to her or just utterly bored by her.

"Jackie himself is close by. A real crowd gathers. Word has spread. Our boy Ivory has become the stuff of legend in the past week. The man who broke the bank at one-one-two. Ivory has eight. Freddy has seven. The next hand. Callaghan has six. Ivory has seven. Callaghan calls banco. Someone has to try to put a stop to this. Ivory's hand is shaking as he flicks the top corners of his cards. You get the sense that he's in the grip of something he knows is so much bigger than himself. His girl wants to see his card. Ivory doesn't show it to her. Pays her as much attention as you'd show a librarian in a brothel. He considers. Anthony calls over to him, yes he's back, but he can't afford to play. 'So, Willy,' he detested being called Willy, 'is it over?' Ivory ignores him, he can't stand lawyers anyway. He shows his card, it's a five, and he wants another. Callaghan shows his seven. Ivory shows the three he'd taken. That makes eight. The mulatto pushes Callaghan's stack of chips over to join Ivory's. The crowd gets larger. This next half hour is going to be good.

"The croupier sometimes smiles, Ivory never does. His face is flushed, his hands are perfectly controlled. He looks at his cards and he looks at the crowd around him. He's proud, and he's arrogant, and he's more than a little scared, because for some dark reason he can do no wrong. The others are desperate to recoup and they bet to the maximum and Ivory wins every hand. A sound builds up around him, the envious murmur of an unlucky mob watching one man get the better of fate. His girl drapes her arms around his neck and Ivory shrugs her off. She slides a hand down his chest and tugs at his watch chain and he relents. He lifts the watch, looks at it, he gathers his winnings into a pile. 'Excuse me, gentlemen,' he says. 'That's my gaming over for the evening.' Half an hour has passed. The two of them walk away from the table and the croupiers change over their shifts.

"Ivory and his girl walk off like two people who don't know each other but who happen to be going the same way. She wants him to play the piano awhile but he ignores that. He cashes in his winnings, and he's won a lot that night, many thousands, and picks up his overcoat and umbrella and hat from the cloakroom girl and stalks off into the night. His girl runs after him, her heels clicking on the rain-slick streets of West London, her light urgent voice flicking out after him, as he stalks on ahead, chasing something unknown."

"It's something to do with the croupier. That's the trick, am I right? Fixing the cards. Or it's Jackie, yeah? Laundering money or something? You said no one knew what Ivory did. Maybe he was a gangster."

"Shut up! You don't know what you're getting me into. We don't have long to go. Hear the story out."

"Is he back next week?"

"Of course he's back next week."

"With his girl?"

"That's the curious thing actually. He's there alone, sans girl, sans brolly. Later than usual, he arrives, this usually so impeccable gentleman, and he looks as if he's been out swimming in his clothes. His coat and hat are soaked through and he presents them rather brusquely to the cloakroom girl. He goes straight to the table. There's an impatient crowd to see him, and Jackie himself is playing and has taken the bank. The table is full, but as soon as Ivory arrives one of the gamers, I think it was our Friend Jack, offers his place to Ivory. The club is wild, a hugger-mugger hubbub, like at a prizefight before the bout has started when the local boy climbs into the ring.

"Ivory's still wet, his suit is patched with rain, there's a line of hair around his head flattened down from where he was wearing his hat, he smells of a damp dirty city. He's more nervous than usual, his hands continue to shake long after he's been dealt the first cards, and he plays like a man in a fever. But, of course, he wins. Jackie cracks Jamaican jokes and the crowd jostles around as the ones at the back struggle to see and have to rely on commentaries from the sharp boys at the front. The other players drop out. They're irrelevant now—Callaghan is the last to go. It's just Jackie and Ivory. Ivory looks occasionally at his watch with the expression of a man in a dream, and plays frantically, but always winning. Eight to Jackie's seven, nine to his eight, six to his five. On and on, always drawing to a five. And he keeps winning. Winning against impossible, diabolical odds. He's showing a four and a queen—he doesn't bother to hide his cards anymore—he takes another. Jackie has seven. Ivory flips over his second card. It's another four.

"On and on. Ivory is sweating now. I don't remember seeing him sweat before. He loosens his tie. He gives himself another card and wins again. He looks suddenly back over his shoulder as if there's someone missing who ought to be there. He puts each hand on its shoulder like a child playing a classroom game, and then, abruptly, as if suddenly aware of the foolishness of the gesture, he forces his hands down to the table, just ahead of the next card arriving, it's an ace, and clasps them into a cathedral. A second ace. Then he draws a seven. A lot of money to young sweaty cathedral-handed Ivory.

"A few slip away from the back of the crowd. He's been there for half an hour so he's bound to be stopping now. But he doesn't stop, even though he is in sufficient possession of himself to look at his watch, albeit with a puzzled expression as if he doesn't quite remember what it's for. Someone, it certainly isn't me, reminds him that half an hour is up, but he doesn't seem to hear. He keeps playing. Reckless and wild. Money, fortunes, have been flying towards him so why should they stop now? His hair droops out of its pomaded pretty perfection. He's taken his jacket off and rolled up his shirt-sleeves. His waistcoat has popped a low button but he doesn't notice that. I catch a surprising glimpse of a tattoo across his belly. He strokes his mustache, he clasps his hands together, he flicks corners of his cards like a man in a hurry. Jackie keeps joking, keeps smiling, keeps playing the cards, and Ivory is now no longer winning every hand. He's got a five to his ace but Jackie has a four and a three. He has a seven but Jackie draws a three to a six. He has the seven of hearts but Jackie has the nine of diamonds. Ivory wins two hands in a row, then loses three. He wins the next three and then loses five. He can stop when he's winning but not it seems when he's losing. He looks again at his watch, shakes his head, and he carries on playing. And losing.

"There's just the two of them sitting at that table. An over-head light. The cards shuffling, sliding, destroying. Jackie isn't joking anymore. He doesn't even smile. Ivory doesn't have any more chips in front of him. He writes an I.O.U. Jackie already has a pile of these. He doesn't want another. Ivory insists. Finally Jackie agrees. Ivory is dealt an ace and a four. Jackie is showing a ten, a worthless card. Jackie allows him to raise the stakes and Ivory draws another card. Jackie delivers it face down. Ivory impatiently turns it up, as if secrets are starting to annoy him. It's a seven. He has twelve. Too much.

" 'Last hand,' says Jackie. 'No pay. No play.' Ivory nods, his eyes are fixed on the shoe of cards. 'Deal them open,' says he, and Jackie shrugs his shoulders, flicks the top card up towards him, an ace. Jackie deals himself a six. Ivory gets a two. Ivory, fixated Ivory, fated Ivory, eyes-focused Ivory, sweating Ivory, motions with his hand for another card. Maybe Jackie's for-gotten that they agreed to play open or maybe he's doing it for the punters, for the spectacle, but he flicks it towards his opponent face down. Ivory doesn't look at it straightaway. There's an awful hush, we're watching the ruination of a man. Jackie turns up his second card. It's a king. He's still on six. Ivory pulls out his watch and smiles a rather ugly smile. 'It stopped,' says he. 'I wonder if anyone has the correct time.' Someone shouts it over to him. 'I believe it stopped three hours

ago,' says he. 'I hadn't intended to play this long. Someone—'
He interrupts himself and turns over his card. He needs a five,
six, or seven. It's a nine of spades. He's lost.

"The thing's a mess. Some lad with a head for figures esti-
mated that Ivory lost in those three hours about five times as
much as he had won before."

"How did he take it?"

"Ivory always was a self-possessed man. He rolled down his
sleeves and slipped in his cuff links quite adroitly, without
requiring anyone else's help. He replaced his jacket and
straightened his tie. His waistcoat was still partly unbuttoned
and that was the only signal of disaster. His tattoo looked
sinister shining in the light. He smoothed down his hair and
gulped for air and smiled his typically urbane smile. He waited
for us to part to let him through, and we waited—what were
we waiting for? The final thing, a denouement. For Ivory to
crumble, to rant, for his ghostly girl to arrive. We wanted the
ordering thing, a neat ending. The materializing presence of
the demon of the piece, Horatio. Because that's what this story
is all about. The intrusion for that brief dark-charmed time of
something evil, a power, pulled through past the customary
curtain. But Jackie just said, 'Ladies and gentlemen, if you
please!' in that lovely Jamaican lilt of his, and that shifted us.
We made an avenue for Ivory to walk along. He straightened
his collar as he passed through us. His elbow brushed against
me. I felt him trembling.

"He didn't return to the club. We heard he had settled with
Jackie sometime that following week. And then he disappeared
again. He was supposed to have gone to Japan, to Greece, to
Italy. He was sailing a boat around the southern Mediterranean
with one of his cousins. He was living in anonymous cruelty
in a suburb of London. He was in the Foreign Legion. He was
in prison. He was playing piano in a Cairo bordello."

"And his girl?"

"We never saw his marvelous fetish again. Jack Crew claimed
to have spotted her, dowdy again, or so he said, her brief
butterfly life over. Frankly, we didn't believe him. We all knew
she was something unreal, bigger than life."

It seemed to get darker in there. A thin cold breeze disturbed the surface of the Percy Street flat. The paintings turned creepy in the dark, no longer pictures of countryside and cows.

"It couldn't have been a setup?"

"Magic, dear boy, is the only explanation. A pact with dark forces. The girl the go-between. So long as she was there to wind up Ivory's watch he kept to the limit and he won. When she was gone, after he'd driven her away or reneged on his otherworldly promise, he met his ruin. At least he did it gracefully. He won without swanking and he lost with dignity. That much I'll give him."

"When did you see him again?"

"Ivory returned to London five years later in nineteen fifty-six, and he was a harder man by then but he would never talk about what happened and my glass is empty and my telling is done."

A moral tale about why you should never trust in luck and why men shouldn't drive their women away. I didn't know if the principle worked in reverse. We finished off the bottle. In silence, with Brougham Calder nervously looking at his own watch. A ghost story to scare children with. He was getting more nervous the longer I stayed. When the whiskey was drained he unsteadily led me back out onto Percy Street, pushed me out into the rain, and bolted five bolts behind me.

Anger. Fury. Fucking rage. I wanted to hurt someone—maybe you, maybe myself. Throughout the conversation
with the hotel night manager I kept my hands behind my back.
Maybe he thought I was standing correctly, a colonial aping
an officer of the Guards. He couldn't see what my hands were
doing. My right hand, my daddy hand, crushing the fingers of
my left hand in a hard daddy grip. Pain gives a tight narrow
avenue of sense through anger, through rage, through frustra-
tion, through fear. It gives you a rational path to walk along.
Stops you doing something irrevocable.

When I'd got back to the hotel they were not pleased with
me. A tap on the arm from the night manager and a gentle
steer toward the desk. This was your fault. A severe expression
on the night manager's face. A piece of paper touched gently
toward me. Big figures at the bottom neatly circled. Embarrassing for me. He waited for me to say something. I waited
for him to say something. I was tired. He was implacable. He
was the law. I was a gangster. He was tucked neatly inside a
black morning coat. I was wet, in a sopping linen suit, already
pissed off that I'd left my bag in the car and would have to go
back to get it. He was disappointed with me. I wanted him to
like me. He disapproved of me.

"Your bill."

Breathing deeply, gulps of air to calm myself down. "It's late."

"Quite. If you could settle it?"

If I could settle it, what? The world would settle into its
perfect shape? Angels would soothe us with lullabies? I was a
bad boy. I was stretching the fabric of things. And this was
your fault. I'd arrived in good faith. I'd listened to you in good
faith. Your boy. I didn't like England. I found it difficult. It
didn't make sense to me. The night manager intimidated me

with his repertoire of charm-school moves. It was strange outside. Ugly weather. The windows pelted with hard rain. The streets empty apart from a few unfortunates. I didn't want to be an unfortunate. I wanted to go to sleep.

"Each night accounted here. Room service here, here, and here. Mini-bar here, here, here, here, here, and here. V.A.T. here."

"V.A.T. That's like a purchase tax, yes?"

"The total here. Carrying forward to the next page. The net total here. It's quite a large figure."

"I'd like to settle it."

"We would like you to settle it."

"I intend to carry on staying here."

"We would like nothing better."

He smiled at me. I smiled at him. My eardrums thudded. I looked at the bill. He looked at the bill. We smiled some more. I plotted a murder. Yours. An old boy in pastel blue golfing slacks and a checkered cap drifted into the lobby. I couldn't work out why he wasn't wet. He drifted on past, leaving us a smile along the way. I hated you. Cunt, I thought. That's what I thought. Fucking cunt. I was wet and I was cold and I was miserable and I didn't have the money to deal with this.

"The morning? I'll settle up first thing."

He beamed at me. Nodded his head in polite disdainful chumminess. "That would be appropriate. I'll leave a note to that effect."

I thanked him extravagantly. He told me to think nothing of it. We silently admired each other until he got bored. He turned away. I walked to the elevator with murder in my heart.

I had a shower in my room. I used all the towels—brave boy, I dirtied them all and left them scattered around. I turned on the TV and the radio and ordered room service and drank from the mini-bar. I sat on the bed taking care to disorganize all the sheets. I opened the windows wide and took pride in the wind and rain coming in. I put the photos of Ivory carefully away in my wallet.

Bad emotions have bright colors and anger is deep scarlet

red. I went out onto the terrace and the world was scarlet and all I remember doing is shaking and maybe jumping up and down a little with my hands big daddy fists around the wrought-iron latticework of the terrace. I held on to the iron and tore open my hands and I shouted your name.

Does this surprise you? You are past surprises, I know, but maybe this moves you in some unfamiliar direction. How did you see me then? A good-natured lug to do your bidding. A man with simple and direct appetites. A primitive of sorts to carry your bags and tote your load. Black-haired and green-eyed, exotic Mexican blood rising against the Irish, your own very necessary Negro.

Slow down. Pull back. Control. Take some deep yoga breaths. Anger gets us nowhere. The memory of anger—but I want you to know. I want you to understand the way things were and the way things are. But all the same this gets us nowhere. Let's not allow emotions to get in the way of the story. Stop. Chill. Let me just take a walk around the room. Consider its perimeter. Open the curtains and look out on the street. Go into the bathroom and rinse my forehead and wrists with cold water. Open the apartment door and sniff the silence in the house below. Close it again with a soft click, sit by the table, poke my fingers into the rotting oranges and apples. Turn on the oven and be satisfied by the demonstration of power. Back into the bathroom, appreciate the careful beauty of the jars of cosmetics. Examine my reflection in the mirror and think about having a shave. Time to do that tomorrow. Return to the bedroom and lie down on the bed and be soothed by contemplation of the ceiling. Sit on the bed, feet pressed against the floor, and be reassured by the necessity of gravity and weight. Carefully ignore the place in the corner. Don't even look at it. Don't even think about it. Get up off the bed and draw the curtains again. Keep this place secret and quiet. Pour a glass of purified water. Light a cigarette. Maybe go out and take a walk around the city. No. Don't need it. It will only confuse things. Relax.

Hard to remember. The events are easy enough. But maybe I wasn't that angry after all. Maybe I didn't have murder in my heart after talking with the hotel manager. The emotions we paint in afterward, like primary shades in a child's coloring book.

It was convenient that I'd left my bag in the trunk of the hire car. I could wear the rest of my clothes, my second linen suit, a pair of jeans beneath, two shirts, a heavy fisherman's sweater, and the rest of my shit crammed into pockets. I rolled out of my room like a hot Egyptian mummy in modern clothes. My movements inhibited by cotton and wool, I staggered out into the elevator with mini-bar whiskeys in both my hands.

My friend the night manager was at the desk, reading the early-morning edition of *The Sun*. He glanced up at me as I waddled past. His eyebrows lifted. I gave him a stiff cheery wave.

"Just slipping out for a stroll. It's a cold night."

I kept on walking, didn't give him the chance to say anything more. As soon as I'd struggled my way through the revolving door I rolled fast out of sight. Clambered into my hire car and drove random miles.

Driving through London sweating like a pig, sweltering in my many layers of clothes which I couldn't be bothered to remove. Streets and roads and avenues wet from the storm, sleeping gray suburbs, streetlights flickering. I once knew a girl who claimed she'd had to move out to a farm because she turned off each city light just by standing under it, and I wondered if she was in town. I drove up Portobello Road and I drove onto Harrow Road and then turned back on myself and headed west along a six-lane blacktop. I rolled down the window and that took an age. Too many clothes on for my elbow to work. Sped past a car supermarket, past the Hoover building, art deco white. Along to signs to a Polish cemetery. The pull of the city got less and that disturbed me so I turned around and drove back to the city through gray suburbs. It was like when I was a teenager, when I'd go stay with my cousins out in

Virginia, and we'd steal into my uncle's car after midnight, drive out of Frederick and head into D.C. Cruise Southwest, mean boy racers looking for trouble but not able to recognize its shape, stop off for a soda at a 7-11, the only white boys in the neighborhood. Radios blaring disco-funk, relaxed threatening smiles and rolling papers. Get back into my uncle's car, tune the radio to a college punk station and sing along, grinning with adventure. Keep driving back down around Maryland and Virginia until we felt ready to fall asleep. Driving in straight lines always helps me to think straight.

I drove the Ford through narrow streets with video stores, bathroom-accessory units, bookies' joints, pubs on every corner, displaced corner stores next to them. Look at the few people out at night. The kids on bicycles joylessly patrolling their territory, bums picnicking out of trash cans in the pleasant spring night, occasional clumps of drunks rolling back after a party or a pub. Teenage girls in short white skirts swinging little white handbags, walking drunkenly with city bruises on their sturdy legs, hungry for sex or just disappointed in it, weaving their paths home where their parents waited up to give them hell and remind them of shame.

I kept driving. Watched the fuel gauge flicker down to red. Wondered, hoped for a magical series of tunnels that would take me back home to my childhood place. I felt no part of this city. It was too big and narrow and cramped and it was too sad and all the important things had happened too long ago. But back home was a place to leave as well, and I'd done that, and at least certainty was offered here. A man's life is fixed. Interpretations can only be applied after the facts which remain cold and aloof and still. I'd found out little about Ivory, less than I'd have thought, and there was more ambiguity than I'd expected, but the facts of his life were there to be found, the secret pattern waiting for my hand to trace it; the clues lay here in this city, hidden or buried, and I'd be able to dig them out. A faithful sleuth, history's snooper, the man with the magnifying glass and a coonskin hat: just focus on him, William Ivory, man and monster, to unearth, to prop up in the light of the living. To ask questions of without a dictionary of the dead. Just tune out everything else and listen to him alone and hope to hear it all.

I drove back into the city, turned left and right and left down random streets, and kept going until I could hear the sputtering of a motor about to snuff. I was down near the river, rolling in neutral on a street full of shabby hotels, and when the engine died I was outside one which displayed a tattered VACANCY sign propped up in the window.

I rolled to the door sweating in my swaddling clothes, pressed a bell which didn't work, banged a knocker which did, and waited. It took a while for the long-haired Australian in cutoff denims and rock-tour T-shirt with an aerosol can of lily-of-the-valley perfume spray in his hand to pull open the door a touch. I probably looked like a Michelin Man fetishist, but I asked for a room and he reluctantly acknowledged he did have one to spare. I followed him through to the desk, where I signed my name while he sprayed more lily of the valley to cover the scent of the reefer he'd been smoking.

It was not an attractive hotel, the Continental of Belgrave Road. And my room was not an attractive room. Brown-painted walls aged to beige. White sheets with yellow stains, a plastic one over the mattress. A watercolor of a horse inside a broken unpainted frame above the teak-veneer dresser. A window covered with grime looking out onto the street where a few scared whores in patent-leather skirts offered their cleavages to cars dawdling along the curb. A bathroom down the hall and, down below, the basement containing some kind of English-language school that was probably a cover for a Hizbollah terrorist cell.

I stripped off all my layers of clothing like a snake sloughing off many skins, climbed into bed, switched off the flickering bedside light by tapping the loosely connected wire, and lay there, throat sore from cigarettes, body stiff from driving, an exile a long way from home with only the ghost of William Ivory for company.

It was sometime after noon that I woke up. I lit a cigarette. It was something to hold on to. Then, unshaven, went downstairs to endure what the hotel was pleased to call its traditional English breakfast (delivered by the Australian and noisily prepared by a Pakistani) of raw bacon, egg fried to rubber, burned toast, and canned tomatoes, served cold for the discerning epicure. The food made me gag so I smoked another cigarette and that made me feel stronger. Cashed up a pile of fifty-pence pieces and went to the pay phone in the cupboard the hotel was pleased to call its lobby. I dialed numbers to chase you down to ground.

I called the office number you'd given me. The same machine message as before telling me the line was being repaired. I called you at home. A machine message saying you were at work. I called international information and they gave me three numbers for your company on Milk Street. I called all three. The same receptionist answered each time. The first time he politely said he'd never heard of you. The second time he was quite firm on the subject. The third time I called he hung up on me as soon as he heard my voice.

I called you at home again. And again. And again. Left messages on your machine. You'll remember those messages. They were not very polite. Then I went upstairs and shaved and came downstairs to try you again. I left another message. Then I looked up Harkin, J. in the telephone directory, hoping to find the blushing man humiliated at Ivory's table. Four Harkin, Js. Three of them at home, each of them abusive. The fourth, if he was my man, if he wasn't, as Brougham Calder thought, dead, wasn't around to answer his phone. I was nearly broken by this time so I called Helen Ivory and she remembered who I was and she invited me round. I put on my other linen suit and caught a tube train uptown.

The house of Helen Ivory was not what I had expected it to be. With a clutch of white lilies in my hand I waited for her to answer the door of a terraced building off of Holloway Road. It was an Irish trash neighborhood like the part of Boston where my Uncle Eddie used to live. My father's sister's sometime husband who was mysteriously called Shiny Eddie by everyone outside the family. He used to fix up cars in the street by his house and played cards for money Friday nights. He made a pass at my mother every time he came over, and each time he was rebuffed he'd good-naturedly go to the icebox for another beer, usually whistling "Cucaracha" to annoy my dad. Uncle Eddie was whispered to have a shady past. Some people said he'd come by his Shiny nickname in a federal jail, but still they'd never say what it meant. I liked Uncle Eddie. He took me sometimes to Fenway to see the Red Sox play. I called him Shiny under my breath, not loud enough for him to hear, just to try it out. And I liked his neighborhood. I used to go there whenever I could. It was fun. Things happened in the street. I'd have liked to take you there. Not the kind of place for a Helen Ivory though. I had imagined turrets for her, crowning the wings of her seat. Landscaped parkland all around. A folly. A domed temple for moonlit trysts. Servants in attendance. A smoking room. A place for billiards too. Not the narrow nineteenth-century building which she opened the door of. She stood there, genteelly shaking in a blue silk dress, careful to interrupt her spasms long enough to offer her hand and smile.

Where were you? What were you doing now that the wheels were finally turning? At your makeshift home in Boston listening absentmindedly to my machine messages while you cut out animal shapes from newspapers? Reading your correspondence from a country lawyer in an English town? Playing cheater's solitaire while a late-spring storm attacked your windows? Walking the streets of an alien city while you tried to reconcile your life to the facts? Picking at your food in a fashionable eatery while a balding lawyer or architect in a French suit bored you with magazine opinions and added more wine to your untouched glass? Combing your long hair in the bedroom mirror, your answering machine flashing futile red lights, a record filling the room with hard jazz or nostalgic punk or maybe the *Siegfried Idyll*? Or slowly piling your hair on top of your head, your neck seeming too slender to support that pile of hair, pins and an ornamental comb between your teeth while you plotted the gulling of another unfortunate lug?

Helen Ivory led me to the dusty tousled place she called her sitting room. She invited me to fold myself into a sofa while she perched on a straight-backed chair.

"Over there are decanters and glasses. You will have to help. Yourself, I am afraid. I give crystal a wide berth."

She was diminished by this place. The cardboard boxes and packing cases with the same address in Tirana stenciled on all of them, dying insects wriggling in the spider's web in the corner of the room, the dusty decanters on a silver tray on the coffee table, the obscure trophies on the mantelpiece, the photographs inside beaten frames.

"May I?" I went over to the row of photographs. Ivory was in most of them, a handsome man. An almost beautiful woman with that weird crinkly blond hair they used to have joined him in two of the pictures. In the first she was in her wedding dress, full length with a mermaid tail, her husband next to her diffident and relaxed in a black frock coat. In the other she sat with two small children cross-legged on the grass in front of her, carefully composed and stiff, she in a coat with a fur collar, sitting on a low bench, a stately home behind her. The two children, a small boy with the same hair as his mother and a younger girl who takes after the father, look at the camera as if it had the capacity to hurt them.

"He. Took that picture."

"You were very beautiful."

"It is hard to remember. It was. A very long time ago."

Ivory once published a poem in *The Listener* magazine called "Accidental Beauties" in which he remarks upon "the chanceful meeting of time and flesh/promising exemption/from love's physical decay." It was written when he was a young man.

"He. Never lost his looks."

I poured myself a glass of something I hoped was Scotch. It turned out to be an acrid brandy.

"You look tired. I hope our climate agrees with you."

I was unused to sympathy. My throat went self-piteously sore. "It's hard work," I said, "chasing a dead man."

She might have winced. Maybe she didn't. A sudden mad suspicion hit me. "He is dead, isn't he?"

"Indeed. He is very dead."

"No one has been able to tell me what he died of."

She gave me one of her lopsided, body-decaying smiles. "I'm afraid I can't do that either."

I poured some more brandy down my throat. "I've been finding some things out," I told her, as if it was a warning for what would come next. "He wasn't a war hero like the obituary said. I'm not even sure he was noble-born."

"Your name is Irish. But you do not look entirely. Irish. Too dark-skinned."

"My father was Irish. His family were from Londonderry."

"Perhaps you have Spanish blood. Many of the Irish are reputed to be descended. From sailors of the Spanish Armada. Unknowing progenitors. Shipwrecked along the coast."

"I couldn't tell you about that. My mother wasn't Irish. She was Mexican."

"How marvelous. Where did they meet?"

"In Boston. She was a student there, at Boston College. It's a Catholic place. But listen. I'm here to talk about your husband, not my parents."

"Please. I receive few visitors. And you do have to understand the family. To appreciate the individual. Is that not so?"

"I guess that's true."

"Then indulge me a little. The better I know you. The more I shall. Trust you. And the more I trust you. The more I am likely to tell you. Don't you believe that to be so?"

I don't like talking about my parents. From myself I sprang immaculate. "Sure. What do you want to know?"

I had to repeat the question. She'd drifted away, as if she'd managed to steer me away from the dangerous thing and, satisfied with that, she could retreat into a different place.

"Tell me about them. Who they were. How you liked or. Hated them. What manner of people they were."

"I don't remember feeling that much. A little contempt for my dad, some pity and—I don't know, maybe love for my mother. Dad was a bigot. The only Protestant Irishman in Boston, and that made him mean. He was a tall man, worked in a car lot on Massachusetts Avenue, looked smaller than he was. Still does. He's alive as far as I know. My mother was small, beautiful, and dark. She changed her religion to my dad's, became the perfect wife in everything but feeling. My dad was a racist. A quiet racist but a racist all the same. He believed in the instability of blood. Temperamental Latin blood, my mother's and mine. My mother did her best. She lightened her skin with powder, dyed her hair mousy gray, was a head-down, hand-wringing member of the Anglican congregation. There were no guitars or ponchos in our house. My brother played his Standells records and later on, Hendrix and Led Zeppelin. Downstairs, when the curtains were drawn so the neighbors couldn't hear, ugly Orangeman hymns and wild symphonies from the Celtic revival. Pictures in silver frames hidden in their bedroom of King Billy and Queen Elizabeth the Second."

She stared ahead, blue eyes unblinking, face shaking from her disease. She gave no sign of hearing but the recollections tumbled out.

"I had a photograph of Lupe Velez, xeroxed from *Hollywood Babylon*. The Mexican spitfire sitting on a sun lounger, holding a chihuahua up to kiss some black-haired meat-headed hairy-chested lug. He's in swimming shorts, she's in a fluffy angora top and white shorts with a dumb beanie-beret on her head.

I stuck it to my wall, in between photos of Lou Reed and Iggy Pop. My mom took it down. In front of me. She folded it up sadly and put it away at the bottom of my socks drawer. They named me Richard."

Yeah. Richard. At grade school I insisted on it, the full name, dignified. No Ricky or Dicky or Rick or Dick. Or try Spic and see where that led. Down to the corner of the schoolyard where fights take place, that's where. Open the door, Richard. Richard. It's a solid sturdy name, but dimly, guiltily, from moments when I was young, I can still remember her whispering "Ricardo." I ignored her when she did that, when her voice reverted to a sudden Spanish whisper. I always pretended I couldn't hear, frightened, I guess, of the strange-sounding name and the obvious emotion on her face.

"Why am I telling you these things?" I said it out loud, more to myself than to her, not expecting a response.

"Perhaps because you don't think. I'm listening? Your mother. Is she still alive?"

"She died a few years back. Worn out from make-believe. Anglo-Irish Protestant make-believe. Boston housewife make-believe. White-man make-believe. Like a lot of Mexican women she had a little bit of a mustache. I think it was the effort of trimming it and bleaching it every day that killed her."

This was too much. The bitterness of the orphan. The motherless child. Out of myself I sprang immaculate. I downed more brandy and stretched out legs which had become suddenly drunkenly long. Close the door, Richard. I reached into my pocket and busied myself with a tape recorder. Self-possession.

"And what brings you. Here?"

"A job."

"More than that. I suspect."

Yes. A lot more than that. See? I used to have secrets too. Once upon a time I was due to get married to a girl called Mary who taught Eng. Lit. at Boston College. We'd been together for the longest time. She was Irish. Black hair. Blue eyes. Everything was set. I was dragging my heels but it was the right thing to do. There seemed no decent option. Then I lost my job. Then an English girl who called herself Dorothy Burton blew into town.

"I'm sorry for going on so long about myself. Please. Can we talk about him?"

"Perhaps we should have a bite to eat?"

We had a bite to eat. We ate in the dinette, at a round Formica table. Dry toast with randomly scattered sardines dripped in tomatoey brine. Off delicate china smeared with ancient stains and pockmarked by chips. A layer of dust covered everything, like an extra skin, for protection.

"I love fish. Sardines, yes. But fresh sprats are becoming something of a passion."

What do you say to that? If I were British I'd have countered with a "Quite" or an "Oh really?" As it was, Yank in town with a vocabulary naked of diplomatic nuance, I had to just try to coax her back to the subject of her husband.

"I've been looking at your husband's books. They're very good. What was he working on at the end of his life?"

She paused with a precisely cut red triangle of toast and fish dripping halfway to her mouth to consider my question. That was a mistake. Her shaking hand threw the food off the fork and splashed tomatoey brine onto the front of her dress. She answered as she went to retrieve the mouthful which had fallen neatly beside her plate.

"He believed. In the rottenness of the world. The corruption of men. And his own superiority. As did I."

"And do still?"

"And do still. Although if you spoke to his childhood nurse or one or two of his friends and cousins you might hear a different story. I wonder if after we finish. Our tea. You might do me a. Large favor? My daughter might soon be arriving. She stays in the flat at the top of the house. Which is, I'm afraid. Terribly cluttered with Albanian things. Would it be an awful bore for you. To shift some of them. Downstairs? I wouldn't ask, but I am not. Especially strong."

I told her I would be happy to shift some Albanian things and she rewarded me with a gentle smile. She finished her bite to eat. I had managed about half. The brandy, I claimed, had taken the edge off my appetite.

"And where did you meet?"

"I think I shall delay the washing-up. I sometimes indulge myself like this."

"Was he a good husband?"

"Are you sure you are quite full? There is cake."

"Was he a good father?"

"Would you like some tea? Or do you only take coffee?"

"Tea will be fine. How did he die? Where?"

"I usually drink Lapsang Souchong. I do have Earl Grey as well. Americans like that. I believe. The taste of. The old country. My mother was an American. Did you know that? She was from New York City. Or Darjeeling. Which would you prefer?"

"Whatever you're having is fine by me. You're not answering my questions."

"I take Lapsang without milk. How do you like it?"

"As it comes."

"I'm afraid I don't quite know. What that means. Like apple pie à la mode. It's rather the same. Sort of construction. Don't you think? It leaves me absolutely. Nonplussed."

"I'll take it black."

"Without milk? Or sugar?"

"Quite."

She grinned. That's the right word, grinned. It wasn't a smile, and it was far from a smirk. It might have been me saying "Quite," an absurd Anglicism that sounded fucked-up and pretentious from my mouth, or maybe it was because she had decided to show me how happy she was with the game she was playing. As if she was taking pity on me. Letting me see that she wasn't senile, or crazy, just a woman, once almost beautiful, flirting and teasing from inside a crumbling body.

I carried the tray of tea things and we went back into the sitting room. She switched on the TV and fidgeted with the sound knob.

"Forgive me. I know this is terribly rude. But it's time for. My Australian soap opera. I'm an absolute slave to it. I'll keep the volume off so we can continue. With our conversation. I can follow the story just by the pictures. In fact, I rather prefer it. That way."

We sat side by side on the sofa, balancing dainty cracked cups on dainty cracked saucers on top of our knees. On the TV, a pretty blonde girl in a psychedelic T-shirt over her bikini was crying as she kicked her way across a beach.

"Her boyfriend has just dropped her. He doesn't know she's pregnant."

She put the tea things down on the coffee table and turned up the volume cruelly loud and leaned back on the sofa. She rested her head on my shoulder, and her shaking, which had gotten worse as the afternoon wore on, suddenly stopped. I had a crazy virginal panic that I was about to be molested by an ancient woman with Parkinson's disease. A weaker man might have screamed. For a moment, we stayed like that, a parody of lovers, and then she softly started to snore. Gently, I managed to lift away her head and ease it against a cushion. Her legs fell together and it was an easy job to silently arrange her full-length across the sofa. I tucked my jacket around her and she seemed to like that. She smiled, fully, not lopsidedly, in her sleep.

On the TV, a couple of tow-haired kids were scaring themselves shitless exploring a creepy old beach house. But give me a little credit for skulduggery, I'd have probably figured out the best way to spend my time without that as a spur. Ma Ivory was sleeping soundly, and I decided to have myself a little poke around. Dead men have a habit of leaving clues in the homes of the living. And if the old lady should stir, I could always just look choirboy-lost and apologize for having found myself in the wrong room while shifting some Albanian things from her daughter's apartment.

I can see the house, a narrow Holloway house, cluttered and dirty and shabby and uncared for, except for the medical shrine at its center.

In the cellar: a small kitchen containing more dust than food, appliances which had once been white, peeling Formica surfaces heaped high with dirty dishes and pans and the dry remains of scrambled egg and tiny fishtails. The window was besieged by a garden, high grass and mad sunflowers twisting painfully up. On the door of a food cupboard (which contained jars of honey and bottles of lime juice and Sanatogen tonic wine) a church calendar with an airbrush painting of a flock of children atop a hill, their faces raised to heaven, and the pious slogan below, GOD IS DAD, with Helen Ivory's appointments inscribed in garish red ink. Next door, a bathroom with walls covered by fading floral tiles, the floor and toilet bowl in need of a scrub. A storeroom with a couple of rusty children's bicycles with flat tires, crates for Albania, supermarket boxes containing the children's long-ago school things, the boxes marked either D or M. Essays, report cards, name labels to sew into clothes.

Upstairs: past the sleeping figure on the sitting-room sofa, through the dinette into the dining room which hadn't been used for a very long time. A long oval mahogany table with tarnished silver candelabra at either end. A drawing room with matching wooden chairs surrounding a grand piano. Debussy sheet music open on display. Hit a key, wince at the tuneless sound, hope it doesn't stir Ma Ivory. Up another floor: bedrooms full of crazy things, old people's things. Piles of back copies of *Psychic News* and *The Radio Times*. Teapots, thousands of teapots, china teapots, stainless-steel teapots, teapots in the shape of cottages, of castles, a teapot in the shape of a gnome smoking a hookah on top of a toadstool, teapots with painted pastoral scenes, Georgian-garden teapots, the-crowned-heads-of-Europe teapots, battle-scenes-with-muskets-firing-like-the-War-of-Independence teapots. And in all the wardrobes in all the bedrooms, she had dresses, hundreds of the fuckers, silk, damask, cotton, chiffon, organdy, dresses that had gone in and out of style so many times that a fashion magazine could strut through the next couple of centuries draping its models in them. Hatboxes piled high higgledy-piggledy in each corner of the room like tottering temple pillars made of card.

In the master bathroom, the walls were covered by photograph montages under glass. Kodak snapshots of men with mustaches, artistocrat hoodlums, men in swimming shorts with beach balls beside sand castles, men in tuxes who aren't safe in taxis with shiny women on their arms, men in panamas on the running boards of automobiles, men playing tennis, men playing cricket, old crows in wigs and judicial robes sending the Irish to their deaths; and women too, women cut out of newspapers and magazines, mostly from what look like the '50s, but English '50s ain't like our kind of '50s, we're talking drab, honey, and mostly one woman, a girl at first, Helen Ivory with that weird crinkly blond hair. Fresh face, English rose I suppose, a kind of innocence and purity that suggests inadequacy with men but a good rapport with horses, a few freckles around the nose, something a little strange in honey's blue eyes, something a little askew, some strangeness behind her eager-to-please smile, which doesn't quite fit with her spreads of elegant clothes, but which makes her more sexy than she would otherwise be.

Moving along: past a small bedroom already filled with boxes for Albania into m'lady's chamber. Wooden furniture all dyed the same ugly shade of lime green. A lime green four-poster bed built to die in not to fuck in, with curtains hanging down the sides and drawn open at the foot, big mattress, thousands of pillows, makes you want to climb inside, draw the curtains shut, safe in your funeral tree house. The vanity table is lime green, and no surface is free of debris. Coming a close second to teapots in her taste are music boxes. Music boxes clutter up the dresser, a mountain of knickknacks with two at the peak —a broken ballerina on pointe with one hand up in the air, the pink of her tutu deadened to a dull strip across the urine ceramic, and a tweeting bird to tweet no more with a spring dribbling out of its butt.

Open the boxes, a game show of ancient ornaments, most of them open with a crack and a wheeze their only song, but a few crank out old melodies, uglily familiar from my childhood—"Lillibullero," "God Save the Queen," "Get Me to the Church on Time," "The Surrey with the Fringe on Top," "Danny Boy," a whine of Chopin, a whisper of Liszt. And the large box at the bottom, black-lacquered Japanese design, a delicate gilt bird swooping low over gilt bulrushes, a gold key in its tiny golden lock. Turn the key, open the box, bawled on by the studio audience, look over my shoulder at the imagined specter of a horrified Helen Ivory discovering my shameful snooping. The box is full. A tall neat pile of cream envelopes, dry with age, a pink ribbon tied around them.

I touched the ribbon, touched the corners of the envelopes. I lifted the pile up, let it fall again, the expected cloud of dust did not spew up. Unlike everything else in this house, these things have been regularly attended. A vision of the decrepit lady shaking by this box, clutching the vibrating letters to her empty breast, lifting them up to her unsteady eyes, and reading—what? It had to be love.

The fearsome investigator rushed to the door, kicked it silently shut, locked it, returned to the box of letters. The ribbon was not too tight, an easy matter to slide the top letter away and out. Slip the letter out of the envelope, read the dedication quickly, *My Darling Helen,* and below, the initial, *W.* My man. Grand-slam home run. William Ivory, his correspondence, a cache.

Surrounded by a dying cacophony of music-box chimes, I read the letter. Dated 1974, five years after his second marriage, he summons wife #1 up to Norfolk to discuss the matter of the children's education. I reached into the box for the next letter and stopped, froze, when I heard a footstep on the landing. I stuffed the letter back beneath the ribbon, closed the box, ran to the door, listened for a moment, nothing, no sound, then, slowly, turned the key and pulled open the door. There was no one out there. The sounds of discordant springs cranking out their last notes behind me, in the street a police car went by, and down below me in the house the old lady slept quietly, tremblingly on.

I figured it was time to shift a few boxes containing Albanian things. I ignored the final unexplored room and went up the final flight of stairs to the attic rooms. Inside the door to the apartment, on a round table, a pyramid of oranges and apples had been built in a plain white bowl. Farther in, a recently cleaned bathroom waited for an occupant, and on the narrow bed a white-and-yellow rabbit with a missing ear was propped hopefully up. The tall window looked out onto an anonymous street. Albanian boxes filled the floor. I set to work.

Thirteen stairs back down to the previous floor. Another thirteen down to the hall. I counted them forty times, twice for each box. In the boudoir, a broken ballerina kept turning to the fractured rhythms of *Swan Lake*. The counting kept my mind away from the lacquered box containing the letters. I hadn't had to deal with an ethical question since I was in college.

When I was done I ran softly downstairs, already feeling like a thief. She lay there still on the sofa, her face softened by sleep, the lines eased away. In her sleep she'd shaken off my jacket. I picked it up off the floor. The TV was still on, a pop promo loud enough to wake the dead. I couldn't risk turning it off. I snuck back upstairs, an outlaw before the fact. Stood on the threshold of the sleeping woman's bedroom. The ballerina had stopped revolving. I moved forward, moved back again. Stood in the hallway, ashamed of my hesitation. There was still the unexplored room next door, a legitimate reason to delay.

The room was surreal. Transplanted from Beth Israel Hospital (did you ever go there in your time in Boston? Did you ever need treatment for a sprained ankle or broken limb? Were you ever concussed? Did you ever take an overdose? I was born there—my father decided that even a Jewish hospital was better than the Papist Sancta Maria), a surgical chamber gleaming antiseptic chrome and white, perfect and sterile. She'd have needed to clean this room twice a day to keep it in that hygienic state. A medical gurney at the center of the room. A narrow mattress dressed military-neat with a white sheet and red blanket. A chrome desk in the corner, a doctor's bag on top of it. Each compartment of the desk packed with medical paraphernalia, a junkie's dream—unused pads of drug scripts, sterile needles wrapped in cellophane, shiny brochures from pharmaceutical companies inviting you to sample their barbiturates, their brand-name Paracetamol, their amphetamines and opiates, poultices and splints. The doctor's bag opened to reveal all the things you'd expect, this woman must have been a powerful hypochondriac or else a medical fetishist, with her stethoscope and emery boards and blood-pressure kit, the asthmatics' inhalers and rows of pills neatly labeled. A medicine cabinet on the wall, full again of rows of pills, arranged perfectly straight. Free-standing against the wall, between the desk and the patient's chair, two oxygen tanks with breathing apparatus dangling down. Spotless and gleaming, the room promised light and eager sterility.

Suddenly, a noise from below. A footfall that broke through thoughts and ethics. Ran from the surgical chamber back into the Havisham room, opened the box to cheers and whoops from the audience, hysterical now with delighted vicarious greed, knocked a couple of music boxes onto the carpeted floor. To the broken chimes of "If I Were a Rich Man," I gathered about half the letters in the box, closed the lid, a gasp from the audience, they wanted more daring, more avarice, more *dash*; then the casual stroll downstairs, wander into the sitting room where still she lay, sleeping, snoring, gentle, unworried. I didn't like to wake her. It would have been like breaking something. With booty crumpled in my pocket I walked out of the house into a twilight London.

A gang of black youths on the corner of Holloway Road, secret designs shaved into their hair, tough fighters' bodies draped for some crazy commercial reason in the sort of clothes I used to wear when I was six, boom boxes blasting urban funk aggression, drugs for sale. Lord, give me some. Beam me up. Get me out of this place. Went toward them, shambled toward them, feeling white and big and ugly. Money for old dope. Vaudeville street back-chat. Hassle me, I'll hassle you. My blood is unstable, that's what my dad said. My touch like my country's is rough and clumsy. No delicacy. A nation of prizefighters, not duelists. Ivory had delicacy. Ivory had poise. Ivory had cruelty where we only have carelessness. You have decadents, we only have dead heroes.

Out of my head on an alphabet soup of narcotics, I shambled around the city. A semi-stolen car empty of gasoline waited for me uselessly on hookers' alley. A long way away. In my pocket clues to the past. Beneath my feet uneven sidewalk paving stones. Don't let me get picturesque about London. London's a ghost town. A dirty wasted river in its middle. Losers in the rain pushing supermarket handcarts containing the things they've chosen to hold back the world. Velveteen pubs full of pinch-faced office boys, mean on beer. Loud West Indian girls, saucy in denim, arguing with their boyfriends, the arguments just a form of foreplay; Indians and Pakistanis in their corner stores, bellies swelling under loose button-up shirts, everything's for sale; and over everything, invisible and huge and sinister, above the red tourist buses wavering through the center of town, above the cartoon tattooed punks hustling for cash in the few West End streets where the cops leave them alone, above the closed doors of the marble-paved gentlemen's clubs, above the suburbs, spiky with TV aerials, the rooms filled with bright color signals and not much else, above all this, grotesque and dangerous, up in the sky, dwarfing us all, the cloudy muscular figure of a senile Bugs Bunny dressed as Captain America, jeweled ears priapically up, body heaving with hysterical good fortune, hands flicking down frisbees and guns and fried-chicken franchises. A pallid conspiracy of a town. Long days, the pale light fading but refusing quite to die. Didn't have enough cash for a cab, didn't want to go down into the underground warrens of the subway system, kept on walking.

Nick Wheel was waiting for me at my hotel. He'd tracked me down, I couldn't figure how. Waiting for me in the lounge, drumming piano scales on the arm of his chair.

"You don't call. You don't write. Let's have a drink, I'm parched."

He was dressed for sport and I was seeing two of him, shabby incongruous twins in sweatpants and running shoes and Chicago Bears T-shirts, headbands bunching up their thin yellow hair.

"I'm a little tired right now. Maybe this isn't the best time."

"What you need is a pick-me-up. Or a hose-me-down. Come on. Don't be a stranger." He went around the side of the bar and poured several measures of whiskey into two tumblers.

"How are you getting on, then? Come on, don't be shy. That reminds me of a joke about coconuts but I don't remember what it is. Look, I've finished mine. You're not a very fast drinker, are you? Oh all right, you're twisting my arm. Thanks very much, I will. Come on, I want to take you somewhere."

He downed the second glass and grabbed me by the arm, tried to tug me out into the street like a child taking a grownup to see his childish discovery. I was too tired and addled to resist.

"Where are we going?"

"Sanity Towers. The house of pain. Where's your car?"

"I don't remember."

"Don't worry. You worry too much. Worry, worry, worry, worry, there's more to life than anxiety, you know. Come on, I'll take you, it's all right, you can pay for the petrol."

Wheel's car was a beat-up MG Midget. We crumpled up inside it and he eased gradually out into the road. He drove frighteningly slow. Like a TV replay, taking an age to execute each maneuver. It was as if before he did anything he had to consider every possible alternative and imagine each possible way to die. I shut my eyes, gripped my hand hard around the pile of Ivory correspondence in my pocket. Wheel kept up his end of banter. I fell asleep.

Felt even worse when his fingers poking around mine in my jacket pocket woke me up. I slapped them away.

"Oops, sorry. We're here."

"Where?"

"Our destination. Lovely. That's three pounds fifty you owe me. And don't forget the tip."

Climbed stiffly out. A residential street lined with trees. High ugly terraced buildings, stout with respectability.

"This is the place. Number forty-two. That's X-L-I-I in Latin. In French it's quarante-deux, or is that fifty-two? Maybe I don't give such excellent French as I thought. Do you know the one about the blind man going past the fishmonger's shop?"

"What happens here?"

"The usual. Cat feeding and nose bleeding and garden weeding and book reading and—"

"Why are we here?"

"We're here because we're here because we're here. This is where the raping used to go on. I thought you'd want to see it."

"This is where Ivory's office used to be?"

"My, you're quick. Like lightning. The way you love me is frightening. Never strikes twice in the same place. Or does it?" He thrust a pantomime meaningful face into mine, and that made me hold on to a tree to keep my balance. "Let's go to the pub. Your round, I think. Or do you want to go in and look around? They don't like me here."

I inspected the door, cracking paint, yellow, the same, said Wheel, from Ivory's day, ran my shaky fingers along the darker area in the middle where his shingle used to hang. Wheel stepped ahead of me, rang the doorbell, tried to spin a line to a girl with a kitten cuddled up in her sweater. She threatened to call the police if he didn't go away.

Wheel took me by the arm and led me to an Irish bar a

couple of blocks away. He ordered two pints of Guinness. I paid for them. When I was safe in a seat I asked Wheel about his flipper friend.

"Bob? He's in prison. Go directly to jail do not pass go do not collect two hundred. He'll be having fun in there leading the life of Riley. Who is Riley? And where does he go when other people are leading his life?"

"You been back to this neighborhood since your Ivory days?"

"I come back every day. It's my pilgrimage. You see that barmaid? The fat boiler? Do you think she'll fuck me if I ask? I love fat women mountains of flesh it's like swimming. I could lose myself in there."

I was fighting to stay in control. I forced it back to the concrete thing. "Tell me about therapy with Ivory."

"The rapist. He raped me."

"You've made that joke before."

"I'm sorry. I don't like to repeat myself." He made himself belch. "Pardon I'm sure, I don't know where to look. What are you drinking? Why thank you, mine's a pint. God I fucking fancy that boiler. Oops. There's another ten pee in the swear box. Am I tiring you? Am I trying you? Your Honor, my contention is that this is one confused American. Do you like my gear? I vow to get more sportif. Behavior follows the clothes. Dress right and that's what you are, don't you think? Don't you know."

"Ivory."

"Danger. Danger in a room. One small room, a couch, a lampshade on his desk, a few books, a painting on the wall of a fat lady in a circus, a photograph on his desk of two small mites in a silver frame. Me on the couch. Him on his chair. Together we go places I'd never imagined before. He never changed his expression. He used to make me cry. How did Ivory die? Tell me please. I'm going to ask the barmaid if she'll let me fuck her. Whoops, that's another ten pee."

I felt like puking. I shut my eyes, held on for comfort's sake to Ivory's letters in one pocket and my cassette recorder in the other. The last thing I saw before I fell asleep was Wheel putting a move on the barmaid, who was three times his size and probably twice his age.

Surprising kindness. He was looking at me when I woke. I was back in my hotel room.

"Here. A glass of water. Drink. You collapsed. You're not much of a stayer are you? I think you peak too soon. You won't believe the trouble I had getting you into the car. The boiler helped me. I think I'd have been in there if it hadn't been for you. Well in there. Welwyn Garden City."

"I'm sorry. Thank you."

"You could do with some more sleep. I'll be off then. Do you want me to stay? I will if you want me to. Don't worry, I didn't take advantage."

I watched him go. He shut the door quietly. I got slowly out of bed, went to my jacket. The cassette player was still there. The letters were gone. I would have cursed if I'd been able to remember the words to use. Then I saw them on top of the dresser, the Ivory correspondence, neatly arranged in chronological order.

S he was rich and she was beautiful. She had no shortage of suitors.

3 March 1955

My dear Miss Newell,

I should ask you to forgive my rudeness. In other circumstances my outburst would have been unforgivable; but I would rather have understanding from you than pardon. That dreadful lawyer who was assailing you with his dreary romancier prattle offended me because I felt that he must be offending you. I had no intention of upsetting you and I had no intention of creating a scene. There was once a simpler time when the matter would have been simply treated as a question of honour. Does this notion appal you? —I know you are a modern woman. The dreary lawyer and I would have decamped to a discreet open place where one of us would have run the other through with a sword or discharged a pistol shot into his body. It is a Darwinian principle which, to my mind sadly, has fallen out of favour. When males of the species squabble over the beautiful female, then trouble must inevitably follow. It would be quicker, more natural, more seemly if that trouble was concluded in a simple manly battle. Without wishing to descend into the language of the barrack room, I for one would rather that dreary lawyer was prevented from engendering a race of dreary legal children.

I am sorry. This letter had been intended as polite apology. It seems to have taken the form of archaic chest-beating and sword-waving. It intends no disrespect and I remain

Your devoted servant,
William Ivory

Do women go for this kind of thing? Antelope horns at dawn, Lancelot posturing. I'd sort of hope that women were a little more sophisticated than that. I don't know if the dreary lawyer wrote a rival letter. If he did, Helen Newell wasn't impressed enough to wrap ribbon around it and hide it inside a black-lacquered box.

16 June 1955

My dear Miss Newell,

I am sure your party did not miss me. I am sure it did not require my presence for it to be a success. None the less, I would have liked very much to be a part of it, and I thank you for your charming invitation.

I have been travelling for much of the past few months and therefore quite missed both your invitation and your party. They were rather dull travels—to the Orient and North Africa—but if it would amuse you I would find it a great happiness to recount one or two of the adventures that came my way.

The next few months are unpredictable. I may be off again at a moment's notice. As you know, a traveller's correspondence inches after him, like a crab on a beach splashing after a steaming ship. If any message from you goes unanswered for any length of time please do not consider it a sign of any lack of regard from a man who would like to be

Your friend,
William Ivory

29 June 1955

Dear Miss Newell,

You write so wittily, your intelligence and charm shame
the reader. I laughed out loud at your description of the ball
and attracted some florid-faced disapproving looks from
several previously dozing gentlemen at my club. All the
same, I'm sure (reading between the lines) the attention of
so many captains of Guards can't be <u>such</u> a tedious business.
If it is, this pleases me. If it is not, then I shall rush out for
my commission straight away.

I don't know who's been filling your head with loose
gossip. I wasn't aware of enemies—except perhaps a certain
silk of our acquaintance and a Jamaican with whom the
score was settled a long time ago. Simply: these things are
not true. I shan't dignify the mongerers with a point-by-
point refutation, but let me tell you two things. I have never
claimed a George Cross, and nor did I "pay my way" out of
service during the War. Owing to reasons of ill-health I did
not in fact pass my Board and instead served in the Auxiliary
Fire Service throughout. I did happen to be awarded a
George <u>Medal</u> for my work in the Blitz, something I do not
ordinarily brag about. I hope you only tease me with the
story to get a rise out of me. I would be hurt if you gave it
any credence.

As to the other matter, I have nothing to say. It is too
absurd and too ugly. I should be grateful if you would pass
on the name of the "careless individual" who told you of it.

No, I don't think I will be at the regatta. Certain matters
prevent my appearance. I trust you will enjoy yourself there
and perhaps spare a thought for someone absent who
remains

Your friend,
William Ivory

5 July 1955

Dear Miss Newell,

William Ivory requests a moment of your time, tomorrow, the 6th of July, at 5 p.m. at your home address. He hopes this is convenient.

7 July 1955

My dear Miss Newell,

Some things we do not ordinarily speak of. Do I offend you? Did I offend you? The myth of the passionless Englishman is only a myth. Stultifying convention and puerile repression alone prevent the most courteous empty-headed dog suitor from acting as I have done. If you choose to sever our friendship I should understand it but not forgive it. Please do not misunderstand, dear Miss Newell: I am not seeking to excuse, justify, mitigate or even explain my actions. They were entirely natural. The darkest pagan would act as I have done. The effeminate bishop would not. I know where my sympathies lie. Where do yours?

You are rich and you are beautiful. You have no shortage of suitors. You say no man has behaved to you in the way I have. You are thirty-five years old and yet unmarried. Perhaps this is why.

With most respectful regards from

Your admirer,
William Ivory

7 September 1955

Dear Helen,

I have been away. To Japan compiling a report on post-war reconstruction for our government. I have thought of you often. Did you receive my card from Osaka? With the widow of a kamikaze pilot acting as my translator, I toured the city there, and in her company went to Nagasaki, to Tokyo, to Kyoto. She wears his medal still, the three-petalled cherry blossom commemorating his foolish brave death.

I should like to take you to Japan. It is a cold perfect place. Extremes of activity—far beyond our own decadent notions—adorned with artistic correctness. A pale harsh centre. Brittle and strong. Being there fills me with sadness for our own anaemic culture. Takao, my guide and translator, is, I think, typical of Japan after defeat. Deferential to the American oafs, polite to the gaijin, diligent in her guide-translator duties even to the point of—
. . . No, I shan't try to shock you. She has no conception of happiness. Duty, work, struggle, success, momentary joy, melancholy. Those are her expectations.

London seems unreal to me. People ask me if I am happy and the question sounds absurd to my Japanized ears. Something is lacking in this city that I am sure once was here. I can not describe it, I can not even name it; but the last time I remember being in its presence was one bright fire-filled night in the Blitz.

I am sorry if you find this letter strange. Perhaps it is. I have been quite solitary since my return and when I need to share my thoughts with someone, you are the only one I think will understand.

Why don't we meet for lunch next week. On Tuesday I shall be at the Fountain Room at about one o'clock. Perhaps you might like to join me there.

With fondest regards,
William Ivory

13 September 1955

Dear Helen,

Was I rude? I had not intended to be so. I was surprised by your bringing-along of Anthony. I was surprised too by his proprietorial handling of you and I was disappointed by your allowing of it. I have never been impressed by rudeness to servants or waitresses and have always intervened when I saw fit. The girl was weeping and I just did what any gentleman would—or should—have done.

So Anthony considers me a "dangerous character". What of it? I am flattered. "Dubious background". What does that mean? If I cared I could tell you one or two things about the suburban roots of the Brougham-Calders. I used to have an acquaintance with both Anthony and his brother. Julian, I knew slightly better; he was a rebellious young man, so rebellious he has never earned a living and dropped the hyphen from his family name; but as far as I can tell they are much alike in their mediocrity of mind and spirit. It is a dull crowd you travel with.

I shall be off to Japan again shortly. I should have liked to invite you along but I realize that is impossible. Perhaps coincidence will cause us to meet after my return. Until then, I remain

Your fond servant,
William Ivory

7 November 1955

Dear Helen,

How charming that we should meet and in such an unexpected melancholy place! As you know, I am not entirely devoted to the tenets of Christianity; none the less, when the mood is on me, I like nothing better than meditation in the beautiful surrounds of a cathedral. You were breathtaking in your black outfit. Sorrow becomes you, as it becomes us all.

I did not know your brother, yet I am sure I would have liked him. I tend to get along with those who are not ashamed to live on the margins of things. If you would like a sympathetic ear I would like to offer you mine. I do not wish to intrude upon your mourning so I will leave it to you to contact someone who will always be

Your friend,
William Ivory

11 November 1955

My dear Helen,

It was a tender time we shared, that afternoon. For myself as well as you, so please do not be ashamed of your tears. You worry that I will think the less of you: the reverse is true. It seems to me that when we are in touch with death, when we are in its presence, we become somehow both stronger and softer. You were extraordinarily beautiful that afternoon. I have never loved you more.

I shall let that stand. This was intended as a letter of companionship, showing you my understanding of your grief, my ability to share some of it at least, to help you. I had intended no declarations, no protestations to confuse you in this vulnerable time. But when the truth is written only the coward dares to erase it. For all my faults, I am not a coward.

I am sorry if this comes at a bad time. I cannot retract it. I shall be dining at the Café Royal on Thursday evening at eight o'clock. I would be delighted if you joined me there.

Warmest wishes,
William Ivory

14 November 1955

My dear Helen,

There have been times, yes, when I have hated London. Times when I have raced overseas tight as a spring to breathe deep only when I was steaming across a foreign ocean or strolling along a strange avenue in a strange city. London was a shabby ordinary town. It was a decaying place. It was a pale circus full of properly dressed mediocres jumping through threadbare hoops for forgotten purpose.

And then there are the moments, like yesterday. Walking along the boulevard of Piccadilly, stopping at 105 to look up to the balcony and imagine Old Q, the Rake of Piccadilly, raising his spyglass to his eye to pay tribute to the young ladies making their promenade. When concrete London becomes a benevolent magical place, when the heaviness lifts, and things become possible. To Hyde Park, a place where lovers can make their accord.

You say you are confused and, yes, I know you are. You are confused by contrary feelings, by sorrow and joy and anticipation and fear all mingling and doing battle. You are experiencing one of those rare moments to be cherished, when every perception is heightened: each contrary emotion is thundering your body; you ache, don't you? with the twin passions of desire and shame.

And now if things were allowed to follow their perfect course I would lay my siege. I would issue a fusillade of flowers, blast bombshells of promises; with my artillery of compliments and a propaganda machine devised for love-making I would play general and you my desired city.

But we are not solitary makers of our fates. The world has its call on us and at this perfect moment when everything is poised and waiting I am pushed overseas, for once against my will. It is midnight and if I had time to reread this in a sober morning I might wince at my florid language; I might crumple this poor piece of paper into a useless ball and set light to it and watch it flame and die. But it is night and we are different creatures at night. When do you read this? Does sunlight break across the page? Please do me the charity to read it again at night, when the house is sleeping.

By the time you have this, I will be beyond England. The reluctant traveller will be approaching a distant curious shore where a translator-guide waits with Oriental patience to help him compile a dry report. I can't say when I will be back. I can only hope you will be there to welcome home

An aspirant,
William Ivory

And in reply, the first letter of hers that I have. The first, I suppose, he considered important enough to keep.

18 November 1955

Dear Will,

Is England as gloomy as all that? I can't help but think you are over-savage in your description. I have listened to you talk long and tenderly about Norfolk, its beauty and character.

Yes, I read your letter in the daytime. I read it again at night and then again the following evening. I am flattered, touched, startled by its strength. You have the vision to look very deep into another. That must be an awful responsibility. To be the object of such a gaze is both a relief and a worry. A relief that there is someone with whom the playing of silly emotional games is entirely irrelevant, and a worry because there is a power involved. How can one predict how power is likely to be used? Dear Will, the last thing I have been looking for is a despot of my heart. I don't accuse you of wanting to be that, but the possibility of anyone being that is almost sufficient to push me onto a different course.

I have avoided marriage for many years. I have steered my

own safe course between the silly boys with their silly
traditional ways and the passionate spivs with perfect
manners who haunt the balls and hotel bars on the look-out
for any rich girl with a bored expression on her face. You
are different from any man I've ever known. For a start,
you're cleverer; and for another thing, I don't understand
you at all and that's a delight to me, and yet . . .

What <u>do</u> you do overseas? For whose eyes do you
compile your dry reports? You are such a mystery man. If
you were less than you are I should be tempted to think
that you make up all this mystery, that you use it as a
glamorous cloak to cover some guilty or ordinary secret.
You remind me sometimes of my father. You would have
liked each other, I think. Anthony has asked me again to
marry him. I am getting almost too old for marriage and I
think if you had not popped up I would have gone for being
Mrs Brougham-Calder. He is steady. He has a distinguished
career ahead of him. He loves me and I am sure of him.
Sometimes I feel very lonely. Too many people around me
are dead. They would have been able to advise. I wish you
had had a chance to meet my brother. Despite what the
world thought of him, he was a very wise soul.

There are so many difficulties, so many doubts. You mock
the Church and I think that means you mock my Faith. You
are a wanderer and I only want a fixed place in the world
surrounded by people I can call my own. You are so
scornful of so much and I doubt my own capacity to soothe
your pain. The only thing I can be sure of is that London is
a dimmer and colder place when you are not here. How
long will you be out in the East? Are you in one place or
travelling around? Do you have the same translator-guide as
before?

Please write if you can. I hope your London address will
forward this on to you before too long.

Warmest good wishes,
Helen

He has her. The next letter from him will consolidate. The one after that will close the deal.

3 December 1955

Dear Helen,

The Japanese have a word "haragei". It means "the art of the gut". It is the act, inductive yet intuitive, of going beneath the perfect surface a man presents to the world to apprehend the truth below, the grand or shabby or lunatic or bestial needs that <u>really</u> drive him on. I sit cross-legged in an English suit in the largest room of a fragile house in Kyoto. Demure and efficient Takao sits near me, on her knees. Industrialists, poets, the betrayed children of once high-ranking army officers come to my house to tell me proper-sounding lies for my Report. I am becoming an initiate in the art of the gut.

I do not know when I will return to England. It is a fusty musty place, you know. Perhaps—does this sound too unpatriotic, too societal-masochistic?—we needed a defeat, an invasion, a massacre to revivify our culture. Like the neurasthenic French at the turn of the century longing for barbarians to storm the city walls and rape the women and slaughter the innocents so that the tired blood would flow and the culture would be renewed, I too have some of that feeling for London. Here, I find a peace filled with possibility which I have never encountered before.

I shall write again soon. With warmest good wishes, I remain

Your friend,
William Ivory

27 December 1955

Dear Mr Ivory,

I am not used to this. I send you a letter replying in the spirit of your own in which I open my heart to you. You ignore it and in so doing belittle me. London may feel dying to you and a long way away but there are people here, with feelings. I had not thought you were a cruel man.

Helen Newell

19 January 1956

Dearest Helen,

When a traveller is a long way from home sometimes he misjudges his words and effects. I do not ignore your letter: I cleave to it. It comforts me when I am lonely, it brings me cheer when I am feeling low. In short, it sustains me. In my last letter I had merely intended a word picture of my state of mind and state of being in a place you do not know. The solemnity of my feelings for you had, I thought, no place in such a letter. Do you think so little of yourself that I might forget you? My love for you sustains me in the same way that your purported love for me sustains me. My Report is not yet finished; nevertheless I would drop it now and rush home to be by your side if that is the reassurance you need. I am

Your own
Will

29 February 1956

Dear Will,

How your words comfort me and reproach me. I am sorry
to have created such a fuss. "Purported love"? It is much
greater than that. I would not dream of making you return
before your Report is completed. You once laughingly
accused me of being a "modern woman". I still believe that a
man must work and a woman must respect that. No: stay in
your fragile Kyoto house; continue your work. I will not
devalue your feelings again.

London is dreary without you. I wait for your return.

Your
Helen

(PS A certain lawyer of your acquaintance continues to
"sniff". He makes extravagant declarations. He receives no
encouragement.)

19 April 1956

Dear Helen,

The Report drags on. I have become associated with a
Unesco study of Japan. Time-serving bureaucrats, Embassy
flunkies, pompous progressives, sociologists who preach the
dialectic between pursed colourless lips, these are my
supposed colleagues. The real Japan goes hiding when these
spiritless men and bluestocking women go stamping. The
Japanese educationalists involved with Unesco are, as you
would expect, as polite as could be: they know how to
butter their bread. Paper piles up into statistical mountains:
railway line dimensions, ceramic industry figures, tables of
the most favoured radio programmes, lists of the

representative wildlife of each region . . . it goes on. And on.

You continue to see your lawyer? It is your decision. We are not formally attached. I can issue no decrees over your friendships. I can only hope that when I finally return to London I shall find welcome.

Until then, surrounded by paper mountains, I remain

Your
Will

7 May 1956

Dear Will,

Poor Will! It must be so desolating to see your work taken up with so many mundane tasks and by so many little people. I am sure you will triumph. You are not misnamed Will.

The lawyer is banished. I find now I go out less and less. Parties, charity balls have lost their flavour for me. For a little while, I went on with them—out of habit, I think. Now, after Johnny's death, I find myself encumbered with a great deal of paper-signing. I will have to go to New York soon to sign some papers over there. I have been engaged in a dull correspondence with an American "attorney" who frightens me rather with his dry precise ways. Money creates its own industry. I had no idea how many people work in the financial factory.

It is dull here in London. I need your eyes, to see the city through them. I had given up on parties already, but now that people are aware I'm "spoken for", I get invited to fewer than before. This does not make me miserable. I read, sign my papers, I listen to the radio. I walk each day in Kensington Gardens and have struck up an odd friendship with a very peculiar woman who walks dogs for the ladies of the area. And I wait, patiently, for your return when life will start again. When do you return?

With all my love,
Helen

1 June 1956

Dear Helen,

Takao and I went on an expedition up to the island of Hokkaido which is a strange primitive place whose inhabitants are rather despised by the smart mainland types. We stayed in basic village accommodation and interviewed brutish types who grow tobacco and potatoes on volcanic ash-land. Then we went into the city, Sapporo, and contemplated the future with young men who make beer. I had not seen Takao ruffled before. Like a great snob lady doing good works in the East End of London, she talked a little too loudly, never met anyone's vulgar eyes, and was clearly bothered by the smell of these people and their living quarters.

We returned to the mainland, and the rainy season. I write this from a drenched Tokyo where neon lights refract through the rain into my hotel window. It is a Western-style hotel, sturdily built, whose ceilings are tall and all the furniture is higher up from the floor than I have grown accustomed to. Takao will be arriving soon with a bottle of warmed rice wine. How I wish it was you who would shortly be knocking at my ersatz oak door, wearing a silk kimono that draped to the floor, with a lacquered tray held in front of your breast. Takao is a strange creature. She wishes to accompany me to England when it is time for me to go. I of course tell her that is impossible.

When do I return? If it were not for you I might not return at all. I look through the glass at the city outside and I see your face reflected back. I try to remember London and all I can think of is you, your face, your voice, your scent, your wise indulgent smile. If it were not for you, London would be a phantom to me, the dead foundations for my city life here.

Your life as you describe it sounds a little bare, a little plain. We shall have to spice it up for you.

With love,
W.

17 July 1956

Dear Will,

Be careful, dear Will. You are going native. Before we know it we will find you a Eurasian; your cheekbones will grow high, your hair will quite lose its sweet brown curls and become black and Mongolian-straight—you will turn into what my Grandfather de Noull called a chee-chee.

I enclose a photograph for you. It is a poor shot but a likeness. I know the power of your imagination and I fear that the face you see which you call mine will over time lose any correspondence to the face I see in the mirror.

How much longer is it to be? I am maybe not as strong as I once thought; or maybe it is you who have weakened me. I find myself assailed by boredom, the hours of the day tyrannize me, the sight of a clock makes me start like a rabbit. I think of you out there in the Orient, and I wonder and I doubt if you will ever return, and I can't remember what my life used to be before you were in it. I am sure Takao is a stout woman with the face of a tuna fish but I hate her, I am jealous of her. I am jealous of anyone with whom you pass the hours of the day that you cannot spend with me.

Don't despise me but I go to church and that is my way of fortifying myself against your absence and the horror and doubt it leaves, like a vacuum in an airless room. I tell my

Kensington Gardens dog-lady almost everything and she advises me to play you like an instrument, to make you jealous, angry, loving, returning. I am meant to make things up, to tell you of the parties I go to, the men who gather around me, the tributes I receive. We are too old for that kind of débutante behaviour, aren't we Will? All we can do is tell and describe and wait. Sometimes I fancy myself a tubercular heroine of a nineteenth-century novel. I sit at the window and think of you and wonder if you will ever return to marry me.

Please come back.

All my love,
Helen

31 August 1956

Dear Will,

Are you alive? Are you ill? I have not known such a long time to go by without a letter from you. Has Japan swallowed you up? Has your curiosity led you to a dark wretched alley and onto the knife-point of one of those tattooed gangsters? (You see: I have been doing my Nipponese research too.) It's ridiculous, just to see the words written down makes me laugh. You cannot be dead. It would be too unfair. Too many people have died near me. Is it my fault? Should I have been firmer with you? Should I have made you come back to me? Begged you, ordered you? Or did I put too much pressure on you? Too much responsibility worries you, doesn't it, Free Will? Have you been hiding from me all this time? Kept away from England by a demanding spinster lady with her wretched romantic schemings?

Are you feeling guilty about something? Is it your exotic Takao creature? I know what men can do in carelessness and in darkness. I am not such a naïve. Have you done something you think might hurt me? Is there something that shames you? Something that makes you turn my photograph to the wall? I forgive you. I forgive you everything you have done and everything you might ever do.

Please come home. Please write. She waits for you and each moment of your silence gets harder to bear.

Helen

Hey there, Bad Bill Ivory, the demon king of the correspondence course of true love, nice going. You fished her, you hooked her, you caught her good. In the playful parlance of old Boston-schoolyard Lochinvars, you got her begging for it. The next item is a newspaper clipping, society pages, under the bold-print heading,

IVORY-NEWELL:

> On September 19th 1956, at Brompton Oratory, London, William Stuart, of Norfolk, to Charlotte Helen Yorke, only daughter of the late General Newell and the late Emily Newell, of Kensington, London.

We have the wedding photograph, Ivory in a tux, carrying a top hat, hair slicked back, mustachioed, almost smiling, Helen, the first Mrs. Ivory (does she know there's going to be another?), bridal in a well-chosen cream dress, a virgin who isn't pretending to be.

Put the letters away. Ivory's bold strong script dominating the yellowing paper. Tie a fraying length of pale-pink ribbon, faded through time and touch, around them. Lay them on the table. Fold the newspaper clippings alongside, and Ivory's journals too. Leave them all for the moment, along with cassette tapes of interviews with Ivory associates and intimates and enemies, and notes of mine, scrawled across several piles of yellow legal notepads. Leave them all on the white round table at the window overlooking the street below. Block out the red-lipstick words painted over the living-room walls. Could paint them out. Prefer not to. Don't ask why. Cast back to the Pimlico hotel where I was then. Before you came back. After I'd returned with pockets full of purloined letters.

I was on my bed, heartened, triumphant, surrounded by letters, picking my way through a historic seduction. The Australian night manager knocked on the door. He had a message for me. A Dorothy Burton had called. She'd left a number in New York. I went downstairs. I dialed it.

"Yes?" Your voice. Distant, reserved, and cold, ready to find a reason to hide. Protected by miles and your fingers poised to break the connection.

"It's been a while, Dorothy Burton."

"Who is this?"

"Your devoted servant. An admirer. A friend." Corny? It had worked for Ivory, which was reason enough to suppose it wouldn't sound true from me.

"Tierney?"

"Yes, Tierney."

"You got my message? I was trying to reach you." Your voice got earnest and actressy-clear—relief at having got me at last, irritation at not having found me at home earlier. Hypocrisy? Sure, that's what I'm implying. Indeed.

"It's been a while."

"How is it getting on? Your work."

"Coming along. Money's something I could mention."

"Tierney, I'm sorry. You wouldn't know how difficult things have been over here."

"I couldn't know. You've been out of touch so long."

"Things have changed. It's been a confusing time but nothing's changed."

"What's that supposed to mean?"

"Things have been in flux. I'm living in a different place now."

"I left messages. Many messages. Your company said they never heard of you."

"I can see why they'd do that. I've changed jobs too. I left under a bit of a cloud."

"I'm broke. Cleaned out. You should see my place where I'm living. A penthouse on Skid Row. Do you know the neighborhood? It's a suburb of Palookaville."

"But you're still researching Ivory? The commission stands —it just took a little red tape, that's all. What have you found out? How much more is left to do? I might be coming back to England soon. Tell me how he died."

"I couldn't do that."

"Why not? You'll get your money."

"You wouldn't like how I'm living. It would distress you, I'm sure."

"You're still working on Ivory? You haven't stopped? Did you see his wife?"

"Helen? She's a game old bird. Don't worry. Night and day I've been working. Honest."

You might have sighed then. You certainly stopped for thought. When you started to talk again you sounded less anxious.

"Listen. Give me your address and I'll send the next installment directly. I'm sorry about everything that's happened. I'm very glad you're still working, I knew you were right for the job. I'll be coming to London soon but you'll get your money before that. What's your address?"

I told you. You wrote it down and repeated it back. You said something else that flattered me and I returned the compliment, which you accepted, clumsily. Then you gave me a name, Martha Brennan, and an address, Hobart Hall outside Norwich. Martha Brennan was an old woman who would be able to tell me more of Ivory's early life. I promised I would go see her. We got ready to finish the conversation with a few facetious remarks about the weather. William Ivory weather, we called it. You asked again how he died and I said I wouldn't tell you. I didn't admit I hadn't found that out for myself. I enjoyed refusing you something, I admit that freely. It evened the score a little. It gave me a feeling of power.

After making my regular failed morning call to Harkin, J., my long-overdue rental car took me up to Norfolk powered by gasoline purchased with the last of my money. I drove up a long dull highway which became a single-lane road as I approached Norwich. I got stuck behind a tractor and I got oppressed by the view. Desperately flat country pressed down upon by an ugly enormity of sky.

In the market square I exchanged fifty pence and a handful of cigarettes for directions to Hobart Hall from a band of tattooed denim boys who were killing the day with beer. I got through to them in the end, after they were done laughing at the way I pronounced Norwich, and I left them taking it in turns to dribble strange rural curses from the corners of their mouths.

It was like driving across the back of a giant flattened wasp. The road out from Norwich to the Hall was a straight black line through fields of bright-yellow rapeseed. You'd prefer America, wouldn't you? Americana myth, beatnik hobo heroes. Once you called my name softly and asked if I'd ever hopped a freight train. I can't remember what I said. I might even have said yes. But that's not the way anymore, and I don't know if it ever was. In the States you'd get truck stops with video porno handjob shacks, one-street towns (where the single horse would have long since died and the body been sold to a dog-food company), plastic-food joints and a soda-pop bar with a pool table that slopes and cushions that cheat (did I ever tell you about my adventures in Bogue Chitto, Mississippi? It's too late for that now), and stores selling satellite dishes and guns. Here, there was just the occasional hand-printed sign inviting you to *Pick Your Own Strawberries*, or *Potatoes 15p a Pound*, or directions to Royal Air Force bases. My red sedan, a blood spot on the wasp-stripe road, drove through the plains of rural Norfolk, Ivory country, and puttered to a stop, dead out of gas, in the National Trust parking lot of Hobart Hall.

It was the perfect setting for myth. A path between yew hedges the size of dinosaurs led the way to the sexy Jacobean sprawl over a stone bridge toward turrets which pricked the sky ahead. I tagged along with an army of Germans shivering inside canary-yellow leisure wear who were crossing through the large courtyard, drifted into the middle of them when their tour guide bought the entry tickets from a tweedy old dame who looked like a drag queen. I exchanged good-natured puzzled smiles with my neighbors and pigeon-stepped along with them as they entered the hallway. The Germans stomped away and left me to admire the Great Hall. Do you like grandeur? I like grandeur. And this was a grand place. A curved ceiling that billowed up to reach halfway to God. Paintings of gaily costumed hard men hanging on the dark paneled walls. A wide wooden staircase, wide enough for ten pear-shaped beauties to make side-by-side Hollywood entrances. And at either side of the base of the staircase, the face and body of a woman carved out of the wood like figureheads on a pirate ship.

Below a window by the side of the staircase, another fierce drag queen, a string of pearls rubbing disconsolately against her ruddy neck, sat behind a table of guidebooks. I fiddled with the English version and politely, trepidatiously, asked her where I might find Martha Brennan.

With a jowly shake she barked something that sounded like "Brine Droing Rm."

"Excuse me?"

"Brine Droing Rm. Heah. Look. Mep."

Ivory in 1961 wrote a review of an anthropology book for *Encounter* magazine in which he implied that there was something less than wholesome in the relationship between the English country lady and her animals. He wrote of "rural fidelity and innocent fun between the indulgent dowager and her willing Dobbin and wet-nosed Rex." I have seen the original draft and the phrase that stood in the place of "the indulgent dowager," which the magazine's editor apologetically excised. The phrase, a little too blunt for those genteel dissolute days, was "the good lady's pleasuring finger." It was the good lady's pleasuring finger which stamped down hard on the map in the guidebook.

"Heah. The Brine Droing Rm!"

"The Brown Drawing Room?"

"Next to Ler An tir'm. Daw through Great Hll!"

"Next to Lower Anteroom, door through Great Hall?"

"Aver the!"

"Over there." I thanked her. She shook her jowls, brutally.

I've never been too good at following maps. I thought I'd got to the Brown Drawing Room but instead I was in the Library, the shelves filled with books bound in leather and printed in Latin, mirrors on all the tables so you could admire and be improved by the friezes on the ceiling, allegorical figures of Vice and Virtue strutting their Vicious and Virtuous stuff. Took a turn away from there and I was in the Music Room, a circle of chamber instruments propped on stands as if the players had just gone out to take a leak and would be back if you waited long enough, sheet music on the grand piano, something by Bach, open in the middle at a particularly tricky passage. (The piano stool had once received the impression of Ivory's prodigy ass and I was about to try it too until I saw the look I was getting from the drag queen in the corner.)

Then I found myself in the Japanese Bedroom and I stayed there awhile; it was queer in there, and peaceful, flawed vases on plinths, and a four-poster bed built for Junior, and the best wallpaper I've ever seen, a story in every part of it just asking to be told: old Japan, villages and volcanoes, and steamships in harbors, and stretched-out girls startled from their sleep by men in metal with pins in their hair and swords or poems in their hands, and market squares and discreet bedchambers behind paper walls, and little guys tending temple grounds and big guys cutting open their bellies; there was a whole world pasted around that room and I was reluctant to leave it but finally I did, and I finally found my way to the Brown Drawing Room, which was, in fact, yellow.

Some of my yellow-shelled German friends were there, and a few Japanese too. Everyone in the room, except for me and the little old lady custodian, had a camera, and all of them were snapping pictures. The Japanese did it efficiently, taking one polite shot of each notable thing in the room, to be annotated and filed once they got home, part of their archives, their grand plan to make sense of Europe, but the Germans really got to it. They took photographs of green velvet chairs behind red velvet ropes, and they took photographs of a long velvet reclining chair, and they took photographs of a side table with a marble top and a rough marble base, and they took photographs of each other with grim happy smiles and fat arms around fat spouses. And they set their timers and laid their cameras at angles on the floor and took photographs of themselves (nylon leisure suits rustling with the sudden rush of activity) in front of the Canaletto painting of the river Thames that was next to the fireplace; and they took photographs of the fireplace itself, murmuring as they rubbed their fingers against the stone angels carved into it when the little old lady custodian's back was turned; and they took photographs of the little old lady custodian herself, sweet face, sweet as any stone fireplace angel, with red-apple cheeks and soft white hair clipped into a side parting, a National Trust badge pinned to the jacket of her green tweed suit, who sat beaming at all passersby from her perch on a straight-back chair, tiny under the high ceiling, and who in a soft Irish voice was gently lecturing to a beatnik in an electric wheelchair on the subject of the perfection of family life at Hobart Hall in the mid-twentieth century.

I waited to one side until the beatnik whirred away, scattering photographers as he sped to the Lower Anteroom, and I stepped forward to inquire if the sweet old lady custodian might happen to be Martha Brennan.

She beamed at me and she acknowledged that she was. I asked if she might be able to spare some of her time, and she replied that she would be delighted to do just that. I asked if she was likely to find the time to take a break from her station, and continuing to beam she also managed a frown and said that she would not—there were treasures in this room and her job was both to guard them and to explain them to the interested visitors. She was afraid both for security and for education if she should desert her post. I asked her if she might spare me some time at the end of the day, and again a frown clouded her beam, and she told me quite firmly that it was not her rule to fraternize with visitors.

"You see," I said, "I'm doing some research—writing a book, in point of fact," somehow, call it blood memory or the power of the father, I seemed to be reverting to an ugly neo-Irish tone, "into the life of William Ivory."

The beam departed entirely. She said nothing, but the similarity of her face to the fireplace angels got worryingly close as her features, old, very old, older than Brougham Calder's, older even than Helen Ivory's, older than maybe anyone's I'd ever seen before, became fixed, like stone.

"You remember William Ivory?"

The stone nodded.

"I'm writing a book about him. I'm speaking to people who knew him."

She made a noise in her throat. It might have been a cough, it might have been a grunt, it might have been just a pocket of air hiccupping through the ancient passages of her throat. I started to repeat what I'd said and she interrupted me. Her face became human again.

"And tell me one thing—why would anyone choose to write a book about a nasty little boy?"

She put up a struggle, she was worried about jeopardizing security and education, but I managed to persuade Martha Brennan to leave her post.

"We'll go through the Wilderness," she said, "and out towards the Temple."

She led me out of the house into a woodland garden. She talked briskly as we walked briskly along a tree-lined path toward the solitary building at the end of the park. It looked the perfect trysting place, a Hellenic domed arena for secret scandals.

"There was a terrible storm in nineteen eighty-seven. A hurricane. So many trees died. It is a sad thing, the dying of trees. And what is your name?"

I told her.

"That sounds an Irish name. We planted many more to replace the ones that died. Over there is the secret garden. You can't see it through the trees. After the storm it was horrid and bare. Not secret at all. You do not sound Irish. Where do you originate?"

I told her.

"I have family, I understand, in that town. I have never been there. I don't think I should like to start now. Here is the Temple. Why don't you sit?"

She sat beside me with her handbag on her lap after first spreading out a wad of paper towels.

"I have certain problems of a medical nature to do with my seat. It is not painful just so long as I take some necessary precautions. Why do you come here?"

"To see you. To talk about William Ivory. To see the place he was born."

"You see me, I have a little trouble seeing you. Not too long ago I was diagnosed with cataracts. The milky thing is particularly developed in my left eye. I am meant to be wearing glasses but I find they play merry hell with my sinuses."

"You don't seem to have any trouble finding your way around."

"I know every scrap of this place. I could navigate by the sense of smell alone if it came to that."

"Even with your sinuses."

"Even with my sinuses—Are you cheeking me?"

"Only a little."

She considered that for a while, then shrugged it off. She looked out toward the Hall. I don't know what she saw or which decade she was looking at.

"If you have questions to ask of me, please would you just go ahead and ask them. I do not enjoy the luxury of dilly-dallying. I have a responsibility to the Hall and I do not entirely approve of giving the public such free rein. Especially our foreigner visitors, pardoning yourself. They use it as if it was a stage for theatricals. They imagine Agatha Christie lived here and that man with a mustache who was in all those war pictures. They take photographs as if they were on Cromer Pier—those paintings on wood with the face removed so these Fräuleins can stick in their own with a fat foolish sausage smile and pretend they're a bathing beauty. It was a sad large day when the house went out of the family. This is too grand and heavy a place for two old ladies to inhabit it alone. But the visitors don't understand. This used to be a family house. They don't give the place its deserved respect."

"It's a very beautiful place." And I suppose it was, elegant and manicured and halfway to dead. Apart from times in the desert, I never did feel all that comfortable away from the city. Too many strange noises. Too many ugly animals bigger than me. I wanted to be back in London, and out for a good supper when your money arrived, and I wanted to be back with Ivory's correspondence. (I only had a couple of letters with me, for luck.) But there were things I needed to find out, diligent biographer that I was. I wanted to know how it was when Ivory roamed here. What he used the Temple for, the Wilderness, the Secret Garden. Did he chase chambermaids along the narrow echoing corridors behind the kitchen? "How long did the Ivorys live here?"

"I beg your pardon?"

"I imagine for centuries. The Ivorys. How long did they have this house before?" I was bored by the slowness of this woman. "You were described to me as an expert. When did you come to this house?"

She drew breath. "Nineteen twenty-six. I was part of a family outing to Holkham Bay every summer between nineteen thirty-three and nineteen fifty-one. I visited London in nineteen forty-five and nineteen fifty-three. The first time for VE-Day, an occasion you have probably never heard of and nor would understand. The second time for the coronation of the Queen.

I have been treated as an inpatient and an outpatient at the Norwich and Norfolk Hospital twice a year since nineteen sixty-nine. Other than these occasions I have not left the house. Not ever. And you are in grievous error. This was never a house of the Ivory's. It has been in the Glaven family since seventeen ninety-three. Before that it belonged to the Hobarts, Lords of Buckinghamshire, who purchased it in sixteen sixteen. The Honorable Miss Sophie Glaven presented it to the National Trust in nineteen seventy-six. You say you came here to see the house William Ivory lived in as a child. Unless you have already been to an ugly road in Norwich near to the Roman Catholic cathedral I don't think you could have done what you set out to do."

"But you say you knew William Ivory? And he lived in this house. He was the son of the ambassador."

"He was most certainly not the son of the ambassador. He was the son of Thomas Ivory, who ran a large hatter's shop which used to be just off the market square right next to Jarrolds until nineteen fifty-something, I don't remember the exact year it closed. It might have been the time of the Festival of Britain. I think it was—there was talk of the household traveling up to London to view the festivities. In the final event I think it was only Sir Philip and Lady Sophia who went."

I stuttered out a question. "Sir Philip. He was the ambassador?"

"Indeed. I think the Festival of Britain was in nineteen fifty-two. No: it was nineteen fifty-one. King George with a beard was still on the throne. Sir Philip was the Ambassador to the United States of America. He was a fine, distinguished, and handsome man. We mourned him dearly when he died. The whole family was desolate."

"I don't understand you. What was the connection to the Ivorys?"

"Missis Ivory, who was a good woman, painted, but good, very quiet, very pure, spoke so well and so soft you would strain to catch her words, she was the sister to Lady Sophia. She married beneath herself, as women often do, to a man who claimed to have been a captain of Guards in the First War, but

I for one never believed that for a moment. Therefore, your precious little William Ivory was nephew to the ambassador and his wife, cousin to Mattie, Sophie, and John. Better children than the Glaven children you could not find. Even now, Miss Sophie doesn't forget me. She always comes out with a cake for us to share on her birthday. It is a sad responsibility to find myself the last one remaining in the house. People who come to visit, I tell them about my family. Naturally, I answer their questions about damask drapes and Thomas Gainsborough and beautiful martyred Anne Boleyn, and the Empress Catherine the Great of Russia, how she was charmed by the dancing of John Hobart, the second Earl of Buckinghamshire, dashing stories Sir Philip used to tell to us in the old days on winter nights in the Brown Drawing Room, but I try to keep the memory of my Glavens alive, I talk about them to all our visitors, even the foreigners. Maybe one in a hundred understands. Would you like to see a picture?"

It was getting cold out in the garden. The sun was setting over the Wilderness. The yellow-shelled Germans were lining up for group shots between the trees. The spring wind was brushing newly mown grass along the path toward us. The old lady didn't seem to feel the cold. She opened the clasp of her handbag and pulled out a black-and-white photograph. She held it carefully between white wrinkled fingertips. I reached out for it and she pulled it away, then brought it forward toward my face and held it waveringly still. A family group shot, formal, posed. The grownups sitting on chairs in the center: mother, pale and fragile; father, stiff, balding, louche, and proud; the old nanny (she looked old even then) by the side of Lady Sophia, still in her overcoat, fixed false-tooth smile, handbag, I think the same handbag, firmly planted on her lap. Next to father, standing, a boy, handsome in the English way, in a stiff formal suit, blond hair slicked down, something out of sorts about this boy, something defiant. And in front, cross-legged on the lawn, a sweet little boy with a mischievous grin, and a graceful girl, aping her mother and old before her time.

"Which one is Mattie?"

She didn't need to look at the picture to tell me. If she had

I don't think she'd have seen it any better. "There. Standing. Beside Sir Philip. If they were the same age you'd think they were twins. He would have grown up straight and tall like his father. And in front that's Jack and Sophie."

"And Mattie and William Ivory were friends."

She might have snorted. "William Ivory was a nasty little boy. A schemer, a corrupter. A devil when he looked so charming, butter wouldn't melt in his mouth in his blue sailor suit. Did you know that he was banned from the Hall? And a good thing too. I argued to the death that the ban should remain, but Lady Sophia was an angel and she relented. Sometimes good people do what they think are good acts, but the acts turn out to be evil because they judge people by their own standards. Lady Sophia was too good for this world. So was Mattie. So was brave Jack. Only the good die young. The ban should never have been rescinded. Not ever. He didn't come back for long. Just long enough to do his damage. You can never keep a villain away from the scene of his crime. He returned here, I saw him, it was around the time of the Queen's jubilee. Nineteen seventy-seven. Skulking around the Japanese Bedroom. Unmistakable. I acted as if I never saw him. It would have been a believable excuse. My eyes were bad even then."

"What was so nasty about him?"

"He was thoroughly wicked with a dark soul and no heart at all. He drove Mattie against his family. And even before that, you could see the signs. My family was so generous to the hatter's boy. He was even permitted to share family holidays, be part of Christmas festivities just as if he was a proper member of the family, just as if he was one of us. Even then he'd always be doing something bad and wrong and wicked. Devising evil games that made the children squabble and bicker and fight with each other. Bullying Jack, doing strange cruel things to sweet Sophie that she still won't tell her Nanny about. He was cruel far ahead of his years. Spending hidden time with Mattie. Out in the yew hedges in the front of the house, that's where they'd always be, hiding like snakes. I'd take my broom to them. Mattie would never have run away from home if it hadn't been for his cousin. Who can say whether he'd still be alive today? And this house would have continued as it was meant to continue, and I'd have another generation of Glavens to nanny and care for."

You'd expect her to be crying. She wasn't crying. Hard-faced, vindictive, hateful. Despising the bourgeois cousin with a snobbery borrowed from her employers. I could imagine this woman's life. Plucked from a village in rural Ireland to care for children whose parents didn't know how. A hard-bitten virgin slave who remained part of the house, keeping "her" family's memory alive. I doubted if sweet Sophie ever visited at birthdays. Or on any other day.

"You couldn't have been mistaken?" I said, gently. "I understand your loyalty. It does you credit. But couldn't things have been different from how you say? I've heard stories—"

"What, kind, of, stories?" Hard staccato words. She replaced the picture quickly in her handbag as if any more of my attention might spoil it. She stared at me, her milky half-blind eyes alive and deadly in her dead face.

"Stories about Mattie in London. Things Mattie did. What he was."

She got to her feet. Held her handbag to her chest as if it gave strength to her heart. Kept staring at me—it must have been the look she used to save for William Ivory, and that pleased me.

"May, God, strike, you. Dumb! How dare you suggest such a thing in this place. Hasn't this family suffered enough without having the likes of you, fake Irishmen with dark tainted blood—yes, I see what's inside of you, you're more a gypsy than a Cork man. I command you to leave this place. You get the hell out of this place! (May God pardon my tongue in my rage.)"

She even crossed herself. I waited for the old witch to totter and fall. To pay finally for the abuse she must have heaped on the head of little William Ivory for no other reason than he was a hatter's son from Norwich not good enough to play with her borrowed children. I wanted to avenge the boy in a sailor suit. See her bile stop her heart. I got to my feet.

"If Mattie was a homo that had nothing to do with Ivory. If you ask me—"

"Out. Out. Out out out Out Out OUT OUT OUT! OUT

Out OUT! OUT OUT OUT OUT out out out OUT OUT out out OUT!! OUT!!!!"

She was struggling to breathe. The few Germans left jerked their heads alarmedly our way and shot a thousand flashlit photographs of us in the fading light. Illumined by the lightning flashes of their cameras, Nanny Brennan lifted up one biblical arm and pointed toward the house, a terrifying command from a statue about to crumble. I figured it was time to go.

They were getting ready to shut the house up for the day. I walked back in through the stone part of the garden, took one look back at the tiny figure of Martha Brennan still out there in the same pose, an allegorical sculpture of sightless, bigoted outrage, got back into the house along with a group of Swedes being kicked out of the Tea Room, and we were all ushered away along the corridors, through the servants' rooms, the Kitchen, the Dining Room, the Outer Courtyard, and away across the bridge by a busy coven of tweedy women with fake tour-guide smiles on their lined, aging faces.

S hould I have hunted for his childhood house? Investigated that suburban street near the Roman Catholic cathedral where the hatter's family used to live? Opened my eyes and ears and tasted the scene? And what would it have taught me? The place he escaped from. The life he rejected. I wanted to find the man he was, not the person he chose not to be.

I know I should have tried to find my way out to his house near Binham. Ignored my empty wallet, the darkening Norfolk sky, but there was money waiting for me in London and that was where I had to get to, so I walked out into the carpark, gave a kick to the useless hired sedan now safely hidden a long way from hookers' alley, and, with my collar turned up, joined the end of a line of Japanese kids waiting to climb their tour bus back to London. I found a seat near the back, curled my large occidental body on the seat, and pressed my white-man features close to the glass.

A girl came to sit next to me just before the bus pulled out. She paid me no mind, she was chattering with her friends on the nearby seats, all of them sitting toward each other, feet and knees tightly together, heads nearly touching. When the bus left the grounds of Hobart Hall and gathered up speed along the darkening wasp-stripe road, lights flickered on inside. No one came round to count heads. No one came to check for large-boned intruders. I relaxed slightly and pulled out of my pocket two letters from William Ivory, the ones I had plucked at random from my stolen pile.

4 March 1973

Dear Helen,

I had not meant to cause you pain. The poetry of
coincidence, that our little picnic should happen to occur
with yours. Thank you for your charming letter. DB is
grown very pretty. I do believe she takes after you more and
more each day. I have done some beastly things. I hope you
can find it in your heart to forgive me, your errant, your
once and future

husband

Once and future? What did that mean? Was it just a formula
that had worked before, a way of hooking her to him? Or was
it sincere? An expression of a love that was true, thwarted one
time, and now ready to clench back together? DB, her daughter.
Had to be his daughter too. We know that Helen Ivory believed
marriage was forever. She'd told me that her daughter's name
was Deborah. What did the B stand for? And picnics, always
such a fuss over an outdoor spread. What is it with the British
and your picnics? If you hate them so much, if trouble always
arises, then why the fuck don't you just eat indoors?

17 April 1972

Dear Helen,

Kawabata killed himself yesterday. Jim Harkin called
from Tokyo to tell me the news. The Nobel laureate was
discovered in his house last night, dead, gassed. I knew him
very slightly, admired him more, but always rather resented
his being awarded the Nobel ahead of Mishima. The reasons
were clear: the veneration due to age, the feeling no doubt
that Yukio had time on his side and would get it, say,
twenty-five years on, when Japan's turn came around again.

Why did Kawabata kill himself? He was old. His body was sick and en route to death via decay. That is enough reason in itself. Jim says that he went into a decline after the death of Mishima: he knew just as well as you or I or Yukio that the Nobel had gone to the wrong man. And then he followed the greater man down the same sickly path.

Why do writers kill themselves? That mad Berryman in January was the most recent. But look at this list. It is by no means complete and it excludes the cowards who murdered themselves with religion or alcohol:

Kawabata Yasunari, John Berryman, Mishima Yukio,*
Paul Celan, Sylvia Plath, Stefan Zweig, Malcolm Lowry,
Ernest Hemingway, Frank O'Hara, Akatugawa Ryunosuke,
Cesare Pavese,* Dazai Osamu,* Jack London, Vladimir
Mayakovsky, Stanislaw Ignacy Witkiewicz, Hart Crane,
Heinrich von Kleist,* Thomas Chatterton, Petronius.

*Dazai and Kleist killed themselves in love suicide pacts!! So did Mishima. Cesare Pavese—"No one ever lacks a good reason for suicide", "Women are an enemy race, like the Germans"—would have too had he the capacity to make anyone fall in love with him.

I have often alluded to the following story. I shall tell it to you now.

It's the winter of '66. I'm at one of Mishima's Wednesday-night parties at his Tokyo house. The house is built Western-style but with smaller rooms and lower ceilings than we are used to and that's so Yukio can appear taller than he really is. We're in the upstairs living room which is as provocatively vulgar as a Hawaiian shirt, and we're all getting sloshed on American whiskey. Mishima has taken the floor to lead us in a selection of tunes from Broadway shows. (Japanese intellectuals—you can spot them by their berets and goatees—affect an inexplicable fondness for this bastard genre.)

The top of the author's shirt is unbuttoned. His tie is half unknotted. He's yowling out one last encore chorus of "Oh, What a Beautiful Morning". The Japanese copy of a Victorian grandfather clock chimes out midnight. Mishima pauses. He nods to some interior thought and releases the last few sounds in a swooping breath-held line. Then he bows to our over-generous applause and quietly exits by the ivory white staircase to the dining room we overlook. Enthusiasm for music diminishes without him for our focus, and we return into little groups for conversation. I'm leaning against the iron gallery rail, talking on one side to Yoko, Mishima's wife, and on the other to his American translator. The author is in the dining room below. He is dressed now in a kimono tied by a dandy's scarlet sash. He crouches by the dining table and picks up several long, obviously heavy cloth-wrapped bundles. He straightens and he meets my eyes watching from above. We hold that look for a moment, he always enjoyed those duels of the eyes, before he half smiles and breaks the contact. I watch him climb slowly up the stairs and retake his position in the centre of the room where he lays his bundles across the floor.

Conversation falters and stops. A Times correspondent and a Jap military boy are the last to notice, but cease their snaky whispering just as Mishima is about to look their way. A semicircle forms around our samurai conjuror. He's on his knees, solemnly, lovingly, unwrapping each bundle to expose another gleaming perfect blade. Hunch-shouldered, he contemplates each one in turn. All of us are silent. We too are part of this ceremony.

These are the marvels of his collection. The swords range in shape and age and all are fatally sharp: naginta blades, single-edged, swelling and curving deeply to their points; the flat, straight-bladed hira zukuri; the selection of katakiri ha, one of these is very old, fourteenth century, I'd say. Finally, he selects. A dagger, yoroi doshi, an armour piercer, with a double-edged hira zukuri blade. He lifts it into the air and we are silently commanded to admire the play of light across the blade; the black-and-white inlay on the hilt; the glittering hamon. Mishima draws the dagger lightly across the fingertip of his left ring finger and displays the wound for our attention.

He holds the pose: the lights have him in an artful half-shadow; blood drips in a slow trickle of black down to his wrist. He stays there like that, on his knees, one arm held high, his torso half twisted: the proud body-builder delighting in his awkward pose: the poetry of flesh aching to be marble. Then he calls my name.

The crowd parts to let me through. I stay where I am; I have no desire to play the straight man in a Mishima performance. He calls out my name a second time. He rises. He finds my eyes with his and he doesn't let go of them this time. I have no choice; I walk towards him; I join him in the centre of the ring. He stands fully up now; he bows to me and I to him; he raises his right hand to place it on my left shoulder and exerts a gentle pressure. He's playing courtesan and this is a seducer's command to kneel. There's an appreciative murmur from our connoisseur onlookers. I don't know what to expect—I have not seen this performance before. I kneel.

Black shiny shoes and narrow-trousered legs surround me. The naked feet of the man with the dagger, his girlish thin calves, the thick blue silk of his robe, and up: the scarlet sash, the chest he is so proud of, hairy for a Japanese man and decorated so perfectly with fairy-tale muscles. A vein pulses in his scrupulously developed neck. His mouth is clenched shut. His dark eyes have never left mine, not for a moment. Suddenly: the gleaming fish-through-water slash of the dagger swooping down: the point quivers and holds against my shirt-front and rips: my stomach is bare, my shirt is hanging open, torn. A gasp from our attendants, breathing all with the same nervous rhythm. I keep my eyes on Mishima's. Anything less would make this thing ugly to him.

He slides the gleaming side of the dagger down to the centre of my belly and the hamon shines a zigzag pattern; he holds the point against my navel: this is the beginning of ceremonial death. He whispers loud enough for just me to hear, 一瞬の生命の燃焼 : "Isshun no seimei no nenshō" (a moment of burning life) and, louder, "Are you scared, Englishman?" I give him no reaction, that would be weakness. He digs the point of the blade into the tuck of

my belly with enough delicacy and strength merely to break
the skin and coax a thin flow of blood to drip slowly down.
He pulls the dagger away and holds it above his head. He
closes his eyes and whirls the blade in a perfect circle; the
gleaming point cuts a halo in the cigarette air. He opens his
eyes, whispers again, 陶酔: "Tōsui" (rapture): then abruptly
laughs. This is the cue for us all and our audience takes it. It
laughs. I do not laugh. I climb slowly to my feet and bow.
He returns the bow. I stand straight and still. He slowly
wraps his daggers. I wait there in the centre of the room.
He leaves to fetch me a replacement shirt. It is made of a
finer silk than my own and would have been too large for
his weight-sculpted shoulders and chest. I do believe he had
laid it in store specially. I change in the dining room below.
The party drifts on, but the host is gone: up to his study for
a night of writing.

Was he attempting to explain something to me? Was he
promising the manner of his death? Was he to perform this
same pantomime with Kawabata and, later, Morita? (Because
it was with the same blade that he performed seppuku four
years later.) Was he testing me? Was he performing a
narcissistic fantasy for the benefit of his guests and, more
important, himself? Or was he merely choosing to drive
himself into the emotional state he required for the literary
work he had to do that night? I believe all of these are true.
Increasingly as he got older he chose to inhabit a dark hard
place, a cruel country whose willing maroons spoke a
language of fetishism, Wagnerism, history, and death. He
needed followers to assure him of the truth of his way, to
convince him, because he didn't ever really believe it, that
the Sodom in his soul was something more than a
psychopathology rooted in a woman-smothered childhood.

There was a cult of him before, and there is a cult of him
now. Young provocateurs carry the warrior-clown image of
him around in their life-denying hearts. I cannot share that.
(And he would have said that is because I am not Japanese.)
I do recognize his greatness.

But it is interesting, is it not, dear Helen? the way writers play kiss-chase with the dead men of the past. Look at how Kawabata chose Mishima for his assassin. They do, all of them, have one historical figure, recent or ancient, as their exemplar, their archetype and unknowing precursor, whose glamorous or seedy cloak of fame they wrap around themselves (and some suffocate in the process): the fragile poets with their pashes on Byron or Shelley; the acned hippies with their Jesus guitar fantasies; the silly girls who dream themselves to be fated queens—Cleopatra, Anne Boleyn, Mary, Queen of Scots—tantalizing historical mermaids; and I have my Prince Boothby, Regency fop, of whom I know little and care to know no more, just this one salient fact: getting dressed and undressed every day became such a bore that he killed himself. It is a curious road. I could walk down it with you.

My book has been published. After a slow start it is now going rather well. (I confess a little newspaper manipulation.) We might even have a best seller on our hands.

Yours, from the midst of life,
W.

Outside the bus it was dark. Norfolk night interrupted now and then by the glowing windows of another TV-watching village. Inside, the lights had dimmed without me noticing. The girl next to me was sleeping. A bandy-legged doll in black curled up on her seat, her face toward mine. I folded the pages of the letters flat, touched my fingers against the raised surface of Ivory's big dominant scrawl, and looked out of the window, like a blind man reassured by a history lesson in Braille.

Things look different at night, Ivory said so. I didn't recognize the route, the sudden line of lights that appeared by the side of our road, the steep banking curve the bus took which jolted the sleeping girl against me. I eased her over with my shoulder to try to replace her to her position and her eyelids flickered open. We looked at each other for a very long moment, she and I, like Mishima and Ivory; and when I reached over to give her a reassuring, everything-will-be-okay, don't-worry-honey pat on the knee, my inadvertent thumb poked beneath the silk lining of her little black skirt, and she blinked one time, pulled her body slowly away, and covered her mouth with her hand.

And screamed.

High-pitched young crow shrieks. Eyes screwed shut to give more power to the throat. Hands waving in the air like a minstrel mama. I lay my hand on her arm and she opens her eyes. I smile at her and she closes her eyes again and screams some more. Louder even than before. Her friends wake up, see her screaming, see my calming, weak sick smile, and they join in, they scream too. Lights glare on in the cabin. A wild commotion of noise and light and speed. Everyone jumps up around me, ready for war. The bus lurches and grinds to a stop at the side of the road. Wheels churn up gravel past my window as everyone either falls back into their seats or else rushes on down the aisle like eager contestants on a mobile game show. She carries on screaming next to me. Every moment gives her more fuel.

If there's one thing I hate, it's people who've learned their English from American cop shows. The sumo-fat thug with the wispy adolescent's mustache who pulls me out of my seat, repeating time and again, "I'm taking you to jail, baby." *Kojak* episodes, I guess, must take a long time to get to Japan. Screaming all around me. The middle-aged woman chaperone nodding at her pet thug. "I'm taking you to jail, baby." The English bus driver, sitting yawning at his wheel, not bothering with me, bored, waiting to set off again, probably hungry, probably wants to dump this load and drive into some sleeping suburb where his part-time squeeze is all dolled up in corset and garter belt and pancake makeup waiting for her demon bus-driving lover. "I'm taking you to jail, baby." Sumo-kid gets me in an arm lock and marches me down the aisle, his friends offering me ineffectual kicks and punches like going-home gifts after a child's birthday party. Without bothering to look, no white-man solidarity here, the driver operates the door and it pulls open with a steaming hiss. "I'm taking you to jail, baby." I manage to hold a last stand in the doorway, sumo-kid struggling to get both my shoulders past the metal ridge. The chaperone, confident in her victory, looks at me mildly. This is my moment, now I can say the thing that will make them understand, might even make them my friends. Sumo-kid gets one shoulder out, but when he sets to work with the other, like a tugboat heaving against a barge, I manage to get the first one back in. I look over his head at the chaperone and she looks at me, and this is my moment but all I can think of to say is "I'm a friend of William Ivory" (big in Japan, that's what you told me), and the chaperone is polite enough to say "Who?" and I'm about to repeat the name but the kid gets both my shoulders through into the night and says, "I'm taking you to jail, *baby*," and kicks me off the bus. I land with a jolt on the side of the road, and those cute Japanese faces press against the glass to stare out at me as the bus pulls away.

Lying in the dirt at the side of a strange road at night is not a good thing. Linen suit soiled with gravel. Stones pricking up against my shoulders and legs. Boy racers practicing for the Indy 500—or what's your British equivalent?—taking the bank of the road in high gear, shuddering screeching past. I stood up and contemplated my state. There are low moments in every man's life and I'd had plenty of those since arriving in your country; but this was my lowest—and of course I blamed you for it all. I was cold; I was lost; I was hungry; I was broke; and I needed to piss very badly: and only one of these conditions was in my power to do anything about. Defiantly, it was one of those moments that defines the hero, that separates him from the common herd, I opened my zipper, pulled out my dick, and pissed into the road, and I took great delight in the metallic splash of my urine against the sides of the boy racers' cars, and I cared not a fuck about the splashback on my shoes.

This gesture lifted my spirits. I was taking responsibility into my own hands, like all the best self-help manuals advise. Hardly had I zipped up my fly and stuck out my thumb when my lift arrived. A sweet middle-aged couple in heavy-metal fetish gear driving a Mini Cooper held together with chicken wire came to my rescue. He rolled down his window and I muttered something about getting beat up, robbed, and having my car stolen by a tour group of Japanese, and my rescuers said, in unison, "Fucking Nips." She climbed out with a jangle of metal and a groan of leather and told me to hop in. I got in the back and pulled the seat down. She sat back down and crushed my knees and I grinned. They told me their names (Doug and Dee Dee) and I told them mine. They offered me some drugs in gelatin capsules—they didn't say what was inside, just, "Do you want some drugs?"—which I refused, and a jug of cider, which I happily accepted. They were on their way to a homeopathic fair in London and, cranking along the slow lane in a wheezing, steaming third gear (fourth, they told me, was fucked), they took me there.

T he next day I was woken by the Australian at my door. He looked spiffy. "I'm sorry about the suit. It's all a circus, isn't it?" His surfer's hair had been pinned into a bun. He was wearing a narrow-cut suit, third-generation threads, Swinging London, Carnaby Street. A thin wool tie had been hoisted up to bruise his Adam's apple. "I've had a bellyful of this place. I'm going for a restaurant job."

"Very nice. You woke me up to tell me that?"

"Excuse me. I'm nervous. You think I look all right? I don't like these jacket flaps. They make my bum look funny. Postie's at the door for you. Recorded delivery."

He left me alone. I threw on a random selection of clothes, went downstairs, signed the Post Office form, received a slim brown envelope with a New York stamp, went back to my room. The Australian was still in the corridor, presenting his profile to the full-length mirror beside the pay phone, twisting his head over his shoulder to catch the full effect of the jacket flaps. I locked my door.

I flicked on the bedside lamp and opened the envelope. A banker's draft for £667 sterling. Not a fortune, nor the amount agreed upon, but sufficient for the moment. I went to the window and pulled open the curtains. Outside, a gray London morning, the city lurching into a half-life. And inside, me, a large American hidden in a small room, reassured by the promise of money in my hand, and reassured by you, for once, being almost as good as your word.

Enough. Maybe I can wrench something out of this after all. Let me get scholarly now. *Serious* biography. Concerned, disinterested, lofty, scandalous. Prize-winning stuff. Ignore the red-lipstick words. Ignore the rotting fruit in the bowl—or maybe succumb one last time to the nauseous temptation to stick a finger through the moldy body of an orange that used to be round. Take no regretful looks at the jars clustered on the bathroom shelves. Certainly pay no attention to your silence in the corner. Instead, take my scholar's seat at the table, put on a metaphorical pair of pince-nez, settle down with legal pads and tape recordings and letters and books, and dryly construct a life, fastidiously annotated by footnotes.

H

e was born in 1925 in Norwich. William Ivory, the hatter's son. Is that too bland? Is that the way to start and go on? Day by day, piece by piece, kiss by kiss, the gathered increments of a dead man's life? Start—how? With a bang? With the loudest of bangs?—the perfect, final collision? Or softly, with a quiet, true moment? A capsule of truth that the rest will surround and explain. Begin with atmosphere and conclude in blood, like all the best stories do. That's what Brougham Calder said.

Norfolk. Holkham Bay. February 1980. A light rain falls on three figures alone on a sea-washed shore. Behind them, a line of trees, a stripe of forest, and a flat green landscape pressed down upon by the enormous sky. But here, on the sand, within the dunes, there is relief from the Norfolk sky. If the three people, the man and the two women, one on either side of him, intimately close, were looking out to the horizon, they would see fishing vessels and a scattering of tugs and one or two anchored barges and a few reckless sailboats tossed about by the whitecap waves of the gray North Sea; but they are not looking out to the horizon. In a moment the light drizzle will disperse and be replaced by a new bright sun; and in a moment the blonde woman will remove all of her clothes and shut her eyes and lie back down again on the fine-grained yellow-white sand and feel the sun touch her skin and feel some of her sadness return; and in a moment the mustachioed man, the leader of these three, will be hatching the next game for the party to play; and in a moment his Japanese wife will inspect the chamber of the gun: because this, the gun, World War II Home Guards issue, cocked and aimed, is what the three of them are looking at, because William Ivory is slowly moving it up to his opened mouth.

Too doomy? Too staged and solemn? Too much strained-after style getting in the way of things? Begin with the family before he was born, that's how to do it, play to the eugenicists in the audience. Take two.

Captain Thomas Ivory adjusted his trilby (company stock, a popular line) and stepped outside his store into a pleasant winter evening. It was late January 1925, a Wednesday, and the retired army captain should have been happily, and usefully, engaged for the evening drilling a khaki parade of schoolboy cadets. Instead, and this irked him, he was due back home for cocktails and dinner because his wife was going to be acting the society hostess tonight.

He didn't resent his wife's brother-in-law. He didn't feel in any way inferior to him. For one thing, Glaven was a Catholic and for another, Thomas had been a fighting officer in the War while Sir Philip was sitting safe in Whitehall doing sneaky stuff in the Foreign Office. But Joan, the wife, Mrs. Captain Ivory, that was another affair. She'd been rich once, as a child, and had expected more of the gaudy stuff when she got older, and position too; and her sister, her *younger* sister, had done all right for herself: Lady Sophia, Mrs. American Ambassador Glaven; and the captain had seen on too many occasions that comparing look breaking the pretty powdered frost of his wife's customary expression when he and her brother-in-law were made momentary companions at cross-class dos. So a night of boredom was to be expected; but maybe there would be benefits later on, after the guests had gone home, after the cocktails had been drunk and the wineglasses emptied: perhaps a marital rite observed in the chill of his wife's private bedroom—there had been all too little of that, ever since baby Thomas had been delivered stillborn in 1922 . . .

No no no no. This reads like the worst kind of opening to the worst kind of historical novel. It's crap to try to get inside the head of Captain Thomas Ivory circa 1925, it's crap to try to reconstruct the night when the sperm hit the egg and little William Ivory was conceived. The only way is to chronicle the unarguable facts, to describe the surface, the rest will follow.

Begin stolidly at the beginning, with the date of his birth. Work through from there. That's the only way to make sure of getting it all.

In a rare autobiographical moment, William Ivory remarked that his decline began on "a late autumn day in 1925."[1]

To Captain and Mrs. Thomas Ivory, a boy. William Ivory—soon to be dressed up in sailor suit and shown his first sight of the sea, and soon to make dangerous friendships at Hobart Hall: the shy boy who played the piano so fancily; adventurer, yes, and author too, and mow-'em-down war hero, and luck-crazy gambler, and Englishman and monster—was born on October 30, 1925. William Stuart Ivory, the philosopher of decadence, began his decline as William Sidney Ivory, the hatter's son, of Norwich.

[I should have gotten one of those *Norwich: Portrait of a City* books.] The county of Norfolk is notable for its unkindly heavy sky and grand northern coast. The capital of Norfolk is Norwich, and Norwich is a two-cathedral city, crammed tight with pubs and churches, the proud possessor of a mean temperament and a market square at its center. And just off the market square, beside Jarrolds department store, there used to be a hat shop, a sturdy Victorian construction, Ivory & Son (est. 1854).

Its owner, Thomas Ivory, was an extravagantly mustachioed man who had been a captain of Horse Guards[2] in the First World War and then resigned his commission to return home and assume command of the family concern. He married well, the retired captain, taking for his wife the Honourable Joan Sidney in 1921. William was their second child out of three, but the only one to survive birth.

The Ivorys were a middle-class suburban family, well-to-do, securely supported by their long-established business, short of

1. The penultimate paragraph of his essay "Game-Playing with Schizophrenics," *Psychiatry Now*, December 1974.
2. Although there is some doubt over this: Captain Thomas Ivory of the Horse Guards is not mentioned in the Army Lists of the time. It does seem clear, however, that he *did* serve in the Great War (although of Thomas Ivorys for that period, I have unearthed only a second lieutenant of the Horse Guards and a captain in the Army Service Corps), so we shall keep, skeptically, to the official version.

being rich. They lived at 7 Heigham Grove, a detached house of
three stories, with a small garden at the back for the child to
play in, had he been that kind of child. It was a brisk morning
march to work for the robust Captain Ivory, and a comfortable
if disagreeable surrounding for his wife.

Joan Ivory was a disappointed lady who found refuge of a sort
in an excess of makeup and costume and hair dye when her
fragile looks faded. She was a would-be, had-been socialite who
dabbled in causes and good works, and froze out her husband,
who was never permitted to forget that he was born a class below
her. Ivory recorded no opinion of his mother in his journal (he
mentioned his parents seldom, and when he did, it was usually
just passing spite or a stab of contempt aimed at his burly father), but there was some sympathy between the pair: the artistic boy and his slightly ridiculous mother, who felt herself so
acutely to be lost with the wrong man in the wrong world. Joan
Ivory's antecedents were Yorkshire textile millionaires, enno-
bled in the late nineteenth century, financially ruined in the
early twentieth, and her younger sister was a permanent, neigh-
boring reminder of her own decline in status.

Lady Sophia Glaven, née Sidney, was wife to the onetime Ambassador to the United States, Sir Philip Glaven, who owned the
nearby Hobart Hall. The Glavens were the most prominent family in that part of Norfolk, and Mrs. Ivory's work with the Children's Country Holidays, a charity set up to allow urban children
the brief pleasure of rural visits, could hardly compete with her
sister's role as ambassadorial hostess.

William was a sickly child, asthmatic from the first, awkward,
but with a surprising talent for the piano. We have seen the
formal portrait taken by Gerald of Norwich of the young prodigy:
the pale solemn boy, hair sticky with pomade, who sits, blank-
faced, in a formal suit on a piano stool. And this boy virtuoso
seems to have inherited or learned his snobbery from his mother.
As his imagination grew, cramped, perhaps even a little twisted,
by the boxrooms of the suburbs, his richer, titled cousins out in
the country became the focus for his early aspirations. Cut to
Hobart Hall, director.

An imposing dead pile, once home to Anne Boleyn, the house

survives as a tourist property and is still presided over by Martha Brennan, nanny to the Glaven children. A long avenue of yew trees to the front courtyard door, an ornamental garden, an over-grown field of weeds called the Wilderness, internal acres of grand cold rooms, Hobart Hall was home to Sir Philip, now back in Whitehall; his saintly wife, Lady Sophia; and their three children, Sophie, Little Jack, and doomed Mattie. It was William Ivory's favorite place.

Shortly before his twelfth birthday, William caught rheumatic fever and nearly died. This was his first major illness, and he was going to suffer repercussions from it throughout his life. It affected his heart.

He began his journal[3] at the moment (October 26, 1937) when his spirits and his health were at their lowest. "If I am to die now or in the next few days then it will be an extrordinry record of the mind of an extrordinry boy who died a solemn death mis-understood by his parents and his town."

It is a precocious record, the young Ivory journal. It imagines exotic locations where his fortunes might flourish, it lists his ambitions, it abuses his father—"He tried to make me cry but I did not cry. Instead I imagined him dead on a parade ground with bayonets piercing his uniform"—and it carefully chronicles the symptoms of his disease:

My whole body hurts and my hand hurts as I write this. It is a brave thing I do. When I try to stand I can see that the world is moving as Isaac Newton said and for once gravity has not an effect upon me. I spin with the world and tumble to the floor which rises up from the perpindicular to stop me. [. . .] When the curtain is open I look out at the branches of the tree where sometimes there is a small bird who makes such a racket with his song. I like the tree better when it is bare. I am sad to die in such a small mean place. I wish I could be somewhere more elegant like London or Paris

3. What survives of the (previously unpublished) journal is in the personal care of the author.

or Saint Petersberg or somewhere I could feel at home or else lying in rest in the Japanese bedroom at the Hall.

But he had been banned from the Japanese Bedroom, and he had been banned from the Hall. However, on the day of his twelfth birthday, October 30, 1937, his cousin Mattie was allowed to visit him. Stern William didn't relax his guard to display any pleasure in the visit or in the sketch pad his best friend had brought for him, but when Mattie left the sickroom, Mrs. Ivory arranged the few birthday cards that her son had been sent and, under William's instructions, put the card his cousin had drawn for him ("a green odelisk") in the most prominent place, on the window ledge.

And when the symptoms of his illness began to alleviate a little, the sickly diarist discovered that he missed them:

> After the fever and the pain had gone there was nothing. I was dissapointed. I had prepared myself for Death and was curious to see what It would be like and whether I would be allowed to come back in spirit form to haunt Mattie like he had asked me to do and like I had promised. [...] I rub myself harshly against the blankets to make the shoulders and the knees hurt again. The world does not spin as much as it used to and things will get ordinary again. There is something dissappointing about being on the mend, as if the grand adventure I had been about to embark upon had been cancelled by a goverment official through a whim. When I am older I intend to be a great comic novelist like Mr. Aldous Huxley or Mr. Evelyn Waugh.

Sir Philip was occupied in some Czechoslovak discussions over in Paris, and the regime always relaxed in his absence. So, before he was much older, recuperating William was permitted to visit Hobart Hall again.

> Today I went to the Hall with Mother, who took me there. We sat discretely in the Long Gallery, Mattie and I,

until Mother and Aunt Sophia left us to our own devices. Then up to the Japanese Bedroom where we lay upon the floor and slanted our eyes with our fingers and took it in turns to tell cruel Japanese tales from the paper on the walls. Then we ran pell-mell out into the garden to our place inside the yew hedge at the front of the house. For once Mattie got there before yours truly. I was slow and out of breath and Mattie took pleasure in remarking upon it. I am a convalescent and an asthmatic, I told him after I recovered my breath, and I think that made him jealous. I think he wanted to be a convalescent too. He said he had come to the house every day of my illness but had not been allowed ingress except on my birthday because of instructions. I did not lower myself to respond. Mattie has dark hair on his upper lip. I chaffed him about it. I made him show me his underarms and there is hair there too. The pain has returned fully. It is equal on both sides of my body. My wrists and ankles and shoulders are very thin and very delicate nowadays. We lay there very tightly together ~~didnt~~ did not say anything more.

My name is William Stuart Ivory. Mattie is the Honourable Robert Matthew Lothian Glaven. My name used to be William Sidney Ivory but I prefer Stuart because it is more redolent.

The friends didn't stay in their hiding place for as long as they would have liked. Martha Brennan ("foolish old Nanny") went hunting for them and the two boys were driven back inside the house to take tea in the Brown Drawing Room. The sisters, the ambassador's wife and the shopkeeper's wife, were there, and Mattie's brother and sister, older Sophie and younger Jack. William noted his delight at the way neither of those children would meet him in the eyes "because they were scared. Aunt Sophia told Sophie to pass tea to the convalescent which she did in a downcast way and the way Aunt Sophia pronounced the word convalescent made it ugly and without dignity and I shan't use it of myself any more."

Some have argued that young William was a malign influence on the family at Hobart Hall. The child who practiced his Chopin and Debussy pieces on the grand piano in the Music Room is described by Martha Brennan as a "schemer and corrupter."[4] But a motor of snobbery drives the emotions of all great families, particularly British ones, and the worst snobs of all are those who aren't born to it and have to fight tooth and nail to protect their own questionable status. Certainly, the boy William had been banned from the Hall. Whether this was due to his corrupting influence on his close friend Cousin Mattie, and also on his cousins Sophie and Jack, or just the effect of childhood games carried too far, with the suburban cousin as the convenient scapegoat, is open to conjecture.

Of course, childhood games can be vicious. William admits his delight when Sophie and Little Jack appeared too frightened to meet his eyes in the Brown Drawing Room that day of his readmission to the Hall. Was their reaction the terror of the persecuted when they see their oppressor? And his, the tyrant's simple delight at the sight of fear in the eyes of his victims? Or was it much more innocent than that? Was it merely their guilt over their part in his social martyrdom, and his, the feeling of small revenge on the part of the one who was wronged? William was a boy more sinned against than sinning. The victim of adult incomprehension of the child's games of sexual curiosity and adventure.[5]

Two years pass. Two years in which William and Mattie hold on to their fragile embattled friendship. The prodigy piano player distinguished himself in several public examinations. He won second prize in an under-eighteens' music competition held at the Assembly Rooms in Norwich. He continued to practice on the concert grand in the Hobart Hall Music Room and, less often, on the undistinguished one in the drawing room of 7 Heigham Grove.

4. In conversation with the author.
5. It is a little unclear what these games actually were. Young William doesn't describe them. I can find only one reference—March 16, 1940—in which he refers to Sophie's "shamed blush" when Little Jack reminded her of the game of "forfeits" played two Christmases before.

And then, on September 1, 1939, Britain declared war on Germany. For the British, the first year came to be known as the "Phoney War," when the apocalypse was always imminent but nothing much actually happened; and the only change to the lives at Heigham Grove and Hobart Hall was the arrival in the early spring of 1940 of a party of East End evacuee children for whom Joan Ivory arranged accommodation on the top floor of Hobart Hall.

In the words of one family member: "They were exotics, these children from London. They displayed a different way of speaking, of dressing. They were like stragglers of a defeated foreign army encamped on our top landing: a wild pack of refugees, feral, violent, bold with curses, shy, smudge-faced and scared, who became objects of fascination for us all."[6]

These East End children, who must have been terrified by their abrupt separation from their families and their sudden relocation to a chilly country house in Norfolk, became particular objects of fascination for Mattie and William.

Secretly, against all orders from their families, the two cousins would go up to the top floor of the Hall. They conquered the evacuees' resistance with apples. They won their confidence with scraps of food from the family dinner of the night before.

As William wrote in his journal:

February 3rd 1940

We went upstairs again today. Sophie was in the Long Gallery practising her dancing steps and falling over greatly, and Aunt Sophia was busy somewhere else in the house. Nanny was safely out near the yew circle, where she fiddled about with weeds. Little Jack had been bribed to keep watch half-way up the staircase with a pea-whistle ready in his mouth to sound the alert if any

6. Sophie Glaven, *A Journey* (London, 1954). Sophie was the oldest of the children at Hobart Hall, and her book, an eccentric, somewhat rambling, anecdotal account of her wartime experiences—as a teenager at the Hall; then as an aspirant at a closed order of nuns; later searching for her brother in London; and subsequently serving in the WAAF (the Women's Auxiliary Air Force)—is the primary source for information about the family during this period. Unfortunately, Miss Glaven has not been in the best of health and was unable to meet the author.

of the others came to pry. They had sentries on watch too—two sullen girls who swore at us and tried to kick us when we muscled through. Then out of the old servants' sitting room that's become their school room, Vic came out, and Eve, and George, and Stanley. We stood before them looking cold and aristocratic. I do not know who is their leader. Vic acts as if he is, but yet he kowtows to George in the event of a disagreement. Vic has a round fleshy face, dark hair, hulking shoulders and a broad back. He delights in showing off his strength; sometimes he will carry two school-desks, one balanced atop the other, all the way round the servants' sitting room. He has the strangest voice I ever heard: loud and hoarse, like a very large crow. Mattie says he has a cabbie's voice. George is wiry and sly-looking. He has fine blond hair above a very pale face (a slum face, says Mattie). He is the same height as Mattie and in truth the two look very much alike. If I were a philosopher I might say that George is Mattie's doppelganger, his diseased-looking secret double.

Vic folded his big arms across his grey-shirted barrel chest and asked us what we wanted. Mattie did not speak. I said that it wasn't for him to deny us entrance. It was our house, I said. They were all our guests. I spoke in a tone of flattery mixed with condescension. I could see that Vic took exception to what I said but could not find a point over which to make a fighting stand. George whispered something to Vic, who listened to him with an arm over his shoulder. Mattie affected an air of boredom but underneath I could detect that mood of desperate keenness which he used to reserve solely for me. You can come in, said Vic in the end, but you'll have to agree to play the game.

Inside the room that used to be the servants' sitting room, they were busy fighting. All the desks and chairs were against the walls and a ring of children made a ring for the battlers to use as their impromptu arena. Two barefooted boys, stripped to the waist, were having at each other. Punching and kicking—I even saw one using his teeth to bite. It was dirty fighting.

All right, said Vic, when the bout was over and the smaller nose-bloodied boy had his victorious arm lifted in the air by the girl referee, which one of you is going to give it a go? I made to remove my jacket but Mattie stopped me. Remember your asthma, he said in loud enough of a voice for the others to hear and made me embarrassed. *I* will, he said, and his voice rung out like a hero's.

Vic started to pull at the buttons on his shirt, but sly George stopped him. Leave it to me Vic, he said, I'd like the privilege. I'll ref then, said Vic. I looked at Mattie. He had already removed his jacket and was now unbuttoning his shirt and he appeared very distant from me. No, I said, I want to referee, keep it fair. Mattie had exposed his thin, sparsely-haired chest by now, and he was untying his boots. Someone from the crowd shouted "Silvertown rules!" and then more of them took up the cry. All right, said Vic, you can be referee, but it's Silvertown rules—hands must be fists, no clawing, no biting, no butting, and no kicking in the face or the goolies. I started to argue about using Queensbury rules, but Mattie stopped me without even bothering to look. I accept those rules, he said. He stood waiting there in the middle of the ring, looking noble and frail in his black gaberdine trousers.

George yanked off his shirt and he kicked off his boots and he ran through the crowd into the ring and everyone cheered. Mattie took his body into a crouch and he held his fists in front of his face and he watched his opponent circumspectly. George scampered round the circumference and hands kept lifting up to pat him on the shoulders and his friends kept chanting "Come on George," with the first word the loudest. I kept to the edge, leaving space for the two of them, but made sure I stayed out of reach of the crowd because whenever I strayed too close I'd find myself pinched on the bottom or prodded in the small of the back. Mattie stayed wary, he stayed in his crouch, but he took the centre of the ring and kept turning to keep George in full front view. He aimed a couple of try-out punches at George's chin which George slapped away with open hands. "Fists!" I warned. "Use fists!" and all the onlookers laughed in derision at me and I heard some girl make a remark about my asthma.

George started to move nearer Mattie. He sent a couple of punches to Mattie's rib-cage which Mattie easily parried, then he kicked Mattie in the shins and I could see that hurt, but Mattie paid it no heed. He hit George in the shoulder and then in the chest which George only half slapped away. Both of their faces were red and Mattie's hair was flopping over his eyes and I wanted to scream at him to be careful, but at the same time I wanted to see him hurt. George feinted once with his left which Mattie followed but then George poked him a good one with his right on the left-hand side of the face. Mattie jerked his head back and George kicked him three times hard in the shins and Mattie staggered back and I could see tears in his eyes smarting with the pain, but he kept on. He went for George, hobbling forward at him, and George smiled. George hit him, a good punch, nothing the referee could argue with, in the belly, and Mattie folded forwards, his arms across his belly, but with his face up in the air looking at George. George smiled again, and waited. He danced on the spot with his knees going high in the air like a soldier, and Mattie winced, then gave George the expression that troubled me, it was a beseeching expression, asking for it, the punch to be delivered with all his might, and George wound up his left arm with a windmill action and he punched Mattie on the chin and floored him.

I started to count, as slowly as dignity would allow, and I watched Mattie. He lay on his back on the wooden planked floor. Blood was trickling from a cut on his cheek, and it dribbled down to his lips and I watched him lick it and clearly enjoy the taste. I counted up to ten and counted him out and I lifted George's right hand in the air and I hated the touch of him. Mattie got up slowly. He got to his knees and shook his head a few times to clear it. Then he climbed to his feet and assumed a stern expression. Well done, he said, offering his hand out to his victor. You won fair and square. George smiled and it was a sort of tender smile and he held out his hand as well and the two of them shook, and that's when I left.

I'm writing this out in what used to be our place in the yew hedge. It's cold and I'm shivering with the cold but I wanted to get this all out on paper to record it. It seems to me there has been a parting of the ways, and Mattie is wilfully heading for a place I don't understand.

An eerie friendship grew up between the aristocrat and the cockney, a friendship that would take the two of them into London and to their own, separate deaths, which Ivory would witness and one of which he would be able to do nothing about.

I t was the summer of 1940 when George made his break for London, for home, Silvertown. And Mattie was on that train with him, and Ivory was there too, no longer his cousin's favorite friend, just his jealous protector.

They slipped away from Hobart Hall before sunrise, the ambassador's son and the Silvertown boy each with a carpetbag in his hand, looking like private-school boarders on their way to a mysterious summer semester. Mattie had dressed his "diseased-looking secret double" in his own second-best suit. Ivory joined them on the platform of Norwich train station sometime after they'd completed their long hike into town. The three of them were alone there on that platform, looking cold and lost in the morning. The two conspirators sat silent and close together on the single wooden bench. William stood, a little apart from the couple. He hadn't been invited, but they could not refuse him. There is some conjecture here of blackmail, of Ivory threatening to inform the ambassador's wife straightaway if he wasn't permitted to join their great adventure.[7] Perhaps this wasn't necessary. Perhaps Mattie would have wanted William to come along anyway. Probably not.

At Liverpool Street Station they hopped a bus to Silvertown, a dockland industrial area so named for Silver's rubber factory which dominated the neighborhood. They sat it out there for a week or so, hanging out by the docks, wandering the streets, probably not quite knowing what they were doing there but knowing they'd left Norfolk far behind. The city had been ready for enemy attack for so long that nobody any longer believed it

7. For details of the wartime adventure I am relying on a combination of my own reading of Ivory's contemporary journals and later letters (which sometimes conflict) and Matthew Ivory's recollections of the few childhood stories his father told him.

was going to happen. Somewhere a war was being fought but that was far away.

And then, in late August, it happened. Two German bombers, lost in the nighttime sky above London, with their payload, which had been destined for ammunition depots along the river outside the city, still undropped. We can imagine the two German pilots: young (underneath their pilot's masks and oxygen mouthpieces, they probably've got teenage zits), muscles complaining in their cramped cockpits, exhausted from their flight, aching to get back home but too scared of the bawling out they're going to get, and panicked by the dark with only each other's shadowy plane for company. They dropped their bombs, just to get rid of them, over the docks of far east London. Churchill authorized a retaliation raid over Berlin. The Blitzkrieg starts here. On September 7, 1940, the first wave of German bombers came over to bomb the city. The first bombs in London landed on Silvertown.[8]

George was there in Silvertown, he'd been waiting for it to happen, the pawky disaster prophet, and Mattie was with him. Ivory they left behind after the first wave of bombs. They lost him in the fires. Ivory spent the next few months chasing after them, sniffing for them, the couple queer as Dick's hatband, in the decadent basement bars of smart hotels, on underground tube platforms, on the towpath by Putney Bridge, up on Hampstead Heath, and he caught glimpses of them for sure in the ruins, teenage sex-disaster babies.

Toward the end of December 1940, Ivory signed up with the Westminster branch of the Auxiliary Fire Service. He was underage, but the A.F.S. was taking what it could get.

---

8. Let's not get sentimental over Silvertown. Silvertown was a fucking slum. White trash crammed into black soot-soiled buildings beside a filthy river. The myth of the chirpy cockney that Brougham Calder spoke about, *My Fair Lady* joie de vivre, that was all a lie. Low-rent gangsters, men in flat caps dreaming of owning greyhounds, fat women old with joyless child-rearing, kids who probably welcomed the chance of war giving them a quick easy death, with free food along the way, cartoon industrialist-tycoons, mean little terraced buildings with a toilet out back in the pocket wilderness they call a garden. The whole place was bombed to shit and no one mourned a single brick.

January 11th 1941

It is a metaphysical struggle, our combat with the raw
element of fire. We fight it from within, from what is
technically called the <u>seat</u> of the blaze. It is exhilarating
and it is desperate. You stumble inside charred-out
buildings, you skip over sizzling electrical cables, you
dodge coffin-sized chunks of falling masonry that might
have your name on them; you're already wet through
with a dripping hose and you fight your sodden way into
the heart of the fire, walls tumbling down around you, no
air to breathe, only the hydrated oxygen around the jet
of water, you feed your agonized lungs from that pulsing
jet of water.

George is a creature of war. I see his glee from afar
when fiery buildings light up his face, and I see Mattie
beside him, trying for the same delight and fury but not
quite managing it. I saw them on the roof of Silver's
factory, the only ones in the district not in gas masks as
the sinister sweet perfume filled the fire-torched air. It
turned out that it wasn't poison gas after all, only a
warehouse filled with rotten pears burning to the
ground, but they weren't to know that. I suspect that the
enemy bombs aren't the only agents of chaos. I suspect
that George and others like him are doing their fair
share of destruction. You can see the appetite and lust
dripping like blood across their faces. I need to find a
way to rescue Mattie from his sinister friend.

And when he caught up to them, one night, March 8, 1941, at
the Café de Paris, he did his best for his favorite cousin Mattie.
It was the night that the bandleader Snakehips Johnson died,
when two bombs hit the crowded nightclub. In the wreckage of
that place, in the smoking rubble and blood-spattered plaster,
and under the watching, mistaken eyes of his cousin Sophie,
William Ivory covered the trapped body of enemy George with
the corpse of Martin Poulsen, nightclub owner and champagne

king. And over both of them he built an airless shelter of broken bandstand wood.

It was a noble, murderous attempt, risking jail or worse, to pull Mattie back. It didn't work. George was dead, but Mattie was farther away than before. He joined the Heavy Rescue Squad. He became a reckless hero, written up in all the papers,[9] the anemic aristo throwing himself into the ruins of bombed-out buildings to reappear long after with a buried child on his back to justify the risk he had taken. He shared an apartment in the ruins of Silvertown with the leader of the squad, a man known simply as the Sniffer for his strange talent of being able to smell live bodies beneath wreckage—a talent that Ivory had tested, and bested, in the ruins of the Café de Paris. Mattie's luck held out until close before the end, when he died in a V2 blast on a perfume factory on the outskirts of Silvertown. After the death of George he had never spoken to Ivory again.[10]

Ivory had been taken in by Eileen, the Countess F—, a decaying half-mad inheritrix of a Middle European title who had a candy-floss puff of peroxided hair and an enormous appetite for cream puffs and Benzedrine pills. They lived together, the drug-addict aristo and the war-hungry arriviste, in an upstairs flat on Percy Street.

9. "The Honourable Hero," "Aristocrat Saves Dozens in Waterloo Blaze," "Matthew Glaven, Gentleman Hero," "Nazis 0, Glaven 7?" are among the headlines of the time. *The Daily Mail* was particularly partial to stories celebrating Mattie's exploits.

10. I'm losing sight of the man. I should be plodding on, not racing about so fast. And you know why I'm doing this, don't you? It's not London in wartime I'm thinking of—and God knows I've done my diligent Sherlock best to uncover that world: I've trekked through the streets of Fitzrovia and Soho; I've drunk at the Marquis of Granby, at the Wheatsheaf, at the Bricklayers Arms, hungry for the buffoon shades of Dylan Thomas and Julian Brougham Calder. I've searched for the Gargoyle Club on Meard—Merde—Street and failed to find it, but that's not the London I'm thinking of, it's the London of now, or rather several months ago. When you returned. Go back? Stretch it all out? Fill in the gaps? Go on. Keep going. Ivory. The story.

6 April 1943

This place smells of degradation. Eileen has developed
a problem with her bladder and wears sanitary towels
all the time beneath her dress. Sometimes in her
Benzedrine madness she forgets about them and leaves a
rectangle stain wherever she sits, when she does finally
consent to sit still for a moment. Because of the
Shortages she has to reuse the same towels over and
over; she washes them in the kitchen sink and leaves
them to dry on the electric heater: she fills the flat with
the stench of her infirmity.

There must be something in me that likes this
weakness and ugliness and dirt. Then there is the
outside: the ruins, the fires, the splendid enormity of
destruction, the chance collisions of shattered fragments
resulting in a strange and terrible beauty. Mattie is
living with the Sniffer now. It is part of his campaign to
lose himself in the death games George initiated him
into. He surely is lost. I am no longer sorry for him or
even worried for him. He has found his destiny.

A young bohemian, Julian Brougham Calder, was part of this
messy ménage. He had been Eileen's single boarder until Ivory
arrived, whereupon he was dispossessed of the guest room and
shifted to the living-room sofa, except for when the countess was
sleeping off one of her Benzedrine jags.

And for a while London presented a grand fruitless adventure,
a fluid place overflowing with possibility. But before the War
was ended, things had settled back into their accustomed shape.
Ivory wrote in his journal in December 1944:

Poisoned images: the flâneurs of Fitzrovia and Soho,
intoxicated with uselessness, make dainty ornate
blustering figures of speech to bellow them out into
neglectful bomb-blasted streets. Dylan Thomas, a fat
Welsh boy, a drunken poetry spider, he spins out fanciful
metaphors like diarrhoea, and then, as if that wasn't

enough, spews out sickly sentimentality. (We are meant to be collaborating on a documentary scenario together about the AFS. I am sure mutual dislike will prevent us getting anywhere with it.) Brougham-Calder, mild and foolish, his mediocrity of mind crabs out a lurid fastidious ambition. Eileen was asleep and Julian was out and I went through his papers in the kitchen. I felt no guilt over this, he probably would do the same if I gave him the chance. I came upon a pathetic list of "future projects" complete with publishers' names and prices, pagination and ideas for dust-cover designs, written down in tiny schoolroom nervous letters. TEACH THE FREE MAN, 192pp., Jonathan Cape, 1946, 3/6d. NECESSARY NEGROES, 270pp., Allen Lane, 1951, 4/6d. AFTER THE RAIN, 210pp., Martin Secker & Warburg, 1954, 3/6d. DEAD YEARS, 454pp., Hamish Hamilton, 1961, 7/6d. LESBIANS OF THE DUST: THE COLLECTED POETRY OF JULIAN BROUGHAM CALDER, 184pp., Faber & Faber, 1962, 8/-. ESSAYS AT TWILIGHT, 612pp., Brougham Calder Press, 1967, 1 guinea . . . books that won't ever be written.[11]

Mattie is dead. I had expected it and I had expected to see it too. The perfume factory collapsed upon his body and I heard his cries through the bomb-blasted air and if I had seen his face I know it would have been glad.

For a few chance-filled fiery years this city was a magical airy place. Now things are fixed again. This broken London is returned to a land-locked matter-of-factness. Before, there was a tropical flowering of sexuality in this city whose every scarred outcrop of

11. Brougham Calder, you never wrote a thing, did you? Those book titles you cited to me, they're the same ones you planned way back then on your wartime kitchen table—your only work on them was to adjust their prices to take account of inflation. And you were spiteful in your failure, weren't you? You unlocked the polite official version of Ivory's war years and showed me a shabby antiheroic story of mistaken murder and revenge; but behind that second story there was another story all the time—a third story that was more nasty than yours and more heroic than the first.[12]

12. But I'm falling down on my task here. What's happened to the good biographer who takes every step in his measured stride? It's not enough to throw a little quoted abuse at dead Welshmen and half-alive Englishmen. To jump from poisoned image to poisoned image.

smashed building was a phallic signal, every bomb crater
a vulvic sign.

Meanwhile, back in Norfolk, Hobart Hall had been requisi-
tioned for an army barracks; and the ambassador had a good
war doing something secret with codes. In Norwich, Pa Ivory,
the retired captain, had been happily occupied with a battalion
of Home Guards who had made the coast of Norfolk secure
against Nazi invasion. Ma Ivory had done good works with refugees, and then signed up as a driver-nurse in the W.V.S. (the
Women's Voluntary Service). But Captain Ivory had protected
them for the future, when the world was safe with democracy
again, by looking after the family hatting business. Throughout
the War, it cranked out soldiers' helmets and officers' caps and
assorted dainties for different regiments, and made quite a profit
doing it. When the War was over and the business reverted
largely to manufacturing civilian trilbys and homburgs and
wide-brimmed, ribboned affairs for dowagers to wear at county
shows, it kept up some of its contracts with the military. That
pleased the company accountant, Mr. Petersens (a Latvian who
had fled Riga in 1938). The business flourished. The shade of
John Ivory, company founder in 1854, looked down on proceed-
ings from his portrait perch up on the wall of the boardroom
on the top story above the shop. His whiskered mouth was even
rumored to smile.

Boy Ivory was missing, believed dead, possibly mourned, another casualty of war. But eventually the prodigal returned, early
one morning in the spring of 1950, a lapsed Fitzrovian, twenty-
four years old. There's a photograph of him from this period (see
facing page?), dapper in a wide-cut suit, far too much cloth for
an honest man's ration book to stretch to—showing the finger
to the face of postwar austerity—and a wide-brimmed borsalino
(supplied, no doubt, courtesy of Ivory & Son, hat makers of Norwich) perched gangster-style atop his head. His body is thin and
rangy, nourished by the thrills of war, bored by the limits of
peace. He sports a trim David Niven mustache.

3 May 1950[13]

I am done with bohemia. I am done with Fitzrovia. I
am done with the drunken sprawling shouting parties of
Colquhoun and MacBryde and Minton. I am done with
Jack Crew and his dreams of a poetic Utopia farmed by
philosopher kings. I am done with the legacy of the
ancient fraud magus Crowley and his magickal tinctures
of heroin. I am done with the Countess Eileen and her
Benzedrine promises of money and position. I am done
with drinking out the night and killing off the morning.
War is over and the century is half dead and it is all just
decadence now. On one side is the fruitless pursuit of a
perfect moment and on the other is the grinning imp of
suicide. I am twenty-four and I am done with these
things and I fear I will never find the thing to replace
them.

I showed some of my stories at last to Ackerley who
gave them a gentle praise for attempting to create an
English vernacular in the American style. That is not
enough. When I got back to Percy Street I burned them
all in the grate. There is something to be chased out
there. I wish I knew what it is.

If he wrote about his return in a journal, that entry has been
lost. But we do know there was a conflict early on. Ivory had
kept up his piano-playing, there was always a call for a pianist
to belt out ironic melodies in the early mornings at late-night
dives.[14] And now that he had returned from the War, with the
family business flourishing, he was eager to be sent back to

13. Unfortunately, the author has no journals for the period 1945–49 (thank
you, Helen). I know that he occupied himself partly in writing short stories. His
son Matthew believes that Ivory investigated the occult. This is convincing in that
Ivory was always a man to kick against the times, and materialism (Marxist or
otherwise) had replaced mysticism as an intellectual fashion. However, I have no
evidence of this. He discontinued keeping a journal after his marriage in 1956.
Letters to Helen took its place.

14. He'd even composed a couple of topical songs, their titles probably urbane
but long since lost.

London with sufficient funds to enable him to study at the Royal Academy of Music.

He received some support from his mother, and none from his father. William's role was to work in the hat shop, to learn the business, as Thomas had done before him, to justify the "& Son" in the company title. We don't need to guess at how much this idea rankled. Ivory wrote about it in his journal:

7 April 1951

Mother is useless and Father insists. I can see little way out short of disappearing again. I would prefer not to do that. I am done with the bohemian life in London for the time being, perhaps for ever, and I have no money to go abroad. They called me a snob. They have no understanding of what happened in the War, the opportunities it presented to those of us with Imagination and Will.

I had conceived a mad idea for sponsorship of my musical studies by my uncle. I even had Petersens draw up a contract that would favour the sponsor rather than the recipient. I tried to visit the Hall yesterday and they would not have me in. They blame me no doubt for what happened to Mattie. They blame me too for him having a destiny they would have preferred to be mine.

So the reluctant hatter settled for a temporary life of commerce. For six months, he served behind the counter of the shop. He traveled to the factory on the outskirts of town and oversaw the manufacture of trilbys and homburgs and ladies' headdresses. And the weary bohemian kept far away from London.

I don't know what the hold was that Ivory had over Petersens. Perhaps he promised liberation of Latvia, more likely he had got wind of some shabby little secret of the aging accountant's and held it up in the air and received complete control of the company finances in return for putting it back out of harm's way. Whatever, he had a free hand in the cash register.

And then he started to go back to the city. While in London, he cultivated a world-weary air of mystery. Ivory certainly was a snob, and nothing would make him admit to his having become a provincial shopkeeper. The thrill he had been given by the grand adventures and mysteries of London in wartime needed to be replaced. So William Ivory became a gambler.

He lived for those weekends in London, those evenings spent chancing his father's money to the whims of fate and luck:

3 August 1951

To know the pleasure of winning. To grab Luck by the throat and watch it grin at you with lascivious recognition. Or the other thing, the failure. To be washed over by that awful self-disgust at losing, at letting your nerve slip, the walk away along streets which echo your self-loathing, the chances missed, those awful moments when your mind loses clarity and you make the wrong decision; or the other, the moment of hungry triumph, when you struggle to stop your hands shaking because it's bad form to show too much excitement, when everything is right and with you, and Luck especially, and you are all-powerful. You are master.

Every weekend he would follow a floating chemin de fer game around the private apartments of Chelsea. And one night he cleaned the game out.

21 August 1951

The most perfect moment of all. It was the final coup of the evening and I let all my winnings ride. I drew to a four and a court card, and the card that I drew was the difference between glory and utter utter ruin. My hands were shaking when that card was revealed—blessed five of diamonds! I am truly a gambler now: I shall have cuff links made up with five twinkling diamonds on each!

I can't conceive of how I would have behaved had the

final card been anything other than a five of diamonds. I
hope I would have retained sufficient self-possession to
walk the gallows road like a free man but I fear not. I
admit it: I swanked. When I turned over my five of
diamonds I laughed and I roared and the Jamaican shot
me such a killing look that I cashed up and made my
exit there and then. Even if he manages to raise the ante
for another game I shall never be invited again. I will
have to watch my back; I am told the Jamaican is
nursing dark dreams of revenge.

Petersens was even more relieved than I. The accounts
are straight once again and he even—with an initial
show of reluctance—accepted a cut of my winnings.
Partners in crime.

Ivory was not invited back to that floating chemmy game.
Instead, in the fall of 1951, he joined some of his old Fitzrovian
cronies every Friday night at an illicit casino in North Kensington. For the first weeks he just watched the action, and then,
with a mysterious dowdy girl beside him, he played chemmy and
extravagantly won.

21 September 1951

I am tempted to believe in something even stronger
than Luck. It worked, as Margaret said it would, as if it
had been predestined. She told me to play for one half-
hour and for one half-hour I played and every hand was
mine. I have heard of houses rigging the deal and I was
watching for that, but everything looked square. I left the
table at the appointed time and I was rich. We celebrated
together and spent the night together and in the
morning I bought her a new outfit from my winnings to
recompense her for anything she might feel is lost. Then
back to Liverpool Street. Back to grey Norwich, order
forms and ribbons and felt.

Ivory played and won for two weeks. Then came the climax.
When the dowdy girl in her new French outfit wasn't there any

longer beside him. When he lost everything he had stacked up over the previous luck-crazy weeks. And he lost more than that.

11 October 1951

The hubris of William Ivory. I was gulled good and proper. Jackie arranged it all for his friend the Jamaican, and Margaret did it for Jackie, and I did it for myself. I admire Jackie for understanding my psychology so well. He knew the kind of girl I'd go for and he knew how to push things just so. The watching fools now believe in the supernatural and no one realizes Jackie rigged the game. Margaret, it turns out, is a drama student at Central. I wish her a good career. I bear none of them any malice and I am glad I was able to take it so well. I lost with dignity. If I had beaten the Jamaican with equal dignity then none of this would have ever happened but if that were the case I wouldn't have learned the things I did. It's a bit of a mess and there might be some inconvenience but the account is settled and I'll be away. No more hats.

He used his power over Petersens to withdraw all the company's money to honor his debt to Jackie (because a gambling debt was a matter of honor, no matter what the circumstances were). To silently and surreptitiously bankrupt his parents—justifying it perhaps in his own mind as retribution for them not allowing him to study music—and skulk down to London. After settling his debt, he had a little left over for himself. He transferred the money into stocks and bonds and slipped away to somewhere in Europe.[18]

Wherever he went he returned much sooner than anyone thought. Quietly he slipped back, to live in quiet anonymity. Just

18. He might have gone to Paris, I think he probably did. Camus still had nine years before his fatal car crash. Céline was expiating himself in the sleazy outer suburbs. He might have traveled through mainland Greece and around the islands. Maybe he went down to Turkey and then across to North Africa. I like the idea of him playing piano in a brothel in Cairo or Fez. I think of him signing on with a merchant ship. As cook maybe, or as a junior officer barking out orders to surly sullen men who hate him and plan his death.

him and his researches, and his correspondence with Jim Har-kin, a retired Fitzrovian turned Nipponist,[16] who had signed up for a Unesco study tour of Japan and remained there to live. London was changing and Ivory stayed very still. He studied Japanese with a patient young man in Tooting Bec who had recently got out of the army.

Ivory lived out in the suburbs himself. He rarely chanced going into the center, he rarely went anywhere fashionable. He bought a dog, a German shepherd bitch.[17] He only returned to Norwich, to visit, when he saw a notice in the London *Times* of the death of his father, who was described as a widower. Ivory hadn't known his mother had died, but he had sort of expected it. Fi-nancial ruin brings social shame. And for the snob, social shame brings private death.[18]

Ivory went to libraries during the day, and in the evenings he would write up his notes, in purple ink, on Florentine stationery. He researched the lives of Gilles de Rais, of mad Ludwig of Ba-varia, of Akhenaten, Caligula, Sir Richard Burton, Louis XIV, and Louis XV. He studied the Hellfire Club, George Selwyn, Francis Dashwood, John Wilkes, Lord Sandwich. He developed a strong admiration for the fop Boothby. He was fascinated by cruel men, by suicides, and by dreamers. He read widely in the French De-cadents. His favorite was Robert de Montesquiou, and he kept the early works of Huysmans by his bedside table. He discovered tastes for Gauloises cigarettes and good red wine. But these were the only indulgences he allowed himself on his small, very pri-vate income. He was planning a book that would not be published for another twenty years, because adventures and illnesses would get in the way. The book would be called *Decadent Pleasures*.

---

16. "A man we knew in Fitzrovia and never heard utter a word"—Julian Brougham Calder.

17. Chosen for him by J. R. Ackerley, literary editor of *The Listener* magazine.

18. Ivory had predicted "some inconvenience." The Ivory & Son company ac-countant, Petersens, shot himself in the head the day after Ivory absconded with the company loot. Unfortunately, the luckless Latvian did not succeed in killing himself with Thomas Ivory's Home Guards-issue handgun, only in blasting away all but the most vital functions of his brain. He lived on for a further eighteen vegetative years in the Philip Glaven Chronics Ward of the Norwich & Norfolk General Hospital.

W hat's that sound, do you hear it? Sounds like a slow French melody. Melancholy fin-de-millénaire stuff. Sounds like from the surgery. Do you hear it? It's the sort of music that Ivory loved. Fuck Ivory. I hope Helen's okay. I don't like to think of her struggling out there in the night. Fuck Helen. Fuck his books and fuck his dogs and fuck his children. Let's talk about me. I batted .318 my first year at college, .297 the second, .301 the third, then fell away to .247 in the fourth (but I was carrying some injuries—didn't tell Coach "Grassy" Noll, I wanted to play every day, making my big run at the majors). My upper incisors are false but the rest of my teeth are all my own. I stand 6' 1¾" in my stockinged feet (same height as my father, always thought I'd get another quarter-inch on him) and I weigh 190 pounds. My dancing has been praised by girls from seventeen different states. I worked in newspapers, rock music and sports, those were my beats. I took over Red Kavanagh's weekly baseball commentary in 1989, resigned it three and a half years later when the sports ed. replaced my piece on Red Sox racism with an old one of Red's remembering '41. Mary told me to apologize. I told her to go fuck herself. That was two weeks before I met you. I went on a spree after that, you caught me at a vulnerable time. I've published poems in *Ploughshares, The Kenyon Review, Grand Street*. I'm not such a bad catch. I used to DJ on a college radio station. I've jammed with Nils Lofgren. Jonathan Richman wrote a song about me. Girls used to fall in love with me. I nearly married one of them.

I thought I saw Mary on a street down by the Thames. Ivory got his second dog in 1962, the year his second child was born. I thought I saw the spurned bride in a denim jacket walking toward me along a side street by the Tate Gallery. It was a German shepherd like the first, but a boy dog this time. He called him Gaspard (a name his children would shorten to Gassie). There was the statue of a dancer between us. I hid behind it, crouching down behind a black metal tutu. Shortly after the arrival of the dog, Ivory began to divide his time between the family house in Tite Street and the county of his birth. Mary had friends in London, she'd taught here once, some of them used to come out and stay, any one of them could have seen me, called her up, "He's here, the bum, come bring him back, we've got him trapped. Take him back to Boston and marry the creep and never let him forget how he tried to get away." Ivory bought a house in Norfolk, it was inland, isolated. He bought it from a lawyer settling a rich occultist's estate. The nearest village was a place called Binham. I hadn't written to her, I hadn't called her, we'd had a fight but the wedding was still on and I'd taken a powder, left her in Boston planning an imaginary future, we still hadn't decided which band we were going to hire for the party. Ivory and Gaspard took long walks along the waterfront of Holkham Bay. The dog would chase along the sand dunes after gulls and terns, and be pulled back by the harsh whistle of his master. It wasn't Mary, it was Mary, it wasn't Mary (this doesn't make you jealous, does it? or even triumphant), I didn't wait for her to reach me so I could look at her close, I just ran. Ivory entered his dog in shows organized by the Kennel Club. Gaspard won several of these and placed well in some others. Ivory was mysteriously rich by now—he lived off his interest—and Helen, his half-abandoned wife, was mysteriously poor. I ran along the embankment, fucking coward, fucking runner, the tide was low, bobbing restaurant barges, workmen were fixing the road near the Parliament buildings, Big Ben was locked away in scaffolding. In 1967 the family acquired a Japanese maid. Ivory married her in 1969 and Helen and her children moved away from Chelsea into a Victorian terrace house within earshot of Holloway Road. I left her far behind, the real Mary or the false Mary, whichever one she was, the girl I was due to marry when I fell in with you. He had affairs with younger women (which I knew he would write to Helen all about—I'd already caught some snatches of sly confession). He was writing his book. I kept on running, pains from the sudden exercise chewing away at my belly, Trafalgar Square, Chinatown, Soho, kept on running until I was far away in the back streets of what used to be called Fitzrovia. Ivory might have taken his dog to visit Hobart Hall, I couldn't say. But certainly he loved his dog. Gibbs told me about that. I ducked into a place with a French name near Percy Street, ordered a beer, stared at a menu that pretended to be handwritten, and waited for the sweat on my face to dry. As the children got older, Helen would send them up to Norfolk on their school vacations. And they loved Gaspard too, particularly the girl Deborah.

I ate slowly. Took deep breaths to relax. The meal was sickly-rich, smothered in sauce, and the waiter didn't like my accent or my jacket or my sweat so I left him a large tip to make him feel bad. I walked out and took a stroll around Fitzrovia because for some reason I felt safe in this neighborhood. I had a beer in the Marquis of Granby. And an Irish whiskey chaser in the Bricklayers Arms. I walked out onto Tottenham Court Road and slipped back onto Percy Street. I was tired with guilt. Back in my room there was still a pile of unread Ivory letters and that was really what my day would be about. I would be feeling more resistant to his charm later on, when it became dark and I could return home without having to worry about cheated brides on every street corner.

I went along Percy Street to the building he'd lived in way back in those war years with the Countess F——. No sign of Brougham Calder behind the gray windows. The hardware store had taken a turn for the better. Glistening U-bends and shiny faucet heads in the window to attract any passing plumber trade. I carried on walking, then turned back, thought, Fuck it, risk the wrath of the ancient bohemian, go see if there's any improvement in his state, maybe find some juicy narratives to pick at. I turned around and waited for the traffic to allow me to cross. And then I saw you. On Percy Street.

Now that was a shock. I admit it freely. I stood where I was, one foot off the sidewalk hovering over the yellow parking line of the road. I called out your name. Cars hustled between us. You didn't hear me. I watched you. You were with a man. A long insipid strip of blond who knew how to dress nice and comb his hair just so. You. You were suddenly there, looking in the window of the hardware store. I didn't know you were interested in plumbing. I didn't know you were even in this country. Dorothy Burton, last heard from in New York, New York, U.S.A. You'd had your hair cut, Dorothy Burton. It was just down to your shoulders now. You turned away from the window. You looked pale, troubled. Almost beautiful. You were wearing jeans and a man's leather jacket, a simple affair that was too long for you. It came down past your ass and you'd rolled back the sleeves for your hands to have some room. You were smoking a cigarette. I hadn't seen you smoke a cigarette before. You looked nervous and you looked bored. Charlie Blond-Strip beside you was an attentive type, old before his time and jesuitical-looking, like a decadent priest in a French porno book. Charlie hailed a cab, had words with the driver, and—nice manners, it's good to see such manners—opened the door to let you slide in. He got in. And if it had been the movies, so would I. But it wasn't the movies and I stood in the road until traffic horns shoved me out of the way and I watched you roll up the window and I watched the cab drive away.

I wandered down Charing Cross Road, killed some time in a couple of videogame arcades, went back to the hotel and read some Ivory letters—easy sexual conquests confided to Helen, a few disparaging remarks about his children. The telephone rang in the hallway a couple of times and the Australian wasn't around to answer it and I ran down the stairs both times and neither of the calls was from you. I tried Jim Harkin's number again and this time got a reply. A fresh boy who told me the professor was traveling out East. Expected back in under a month. That cheered me a little. I went back upstairs. I got out Ivory's books again, it was time to read.

You haven't read Ivory's novel *Morita*. It was published in 1976, has a grisly coda. The cover blurb says so and for once it doesn't lie.

The novel is the story of the last four weeks in the life of Mishima Yukio as seen through the eyes of his lieutenant, admirer, and fetish object, Morita Masakatsu. Morita is the straight man. His manner is stolid, unimaginative, humorless, full of the right respect for his master, and more than a little dumb. The two of them wear uniforms together, practice military drills, which includes one that Morita will only refer to as the Perfect One. Mishima also teaches his little sidekick correct table manners and takes him out for evenings in Tokyo high society, where a lot of despising goes on.

In Ivory's version there is no mention of love or sex between the two men, but—and it's masterfully done—the novel is steeped in it, particularly when the telling is broken by third-person apostrophes to nature. That third-person voice re-emerges at the end, at the Incident. Mishima, with Morita dutifully at his side, makes his speech pleading for patriotism and emperor-love and military self-determinism and is cater-wauled down by the soldiers of the Self-Defense Force. Shocked and humbled, the martyr retreats from the balcony to the office where two others from his Shield Society are standing guard over the S.D.F. commandant gagged and bound in his chair.

Mishima unbuttons his tunic, kneels in the proper fashion, and pierces his belly with his yoroi doshi. This is the Perfect One, the performance they have been rehearsing for:

> I step forward in the correct manner and strike with my sword to sever my master's head as we had practised—

Those are his last words in the book. The coda, which runs on for three lush brutal pages, is the account of Morita's failure to behead his master. He tries once, then a second time. No good. This is the big one and he's fucked it up.

The author's butchered head hung forward, suspended by half-severed tendons, by those splendid neck muscles carved into strips. His carotid artery gushed rich betrayed blood on to the office walls, out on to the balcony, and on to the clothes of the three watching men and the tear-smirched face of his wretched executioner. Morita called out Koga's name and Furu-Koga stepped forward and severed Mishima's head from his body with a single stroke. Morita, who had trained so diligently for this most perfect moment, dug his own short sword into the tuck of his belly and, as blood began to pour, he yelped his misery and his pain and lowered his head, to await Furu-Koga's merciful sword.

And so the novel ends. It's grim romantic stuff.

The next day I was all of a sudden the most popular guy in town. People started chasing *me* down. Martha Brennan called, just for a chat, you know, and Nick Wheel, trying to interest me in an insurance deal, and Julian Brougham Calder, who wanted to compare notes on literature, perhaps he could come round to browse through my library? and Roland Gibbs, who had uhm . . . (snuffle) . . . remembered one or two *things* . . . and all of them went for meaningful pauses, giving me the opportunity to volunteer some information, and they all insisted I should keep in touch and they all checked off a little sadly as if I'd let them down somehow. I camped out in the hallway. The phone kept on ringing. Last call.

"Tierney, it's D.B."

It was your voice. I didn't remember you calling yourself by your initials before.

"Where are you?"

"Still in New York but I'll be coming back soon. I might be staying at my mother's."

"New York?"

"Yes, New York. But I'm coming back. Did you get the money? I'll see you soon and advance you some more. We'll talk about everything then. How far you've got."

"People keep calling. I'm the most popular guy in town. This line is pretty good considering you're calling from New York."

"Miracle of progress. Don't worry about anybody else. It's not important. I've got another lead for you. You see, I've been on the job too. There was a woman. A librarian at the British Library in the early 'seventies. There was a connection to Ivory."

"How do you know about this?" I felt a little aggrieved. You were treading on my territory.

"I was speaking to someone today. Someone who used to know him. They told me."

"Someone in New York?"

"What's the fixation with New York?"

"Who was this woman? Was it a romance?"

"Sort of. I don't know her name. She was a spinster. Wore heavy blue eye shadow. That's about all I know."

Then our guards both dropped. Our voices got softer, our words less considered. The world shrank to just the sound of our two voices, touching. And then I asked you where your mother lived and you didn't answer my question.

G ibbs had mentioned her in passing. You set me off on the trail. But it was a letter of Ivory's to his ex-wife that gave me the beginning of the affair.

7 January 1973

Dear Helen,

I trust you and the children are well. Did you receive my banker's draft? Matthew is turned out quite a little grasper. I've been greatly occupied by my Japanese researches at the British Museum, from where I've embarked upon a suburban adventure.

I saw her at the enquiry desk, helping a foreign academic —he may have been Romanian—with his bibliography. He was loudly seeking to track down an artistic manifesto which had been privately published in Moscow in the early 1920s. His nose and ears sprouted wild hair. I watched her with the hairy academic. She kept her eyes fixed on his the whole time; she leaned bonily towards him, pressing her pelvis against the aged wood of the counter; sometimes she pushed back her hair, which was thin and straight and oily. She was a strange-looking woman, skinny and greasy and any age between twenty-five and sixty. She wore artless blue eye-shadow on her eyelids and there was the suspicion of heightened cosmetic colour on her flat cheeks. She was friendly to the academic and professional too but there was also something skittish about her: she was like a small girl flirting with a favourite uncle with a dangerous reputation; and it would be the reputation which thrilled her, which gave life and direction to her solitary fingers under the bedclothes at night.

"People call them Constructivists but they are not Constructivists," bleated the Romanian. "Suprematists."

"Yes," she said, to oblige him. And her voice was from the suburbs, Finsbury Park perhaps, or Cricklewood, a voice confused by books, by the contemplation of words she would never hear spoken but maybe ran around in her mouth on the bus home just to get the taste of them. It was the voice of a woman who had never been told she was beautiful.

I shall keep you abreast.

W.

This is 1973, he'd remarried in 1969, and still he writes to her as if they share a complicity. What are her feelings when she reads about his predatory interest in another? Still, I love the letter. Patronizing to the librarian's awkward figure, yes. And painful in its clear insight, but there is also a compassion here. A compassion that runs close to being sentimental.

An assistant keeper at the British Library remembered her from Ivory's description. Miss P——, she had abruptly resigned sometime in the mid-'70s and, he thought, gone to work in the public-library service somewhere in north London. By bus, on foot, with a copy of the Yellow Pages and a street gazetteer, I searched the suburban libraries of London. Dull, decaying places staffed by vaguely sexed individuals with bad breath and glasses, the anemic descendants, I supposed, of those Victorian missionaries who were always doing weird things in Africa.

Toward the end of the day I found her, at Highbury & Islington Library. It was a pretty building not far from Helen's house, off the Holloway Road, next to some public fields, where, as Ivory might have put it, dogs and children play. There she was, at the checkout desk. Stamping books. Moving them from one pile to the next. She was immediately recognizable from the description in the letter. She wore the same

clumsy blue eye shadow and now a crimson slash of paint
which approximated to her thin lips. Her hair was gray. I stood
at a swivel stand of science-fiction paperbacks, pretended to
be looking at their titles, and watched her. At one point she
looked up and our eyes met before I had time to look away.
She didn't blush or look embarrassed. I think I did both.

I returned the following day, natty and shaved, dressed carefully like a hopeful lover who was also timidly, clumsily polite.
I couldn't just blurt out what I was interested in. I had to lead
up to it and even, though this probably sounds crazy to you,
give her the opportunity to mention his name first. I pretended
that I'd recently moved into the neighborhood and wanted to
join the library. She gave me the necessary forms to fill in and
I made a great show of looking for something in my coat pocket
that would have my new address on it. She said that I shouldn't
worry, that I should bring it in when I had the chance. She
was very nice about it.

"By the way," I said. "I believe you knew William Ivory."

I said it as casually as I could, and waited for the smile or
the tears.

"I'll keep the form here," she said. "Bring in something with
proof of your address and then your membership will be pro-
cessed. Any one of my colleagues will be able to help you."

"I didn't mean to alarm you."

"Excuse me," she said. "I'm very busy."

I returned the next day with an I.D. the Australian had faked
for me. There was a different woman at the checkout desk. I
waited for about two hours—reading through newspapers with
the crazies and drunks, scanning the foreign-fiction shelves for
Ivory's translations—but she didn't turn up. I came back the
next two days and finally asked about her. I was told that she'd
been transferred. It took a few long-winded phone calls with
library-service bureaucrats to find out where.

Highbury & Islington Library was a pretty building on the edge
of fields. G—— Library was on a busy main road and next
door to a fish-and-chip shop. One large ugly room full of old
wooden bookcases where schoolchildren were blatantly tearing

nude color prints from art books. She was there, Miss P——, behind the checkout desk, reading something by Henry James. She saw me, pushed a handful of gray hair away from her eyes and covered her mouth with her hand, a curious oriental gesture. I looked at her, remembering Ivory's first encounter with her. Only the gray hair gave any indication of her age. It was too much of a leap of the imagination to see how "skittish" was a word that could apply to her.

"I don't have anything to say to you." She spoke calmly. "Please. I would be grateful if you left me alone."

I can't remember exactly what I said. Something trite about not wanting to upset her. Followed by something noble about the aspirations of biography.

"Please go away. I do not want to talk to you. It's not a fair thing to do to a person."

I would follow her. From the library to the bus stop. To the flat on H—— Hill. Watch her window light up, and imagine her reading and remembering. I followed her to the supermarket, and stood behind her as she slowly counted out a pile of cat-food cans. I was with her as she walked to the veterinary surgeon, to the pharmacy, and to the house where she would visit on Tuesday and Thursday evenings. I made it clear I was following her, I made no attempt to hide it. The rest of my researches were ignored in the thrill of the chase while I waited to wear her down, and that made my own persistent callers kind of frantic and I liked that. Finally, I think a week had gone by, she acknowledged my pursuit. It was late on a Thursday evening and she was walking home. She stopped under a tree by the Victorian clock tower next to H—— Fields and waited for me to catch up with her. She looked fierce and vulnerable. In her left hand she held a shopping bag full of books.

"I have some coffee," she said suddenly. "You can come up if you like."

We drank instant coffee from fragile cups which we balanced on saucers on our knees. We faced each other across a wood-veneer coffee table piled high with library books. I made a joke about office theft.

"Oh no. I filled out a form for all these. It's perfectly legitimate."

"I'm sorry. I didn't mean . . ."

Her walls were decorated with old maps and copies of Japanese prints. A Victorian screen hid the entrance to her bedroom. I pointed to it.

"It's very pretty."

"You think so? To me it's ugly. Almost monstrous. It was my mother's."

Just inside the door, next to an elephant-foot umbrella stand, there was a photograph in a silver frame on top of a stack of occasional tables. I put my coffee down and went over to it.

"I've never seen this one before."

A teenaged Ivory, wearing just swimming shorts and deck shoes, upper lip bare, sits on the deck of a sailboat working at something with a knife. He is looking up at the camera and his expression is a little shy, as if he has been interrupted in some too intimate action.

"It's a very good picture."

"He was very young. He told me that was the happiest time of his life. Mattie took it."

"Mattie?"

"His cousin. They were great friends. They sailed together. Off the coast of Norfolk before the War, I think. But you probably know all about that."

"Only a little," I said, returning to my seat and putting the photograph on the coffee table at an angle which allowed us both to see it. "Tell me about Mattie."

She shook her head and her hair slid down in front of her face. Before she pushed it away she pressed her hand against her throat to cover for a moment a red rash that had come up since we'd gone inside. I tried to imagine what it was about her that had caught Ivory's fancy. A purity maybe. She pushed her hair away from her face and I thought how young she looked.

"That's not for me to tell. You can find someone else for that one. You're very good at finding people."

"It took a long time. I feel as if I've been to every public library in London."

"I hope it's worth it."

"I'm sure it will be. I'm sure you're going to be a great help."

"That's not what I meant."

There was a silence. Then, I asked, "Do you have any more pictures of him? Do you have any with the two of you?"

"No. It wouldn't have been right." She paused, looked at me, shyly and awkwardly. "Do you have a tape recorder?"

I reached into my jacket pocket. "Would you like to see it?"

"No. I knew you would have a tape recorder. I was sure of that." She settled back proudly.

I sipped some more coffee. We sat in our uncomfortable armchairs. She sat very still and very straight. Her eyes were fixed somewhere on the corridor outside, where stairs led up to another floor. I didn't know how to start.

She abruptly got up from her chair and slipped past the screen without disturbing it. She made no sound in the bedroom. A few minutes later, she came back into the room with a large brown envelope.

"I was going to put your name on this but I can't remember what it is. I suppose it doesn't matter."

I gave her my card.

"Thank you. Would you like more coffee? A tea cake? I can't talk to you. It's all written down. Here, take it. I don't mean to be rude but I'm very tired now."

She led me down the stairs and watched me into the street.

"Send it back to me when you're finished with it. It's all there. Everything I can tell you."

I thanked her. I wanted to kiss her, drink champagne with her, tell her how beautiful she looked.

"And now, please? Will you now leave me alone?" She skipped back inside and looked at me uncertainly through the glass panel of the door.

You should have come that night. I had some booty to
show and share. We could have gone through her confession
together, the scrap of her life touched by Ivory. We could
have taken each a part and acted them out, amateur theatrics,
a history play. Or I could have read it all out to you, examined
your expression every time I turned a page. But you didn't
come, you didn't call, so I settled down alone with a glass of
whiskey and opened the envelope. There were many pages of
unlined cream paper written on in a perfect blue italic that had
probably been archaic even when she'd learned it. The pages
were fastened together with a copper paper clip. The top page
was on a G—— Council memorandum form:

This was written after I saw you that first time in the
library. I knew then who you were. I knew then what you
would want. I knew you would get it too, but I had to try to
hold on to it for myself even though I always knew I
wouldn't be strong enough to keep it. I've enjoyed our
chase.

Then the first page:

I was 39 years old when I met him. I bought my first
lipstick the day of my mother's funeral.
I bought my first lipstick the day of my mother's funeral. I
was 39 years old when I met him. These are the two things
that come to mind.
I love the smell of chemist shops. I always have. Even
when my mother was alive, even when she was suffering
only from minor illnesses and I would take her prescription
to be filled, I would always linger by the counters of rouge

and mascara and foundation creams. The sounds of the
names would make me shiver, but it was the smells that
moved me, so cloying and delicate and full. And the
shopgirls with their pancake make-up and their pink bodies
inside surgical white coats, I would long for them to apply
their lotions to my face and I would watch the glamorous
girls with long hair carelessly trying out dabs of lipstick on
their hands to compare the colour. My own hands, naked,
gripping the doctor's prescription, would twist up in shame
inside my coat pockets, and then before too much time had
gone by, before my mother would begin to grow peevish
over my absence, I would make my way to the medicines
counter, hand over the form, and wait on one of those
plastic straight-back chairs, with the arthritics and the
asthmatics, my shopping bag in my lap, my hands crossed
and, like my mouth, unadorned.

My mother was no tyrant. I do not want to present her in
the wrong light. It was only at the end, when she was in
near-constant pain, when her mind had become loosened
from the present, that she became jealous of my absence.
She didn't bully me into celibacy; in her own quiet way, the
fact of it horrified her. And yet.

My father died when I was very young. I remember a big
man with a black moustache throwing me up into the air,
and then I remember a thin man with a white moustache
wasting away inside an armchair. I remember not
recognizing any identity between the two men. I remember
hiding away from the thin man in the armchair; and I
remember asking my mother when my real father was going
to return. I think I asked this in front of my dying father
and this is the one and only occasion when my mother
struck me.

My father dwindled away until he was very small indeed.
He dwindled and died until he quite shrank away, and then
when his spirit had become too small for even his own
shrunken body, we buried him. I remember holding on to
my mother's hand at the graveside, and the way her veil
stuck to her face in tracks where the tears had run.

We moved from the small house that had dwarfed my

shrinking father into the flat where I live now. It was in the same area and I stayed at the same school. By the time I was about ten, my mother and I had become firm friends. I read my homework out loud in the sitting room at night, and she would admire my work and gently correct my grammar. And on my eleventh birthday she gave me the red Waterman pen with the italic nib which her own mother had given to her; and we said that I in my turn would give it to my own daughter.

I had friends at school and my mother encouraged me to spend time with them but their company was dull by comparison with hers. We read literature side by side in the sitting room, looked at travel books together, and planned imaginary journeys. We took all our meals together. I would rush home each day for lunch, and in the evening we took turns to prepare meals that became increasingly elaborate and artful. At night, in her upstairs bedroom, she would unravel her bun of hair, and I would brush it carefully, a hundred strokes.

And somehow I missed out on boys altogether. We were too busy with each other and I became timid with children of my own age. Even though I performed quietly well at school, I was only relaxed at home with Mother, where together we would shut out the dangerous and noisy world. At times, only occasionally, I would get frightened by my life. I would look at everything I said and felt and worry that it all came from her, and sometimes, only occasionally, I would hanker for feelings that were obviously my own.

She lost touch with most of her friends and relatives, because she had a combative side to her nature, a side which I seldom saw except occasionally, usually in arguments with shopkeepers when she considered herself deliberately short-changed, or given bad measure—"gypped", as she would say. And it was probably her fault rather than theirs that she lost touch with friends.

School did not tempt me away from Mother, and neither did university. We would read my set books together, and discuss my essays together, and at my graduation ceremony there was no one prouder. I took my librarian's qualifications and managed to secure a post at the British Library as a Research Assistant. Mother was very proud.

We cooked a grand meal that night, from the pages of the Alice B. Toklas Cook Book. Aspic de Foie Gras. Salmon Sauce Hollandaise. Hare à la Royale. Hearts of Artichokes à la Isman Bavaldy. Pheasants Roasted with Truffles. Lobster à la Française. Singapore Ice Cream. The truffles were tinned and the lobster had been frozen, but it was a royal feast. We glutted ourselves, and ate until we were full and then gormandized some more. And even if sometimes the two of us did get lonely, that was a wonderful night when we desired no one else's company but each other's. Candles burned and we toasted each other's health with good French wine, and after dinner we drank coffee and then we played charades.

The Alice B. Toklas Cook Book was our favourite. We worked our way through it, from Omelette in an Overcoat to Poached Eggs Babouche, from Gypsy Goulash to Roast Beef for a Rainy Day, from Small Fish in the Oriental Manner to Pink Pompadour Bass.

We were fastidious in our following of cookbook instructions; the most furious arguments my mother and I ever had occurred when she caught me changing the amount of herbs or spices in a recipe. She would grow very cold and very haughty and then take out the breadboard to prepare herself a sandwich. I would argue logically, point out that I had made this dish before and she had pronounced it delicious, failing to realize that I had doubled the proportion of rosemary to mint. My arguments were always to no avail. Stiff-backed and white-lipped, Mother would be close to tears as she spread her own special mayonnaise over the bread. Nothing would do until I had thrown everything away and begun all over again, and then wait for the smells from the kitchen to rouse her from her armchair where she would be sitting with the sandwich untouched on a plate on her lap as she stared at the photograph of my black-moustachioed father smiling inside a silver frame which she would be gently cleaning with a chamois rag.

Our favourite part of Alice was the chapter Recipes from Friends. We would imagine ourselves intimates with Picasso, Joyce, Picabia, Beaton, as we prepared the dishes compiled by the holders of those wonderful, euphonious names. Ibiza Soup from Madame Joseph Delteil; Dr Fernanda Pivano-Sottsass's Gnocchi alla Romana; Harold Knapik's Szekely Gulyas; Fania Marinoff's Pecan Nut Cakes; Princess D. de Rohan's Crème Brûlée, or her Hot Toddy for a Cold Night, with Calvados, cream and apricot brandy, which is attributed to Flaubert. There was one recipe we did not follow: the recipe by Brian Gysen (that is Alice's spelling—in the British Library Catalogue he is listed as Brion Gysin, but it is a pedantic point) for Haschich Fudge.

It made us apprehensive, the prospect of being "ravished by 'un évanouissement réveillé' ", as Alice puts it. Sometimes, Mother would scare me into bed with the thought of it.

And Mother became sick. Like the man who had been my father, she dwindled and shrank. She complained much of the time, became nostalgic and sad. Her pain dictated the rhythms of our household. It was as if I had a child; she would not be able to sleep through the night and would call on me to attend to her. Sometimes I would just sit with her, holding her hand, and she would look at me, eyes empty apart from fear, and I would press her hand and whisper vague soothing words. I bought her a small handbell which she would use to call me to her bedside. She became an invalid.

I bought my first eye shadow—Midnight Blue—after her first seizure. Dawdling in the High Street until it was time to pick her up from the hospital, I found myself at a Boots cosmetic counter. I made the purchase quickly, slipping the plastic case into my coat pocket to hurry out as if I had done something shameful. Later, at night, after Mother had gone to sleep, I locked myself into the WC and smeared the brilliant colour over my lids. I felt suddenly free, and then I burst into tears. I wore Midnight Blue from that time on and if Mother noticed, she did not make any comment until the day of that awful picnic.

Helping academics at the Library with their bibliographies, explaining the Catalogue to new Readers, shopping at the local supermarket, preparing small dainty meals for Mother, and, often, reading to her, such would be my day. Summoned by her bell, I would hold her hand and soften her panic by reading recipes to her long into the night. No other book would do but Alice: sometimes just one recipe; often a whole chapter would be needed before she fell asleep. I read the Recipes from Friends chapter so many times I still know much of it by heart even now, so many years later. Her stomach was not strong enough to digest anything stronger than the simplest meals, and this, I think, saddened her more than anything.

I met him at the Library. I knew him by reputation, of course: "Decadent Pleasures" had already caused something of a scandal. One very firm, very angry letter from a notable academic who was on the Readers' Committee had insisted that the book be classified a Cupboard book and be held under key in the North Library. Surprisingly, this caused more interest rather than less, and we had to purchase several more copies to meet the demand. There was an article about this in one of the daily papers, and the publicity which resulted made the book only then a best seller. He did not look at all as I had expected him to. Most racy academic texts are written by short, stout Americans, whereas he was tall, handsomely built, with an urbane manner, a greying David Niven moustache, and wise, amused eyes.

He wooed me bibliographically. The first words I heard him speak were, "Excuse me, but I'm trying to track down this collection of stories by the American, Robert Coover." His voice was low, and humorous. He pushed a slip of paper towards me over the counter of the Readers' Enquiry Desk. It had the words "Pricksongs and Descants" written upon it.

There was something provocative and naughty in his eyes although his manner was solemn and correct. I walked with him to the appropriate catalogue and helped him fill out his Book Application Form. I kept the slip of paper. I keep it still.

Each day, he would make an enquiry about a different book. "Pricksongs and Descants" was followed by "The Pillow Book of Sei Shonagan"—asked for with a smile and an eyebrow raised—then "One Hundred Years of Solitude" by García Márquez—and there was a solicitousness in the way he wished me a good morning after we had ordered the book together, and as I watched him stroll, stiff-backed like a military man, to the Book Orders Counter I felt vulnerable and alone and apprehensive. Then came "Men and Women", the collection of pornographic verse by Verlaine, and Sade's "Philosophy in the Bedroom" (both of these Cupboard books, incidentally) and "Insatiability" (in its French translation) by the Polish writer Witkiewicz—which was asked for in a quite humble, nearly apologetic way that made me shiver.

Then he didn't appear for a week. Mother noticed my preoccupation but there was nothing I could tell her, just lull her to sleep with a frantic recital of Madame M. G. Debar's Messy Chicken à la Berrichonne and Mrs Gilbert Whipple Chapman's Salzburger Nockerl. Mother's condition was unchanging. She stayed in bed all day now, and reminisced about my father in the days when he was black-moustachioed and strong.

He returned, with a gentlemanly request for "Bliss and Other Stories" by Katherine Mansfield that made me giddy. Then, the next day, wearing a black suit and a dark tie, he asked for Graham Greene's "The End of the Affair" in the morning and Mishima's "Death in Midsummer" in the afternoon. I grieved all night, held close to me the image of something precious that had dwindled and died: an orchid in the terracotta pot of a careless gardener. The next day he invited me to have dinner with him. I accepted.

I very much wanted to tell Mother. I needed her advice; I

wanted to discuss dress and manner and I wanted to giggle
with her while she taunted me with the prospect of kisses.
Even though we were very much friends, romance was an
area we had stopped talking about long ago. Or rather:
romance in my life went undiscussed. As she grew older, her
hair growing whiter and wilder and longer, she would dwell
on dances she had danced at, boys she had dallied with,
kisses stolen and love tokens offered. She had long ago
given up teasing me about the neighbourhood boys who had
grown up to own butcher's shops and second-hand car
franchises. And, before she had become too lost in Alice's
recipes and her own girlish remembrances, when I had used
to return home and in the hour before supper make her
laugh by my imaginative stories of the doings of the Library
personalities, I would always—out of a solicitude for her
sensibility rather than mine—leave out the occasional
clumsy attempts of the Museum Guards to tease me and
touch me in the staff canteen.

I warned her I would be late that night; seasonal
recataloguing would keep me late, well beyond Library
hours. Peevishly, she complained. I brought in a cold supper
for her, covered with foil, and put it on the dressing table.
I'm sorry, I told her, it's something I am committed to do. I
waited until she had complained herself back to sleep and
then I took her black velvet evening dress out of her
wardrobe and stole off to work, feeling guilty and liberated
at the same time, with the dress carefully folded inside a
supermarket shopping bag.

I know my eye make-up is considered eccentric. I hear
the whispers and the giggles of other Library staff. I know
the nicknames they call me; but it protects me. With it as
my shield, I can be a painted odalisque or a harsh career
woman. Maybe no one else notices, but my make-up
protects me. I applied a fresh coat and changed into my
mother's dress in the staff WC and waited for him outside,
in the shelter of the pillars by the Museum entrance. Near
to me, two Guards smoked cigarettes and discussed sport in
low voices and I watched their breath make lively ghost

shapes in the cold air. It was a beautiful night, very grave, and the Museum looked grand in the night. A few pigeons pecked with gusto around the wastepaper bins, and off in the road, men and women walked hurriedly in their overcoats, hunched against the cold. I did not feel the cold at all as I waited, almost bridal, in my mother's black velvet dress.

I remember every detail of that dinner we shared. Every word that was spoken, every gesture used. Oddly, I cannot remember any of the food we ate, or even the wine we drank, chosen by him with a quiet show of taste. I remember everything that we said and did, but it will not be written down here. Some things are too precious to share. I feel as if I am standing now in a cold, drab room and opening an exquisite Japanese box. My back is to you, whoever you are, and I am lifting out of the box a perfect string of pearls, which are warm against my skin. If I showed them to you for any reason at all—be it pride or vanity or even regret—they would lose their lustre and warmth, they would become a social object, cheapened by the indifferent gaze of another.

I will tell you that we kissed goodbye, quite publicly, on a Bloomsbury side street at night, and I will tell you that the chafe of his moustache against my skin makes me lift my hand to my face even now. He found me a taxi cab and told the driver the route to take, and after I returned home I sat for the longest time alone in the unlit sitting room. I sat in my mother's armchair in my mother's dress, half mad I think, sleepless, unblinking, careless of the future, cleaving to feelings that were unmistakably my own.

The next day, I waited for him to appear. I tried to prepare myself for the look in his eyes, for the cool distance I would place between us, for the moment of gratitude I would allow him before making him realize that it was impossible for me to allow him another evening like the one we had shared. I waited for him and dealt with the solemn requests of the Readers and the sly barbs of the Museum

Guards and the careful banter of my colleagues. I waited for him. He did not appear.

When I returned home, Mother was awake but quiet. In a shy, small voice she asked for a glass of water and my hand on hers. We listened to a concert on the radio and we sat together as night drew in.

I almost succeeded in driving the image of him out of my mind. I had almost succeeded in seeing the episode as closed and complete: my great adult love, my grand passion, the romance that was meant to be that was never meant to be. I had almost done these things when he returned. It was only a week that had gone by, the most empty and wretched and lonely week of my life.

He asked me how I was, and the way he asked opened me up entirely to him. He had a knack—no, that's the wrong word: that makes it sound tricksy and calculating—he had a gift for using the most banal formulations of words to convey the deepest sympathy, the greatest respect. He stood there, that slightly anachronistic-looking figure, trim and strong in a hand-made suit, his figure better-formed and more vital than those of men half his age, wearing a club tie and carrying a slightly battered brown leather briefcase. Two of my colleagues were with me behind the Readers' Enquiry Desk, and I think I must have blanched, dreading some slip of intimacy on his part.

"I have been out of town," he said, and he paused, to permit himself the slightest of amused smiles at my trepidation, "and I have an article to prepare that is almost late. I do hope you have this book housed here."

I followed his eyes to the Book Application Form he was holding on the counter. There was nothing written on it.

"I know it is entirely irregular but I was wondering if I could look at it immediately. It is only a footnote I need to check. On page 200. I am in a terrible hurry, and if you could escort me to the shelf I could just check it, replace it, and finish my article. I don't even need to have the book checked out to me."

Readers are never allowed in the stacks and he knew that

perfectly well. I looked at the face of the Supervisor, his inevitable expression of sour disapproval. The audacity of the man terrified me. But the Supervisor only smiled at him and nodded to me. Somehow, I managed to adopt a professional manner and somehow I managed to find the direction towards the book stacks.

We kept on walking. I had enough momentum to go on, and a sinking will dreading what would come next—a difficult, sad conversation—and I had a sense of objectless anticipation that made me feel as if I was sweating with the 'flu. His hand squeezing my shoulder with a cruel pressure stopped me. He turned me around to face him in a narrow lane of books.

We looked at each other with our bodies only a few inches apart and for the first time I was frightened of him, physically frightened. He was a strong man, and his air of infinite amusement and infinite doubt covered something else which I was only now beginning to perceive. I looked away first; I could no longer bear him to examine me in that way, but he reached for my face and slowly lifted my chin so our eyes would meet again. We stayed like that for the longest time, perfectly still, touching, his eyes on mine. It was the most intimate moment of my life.

At any moment we could have been espied. It was madness, and I know that this is the stuff of romantic fiction and will be derided as such, but madness it was. We walked slowly through the stacks, stopping once to allow Gerald, the fat book boy from Stoke Newington, to pass us, and he escorted me back behind the Enquiry Desk. He thanked me courteously for my help, nodded to the Supervisor, and strolled out of the Library, his brown briefcase swinging slightly. I sat on my chair, held my skirt tight to my legs, fought to stay still, and I dreaded the prospect of it ever happening again.

The same event is cruelly described by Ivory in a letter to Helen:

6 February 1973

Dear Helen,

Within the stacks we went, seducer and virgin. She trembling with delicious delight, the anticipation of surrender, of violation, ultimate and cruel: voluptuously, in her way, aching to be disposed of as an empty thing once her precious hymenic barrier to the world had been punctured. Books all around us, quiet, silence, the occasional footfall of a book delivery boy echoing through the chamber. She shivers as if with the flu. She opens her mouth slightly, her wet tongue the animal inside her. I lead her: we stop. This could be the moment, the final outrage. We stand towards each other, she is weak with trepidation, with fright, with a longing she does not recognize. Within the stacks, metal cases from floor to ceiling. She rests her hand on a book as if she needs to gather strength from something familiar. With my eyes I fix her. With her eyes she agrees to be fixed. I had not expected this vulvic moment to open itself to reveal the final, clitoral event. I had not dared to be so impatient. We stand, we look at each other, surprising muscles twitch. We are intimates. It is up to her now. I stand: I wait for her to be pulled towards me, for all the dark physical things to bubble up into her strained voice. I would not be startled by curses. By sudden angular nudity. She is yet strong enough to look away. She might be weeping. I grab hold of her face with a cruel necessary pressure. She looks up at me again. This to her is passion, this sex in the head. The moment holds. She needs me and . . .

. . . resists.

This campaign will have further battles and I am glad. My love to you and Mattie. Deborah requires a spanking.

W.

But here is a thing that puzzled me at the time. In my incomplete selection from Ivory's letters to Helen I found two more passages dealing with his seduction of Miss P—, and in the first of these, only a sentence long, he writes:

The translucent skin that hides the dry, cracked womb of the holy virgin—she carries the articles of her untouched faith in a supermarket bag.

It seemed odd to me that the year of this letter should be given incorrectly by Ivory. It is dated February 7 and that must surely be correct; but 1971 is out by two years. It seemed a surprising slip for Ivory to make. He is normally so precise and correct in his writings.

But back to Miss P—. We've left her dangling:

I held myself together for the rest of the day, somehow. I remember feeling numb and very cold, but I got through it without incident. I prepared supper for Mother and when she had finished it—after complaining about the lack of pepper—I burst into tears and laid my head on Mother's empty breast. She stroked my hair with teasing, slightly malicious fingers and strangely I found this consoling.

After that first time in the Library stacks, I thought I would never see him again. I imagined in him some sense of guilt, or propriety perhaps, that would keep him away; but then he returned, a week later, stopping me at the Museum steps without saying a word to take me to a pub in Bloomsbury. He talked to me and he charmed me, and I even found myself inviting him to the house, where he entertained me with stories from his past in the downstairs sitting room while Mother beat out a rhythm with her invalid's handbell.

He had insisted that he meet her and I had learnt that I was unable to refuse him anything, even if I wanted to. So I took him there upstairs that evening. He courteously held the bedroom door open for me as I carried in Mother's

supper tray, with my dress sticking to my skin in damp
sweat patches.

"There is a gentleman here who would meet you," I told
her, and then I introduced them in a formal fashion. He
shook her hand carefully as if he was scared to break it, and
she primped her hair with the coquetry of a débutante at a
rural dance. They talked of the weather in the most correct
way and then she burst into tears and sobbed with her
hands together as if she was praying. She often cried in that
way in that decaying time, and would sometimes be soothed
by a glass of warm tonic water. I went down to fetch it and
when I returned he was gently stroking her face, a
tenderness I had never found in him, nor known to seek out,
and she was holding on to his other hand, with her eyes
serenely closed. I have to confess that my strongest emotion
was not gratitude but jealousy.

In the morning, when I brought up her breakfast tray,
Mother saw the change in me. She complained of it. She
accused me of neglect. She said I did not love her. She said
she was a burden upon me. She said I was longing for her
to die. I tried to argue, then I tried to interest her in
marmalade and toast, but she drove mercilessly on. There
was colour in her cheeks as her fury lifted her away from
her bank of pillows. She accused me of being jealous of her
because she had the power to attract men. Her hair
streamed wildly and she tore into me with abuse and curses.
She made me cry and she greeted my tears with satisfaction.
Only then did she relent. She ate her breakfast with a naked
hunger, dabbed at the corners of her mouth with the linen
napkin, pushed the tray a little down the bed, and fell
immediately asleep again.

I had hoped to share confidences with her. I had hoped
for her friendship and shared joy. Instead, she made me feel
treacherous and wretched. Mother's ability to concentrate
had shrunk like the rest of her. Only the lines on her face
and body, and her hair, which had grown wild and white
and which she would no longer allow me to brush, remained
discernibly adult. The rest of her had dwindled to the size

of a child. Her attention would drift. Mother would wander through memories of the past, clutch them to her, and gaze sadly at them as if nothing else in the world had any colour. I do not know if she understood what she was saying to me, words that were cruel and without love; they were probably less real to her than the memory of a dance she had been taken to by Ronnie, the boyfriend she had had before she met my father.

I prepared myself for the sight of him. On the 19 bus I practised long looks of polite coolness. A schoolgirl who had been sitting next to me moved away, frightened, I think.

Shortly after, he took us on a picnic, Mother and me. It was a wintry day and he drove us up to Hampstead in his Jaguar with tartan blankets over our legs and woolly hats on our heads. We parked by South End Green and walked slowly up over the Heath to the lily pond. Mother was in seventh heaven. She chattered all the way up to the pond, talking of Sunday strolls with my father, of walks with me, and she held on to his hand the whole time and looked at me triumphantly from time to time like a favoured daughter crowing over her ugly sister.

We spread a tablecloth over the grass and weighed down the corners with stones. He unfolded deck chairs for us, and we sat down and looked at the pond and Mother said something about Monet. It was cold there, and wet, and I was worried for Mother. Her cheeks reddened in the spit of the wind as she guzzled down food that was much too rich for her: salmon on dry toast; German white wine; cuts of beef and spicy Italian ham with soft cheeses from France; thick dark chocolate puddings and sugared coffee. He had brought a portable tape player along and dance sounds from the 'thirties and 'forties accompanied our meal, and Mother talked about life in the Blitz and dancing to Al Bowlly and the Hot Club de France. Her cheeks were flushed with the weather and the attention, but soon I stopped being worried for either her or myself, because he was stronger than both of us. He watched Mother carefully, but not like a suitor, or

even a doctor, his look was like I have always imagined
pioneers of science to look: curious and detached but quietly
and terribly excited as they poke and prod the subjects of
their experiments to drive them into new and dangerous
behaviour.

I think I might have shut my eyes. I listened to the sound
of his questions, calmly insistent—"What did you wear?
How old was Ronnie? Did your parents approve? And you
danced, yes?"—and the sound of Mother's stories, feverish
over the trite clarinet of the Benny Goodman Orchestra, and
the sound of the wind and the drizzle on the water next to
us and through the bare branches of the trees above us, and
I was suddenly somebody else, much higher up. I pushed my
face into the wind and I felt suddenly light and free and
young, and I danced closed-eyed in the rain.

And then I heard Mother's cruel voice, saying, "Look at
the painted lady! She hops!" and the moment was over,
though I tried to make it go on. And when I opened my
eyes it was raining harder, and he had taken Mother in his
arms and they were dancing. Her hair was crazy and wild
and her white shoes were soiled with mud, and her
stockings too, and her white throat was exposed and
stretched, with the two bones sticking out in frail relief, and
I had the fancy that he was a vampire, and she was his final,
bloodless victim.

And the dancing went on, faster and faster, even after the
music had stopped. And he was whirling her around, his
willing, besotted victim, and she breathed heavily through
her open mouth, and thin lines of colourless spittle dribbled
out from the corners and mixed with the crumbs of dry
toast on her chin. And finally he relented and eased her
back to her chair and she clapped her hands furiously, then
let them fall to her chest. He poured her another glass of
Hock, and she turned to me, triumphant and sick and mad,
and said, "I feel a little giddy now. I love to dance."

It was not long after that Mother died. When we returned
from the picnic I put her to bed and when I went back

downstairs he was gone. The next day was a Sunday and I sat alone much of the day listening to the radio, and in the evening I sat with Mother. She was gentle and placid. All the venom that had been distilled from the bitterness and spite of her invalid state had been danced out of her. She was calm and considerate again, and she no longer found refuge in her odd selections from the past. She fretted rather a lot about me and she blamed herself for forcing me into the roles of companion and nursemaid. I dabbed her temples with cotton wool damp with cologne and made no reply. We never referred to the picnic and we never talked about him.

I did not see him at the Library until the day after her funeral. I wore my new lipstick and, probably, an air of confusion. "I will prepare you a meal," he said, "for your mourning." He invited himself to the house and I was not strong enough to refuse him.

I wore Mother's dress, perhaps to pretend that there was something worth dressing up for, perhaps to remind myself of better days, or perhaps just to pretend I was her. He came and I was banished from the kitchen. I sat in Mother's armchair and idly browsed through Alice.

It was a feast that he prepared, extravagant and dark. He had provided his own dishes, entirely black, and all the food served upon them was black as well. We began with a turtle soup, then Beluga caviare served with Russian rye bread and Greek olives. The main course was game in blackberry sauce, with squid-ink pasta on the side. Dessert was plum pudding and pears in a grape-juice syrup. We drank rich dark wines from Roussillon and Valdepeñas, and broke for coffee with walnut cordial, followed by glasses of Guinness for a digestif.

We sat in separate chairs, sipping our stout, and he was the very model of correctness. We talked of Roman emperors, I remember, and he surprised me when he said that Caligula was a bald, very hairy man, which ran contrary to the way I had pictured him.

I do not remember the excuse he used to lead me out to

the balcony; who knows, it could have been something
about the stars. But we stood there, it was the dead of
winter and cold, and I felt his hands crawling up my dress
and I was powerless against him and I remember thinking,
this is what Mother has died for. The action we performed
there was a denial of everything my life had been. It was
harsh and it was bestial and painful, and it was public. I lost
sight of who it was I was there with, and all that was was a
pain and a desperate urgency, and the constant fear of being
discovered. And the pain increased and the urgency grew
and the fear of being discovered became a hope instead. It
was the only way it would ever end, and at the same time I
wanted to be naked and abased and seen, and I hope this
does not shock you.

The ordeal finally ended. He had the sensitivity not to
apologize or enquire after me; instead, as if I had been a
small child and he my father, he ordered my clothing and
stroked my face dry. Then he gathered up his plates and his
serving utensils and left the house, leaving the kitchen a
mess.

The next week, he took me to a rented room off High
Holborn. There we sat, drinking tea from an aluminium
thermos flask, and he massaged my face and shoulders and
whispered gossip of Ancient Rome. Then he made me do
things that were shabby and ugly.

He would not even let me wash. He looked at his pocket
watch, a Hunter, and rushed me into a taxi up to Regent's
Park. We waited, he would not tell me for what, on a cold
park bench next to a vulgar statue. We did not talk. Then,
after such a long, cold and huddled time, he pointed out a
group of people strolling along the grass a little away from
where we were sitting. A thin middle-aged woman; an
elegant, younger Oriental woman; and a little black-haired
girl. "Pretty, isn't she?" he said, and I could not tell which of
the party he was referring to. The black-haired girl saw the
two of us and laughed. She pointed us out to the middle-
aged woman who looked at us; her face suddenly twisted
with a painful rictus, and then she looked away, took the

child by the hand, and they carried on on their walk. "My family," he said. That was the last time I saw him. I think I might have bored him.

I live in my mother's house and her room is as she left it. I clean it once a week and stand in the doorway once in a while. I lost my job at the Library; I think he might have lost it for me, I do not know how, nor do I care, and I hate him for what he did to Mother and I am grateful to him for what he did to me. I was 39 years old when I met him.

Her memoir ends on a separate page:

This has been very painful for me to do. I hope I can trust you with the information I have given. I have been waiting for you, in a way—I knew that one day you, or someone like you, cocky, devoted to knowledge and memory, would turn up and demand this. I knew who you were the first moment I saw you. I knew too that it would be impossible to get rid of you. I hope you don't find this abusive. I know it's not your fault who you are.

I consider our acquaintance now at an end. I think there is nothing here that needs further explanation. Please don't try to contact me or see me. I was happy at Highbury & Islington Library. I am less happy at G——. But, as you probably realize about me, I hate change. I would prefer not to ask the Library Service to transfer me for a second time. It would be irritating to them and tiresome for me.

I would like to be able to wish you luck in your quest. I cannot do that. If your book is ever completed, please do not trouble yourself to send me a copy.

I stayed up reading all night. It was morning by the time I was finished. I was drunk and exhausted, addled with confessions, with booze and speculation and a sudden realization. I returned the pages to Miss P——'s brown envelope. A litany of yelled abuse, of crazed street curses, drifted up to me. I went over to the window. There was a fight going on downstairs between the whores and the pushers and when they lit out I was sad to see them go. I lay down on the bed but I was nowhere near sleep. I sat at the desk again and rested my head on my hands and listened to the sound of drunken blood roll around my ears. I sat back and swung on two legs of the chair and then I went over to the window again and stood there, inspired with pain.

I finally got to sleep around noon. I was wakened a couple of hours later by a loud tattoo beaten on the door. Turned to the sharp light in the doorway. A green cracked Formica tray coming toward me. Toasted bagels, hills of lox, knobs of cream cheese heaped upon it, coming my way. And you, behind it.

"I refuse to eat anything else these days," you said. "Good afternoon. How are you feeling? You look awful. Would you like some coffee?"

"Sure. Yes. Coffee. Yes. I'd love some. Good morning. Where am I?"

"You're in a rather shabby little place that calls itself the Hotel Invincible or something. Honestly, I would have thought you could have found a nicer place."

"I did once. Couldn't meet the rent. When did you get in? I guess I should put on some clothes."

"Stay in bed. Enjoy your breakfast. You deserve some pampering." You trailed off, looking around the room for something to remark upon, didn't find it, and said, for no particular reason, "I'm staying with my mother."

I pulled my belly in and sat up in bed. I tapped on the light. You sat on the edge of the bed. You were wearing a coat.

"I think London's aged you, Tierney. You look worn out. Tell me everything. Eat up."

Of course I looked worn out. I'd been chasing a dead man for the longest time. The food was good. You wouldn't have any.

"I'm stuffed. If you can't finish it we can always give it to that weird Australian downstairs. I wouldn't be surprised if you were the only person staying here. Have you started writing the book yet?"

"Still researching. Still got a lot to find out."

You slipped away from the bed and went over to the window. You passed by the side table packed high with my notes and ledgers of Ivory's letters to Helen. You didn't notice them or maybe just pretended not to, protective, I decided, of my professionalism. Something caught in your hair, a hotel fly maybe, enjoying its indoor summer, which you slapped quickly away. The brief sight of your neck when you did that, the flesh of your nape suddenly revealed, inadequately protected by a few renegade hairs, short dark strands curling down. Then you jerked open the curtain and looked out at the street.

"Nice area. Is that drugs or sex they're selling down there?"

"Both. Sit down. You make me nervous."

You let the curtain fall to cover the street again. You turned back to me and you smiled. It was probably not a sincere smile and I knew that at the time and it was kind of lazily done but it was a great smile all the same. I love your mouth and your teeth—did I ever tell you that? Wide mouth, teeth that look as if you've taken the trouble to sharpen them a little. I swallowed my last mouthful of lox and took care to form a polite, ambiguous question that would reveal nothing of what was in my mind or elsewhere.

"You back for long?"

I'd expected you to be disappointed by my composure. You weren't. You looked pleased. You opened your coat as if you were about to take it off, then put your hands in the pockets and lifted them quickly up and down, like a bird testing doubtful wings.

"It depends. It's strange being at my mother's. We have work to do. Don't we? It's chilly in here, you must be cold. You said you'd found out how he died. Well?"

"I guess I was trying to impress you. I haven't got there yet. I could tell you a lot about the War and I could tell you stuff about Cousin Mattie. Gambling too. You were right about Ivory. He makes an interesting book."

"Why don't you get dressed? I've got some errands to run. I'll be back in a couple of hours."

And you left. I went to the window to watch you walk along the street. A small figure, a dark flapping bird, you swooped through a jabbering crowd of youths as if they didn't exist in the same world as you, and disappeared around the corner along the street that led down to the river. A dark-skinned girl, Indian or Sri Lankan or something, caught sight of me up in the window and pointed to me and smiled. Five bored faces turned slowly up in vague expectation, as if they mildly hoped I might be about to jump, for entertainment's sake. I briefly showed them my genitals and then went out of the room and down along the corridor to take a shower.

You weren't back in a couple of hours. It was about five hours later when you called. Yours wasn't the first call. Shortly before, a strange muffled voice, male or female, I couldn't tell.

The voice asked me if I was Tierney and I admitted that I was. Then, with a pleading kind of menace, it asked, "Do you have it?"

"Do I have what?"

"We're prepared to make an accommodation. We'll require proof."

"Proof of what?"

"Don't be clever. It's not a thing that lasts."

A dead line. I tapped the phone. I shook my head. Neither action made things clearer. I went back to busying myself with notes and tapes and transcripts. I'd eaten the crusts of the bagels I'd rejected at breakfast time. I was drawing lines on pieces of paper, making connections, guessing at gaps. I was looking at the photographs you'd given me at the first, and I was touching my fingers against his face to help me understand.

We finally had dinner that night. Do you remember? Of course you do. It was at a Russian place, downstairs below street level, black-and-gold walls, diners crammed tight together down long tables piled high with platters of smoked fish and carafes of spiced vodka in jackets of ice. I was drunk still, red-eyed, reckless with questions. I stank of stale morning whiskey when I arrived and I washed the smell away with hot peppered vodka. It began amiably enough. Of course you remember.

"Good-looking food, I like it here. Not much room for elbow work but all the same it's not too bad. You're not eating, something the matter? Tell me about New York. What were you doing there?"

"I'm thirsty. Would you like some more vodka? Tell me about the library virgin. Did you ever find her?"

"She's not a virgin anymore. I found her."

I shouted out my pursuit of the library virgin and you warned me to keep my voice down. Miss P——'s story, paraphrased, with all its strange sadness and gratitude.

"You see," you said, crowing after I was done. "He was a monster. I told you so."

"She said he rescued her."

"He killed her mother."

"She was on the way out. Miss P—— was grateful for all that he did."

"He was a monster." You repeated the word again and I noticed for the first time your habit of shaking your head whenever something pleased you.

Then it started to get personal. I asked you about yourself and you didn't like that at all. With vodka swilling through the whiskey inside me I became a bully with questions.

"Tell me about yourself. I don't know much about you at all. Where were you born? When were you born? Did you have a happy childhood? How did you get into publishing? What were you doing in New York?"

You shrugged, looked around at the other diners as if you

were reading their lips in the hope of finding a response to
borrow.

"I went there because I was bored with Boston."

"Why were you in Boston?"

"I was bored with London."

"This could go on forever. Tell me something about yourself.
Anything. What's your favorite color? Do you believe in
heroes?"

You smiled at that. "I've always respected people who don't
stop for death."

"What's that mean?"

You looked down at your pancakes. You played with the
fish, with the dab of caviare on top of the mound of sour cream.
You regretted this for sure. I'd startled you with my looks and
my manner the moment I arrived. It had all gone downhill
after that, hadn't it?

"What's got into you, Tierney? What's happened?"

"Tell me about picnics You don't like them, do you? Why
don't you like picnics?"

"Keep your voice down."

I grinned at you, a wide-grinned teeth-almost-all-my-own
drunk boy smile. "My voice can get louder than this, D.B. It's
a voice that was trained in the bleachers of Fenway Park. We
used to have a competition—how loud can you chant 'Looie,
Loo-*ie!*' when Luis Tiant went into his crazy windup on the
mound? I can get *really* loud if I want to. You enjoying your
food? Tell me about your mother. Where does she live? Do
you take after her?"

"No," you said. Solemn girl. Wide green eyes free of makeup
worried over where the questions were going. "I take after my
father more." There. As if one answer would be sufficient, your
eyes went down to your plate again, your far from hungry fork
playing with the shapes that sour cream can make.

"Your father. He still alive?"

"No. He died some time ago."

"But your mother's still alive, isn't she? You're staying with
your mother?"

"Yes I'm staying with my mother."

"And whereabouts would that be? What kind of neighborhood? Would it be on the south side of town? Or is it more likely to be the north?"

"It might be. Tierney, you're a state. Get a grip on yourself. If you've got a point to make, make it."

Ooh, you shook me there for a moment. Brave defiance. Child of war facing up to the enemy. Stern emotions hidden behind blank face. The face of a girl accused of something by her father. (*Who has seen it? Where is it, girl?! Daddy*—or would that be *Father?*—*I think it must have been the dog. He must have buried it.*) Then silence. Silence is safe. You can't give yourself away under cover of silence.

"D.B.?"

"Yes?" Guarded. Unsure.

"What's that stand for?"

"My name. Dorothy Burton."

"What's your mother's name?"

Silence.

"You had a stepmother, didn't you? What was her name?"

Silence.

"What color was her hair?"

This sounded like a safe one. You shrugged your shoulders. You answered me. "Her hair was black."

"She was an oriental, wasn't she?"

Silence.

"Did you ever meet a librarian from the British Library? An angular virgin in ludicrous eye shadow—Midnight Blue?"

"No."

"Did you ever see her? Did you ever catch a glimpse of her? Like maybe in a park?"

Silence.

"You got any brothers or sisters?"

"I have a brother."

"What's his name?"

Silence.

"Is his name Matthew by some chance? Named after fey dead Uncle Mattie?"

The slightest of smiles. Silence.

"When did your father die?"

"I don't know if he ever did."

That was a weird one. You looked at me very open and very frank. It was the look of a swinging bachelor in a singles bar who demands sex with his eyes.

"What does that mean?"

Smile. Closed-off again. Silence.

We drank more vodka. It made us both more sober than before. Someone with a mustache came to collect our plates, which still contained all our food, just nicely rearranged. You said you were having fun. You suggested going on to someplace else. I paid the bill from the money you'd given me at the start of the evening. A generous sum.

We caught a cab to a drinking place in Soho. Chi-chi. A long-haired hipster with a bony face played jazzed-up show tunes on the piano. A long glass-topped wooden bar with a few drunks looking proud. A restaurant at the back. You said some of the drunks were famous. I said they looked like drunks. We took a table near to the bar and ordered more vodka. There was a folded copy of yesterday's morning paper on our table with a crossword that had been barely started. Clock-circles of letters jotted around from the solver's failed struggle to get the anagrams.

"Where were we?" I asked.

"You were the Grand Inquisitor. I think you were about to try and make me say that William Ivory was my father."

"Was he?"

"I'm sure you were building up to something. I'm sure you've got some wonderful piece of evidence just sweetly stored up. Have you, Tierney? Have you dusted my fingerprints in an incriminating place? Taken a dead man's sperm and matched it to a patch of my skin? Tell me."

"Was he your father?"

"Why? Because I'm interested in him? Because he was English and so am I? Because he went on picnics and I don't like them very much? Is that your conclusive evidence?"

It did sound kind of hollow. I tried to grab onto my thought processes from before but they were far away from me now.

It had seemed obvious to me before and it still did. I just couldn't remember why.

"Or is it because my stepmother's hair was black and Ivory's second wife had black hair? Is that it?"

I smiled at you in an effort to show condescension. I don't know how it came off. Probably pretty badly. Probably looked more a drunk boy's leer than a Sherlock's tight grin of certainty.

"Oh, I know." Heavy sarcasm. Didn't become you. "It's because I have a brother. And Ivory had two children, a boy and a girl." You laughed. "How do you even know I'm a girl? You don't know for sure, do you? Your researches haven't taken you that far. Be quiet for a moment. I want to listen to the piano."

Your face got kind of light and faraway. For as long as the piano player played you were gone. I waited for him to finish. I waited for you to come back. When he took his break you sighed very softly, turned to me again. Waited for my proof.

I breathed deeply. Talked slowly. "The time I went to Helen Ivory's house she told me she was expecting her daughter. Her daughter was last heard from in Canada I think. Shortly after, you return. You say you're staying with your mother."

You nodded. A teacher encouraging a backward child to reach his elusive, awkward conclusion. You might even have yawned. I don't think you did but you probably considered it. There was something to say about Nick Wheel but I couldn't remember what it was. I tried again.

"Oh yeah, I got it. I remember now."

"Keep your voice down. This isn't a baseball park."

"Ballpark. We call them ballparks. What was I going to say?"

Silence. A cold disapproving look. Made me want to stop. I continued.

"D.B.?"

Silence. It was beginning to catch up now. A blur now around me of drunk near-celebrities, of cryptic crossword clues, of your face shifting and changing and darkening and lightening, the constantly repeated all-around chink of bottles and glasses becoming intolerable to my ears, the return of the piano player, jazzy show tunes belting out faster with mad indulgent arpeggios—difficult now, nigh impossible to follow the tight narrow path of reason through all this jungle.

"D.B.?"

"Yes." Impatient. Pissed. Bored.

Closed my ears. Counted up to ten. Established some order in the world.

"D.B.?"

"What is it?"

Jump straight in. Tank on ahead before I lost it all again.

"It's an unusual name, isn't it? An odd thing for a girl to be called. It's boardroom executives in 'sixties movies. Heads of companies. A male thing."

"They're my initials." Defiant. Shifty. This thing was mine.

"Yeah right. Let me tell you something. I have a stack of Ivory's letters to Helen. Did you know that? They make strange sad reading. He told her everything like she was his analyst or maybe confessor, and that's kind of creepy and sinister because he had a lot of hurtful and damaging things to say, but it's also curious and loving, the whole thing." I stopped. Effort of control. I was losing it again. I blocked out the sounds. Stopped looking at you. Looking at you made it harder to think. "But that's not the point. The point is they had a daughter. Her name was Deborah. Deborah Ivory. Maybe she had a middle name that began with a B, I don't know. He writes about her sometimes in his letters. Sometimes he calls her Deborah. That's her name, after all. But more often it's just by a pair of initials. You know what those initials are? Plain old D.B. Now *that's* what I call a coincidence."

I settled back proudly. I took another swig of vodka. I deserved it. I'd earned it.

"You're getting to be a bore."

"Is that it? Is that all you can say?"

Sudden fury in the drunken light. A blush to the cheeks that looked like fire. You stood half up, stretched out a hand. Hair fell in front of your face.

"That's enough. Give me back my money. Come on, hand it right back. You've got some weird kind of obsession that's got nothing to do with anything."

"What did you mean when you said you didn't know if your father was dead or not?"

Nothing. You stayed where you were, fingers involuntarily twitching.

"What does D.B. really stand for?"

You sat down in your chair. You brushed your hair back impatiently like it didn't actually belong to you.

"Why me? Why did you choose me? What were my qualifications?"

"You want to know? Really? Because you're pathetic. Hanging around. Writing your ridiculous sports pieces—what were they called? *commentaries?*—that nobody read and even stupider poetry that no one should have been made to read. I gave you a chance. You've fucked up."

"I couldn't figure it at the time that well. Why me? I knew there were a thousand schmoes better able than me to do what you wanted."

"So why did you do it?" you jeered.

"I guess I didn't take the trouble to think it through. I guess I had reasons."

This was the moment. We looked at each other and it was a pretty serious couple of looks. Like when Bob Stanley was about to go into the stretch to throw what was going to be a wild pitch to Mookie Wilson, this was the turning point. Stanley could have stopped. He could have thrown to third to keep Mitchell honest. He could have balked Wilson. Even that would have been better. Wilson could have taken the hit instead of weaving out of the way and accepted the free ride to first. Gedman could have handled the pitch. Anything could still have happened.

And the same with us. Either of us could have said or done something to give it a twist. We could have chosen, either or both of us, to pretend something else, to agree on any number of acceptable lies, even to break the whole thing off. Both of us probably knew that was the smart thing to do. Neither of us had ever taken much trouble to be smart.

"What does D.B. stand for?"

Spoken softly. You looked away. Looked back to me. A

desperately sober face. The flush fading fast away. Pale. You looked suddenly very very young.

"Let's go out to the car," you said.

London hurtled past our car windows. You drove fast, maybe safely, maybe dangerously, I couldn't tell, in a slick little Italian number painted red. I asked you where you were driving to. I asked you when you were going to tell me where your name came from. You didn't speak, all concentration on the road. You shot through chains of taxicabs, you weaved around night buses pulling out into the road, you sounded your horn to blast cyclists scared as freeway rabbits out of our way. I smoked a number of cigarettes.

Finally you spoke. "Would you mind if I took the top down?" you asked, and when I said I thought it was too cold a night for that, you twisted the wheel, took us jolting halfway up a sidewalk next to one of the Royal Parks, and climbed out of the car and pulled down the black canvas roof. A couple of Japs in American slacks and British raincoats and sporting caps interrupted their midnight stroll to watch you struggle with the apparatus. You settled back behind the driver's wheel, fixed a scarf to your head like it was a racing helmet, and pulled back into the nighttime traffic once again.

I huddled cold in my seat, tried to hug myself warm with my arms. I waited mournfully for us to reach some kind of destination.

What were you trying to show me? That you were one groovy chick? That you knew how to push around an automobile? Or that you cared not a fuck for life, neither yours nor mine? Whatever, I began to recognize the streets approaching the hotel. You pulled up with a handbrake tire screech just outside and turned to me and you smiled. "I needed to clear my head," you said. You waited with your hands on the wheel for me to get out of the car.

"You going to be coming up?"

You shook your head.

"I thought we were going to be having some nighttime stories."

"Not tonight, Tierney. We've done enough talking. I'm sorry. Please don't beg for it. I'll pick you up around lunchtime tomorrow."

"Sure."

"I'm not trying to avoid anything."

"It's okay. Tomorrow is fine. We'll both be a little straighter in the head."

"Tierney. Despite what you think, I am not William Ivory's daughter."

I got out, shut the door. I didn't know if I'd ever see you again, and at that moment, for one moment, I didn't care. You put the car into gear and gave me a wave as you pulled out without checking to see if anything was in your way.

I watched you skid away around the corner, and a couple of whores were watching me. I took one of them, the nearest one, upstairs with me. She was dark-skinned, sturdy, running a little to fat. She wore eye shadow and rouge and bright-red dye in her hair. We got to my room and I switched on the bedside lamp with a tap of my finger. I don't think we did any talking except to agree upon a price and for her to ask me how many of her clothes I wanted her to take off. She spoke English well, with some kind of an accent, and I decided she was probably from Mauritius, I don't remember why. I gave her the money up-front, turning my back to her to pull it out of the billfold you'd given to me. She stripped down to her brassiere and her stockings. I left my shirt on. She gave me a little rubbing and then snapped on a condom with a good one-handed move. She asked if I wanted anything special and I shook my head. We humped for a while and when I came I didn't call your name. She took the condom away with her.

I don't know if Ivory ever took a prostitute. If he did, I've got no record of him ever taunting Helen with the fact of it. You once said he had a horror of other people's experiences. No way. In his final decade he worked as a therapist. He was a virtuoso of the couch. (A dangerous maverick, said the Psychoanalytical Association, a breath of fresh air, said R. D. Laing.) He used role-playing games and sometimes he used narcotics, sometimes he just listened. His West Hampstead office became an arena of the psyche, where patients would try to hang on to the armor of pathologies that had become a necessary part of themselves, where they'd do battle against Ivory's onslaught and most usually lose, crumbling in the face of what he called the apocalypse or the Big Thing or sometimes the Last Thing. He loved to suck the sickness from out of his patients' hearts. Sure he was fastidious in his tastes, yet he was also extraordinarily curious, almost covetous of other people's choices of the strange things they liked to do with their bodies and their minds. As we know, he loved a virgin. That you put down to pure desire for corruption.

Decadent Pleasures makes for good reading. I was going through it while I waited for you in the tiny room the Australian called the lounge. I drank weak bad coffee and leafed through the succès de scandale. Juicy prurient titbits, historico-pathological case studies of cruel refined men (women don't make much of an appearance: a few startling anecdotes about a Ballet Russes androgyne, some snappy shots of the Marchesa Casati leading her leopard by a leather chain, a list of the lusts of the Empress Theodora of Byzantium—otherwise they're pretty much in supporting roles). And lush. Well-chosen pictures, paintings by Moreau, scurrilous political engravings, Japanese S&M cartoons, mug shots of dead men, paintings of banal wooded landscapes made surreal by doomed utopias, photographs taken by connoisseurs of instruments of torture with the blood still drying.

I wasn't expecting you to come. I expected you to run and I expected a chase. And when two o'clock had come and gone without a telephone call or a knock on the door or the sound of your sports car filling the street, I put on an overcoat and stepped outside, not quite sure what I was going to do or where I was going to do it, and there was Nick Wheel waiting for me.

"Taxi, guv'nor?" He tapped the peak of his old man's cap.

"Where to?"

"No no no no no. That's my line. Where to? You see—that's how it's meant to go. Airports are extra."

"I wasn't intending going abroad."

"Maybe you should. A change is as good as a rest. Who said that? Patsy Fagan. Hop in. You can sit in the back and listen to my opinions."

I crumpled myself in the back seat of the MG. He pulled slowly away from the curb and drank from a bottle of cheap vodka while he inched the car along the road.

"Going anywhere special this year? Who do you fancy for the Cup, then? I tell you, I don't care who's in power, they're all the bloody same, the rich get richer and the poor get drunker and the dead get deader and no one seems to care . . . What's the last thing? You tell me that, sunshine. I'd bring back capital punishment in schools, I've got a brother in South Africa . . . I know your face, don't tell me, you're that bloke on the telly, I had that Deborah Ivory in the back of my cab once."

"Tell me about her."

"Nobody's perfect."

"What does that mean?"

He didn't say anything, decided to take a chance and speed up the car a little. We drove for a long time in silence. He resisted my prompts.

Finally, the car stopped and I climbed out. I was on a residential street off the Holloway Road. Outside Helen Ivory's house. I gave my crazy driver a five-spot. He tipped his cap.

"Do you want me to wait?"

"I don't think that's necessary."

"How about a tip?"

"I've given you enough."

"That's not what I mean. Let me give you a tip. That's your arse and over there is your elbow, try not to confuse the two. No one Ivory touched ever forgot him. He changed people's lives."

He drove slowly off. I knocked on the door, just in time to interrupt Helen Ivory making herself comfortable for her first sitting of the day's Australian soaps.

She shook, a little resentfully, I thought, as I inquired after her health. I didn't mention purloined letters and neither did she. She invited me into the sitting room and we silently observed a half hour of Australian beachside doings. There was one actress, I remember, with a particularly bad skin problem. The volume was off, and all I could hear were Helen's breathing difficulties and the rumble of traffic along Holloway Road and, from somewhere at the top of the house or maybe above it, the steady flapping of wings.

Helen fell asleep just before the end credits, when the dreamy theme tune started to roll. I moved her head away from my shoulder and rested it on an oriental cushion. I crept softly out.

The sound of wings got louder as I went upstairs. I walked past Helen's bedroom (what Ivory called her "green-dead room"), past the door to the mock-up of the doctor's surgical chamber, and up the final flight of stairs to the apartment in the loft. The door was open and someone had been making herself at home. A pile of paperbacks on the table beside a round bowl containing overripe fruit—apples, their skins wrinkling like an old woman's face, oranges beginning to go bad. I went past the bathroom, a trail of opened envelopes beneath my feet, stood at the closed door to the bedroom, the sounds coming out, no human noises these, a loud feathered brush and powerful wings flapping, sounded like a childhood night-time monster come to life. I tried the door. The door was locked. I went over into the living room. Tall windows at the end, behind a round table. A battered brown briefcase open and empty in the corner. The walls all cream-colored, prime for defacing with lipstick, hieroglyphs, slogans of abuse. Luggage, still slapped over with airport security stickers, filled the sofa.

When you came out of your bedroom with an empty china bowl in your hands you didn't notice me there. You were wearing a gold-colored scarf and a long brown coat with fur around the collar. I heard you in the kitchen pouring milk into the bowl and when you went back into your bedroom you didn't lock the door behind you.

I followed you in. A weird sight. You laying down that china bowl on the floor beside your bed. The crippled bird, soft brown feathers on its wings and back, blue thin neck, looked like a pheasant or a partridge, one wing pumping like a piston, the other brokenly hanging, its tail brushing frantically and uselessly from side to side against the wood floor. You with one hand at the back of the bird's neck trying to push it down, coax it down to the bowl of milk. Underneath the fur-collared coat was a saucy '60s dress. Polka dots. You were wearing heavy eyeliner—Carnaby Street, acid dreams.

"How's it going?"

"Tierney!"

The bird, startled, tried to fly, and dashed its beak against the wall. You grabbed it around the neck, started to soothe it with your other hand stroking along its back, but then you looked at me and your hands pulled quickly away from the damaged bird like you were touching something hot. It took its chance and went for the half-opened door. I kicked it shut and the bird scuttled away down beneath the bed.

"Bird goes pretty fast. What do you call it?"

"Don't be absurd. It's not a pet. I hit it in the car—it jumped up in front of me—I was in a park. I didn't know what to do with it."

"A lot of people would have just left it there."

"I was going to."

"Doesn't like milk, huh?"

"The milk just happened to be here. I wouldn't have bothered especially. What are you doing here?"

"You were late so I came to find you."

"I was delayed."

"Playing Florence Nightingale to a partridge."

"It's a peahen—and don't get the wrong idea, I wasn't looking after it. How did you get in? Did she let you in? How did you find me here?"

"I've been here once before. You sent me, remember?"

You nodded. That meant the subject bored you. I saw your eyes looking for the bird beneath the bed and I saw your eyes looking quickly back to me when you thought you were being observed.

"Your mother's a fine old lady. I guess she had something to do with your name. Talk to me about your name."

"Don't try to bully me."

"I wasn't. If you circumvent the—"

"Yes, yes. I'm thirsty. Would you like some coffee? Stay in here. Keep the door shut."

You walked through to the kitchenette. I heard you switch on the kettle. You called out to me. "I can hear you perfectly well in here. Talk."

I talked. Ignored the beating-wing sound of the peahen hiding out beneath the bed. I told you about the tragedy of the Boston Red Sox. I told you about 1949 and 1967 and 1972 and '75 and '78, and 1986, when lame Bill Buckner broke all our hearts, again, when he allowed that dribbling ground ball to dribble through his legs. I kept my voice raised while you were in the kitchen and lowered it after you came back out with the coffeepot and a pair of espresso cups on a tray.

"So what are you planning to do with this bird?"

"Forget it. It doesn't matter. I'm sorry I was rude to you last night."

"I can take it."

That displeased you a little, didn't it? An apology sincerely offered merited something less breezy.

"I shouldn't have been rude."

"Fuck rudeness. I just want you to tell me stuff. After I was through reading Miss P——, you know, the library virgin—"

"How many others have you found?"

"Who? What others?"

You smiled. Proud in your knowledge or rather my lack of it.

"He used to call them the Sisterhood—the Sisterhood of Holy Virgins. There were others, not just the library one, he had other women too, my proud f-father—isn't that what the obituary said?—but he specialized in virgins. Isn't that noble and kinky? What would you say about that, Tierney? What would be your words for it? Lonely women crazed with repression ripe for the deflowering touch of the nastiest man."

"He rescued her."

"He fucked them."

"I didn't know there were others. I should have worked it out. There were clues. But all the same he gave them what they needed. What they wanted."

"It was corruption, pure desire for corruption. Finding something to break and ruin. Prove his manhood by taking the most miserable untouched women and ramming it home to them. His poison."

"I love it when you talk dirty."

"Don't try to be smooth. You're not a smooth man."

I went to the bathroom. I had heard the soft click of the cassette reaching its end. The shelves which had been empty when I visited before were now full of shit, overfull. Jars, bottles, canisters, squeezy tubes of makeup goo. Blushers, mascaras, eyeliners, lipsticks, rows and rows of them, eye shadows (I checked for one called Midnight Blue, and found it), skin creams, foundation creams, nail varnishes, the whole range from black to clear, with a real racy one called Scarlet O'Hara in the middle, creams to get rid of unwanted hair, shampoos to refresh tired hair. It was a regular beauty parlor in there. I switched over the tape behind a locked door with the crapper flushing. I didn't want you to know everything you said was being recorded. Long days, long nights of solitary transcription were to come. Your mother's voice, Julian Brougham Calder's, Nick Wheel's, Miss P——'s; the voice of Gibbs, Nanny Brennan, Judge Anthony Brougham-Calder and his wife Jane and all their blond healthy tribe; your brother Matthew, yourself. I have heard your voice in so many ways—speeded up to get through parts I didn't want to hear, slowed down to allow me to get down all the words—your voice disappointed, furious, shrunken, sad, and, most often, level and controlled, slightly husky, like a BBC announcer talking about the trite things which hide large secrets. I would like it if you talked now.

The bedroom was quiet when I came back in.

"What happened to the bird?"

"What are you doing here, Tierney?"

"I was considering asking you the same question. You're kind of unprofessional for a publisher, isn't it like politics or something? Don't you have to declare an interest?"

You shrugged. "Everyone does what interests them. I suppose it was convenient."

"But it's not just the book, that's not the main point to this. What's in it for you?"

You answered, after a long wait. The longest wait. No bird sounds to distract us, just the soothing rumble of traffic off on the main road. And when you finally spoke you said each word so carefully like what you were saying might be about to hurt you.

"Just tell me how he died. That's all I want to know. Forget about the book if you like, it would probably be for the best if you did. Don't worry about the money, you'll get the money, I'll arrange it. Just drop it all, forget about it all, just find out how he died and tell me how he died and you'll get your reward and I'll be glad."

Silently, Ma Ivory had materialized at the entrance to the room. I don't know how long she'd been out there. How much she'd heard. She looked at me like she'd never seen me before, shaking the while, wrinkled head on so easily breakable a neck.

"I'm sorry to disturb. You two lovebirds. I'm making. Tea down below. Would your friend care. For some. Deborah?"

Veneration for age. We walked slowly down the flights of stairs, followed the old woman's shaky gait with tiny muscle-aching steps of our own. Down below, we took our seats in the living room in a semicircle around a TV transmitting the silent opening titles of some old interview program from the early '70s. Helen switched off the VCR and sloshed tea around for us to take. The tea was weak and cold, the sides of the cups sedimented with the stains of generations of cold and weak tea forefathers. Helen twitched an admonishing finger toward her daughter. I tried to see a family resemblance. I tried to imagine you inside a wrinkled decaying body. I tried to remember photographs of the old woman when her skin was smooth. I found no resemblance.

The old woman finally jerked her words out. "There are many things. Young girls like you do not. Understand. You must learn. Deborah. Not to speak ill of the dead." She made what she probably considered a stern maternal frown, which came over like a mad death-mask grin, placed her empty cup on the arm of the sofa, and switched on a news broadcast and turned the volume way up with the remote-control unit.

You looked toward me. You looked tired and miserable and guilty and I felt ready to forgive you everything.

"I'm still going to write it. No matter. I don't give a shit what you say or what you do."

You allowed me the weakest of cheesy smiles. "That's what I like about you, Tierney. You may not be too bright but you don't give up, do you?" You smiled again. Your embarrassed smile you give when you're about to offer too much. "It's a crummy hotel you're living at. You can stay here if you like." And then, louder, "Can't he, Mother?"

"Of course. Dear," said Helen, without looking away from the TV screen or giving any indication that she knew what she was agreeing to.

You put me in the room you called the surgery. Made a bed for me with hospital sheets in that gleaming dead chamber. Shiny hygienic chrome. White antiseptic floor. I was to be on the narrow medical gurney, brake on, in the center of the room. You brought in a towel and draped it over the back of the doctor's chair by the chrome desk in the corner. You sat on the doctor's chair and I sat on the gurney, feet dangling over the floor, and we waited, each of us, for the other to have something to say. I made some joke and you kind of laughed at it, and then you came over, kissed me on the cheek, and left me to it.

I rejected the patient's robe hanging on the door, too flimsy and revealing, the thought of Ma Ivory's midnight horror if she woke and wandered out into the corridor to find my ass shining in the hallway. I stripped down to my T-shirt and shorts, wandered around my room. I thought of going up to see you but the time wasn't right for that, and I thought about going back to the hotel for my things but I could do that the next day, so I read through brochures from pharmaceutical companies trumpeting new products, and I read printed government-agency advice on how to give up smoking, what to do in the case of aneurysms, of ingesting poisons, of electric shock, of choking. I went to the mirrored medicine cabinet on the wall and considered the pills, then shut it again and switched off the light and returned, feeling my way to protect my shins, to my revolving bed. I wrapped my unwashed body, probably riddled with lively germs, inside hospital sheets. In the house it was dead quiet. Not even a bird flapping its broken wing. Helen was probably in the room next to me but she betrayed no sounds of life. You were probably up above me in the upstairs apartment, or maybe you'd sneaked out of the house for some midnight rendezvous trying to make a deal for a book. There was a little gap between the roll blinds and the window, and over against the side wall, between the doctor's desk and the drug cabinet, the two oxygen tanks shone out with a creepy lifeless light. I shut my eyes to that. I wondered if Helen would interrupt my night with a quick sortie for O_2 or pills. Tried not to think about that. There were noises from the neighbors' house next door. The low sounds of people talking, maybe arguing. I listened to those, held on to those, and tried not to indulge my imagination in a twisted haunted house Frau and Fräulein Frankenstein vivisectionist fantasy— to wake in the middle of the night wearing the broken wings and grafted-on feathers of a car-accident peahen—tried not to wonder what the fuck I was doing here.

3 July 1973

Dear Helen,

Gaspard hates my cigars. The metal teeth click of the
clippers you bought for me is sufficient to drive him into a
woeful slink out of the door. He misses the Gauloises and so
do I: nevertheless the olfactory sensibility of an intelligent
dog must take second place to the so-called medical opinion
of a pretentious saw-bones. Gaspard will have to learn
tolerance of new habits yet it troubles me to see the animal
so pained. They hate change, these domestics, and as
Gaspard gets cranky-old it becomes ever harder to inflict
hardship on the beast.

Are the children scrubbed and washed and packed and
ready for their visit? I trust you have managed to drive some
grace into their awkward bodies. I have an expedition
planned to the sand dunes of Holkham Bay. An obliging
friend of my acquaintance is willing to put up with them so
you need have no concern over their safety. Be sure to
include some swimwear in their luggage.

My friend is a new type for me. You would like her I am
sure. Lizzie is sullied by experience yet untouched by it. A
stain on the outside which does not affect the centre. She
has a curious passion for photography: a pathological need
to preserve moments in two-dimensional keepsakes. Another
sign, I tell her, of her essential dishonesty and fear. She
laughs and shows herself to be quite a beauty. She reminds
me a little of you when you were younger.

Please keep an eye on Reiko. She pines and mewls like an
abandoned cat.

W.

I woke up stiff and hungry. (Take that whichever way you
want.) Downstairs in the kitchen—bare feet cautious for the
fishtails and heads beached along the lino floor—a pot of cool
coffee, pieces of dry toast side by side in a silver rack, pots of

unlabeled jelly and marmalade (do people actually *like* that evil bitter stuff?). The scene presided over by an attentive Ma Ivory. You were gone. Destination unknown.

"It is nice to have a man around. The house again. More marmalade? Coffee?"

"Coffee. Please."

"Deborah neglected to tell me which. Morning paper you take."

"I only ever read the sports. Any one will do."

"Was your sleep comfortable?"

"Comfortable enough. Where is Deborah?"

"She left before you woke up. She's always been a girl for secrets."

We bantered pretty soundly for a while and then, when I brought up the subject of her dead husband, your alive father, Helen told me not to worry about the washing-up and went back upstairs to her room with a couple of religious pamphlets.

I waited for you downstairs for a while, then I went back to the surgery room. Locked the door behind me. Pulled out my Ivory file. Spread out the papers on the doctor's rolltop desk.

29 September 1973

Dearest Helen,

I have told you about them before, I shall tell you about them again. The skin of the holy virgins, the glow of their cheeks, when decay and repression and passionless purity evince a superior beauty to the accidental lustre of youth. These suburban saints with supermarket trolleys and library tickets in the place of religious relics: these cul-de-sac madonnas in second-hand dresses, the Home Service played on trashy transistor radios sounds their church bells; their scamp cats form the congregation, worshippers and priests both at the milk dish teat of the Virgin.

And Lizzie too. Naked and self-abasing, the same low

purity shines through her flagellant flesh. We achieved transference early; she dreamed sex-dreams of me after our third session. Now we have passed on to that second stage when hatred for me reveals her utter dependence. She affects to despise me for what she perceives as my vanity. Like any patient mad with ego she is unaware of <u>difference</u>: to her light addled brain everyone in the world is guilty of the same crimes; motives, patterns, all are the mug-book of the same exposed universal criminal: herself. How can I tell her what only you understand? I can not. How can I show her what you know about me, what makes you so all-precious to me? I can not. It is outside the realm of doctor-patient. It is foreign entirely to any of the dark lively things she and I make each other perform at night in our reckless need for a dangerous truth. It is why you and I, dear wife, are and will be for ever married.

She caught me, foolish alert girl, confronting my image on a TV studio monitor. BBC 2, Friday, 10.15, that is when the transmission goes out. You might be interested to watch it. Owing to the eccentric placement of one of the cameras, the monitor image had captured the back of my head. You understand, don't you? That hideous hair-hole of exposed naked scalp: shiny mortality demon, revolting and factual. It is enough to see it on the head of another (why don't these dying men wear hats?), just the chance sight of a balding head is sufficient to induce nausea. Lizzie caught my wince as I saw my own: that grinning hole of decay tantamount to death.

Sometimes the effect of such a moment drives me to charity. I did some good subsequent deeds with mad children and Lizzie dropped her tatty cloak of pretended hatred, and in room number 244 of a smart hotel in Notting Hill she decided I was a saint of some peculiar dirty church of entirely her own denomination. She is a foolish girl but an exciting one.

You can inform DB that her friend will soon be dead. She may come up to witness the truth of it. She will take the opportunity, no doubt. It will allow her the possibility of saving him, and when she fails she will no doubt blame herself. It will provide a harsh necessary lesson.

Your loving husband,
W.

I'd seen a photo of Gaspard at the beginning, the second picture of Ivory, hair lifting in a sudden breeze, smoking an untipped cigarette, his dog, that purebred German shepherd, handsome snout, ears cocked, intelligent eyes fixed on his master, smooth coat, black and white, a testament to good diet and careful grooming. And you loved that dog, didn't you? More than anything. Those childhood summers beside the north Norfolk coast, huge flat threatening sky, your brother already diffident and weak and cruel, a pale dilution of his father, those mad women, strung out with thwarted bodily yearnings, the house itself, cold unless company was expected, an inadequate shelter. Time was always too much on your hands. You read books. You hid as much as possible from the strange hard touch of your father—his sudden intimacy turning always to bullying: *Never cry in public. That'll teach you never to trust anybody.* Or *Shut up!* when you momentarily betrayed yourself with enthusiasm. His strong fingers tickling you in the horsehair armchair in the Little Room, tickling you beyond fun, beyond pleasure, just a tyrannical subjection to the poking hard movements of his fingers, which keep on going until your laughter has long since faded, until you have long since been unable to breathe comfortably, until you are crying and screaming and begging release from the torture of his touch. And then there was the D.B. itself, but we'll come to that later.

And what was your way through all this? Silence. Stillness. Keep your feelings hidden behind a perfect meaningless mask. Learn an acceptable smile that will pass for response. Sometimes stand perfectly still in the courtyard of the house. Just stay there, a statue, feel nothing, not even the salty wind coming in from the coast, hear nothing, not even your brother's taunts or your father's shouted orders, be nothing, not even yourself. And in this world, where everything was threat and danger, you had one ally, one friend on whose love you could count, a dog, Gaspard.

You loved Gaspard and you know he loved you too. You looked forward to his company—sometimes, even, looked forward to going to Norfolk because Gassie would be there. Intelligent and strong and gentle and fast; whenever your father permitted it you'd take the dog out for a walk, proud as you went through the village together, no need to use a leash, you could trust Gaspard not to let you down. Sometimes you'd go out as far as the sands, run into the sea, throw a stick far into the water, watch Gaspard paddle out after it. Or in colder weather, with a frisbee which was sent to you one Christmas by one of your mother's American cousins. Play with that out in the field behind the house and when you were both tired and happy, just lie together in that cold field, hugging each other for company and warmth, and watch the light of the fire flickering out a warning through the window of the dining room, with the dog's breath hot and tangy and reassuring on your face.

Sometimes, if he didn't have one of his strange cranky women with him, he wouldn't let you take the dog out at all and Gaspard would look at you regretfully but obey his first loyalty and respond to Ivory's shrill whistle. And then you would be alone in the house, with that big flat sky outside, with two of your father's sweaters on to keep yourself warm, with your brother there beside you and that was no company at all.

And when Gaspard got older and slower and a little deaf and sometimes forgetful you didn't mind. He never forgot you no matter how long a time had passed since your last visit there. The luster had passed from his coat and some of the shiny intelligence had gone from his eyes and sometimes he'd give you a little warning nip with his teeth if you stroked him in a place that hurt, but those things they didn't matter at all.

What mattered was how Ivory treated the dog. Ivory didn't like it when things wore out. He hated it. He threw out hats when they started to show their age. He dropped friends when they displayed the droop and waste of bodily ruin. And when

Gaspard drifted into old age Ivory started to ignore the dog just like he often ignored you, and Gaspard would slink miserably around the house looking for the comfort of your lap to rest his head on. Before, no matter how much you hated your father, no matter how much he filled you with dread and worry and tears—matched occasionally by a wild hope and a sudden outburst of love and pride and a promise spoken out loud of the woman you would become—you'd had no argument with his way of treating Gaspard. He groomed him carefully, he walked him diligently, he showed him the proper respect and demonstrated, if only to him, a fitting affection. But now that was gone. He shouted at Gaspard when the dog didn't heed his meaningful whistle. You even saw him once kick the dog on their way out of the house when Gaspard expressed a sullen discontent against going out for a walk. How old were you then? Something like eleven, a little younger than the decaying dog.

It was the summer of '73. Miss P——, her hymen broken, had been abandoned not long before and the seducer Ivory was probably sated for the moment. Your school vacation: you and Mattie (his reefer supplies hidden in his Liberty washbag) took the train out from Liverpool Street Station and your decadent father, the sudden literary celebrity—TV interviews which your school friends would see and newspaper profiles which Helen would cut out and paste into a scrapbook with stiff leather covers, which gave you a feeling of unavoidable pride mixed in with some kind of horror—he was there at Norwich Station to meet you. Gaspard was sleeping in the back of the Jag and you cuddled in next to him. Matthew in the front passenger seat, pompous and stoned, got into some debate with his father which he quickly was about to lose, but Ivory kept it spinning out, probably thought it was good training, and that gave you more uninterrupted time with the dog. You hadn't seen Gaspard since just after Christmas and he'd got worse, older, more unsteady—more unreliable, Ivory would have said. But he woke and he saw you and he gave a little whine of recognition and nudged toward you for you to wrap yourself around him, and the drive out to the cottage was an easy one.

The visit followed its accustomed pattern. A polite supper that first evening, when uninterested queries about your lives would at some point be interrupted by an asthma attack of your father's, and there'd be the moment of horror when no one knew where his inhaler was. But then it'd be found and he'd puff on it to open his lungs, and then he would play something on the piano while you were doing the dishes and you liked that. (You still do, don't you? You're a sucker for a man beating out a melody on a piano.) The next morning you drove into Norwich and Ivory bought you and your brother your ugly winter outfits at Jarrolds which you were never going to wear, which your mother would end up giving away to one of her charities, and then you walked around the market square and on the way back to the car Ivory pointed out the place where his father had once had his shop. You always took that same walk on your first day and Ivory always pointed out his father's shop. And that time, that first trip out to the market, would always be fun; and you and your father would kind of flirt with each other and he'd take you by the hand and call you his sweetest girl and despite everything that would make you feel glamorous and proud. Then back to the house, where there would be some kind of fight and either you or your brother would be made to cry.

And the second day, always on the second day, the jaunt out to Holkham Bay. Your mother had forced new swimwear on you especially for the occasion and you hated the powder-blue bikini you'd been made to buy. (Matthew, I guess, was probably in tight black Italian-style briefs—nowhere for him to hide his drugs or his abrupt objectless schoolboy erections, and that would make the fourteen-year-old kind of mean.) The drive out from the village, not far to go, but he wouldn't let you sit in the back with Gaspard, he told you to sit up front. And you sat in your jeans and shirt with your bikini already on beneath, just the touch of it made you feel awkward and awry, and the word that you all would use, the *atmosphere*, was starting to get bad.

Holkham Bay is beautiful. Wild open sea, miles of sand and running hills of dunes. He'd drive as close to the beach as he was able and you'd run out, you and Gaspard, followed by

Matthew aiming for a cool manly stroll in his thin legs, briefs, and sweatshirt, Ivory bringing up the rear. And you'd pull off your clothes and go straight for the water to avoid any comments of your father's while he watched you get undressed, and Gaspard would gallop in and join you there. You were a strong swimmer, you loved the water, and you pretended you were a mermaid and Gaspard the sailor hero you'd sung your sweet song to to drive his ship onto the rocks. And for the moment all would be well.

No one can really remember whose idea it was. You blame yourself, Matthew would probably be willing to take the credit but Ivory blamed you, and you at the time, to your misery and your shame which you will never get over, you blamed the dog.

What moment made it? You were in the water with aging Gaspard. Ivory was sitting on a deck chair in a pair of shorts and a sports shirt and sunglasses and panama hat. He'd have been reading a book, some precious French or Japanese edition protected with plastic covers from the sun and sand. Matthew would have been lying on the sand beside his father, skinny arms straight beside him (arms which Ivory despised his son for) and maybe imitating the rise and fall of his father's belly with every asthmatic breath, while at the same time plotting schemes of perfect domestic murder.

Ivory gets up and carefully places his book on the deck chair. He takes a step toward the seafront. He cups his hands around his mouth and blows a shrill calling whistle to Gaspard. He arches his back and repeats the call, the sound piercing low across the water. Gaspard flinches, lurches away from your hands, starts to paddle clumsily to the shore. Ivory draws himself up to his full height and whistles again, muttering something I imagine about wretchedness and brutes. At the same time, sly Matthew catches sight of the white inhaler dropping out of his father's shallow shorts pocket and onto the sand. Sly Matthew might even have slyly kicked over a little sand to hide the inhaler where it lay. Gaspard struggled clear from the water and you came reluctantly after. Ivory would have yelled some admonition to you about keeping the old dog in the sea for so long. And you have to admit that Gaspard is exhausted. The effort of playing hero to your mermaid takes too much out of the dog. He feebly shakes some of the sea out of his coat and stumbles over to his master. Ivory would have looked at him a little disgustedly, this dying dog, his imperfect companion.

Ivory pulls the dog over by its collar to the shade of the deck chair. He rubs the dog down with a red-and-white-striped towel. Both of them, master and beast, are breathing heavily. A thin yellow line of shit curls slowly out of Gaspard and stains the sand where he is lying. Gaspard looks at you sadly, the indignity of it all, and then looks over at Ivory and blinks. Ivory calls you irresponsible without even bothering to look at you, and puts his hand in his left pocket. He takes it out. He puts his hand in his right pocket. Matthew keeps his eyes fixed on his father the whole time. Ivory feels in his pockets again. He looks at the deck chair. He picks up his book and looks underneath it. He's breathing heavily. *I have to go to the car*, he says. *Try not to act like children.* Matthew turns his head to watch his father clamber over the dunes on his slow way to the hidden road. When Ivory is gone, your brother pushes away a little hill of sand with his foot to show you the inhaler lying there.

You look at each other, brother and sister, accustomed enemies but allies in this particular war. You experience a moment of horror which is usurped by dry resolve. You have one of those white plastic inhalers too, it represents oxygen of the future, you know the rush of panic when yours is misplaced, the way you can't struggle any air in or out of your lungs. You look at Gaspard, at the willing dying dog ignorantly living on just for his master's anger at being betrayed by sickliness. For Gaspard, you think, and for Mother, and for me, and even for Matthew, and for all those funny cranky ladies, who even then you felt a stripe of raw pity for. You and your brother smile sternly at each other and both of you stand up and crane your necks to try to look over the sand dunes and the trees at the road behind. You imagine your father kneeling on the passenger seat of the Jaguar, rummaging through the glove compartment, looking under the seat, staring blindly through the windshield to try to remember when he last saw his gasper, as he calls it. You kick some of the disturbed sand back over it, hiding some of the white plastic under the fine grains, which are almost white themselves, closer to white than yellow. A bird flashes up above your head from the sanctuary just along the coastline and that makes you start but it doesn't bother Matthew. He kicks some more sand over it and suddenly you're both on your hands and knees shoveling sand over the gasper, and when it's hidden far from anyone's sight, even your father's, you press the surface flat with the palms of your hands and then you kick some loose sand on top so it won't look too much like a newly dug grave.

When it's done, the crime, you and your brother fix yourselves into what you suppose are relaxed postures and while you wait for your father to return you pick up stiff handfuls of sand and pour them over your ankles and you almost allow yourself to enjoy the sensation. He's on his way back. He's moving fast. He's striding like a soldier up above the dunes. He half runs, half slides toward you, and you watch the way the wind catches the loose flap of his sports shirt and lifts it to expose his flat hairless belly.

Who has seen it? he calls out, looking at each of you in turn for the inadvertent sign that will give you away. You shake your head in feigned puzzlement. Matthew makes his eyes round and asks what he's looking for and you want to shout at your brother to stop. He's overdoing it for sure. *My gasper!* he shouts, *you brats!* And Gaspard struggles dutifully up to his feet. He mistakes this for the call of his name and limps painfully toward his master. Ivory pushes the dog away with his foot and Gaspard pushes back toward him. He doesn't know quite what's required of him but he's never shirked his duty yet. And Ivory kicks the dog this time and that makes you almost gasp yourself but you hold that down, you don't dare to reveal anything of what's inside. And Gaspard stubbornly holds his weight where it is and lurches back into the shins of his master and that makes Ivory lose his angry balance and he falls easily to the sand and that makes both you and your brother laugh, despite yourselves. *Shut up!* he yells, a weak airless yell, and he scrabbles back to his feet, and in doing so he disturbs the inhaler's burial plot and a flash of artificial white is exposed in the damp sand. *Where is it, girl?* You try not to look at it and you try not to look away either, but Matthew isn't as good a dissembler as you and he looks ostentatiously away and Ivory catches this. He follows his son's gaze and then looks back at what his son is looking away from, and there it is, he sees it, and he drops to his knees to yank it out of the sand and he impatiently shakes the loose sand away and he shoves the capsule into the slider and he puts it to his mouth and breathes heavily, once, twice, three times—and then he pushes down on the thing with his thumb to release the foul spray down his harsh constricted throat.

There's a long silent moment after that. A king in his outdoor court. A sandlot executioner's pyre. An al fresco hanging judge. You're guilty. You always have been in the eyes of this man. Apart from a few charmed moments when you were anointed his sweetest girl, when he declared you a beauty and a brain both, you have always been guilty of falling away from perfection. You look at Gaspard. He's still confused, still waiting to be told what part he is to play. You look at Matthew, skinny and fearful and exposed out in the sunlight in his too-short briefs and too-narrow chest. And then you say it, those hateful words—*I think it must have been the dog, he must have buried it.* And you feel yourself flushing and you look away with poorly disguised hope out to the sea which is the one thing in that harsh bright day that is capable of swallowing you whole.

We, says your father, smiling now in full hard control, *will have to think what we will have to do.* Then he leans down to pat poor Gaspard, who is finally relieved by his master's touch and settles back into the sand.

The necessary punishment hung over your heads for the rest of your summer stay. It was never spoken of but it hung there, waiting for you when you were least expecting it, like the shadow killer that haunted you when you were younger. A woman came to stay for a while, different from the usual sort.

She was a little wild in her habits and often nude, and she paid you a strange kind of distracted attention which made you feel as if she was looking at herself when she was looking at you, and you fell half in love with her.

The punishment finally came some months later. Your mother told you of the sentence and said your father had asked for you to be sent up to the Norwich surgery to witness it. Gaspard would like it, he had said. So you went, wearing black, not entirely sure what was to happen. You stood in the waiting room holding on to Gaspard who didn't know why he was there but still had the smarts to sense that something bad and irrevocable was in the air. He never did like veterinarians. You tried inadequately to comfort him but it wasn't much use because Gaspard could feel through your hands the misery and the shame. And you listened to your father talking to the animal doctor next door, and his voice was unnaturally loud and it took a moment for you to realize that it was staged so for your benefit. *He is weak*, says your father, *and confused and incontinent and he's becoming deaf and, what's worse, unreliable. I think*, says your father, *this is the only way forward.* The doctor didn't know this was a performance for you so he didn't trouble to speak loud enough for you to hear, and then you heard your father say, *My mind is made up. I will miss him but I think it would be best for all.* And then he called your name, *Deborah!*, and you ran out of the surgery leaving them all far behind. You ran eleven-year-old teary steps through suburban Norwich streets and you tried not to think of Gaspard's closed eyes and you tried not to think of your father and all you could think of as you ran until the breath hurt the inside of you and you crumpled to your knees in a tree-lined corner of a municipal park was that it was all your fault and there was something you had done to make your favorite thing die.

I thought the surgery was for Parkinsonian Helen. It wasn't. It was for her once and future husband. He visited it often. That's when you would see him—after you stopped going to Norfolk—a shadow glimpse of your father entering the room and locking the door behind. Or you'd catch him head on and that would take you always by surprise, handsome Ivory sarcastically tipping his hat to you in the hall, his mouth clamped shut to hide his dentures, or you would see him from below as he stopped to have a word with Reiko hoovering the stairs, or you would see him in the kitchen making himself coffee from the cafetière Helen allowed no one else to use, or in the living room sipping brandy and chatting to his ex-wife, your mother. And sometimes you would see him parking his Jaguar and approaching the house, and at first you would never acknowledge him. But sometimes, you would crouch outside and put your eye to the keyhole of the surgery door and watch him inside there for hours.

He treated himself for illnesses real and imagined. He sucked oxygen from the tanks by the side. He wrote himself prescriptions from the pad in the doctor's bag. He brewed concoctions of pills from the cabinet on the wall. He injected himself with adrenaline to help him breathe. He took afternoon catnaps on the surgical trolley before returning to West Hampstead and then back to Norfolk. He might have been there the morning of the day he died.

In 1962 Ivory suffered from bad gum disease. He wrote about it in impressive technical detail to Helen.

1 September 1962

Dear Helen,

The latest entry in William Ivory's catalogue of ruin. The quack Maitland calls it periodontal disease. He's probably right for once. I prefer the more traditional term pyorrhoea but that's fallen out of use. It's a condition fraught with danger. The periodontal membrane is already thoroughly damaged with calculus. And when the disease finishes its gruesome glut on the periodontal membrane its swollen appetite will turn lustily to the supporting jawbone. Maitland assures me that hasn't happened yet but warns me that it is likely to. As it stands, my teeth are loose and the swollen gums bleed at the drop of a hat. In the library the other day I presented a ludicrous figure with my handkerchief up to cover my mouth as blood dripped from around my upper front teeth. The condition presents the likelihood of awkward social moments but far worse than that is the worry of the injection of micro-organisms following trauma on the gingival margins. As you know, my heart valves were not undamaged by the rheumatic fever I had as a boy. The inadvertent chewing on damaged teeth releases bacteria into the bloodstream and there is the consequent danger of further damage to my weak pumping heart. The quack advises immediate removal of all teeth bar the back molars. It seems I have no choice. Ivory will shortly have a mouth of gleaming synthetic ivory choppers. Will you still want to kiss that mouth?

Gloomily,
Your Will

PS I am glad to be finally free of your grateful vampiric friend but your old paramour Anthony Brougham-Calder has blackballed me from the Reform Club. What do you think to that?

PPS I enclose something for the girl.

I woke up in the night, a liquid circle around the base of my cock. Either it was leaking through disuse or a mouth had been around it. Yours? The white puckered lips of Helen Ivory? Or was it a lovelorn succubus searching for Ivory, her dead, hypochondriac paramour?

Struggled to go back to sleep. The oxygen tanks were eerie in the night light. Bulbous malevolent spirits in perfect repose, watching me impatiently. Somewhere in the house, maybe next door, there was a scratching noise like a rodent at play. I missed the reassurance of Pimlico, the certainty of hustlers and hookers outside, the buffoon Australian inside. I didn't know how long I was going to be here for. I didn't even know what I was really here for. To write a book? To be in a convenient place for female Ivory supervision? (And how much in cahoots were you anyway?) To fuck you? To discover the truth of your name? To find out how Ivory died? You can laugh at me now if you want. You can giggle comfortable schoolgirl abuse and throw lies and laughter in my face. But this was a fairy tale and you were the heroine and he was the monster and I was some kind of a hero.

I wrapped myself in a towel and went downstairs to the kitchenette. Ma Ivory had beaten me to it. Her body was somewhere inside a loose kimono and she was sitting at the table and jerking pieces of toast smeared with soft cheese into her face. She saw me come in and there was no running away. I sat down at the table and tried a smile. I told her I was having trouble sleeping. This made her happy.

"I call these the empty hours." She casually dropped some dry crusts of toast to the floor. "Have you read my husband's history book? He writes of mad Ludwig. You know, Ludwig the Second of. Bavaria, the Swan King. Ludwig had an Aunt Alexandra who was convinced that she had swallowed a grand piano made. Of glass. Imagine the trouble this caused her. The difficulties of eating. Or of walking through narrow doorways. Poor lady, I presume the strain must have been. Intolerable. The fear of damaging it. Of feeling it break inside her. Imagine you had a grand piano made of glass. Inside you. Imagine it broken. Imagine the pain."

"Nasty."

"Are you hungry? No? I had not intended to talk of Ludwig's aunt. I had meant us to talk of Ludwig. Himself. The mad innocent living in a fragile. Perfect world. You know of course that he slept during the day. Night was his time for life and. Imagination, which my husband points out. Comes to much the same thing. Ludwig would take his travels at night. Mount his favorite horse and ride it. Furiously around the grounds. Of the court riding school. Around and around. Dreaming himself a traveler. He knew the dimensions of the grounds by heart. He would calculate the distance traveled as if he was on a straight road in the world. Outside. Break his journey at an appropriate point. Return to his room. Tired. Joyful. To travel hopefully is better than to arrive. Who said that? Write in his journal—Today I left Cologne. Am halfway to Leipzig. Will continue my journey tomorrow. Are you sure you are not hungry?"

"Yes." Trying to work out the point of this. Or was it entirely without meaning altogether?

"You have read my husband's book?"

"*Decadent Pleasures*? Most of it."

"And what is your opinion. Of it?"

Steady now. Give her what she wants. "I think it's a masterpiece."

"Yes. Of course it is. Is that all you can say? I expect that's all anyone can say. He was a genius, you know. Of course. In so many ways. You are going to give him his due. What else have you read of my husband's work?"

This was the point. You bastard, she was saying. You scheming colonial cunt. You stole my fucking letters. All I have of my monstrous loved man.

But it wasn't the point. She was getting at something else entirely. Casually, she inquired, "Have you come across. His *Last Things*?"

And in you came. As if you were waiting for the cue. And at first I was relieved that you were here, to break it up. Second opinion, you were breaking something up that was about to go somewhere. Get through any difficult parts and we were about to talk about him truly in a way she'd forbidden me before. All I had to do was keep courteous, to answer her pride with admiration, and I was into nighttime truth. But no. In you came, saying you'd heard voices. You were in blue silk pajama pants and a loose man's undershirt and you walked around the kitchen in a distracted almost beautiful way, with your hands flat inside the waistband of your pants and showing me your breasts through the armhole of the undershirt, and you smiled at your mother and you walked behind her around the table and absentmindedly you pulled one hand out of your pants, a flash of white midriff skin, a curl of hair at your pubic bone, and you smiled again in an absent sort of way and said you were going to have a glass of water, would anyone else want any? And then both hands went to the refrigerator and the water filter inside it and you drank straight from the spout, your shirt riding up to show me your pelvis, your tits against the cotton to show me your nipples, and there was nothing more I was going to learn from Ma Ivory tonight. You replaced the water filter and closed the refrigerator door and announced you were returning to bed, you hoped you could sleep now, and your mother sort of grinned and shook and I probably did the same, and I followed you up the stairs, a few steps behind you, watching the shapes your buttocks made against the blue silk of your trousers, and we went all the way up to your attic flat, and you sat cross-legged on the bed and looked at me in a kind of disappointed fashion. I came over to sit next to you and we kind of wrestled around for a while until you got tired of that and gave me an open-mouthed kiss, just the slightest touch of tongues, and handed me my towel to wrap myself in again, and packed me off back to the surgery again. And I felt like an adolescent again, back in Boston again, when I'd return from a high-school date sometimes with blue balls and go silently into the living room and sit on the sofa beneath a pair of paintings of rain-spattered, vaguely European streets and masturbate into a handkerchief in a joyless, aching-for-relief kind of way. I lay there, on that hospital gurney, and I struggled impotently for sleep, and when the door pushed open and a shape slipped past to enter my medical kingdom I was sure that this was Nurse D.B. come to pay an everything-will-be-okay ministering call. But you were upstairs, foolishly plotting (you never matched your father in blackmail, did you?), and when my eyes adjusted they saw it was Helen. She had a pile of books made from Florentine paper in her hands. She sat down on the doctor's chair. She threw a prescription pad over at me to make sure I was awake and then she spoke in a harsh bird whisper. She was offering me. A deal.

"These are. His. They could be yours."

"What are they?"

"His journals. From childhood. Onwards. They are very precious. They will help you."

"Thank you. I'm very grateful."

"But you must promise two. Things."

I nodded, waited for her to hiss some more.

"There is a book. His *Last Things*. His final. Book. It is lost. You might find it. I would like to own. It."

"It's yours if I get it. And the other thing?"

"Please do not tell Deborah. Of our. Plan. There are reasons. Good reasons. I may. Trust you?"

She waved the journals in the surgical air. I wrapped the hospital sheet around my body and relieved her of her load. She pecked me on the cheek and withdrew. I climbed back on the gurney, listened to your mother settling into her green-dead room next door, and hoped for the return of the succubus with a yen for hypochondriacs.

Y ou told me about your nickname the next morning over the breakfast tray you'd brought in. You surprised me with it, waking me up from fitful dreams spiced with Ivory. A tray of coffee and toast and jars of inedible spreads, you bringing it in like we were married or maybe just because you were sorry for something. You laid it on top of a carton of syringes and watched me while I ate. We didn't talk about what had happened in the night. You didn't seem to want to talk at all. I asked you about the *Last Things* and you brushed it scornfully away. You said it was a myth, a book that didn't exist at all except in the gullible imaginations of some dying people.

I was on my second cup of coffee and on my third cigarette (making you wince by using a surgical tray for my ashes) when words suddenly began to pour from your mouth and your face looked sort of surprised to feel it happen.

"My brother started it," you said. "He's coming over in a day or two. You'll meet him then. We'll all be having dinner together and that should be cozy—you're not a vegetarian or anything? No, you wouldn't be. It was Matthew's nasty taunt, he made up the word because I was littler than him and that gave him the right to bully me and my breath smelt—my father had cooked us something with garlic in it—he was a great cook. I think I was about six. It was in Norfolk. We were already going up there for our summers. No, I was probably about five. Matthew pointed at me and called me 'Death-Breath.' We were out in the field behind the house and I think one of Ivory's women was out there with us. It was my brother's idea of a joke, and he kept on repeating it, Death-Breath, and Ivory liked that. He called that kind of thing polishing our gifts. He approved of competition to sort out the strong and my brother had learnt that and so had I, and Matthew did it for him as much as he did it out of his own meanness, which he still has—don't be fooled by his manner when you meet him—and Ivory seized on the word like he'd always do if something pleased him. He turned it into mythology. He made it into a creature. He used to tell me stories about it. The Death-Breath."

Told after bathtime in a grand way with hushed voice at first and long breath-held lines, with hands flapping the air to make you feel its invisible malicious presence casing the room like a prince of thieves, then the voice gets louder as the D.B. gets faster, spinning in nearer, rushing past you like a bat just grazing the top of your hair, and now you can almost see it as it settles in the corner that the ceiling and the wall make just over the door, shadows around it as it stares at you, its virgin quarry. It pulls its dark powers around itself with an arrogant shimmy and it waits, silent and poised, a thing of the shadows. You better keep your arms hidden beneath the covers, you know how it hungers for the soft white flesh of your arms, shut your eyes and keep them closed, try to keep your lashes from quivering, you know how it likes it to see you move, you know what will happen if it looks you straight in the eyes, its gaze sucking in yours, and your father's voice is loud now, threatening and tender, he's warning you, he's on your side, and you must rush into sleep because the longer you stay awake, the stronger it grows, and keep your window open, it's cold there in the bedroom and you have asthma like he does and the cold air makes your chest tight, but with the window closed the D.B. has no way to leave—it will stay there presiding over your sleep, waiting for a noise to scare you in the night, to pull you awake, and there is always that horrible chance that you will open your eyes and look into that dark horrible corner and look straight into the eyes of the D.B., and it will spread its dark shadowy wings, so large that the span fills the ceiling above you, and it will strike, so quick and deadly, a nightmare hawk, at you, its waiting shivering open-eyed prey.

You told me about it and I listened to the words pull out of you and the expression on your face as if you didn't like them to go, and when you were done your face was flushed and you were breathing heavily and I climbed out of bed and you didn't hide your attention on me as I started to get dressed.

"Your body is a little fucked, isn't it?"

"I used to be a catcher back in college."

"You look as if you've broken a lot of bones. What's a catcher?"

"Baseball. He's the guy behind the plate. Takes a lot of punishment. You have to be a bit crazy to be a catcher. Some big-leaguer once said, How come I'm the only one on our team looking the other way?"

"Were you good?"

"I was pretty good. Probably no better than minor league. I got my ribs and my feet and my shoulder cracked a few too many times to want to take it up for real. Knees too. All that bending. I can tell when there's going to be rain just from the feeling in my knees."

"Baseball is like rounders, isn't it?"

"That's what I hear. Just a little tougher, is all."

"I used to play rounders at school. I never broke any bones. You must have been careless."

I went to draw the curtains to let some sunlight into our medical confessional. You lifted up a hand to stop me. You asked me to tell you about baseball. It's poetry, I said, all of it. You can tell just by the names. I gave you some names. "Darryl Strawberry," I said, "and Harry Colliflower.
Chet Lemon. Estel Crabtree, Graig Nettles,
Zack Wheat, Garland Buckeye.
Carlton Fisk, he was a catcher, and Thurman Munson too,
died in a plane crash. So did Roberto Clemente,
but that's not such a remarkable name.
What about Minnie Minoso? Harmon Killebrew, Dane Iorg.
Urban Shocker, Urbane Pickering, Chief Bender, Chief
    Yellowhorse, Pig House,
Rabbit Warstler, Chicken Wolf,
Doggie Miller, Nellie Fox, Yogi Berra, Possum Whitted.
How about Enos Slaughter?
(one day I'll tell you about his Mad Dash Home,
another nail in the Red Sox coffin),

Carden Gillenwater, Fielder Jones, Orator Shaffer, Tris
    Speaker,
Socks Seibold, Dolly Stark, Sadie McMahon,
Vinegar Bend Mizelle.
A lot of these guys were pitchers, seems pitchers and catchers
    have the best names.
Rollie Fingers, Luscious Easter,
Elon Hogsett, Virgil Trucks, Chuck Churn,
Vida Blue, Whitey Herzog, Rusty Staub,
Sandy Koufax, Dusty Rhodes, Satchel Paige, Johnny Bench
(he was the greatest catcher of them all).
Flint Rhem, Bibb Falk, Jewel Ens, Wade Boggs, Spec Shea,
Welcome Gaston.
Gaylord Perry, Hod Lisenbee, Orel Hershiser, Randy Ready,
    Bill Wambsganss.
Napoleon Lajoie, Victory Faust, Heinie Manush, Clyde
    Kluttz,
Cletus Elwood Poffenberger."
    You laughed. "They sound like made-up names. Groucho
Marx or W. C. Fields. Would my father have been a catcher?"
    "Ivory? Not dumb enough. He'd have been a pitcher maybe,
sneaky guy with a great curveball, or a contact hitter with an
eye to his average who played it kind of lazy and graceful in
the outfield. Like Ted Williams."
    "Who's Ted Williams?"
    I couldn't tell you the history of baseball. Nor the story of
the Red Sox, Boston's choking finest. Harry Frazee. Johnny
Pesky. Denny Galehouse. Luis Aparicio. Bill Buckner.
    I yanked the curtains open like they were Buckner's guts.
And that did it for you. The sun came in on the surgery and
whatever thoughts you were thinking turned to escape.
    "I'll see you, Tierney." You stood in the doorway, looking
fragile and conceited. "You look a lot like Lee Marvin. Did
anyone ever tell you that?"
    Someone once had but I couldn't remember who and I didn't
know what your feelings were about Lee Marvin.
    "Before you go. It's kind of uncomfortable sleeping and work-
ing both in this room."

"So?"

"I thought, maybe—you've got a lot of space upstairs. There's that big table by the window. The rest of the house is too full of junk."

"I don't care. You can work up there if you like. The door's open."

"I appreciate it. Tell me something. What color were your father's eyes?"

A silence. You closed your own eyes. Opened them again. Green eyes, dark eyes, speckled, or so it seemed in that light, with silver. The same, maybe, as your father's?

"Tierney?"

"Yeah?"

"How did my—he die?"

The things you would tell me, on still summer evenings, while we waited, each of us, for the truth to show.

You were a punk in the mid- and late 1970s, taking it up the ass from a mad boy called Nick Wheel, you were dressed in leathers and plastics that looked like leathers, and tight tartan trousers with safety pins and straps, and torn T-shirts with slogans like *Vive la Rock* and *Boy* and *Anarchy*, and you went to places with exes in their names like The Vortex and The Roxy, and you dyed your hair sometimes yellow, sometimes red, occasionally black, and you snorted any powder that was going, heroin, talc, chalk dust mixed with aspirin, amphetamine sulphate (and sometimes you smoked pot but only if you were with Lizzie Sharp), and you called yourself D.B. and no one but your father knew what that stood for, even your brother had long since forgotten.

We had a punk scene in Boston too, based around a club called The Rat, where college kids with Vaseline in their hair to make it spiky would jump up and down on a dance floor that was wet with beer. I used to go there because I was in love with a girl called Emma who was sister to the DJ there, and sometimes we'd do a spot of French kissing in the alcove behind the stage and sometimes I'd get into fights on account of her because Emma had blond hair and liked to wear fishnet tights and that tended to get the boys sniffing her way.

But your scene was harder than that. You had an upper-class girlfriend with a real street accent called Alex, and Alex was shooting herself up with heroin (what did you call it? Skag?) with her homosexual boyfriend Paul who was the son of a priest and used to cut people's hair in exchange for drugs or sometimes kindness. And you lived on people's floors and sometimes in a squat near to Warren Street, six or eight to a bed, not much sex action, everyone too drunk or stoned or sick to do much with their bodies except try to forget them.

And you were all alone on this. School was behind you, you hardly ever went there. And your family was gone from all this. Slimy Matthew was sunk into drugs too, but in a hippy boring way like all his friends from Westminster public school, with their upper-class accents and their clean long hair and their rolling papers and loose strands of tobacco left around proudly on top of record covers by groups like Yes and Genesis and the Pink Floyd in rooms that smelled sourly of socks that had been masturbated into. And your mother was lost in her ancient passion for your father. He'd long since sucked her money away, and he only ever visited to use the surgery, but he still did write to her, his darkest confessions, sometimes every day. And she buried herself in good church works and loud muttered prayers and found some comfort in the first few symptoms of her disease. And she kept the house just as he would want it for the inevitable time when he would make his full return. She didn't notice anything that was happening with you.

But your father did. He loved it. He broke down your hatred of him for a while and he seduced you all over again. He discovered you one afternoon kneeling in leather punk fetish regalia outside the surgery door, and he took you out to a restaurant in Hampstead and he bought you lunch and you didn't know why, but you let him. He admired what you did with your body, he called it art. You showed him the tattoo of a heart dripping blood you'd had done on your shoulder, and in surprising return he showed you his, a blue Japanese dragon curling fiery around his navel. And he admired your attitude. He called it eschatological. And he didn't patronize you, not at all. You still wouldn't go up ever to see him, you wouldn't do that since Gaspard died, but he came to London to perform his dangerous therapy, and often he'd come to the house and you'd meet as if by chance outside the surgery door, and he'd take you out to tea at Fortnum & Mason, the Fountain Room, and the two of you would talk loudly to spite the bourgeoisie, and he'd give you money for secrets.

You told him stories about your life, your friends, and if he liked the stories, like the one about Alex running out of veins to spike a needle into and having to use her cunt; like Paul injecting himself with hashish oil and watching the dark thread run up for a couple of inches in the vein on his arm and then stopping there, stubbornly blocking it, so he had to be taken to hospital and have the arm cut open and the hashish removed and the vein sewn back together again; or the one about your friend who asked everyone to go to bed with him, regardless of age or gender, but never could get it up, not unless he was doing it up the ass (and you liked the fact that this one was a patient of his), Ivory would reward you generously with a couple of ten-pound notes and you would take the money because there were many uses you and your friends could put it to, and even though you felt the money was tainted with Ivory's touch and soiled with the telling of secrets to an outsider, for the first time in your teenage life you felt a kinship with your father.

What made you stop all this? Was it when the music went soft and bad? Was it because too many of your friends were finding stupid ways to die? Was it just because there were too many other middle-class children going around with jungle clothes and art-school ways? Or was it because Paul threw himself into the Thames one winter night because he'd forgotten his name for the past two days and couldn't think of a new one? (You got forty quid for that story.) You said it was because you just got bored, and I believe that. Your father pulled a few strings and greased a few palms and sent you off to a fancy school. He gave you a credit card and a silver stick of French lipstick to take along and you changed your appearance as well as your name. Dorothy Burton. Has a pleasant pseudonymous sound. Dorothy plucked from The Wizard of Oz, that dog-loving innocent, and Burton for Sir Richard, scandalous Victorian, explorer and translator—Ivory writes about him approvingly in Decadent Pleasures—an English adventurer dressed in Arabian finery or rags trespassing on forbidden cities. Dorothy Burton. D.B. Stands for poison, you'd tell people, and they never knew what you meant.

Something was due to arrive, you wouldn't say what it was. But you were always there at the front door in the morning in your blue pajama pants and man's undershirt, waiting for the mailman to come, and Helen was always there too, shivering in her robe, half hiding in the sitting-room doorway, one trembling hand up to her hopeful face, her eyes fixed on you, watching as the letters pushed through the slot in the door; the sudden change in the expression on your face, hungry now, greedy, as you stepped quickly forward, a schoolchild reaching for her prize, picking up each letter in turn, impatiently throwing aside each one in turn, reaching for a package, then tossing it petulantly aside when you felt its shape was wrong, and then returning slowly back upstairs with your mother's fearful eyes never leaving you.

Matthew Ivory didn't have a mustache. Otherwise he would have been the pale image of his father. Tall weak pretty boy in a nice charcoal-colored suit, nice black boots too, and white shirt with a striped tie in a perfect knot. Nice easy trivial manner. Blue eyes, a little too watery for my taste. And then there was the hair. Matthew had his mother's hair, light brown, kind of crinkly. Silly hair for a man to have.

He smoked thin cigars, didn't offer them around. We sat in the sitting room, TV off, Matthew, Helen, and me. You were in the kitchen preparing dinner. I'd tried to help you set the table in the dining room, cleared for the occasion of Albanian boxes and rows of teapots and piles of back copies of *Psychic News*, but you'd sent me quickly away. So we sat there and tried to make conversation. Matthew smoked his cheroots and lolled in an armchair with one leg across the other and a supercilious smirk holding tight to his face. Helen trembled proudly on the sofa, watching her son the whole time except when he looked her way.

It was difficult to get conversation rolling. I inquired of Matthew what kind of work he did and Matthew inquired of me if I had taken to London. I said I couldn't believe in a city where you couldn't buy liquor after eleven o'clock at night. Matthew lifted one eyebrow and suggested I join a club of some description. There are many of these about, he said. I told him I hadn't been invited to join any and his smirk seemed to suggest that this was the point he was making. I don't drink myself, he said, and batty Helen looked prouder than ever and declared herself so glad.

You came in with a tray of drinks. Whiskey sour for me. Bubbly mineral water for your mother, with a bendy plastic straw in the glass to make it easy to drink. You were wearing a jokey kitchen apron with the words *Kiss The Cook* printed in red on it. Underneath was a black velvet evening dress that made you look more than beautiful. You'd done something to your hair too, something intricate with a clasp and a comb that piled some of it high and left some of it hanging there dark, a little forlorn, I thought. You looked High Victorian or else like a debutante from Helen's coming-out days. You gave something yellow and fizzy to your brother that he took one urbane sip of, and then pushed resentfully away to a far side of the coffee table and pulled out another cigar from his pocket. You said dinner would be a while and retreated to the kitchen. I was still trying to figure out whether small talk was over when your brother decided to tell us a languid ugly anecdote. He slid the cellophane off his next cigar and made a little apologetic smile to indicate that the anecdote he had chosen would be an amusing one.

"I hear they arrested a man today round your neck of the woods. Sacramento I think it was. Where is that? Somewhere West, yes? This chap was a serial killer who'd been murdering old dears for the past seven years. He topped one a year, regular as clockwork, always on the same summer day. The case was a curious one and entirely baffled your 'cops.' One a year, remember that, always the same day, and always in the same primitive, rather grisly way. So imagine it—sweet old lady, maybe a retired schoolteacher, pillar of the community, marvelous with charity work. She'd be in her kitchen baking gingerbread men, or whatever it is that people like that do, and then along would come the mystery intruder—rat-a-tat on her kitchen door—and she'd go along to open it. Yes? I think she'd probably squint at him, apologize, 'I'm sorry, my sight isn't what it was . . . Do I . . . ?' —And phoot! A ladies' hat pin straight through the temple. Just like that, neat, precise, rather nasty, don't you think?

"Apparently, his victims all looked the same, all about the same age. All wore sweet granny specs, all had rosy old-lady complexions, all had a small thin build. No enemies, why should anyone want to kill dear old ladies? You're something of a detective, Tierney—what would you say? You must have

a theory to offer. Something that will get us to the heart of
this? Mother. You're something of an old lady yourself. Can
you imagine yourself a target for a crazed serial killer? Would
someone want to kill you? Can you imagine that? Maybe we
should wait for my sister to come back in, she might have a
brainy idea. No? No takers? No smart theories? No one with
anything to say? Shall I tell you? Yes? Well, interestingly as it
turned out, the ladies were all dead ringers—do forgive the
pun—dead ringers for the fellow's mother-in-law. The murder
date the killer had chosen so sentimentally was the day of his
wedding anniversary to his ex-wife. Seems he blamed the wife's
mother for the breakup. The 'cops' traced him through a
florist's shop. The silly fellow had sent the same wreath of mixed
lilies to the funerals of each of his victims. The same wreath
he'd carried himself at the funeral of his own mother-in-law."

"Yeah? Did he kill her too? Whose was the hat pin?"

"Your father did not. Like flowers."

Matthew jerked up his head and his mother for once kept
her attention locked with his and gave him a severe, benevolent
smile that trembled only slightly.

"He described them somewhere. As useless symbols of necessity. They frightened him rather. The way they all point
the same way. Towards the sun. If he gave flowers ever to a
girl it meant he was finished with her. He never gave *me*
flowers."

"I was not aware this had anything to do with my father."

"Everything you do, darling, has to do with your father. It.
Gladdens me."

"Food is on the table."

I didn't know if your interruption was timely or otherwise.
It allowed Matthew to regain his suavity. It prevented what
might have been a childish outburst from the man-about-town.
I should have liked to see a childish outburst from the man-
about-town.

We took our places at the table. You'd done it up very nice.
A silver candelabrum at the center that looked centuries old,
six green candles, aflame. A vase of blue flowers on either side.
Linen place mats surrounded by silver cutlery. Spinach soup

in black bowls to start us off. It was a long table, made of some dark wood, mahogany I supposed. You'd left the ends empty and put us all toward the middle. I was sitting next to your mother and facing you.

Matthew lifted a spoonful of soup toward his mouth and Helen reached forward to place a warning hand on his arm.

"Please. Allow us this instance."

Matthew watched his soup dribble over each side of the spoon in turn and splash back into the bowl. Helen clasped her hands together and closed her eyes and murmured a series of light whispers that I took to be the saying of grace. She opened her eyes, beamed at her son, and grabbed her spoon like a child would, holding it in a fist.

"Now. Let us enjoy our meal. It looks delicious. You've outdone yourself. Dear."

Matthew yawned and started to eat. You kept your eyes fixed on your bowl. I took a sip and admired your cooking.

Matthew smiled toward me. A false charming smile.

"I believe you are a biographer of some description."

"I don't know what the description is. But yes."

Ma Ivory burst in. "Isn't that marvelous? We have needed a book about him for so long. A testament. To give him his due." She stopped talking in order to retrieve the two parallel lines of soup that were dribbling out of the corners of her mouth and down to her chin.

"Warts and all?" Matthew inquired innocently.

"I'd like to find out everything."

"You see, Mother? Maybe it isn't such a marvelous idea."

"We have. No secrets."

You smiled. Matthew smiled. Helen coughed. I waited.

Nothing. The sound of soup being slurped in three different ways. You were still looking fixedly down. I didn't like the way the presence of your brother diminished you.

"Wonderful soup. Deborah."

"It's called Emerald Green."

"One of his recipes? I believe I rather recognize. It."

"I think it's too bright in here. Tierney, would you mind lowering the lights?"

I got up. Played about with the dimmer switch, felt like the bullet-head in *Sunset Boulevard* as I encouraged the shadows to be a little kinder to Helen.

"And how is. Little Ginny, dear?"

"Little Ginny weighs twelve stone, stuffs her face full of Belgian chocolates most of the time, and we haven't fucked in six months."

"That is too too bad. I had hoped for. A rapprochement. This really is. Good soup. I feel quite greedy over it."

"There's more if you want it."

"You're an awful temptress when you want to be. I really think I ought to leave. Some room. Don't you think?"

"Whatever. Tierney, help me with the dishes."

You went back into the kitchen and I followed after with the soup bowls. Despite your mother's compliments, she had left half of hers.

You pulled a blackened carcass from out of the stove and placed it on a carving dish.

"Don't look at it like that. It's meant to be this color. My brother is horrible, isn't he?"

"He doesn't appear to be a happy individual."

"He used to be a junky until last year. I think I preferred him when he was. Do you think he'll manage to carve this without making some nasty remark? Feel free to say to him whatever you want. You won't get through to him."

"You both act frightened of him."

"It's family loyalty. We're just being nice. Can you put this rubbish out? It's in my way."

I carried the garbage bag to the trash cans out the back. The air tasted clean and good and I leaned against the back wall and took a few breaths to fortify myself. Watched the sunflowers in the garden all pointing the same way toward an imaginary sun. Threw the garbage into the pail and nearly slipped as I started to walk away. Soft brown feathers on the wet asphalt. I recognized them, strewn around the trash cans. I never had found out what you'd done with that suddenly silent bird. For a moment I played with the thought that you had baked it for our dinner tonight, then I lifted the lid off the second pail and saw the blue broken-necked brown broken-winged body stuffed inside a supermarket bag. It made me feel sick and I couldn't figure it out. I can now. You killed it, didn't you? With your own sweet hands. Wrung it by the neck because it had betrayed you with weakness and to punish yourself for displaying a moment of compassion for someone else to see.

When I got back inside Matthew was carving, his jacket off, his sleeves rolled elegantly up above his elbows. I think he'd been saving his nasty remark for my appreciation.

"Don't you think I should be just crumbling the ash into an urn? Isn't that what you're meant to do with a cremated body?"

"It's supposed to look like that."

"I'm only joshing you, D.B. Don't get uptight."

Your expression hardened at his use of your childhood nickname. Helen lifted her spectacles up by their ivory hand-rod and held them to her eyes.

"Looks delicious. Darling."

"It's duck."

"And vegetables too. I see."

It was kind of good. Bitter burned-orange taste on the outside. Pink duck meat on the inside. Lightly cooked snow peas, almost raw. Layers of potatoes separated by garlic and cream. You surprised me by how good a cook you were.

"This is jolly," said languid Mattie.

"So," I asked, "when were you last all together?"

Helen smiled merrily. "At the wedding. With little Ginny."

"Little Ginny," said Matthew.

"Was your father there?"

"It was after," said Matthew.

Helen got something wistful in her eye. "I sat next to that nice funny Lizzie. There."

"Don't be ridiculous. You couldn't have."

"No?"

Matthew pushed his plate aside. "Do we want to talk about nice funny Lizzie? Do you, Deborah? Do you, Mother? Tierney, you don't mind if I don't ask you that question? I don't think you ever knew nice funny Lizzie. What the fuck, if I may ask"—grinning humorless smile, thin lips, neat teeth (nice teeth), dead watery-blue eyes—"are you doing here? I don't like you, Tierney. I find you dull and I find you sneaky. What are you doing sniffing after my sister?"

"When—"

"Forget it. Just sit there. Be as you are, there's something quite strangely reassuring about you there; how would you describe yourself? A rough diamond? Sensitive? Lumpen? Lumpen seems quite a good word for you. You're in our country now so you must learn to behave accordingly. Play the white man, Tierney. Are you Irish? It's an Irish name. So sit still, don't shuffle about like that, don't make fists like that—would you like to hit me? Feel free. You can if you like. Maybe I'll hit you back. Sit still, Tierney. Relax. Would you care for a cigar? Be a good guest. I abhor rudeness in people, don't you? Listen to our stories and make something clean out of them. Do you bathe often, Tierney? Your fingernails are dirty. Do you see his fingernails, D.B.? You like that? A little Yankee rough, is that what you like? Where do those fingernails go, D.B.?"

"You're being horrible, you're being—"

"I try. I haven't quite got his utter panache, but I do what I can. While we're on the subject, let's talk about Reiko."

"She was. A dear charming girl."

"Dear, Mother. Yes, Mother. Charming, Mother. Dear and charming, Mother."

"I liked her. Very much."

"Well, she was company for you of course."

"We were. Good companions."

"She relied on you rather a lot, didn't she? What with her errant husband. Her English wasn't of the best, was it? And she didn't really have any friends."

"She was a very beautiful little girl. A china doll of a girl. Allergic, though. To butterflies."

"For the benefit of our guest, D.B., won't you explain who Reiko was."

"He knows who she was."

"Oh, does he? The clever little delver. Tell him anyway."

"Reiko was my father's second wife. She'd been our au pair. She was Japanese. Mother rather looked after her."

"Mother did, didn't Mother?"

"We do. What we can."

"And that often isn't enough. Is it?"

Matthew lit another cigar. Helen sniffed the fumes. You were still looking down at the table, a faint smile of enjoyment on your face.

"He used to smoke. The same cigars."

Matthew shrugged. Helen fanned some more of the smoke toward her nose and open mouth.

"As Mother says, we do what we can."

Softly you spoke. "You haven't got it, though, have you? Are cigars and cruelty enough?"

Matthew flushed slightly and flicked some cigar ash on top of a pile of duck meat. "Let's talk about Reiko a little more. Interestingly, we don't even know that that was her real name. Someone told me once Ivory had renamed her after a character in a Mishima tale. I rather believe that's true. When did they marry, Mother? Why did she stop being our au pair? Nineteen sixty-eight?"

"I rather think. It was the following year. Darling."

"Okay. Nineteen sixty-nine. I was eight. D.B. was six."

"Seven. It was nearly the end of the year. I'd just had my seventh birthday. I think you were nine, actually."

"Does it matter? Does anyone really care? Maybe our biographer here. Important to get the dates right, isn't it? In your line of work. Nineteen sixty-nine, they were married. We moved to this house. All our stuff from Tite Street stacked into this crummy place. Reiko ended up living here most of the time too. She'd been with us for a year or two before that. Ineffectual and homesick as hell. She'd wanted to leave Japan behind her and be trained as a European and Ivory insisted on treating her like an Edo geisha girl. Ivory soon tired of her. He had other fish to fry. There was no real difference between her as our au pair and her as the second Missis Ivory, was there? Reiko was mostly with us, cleaning the house, doing the cooking, except now and again when Ivory wanted a Japanese woman in his bed. To service him. Yes? I don't know why he married her. Why droit du seigneur stopped being enough. Mother had less money than before and had to scrimp rather a lot. D.B. and I were provided for rather well. Generous pocket money from Ivory, he gave us more than anyone I knew. Sometimes withheld it if we displeased him, but then gave more the next time. Mother was scrimping but we were doing all right and we all know where the money came from, don't we?"

He looked proudly round the table. I remember thinking that if Ivory was doing this routine he would have done it better. More subtlety. A higher level of nastiness.

"Anyway. Let's go forward. Nineteen seventy-five. It was the beginning of the year, so I was fourteen. Lizzie was on the scene by now so Reiko was hardly ever called out for service. No, I don't know why I got onto that. I didn't mean to talk about Lizzie. Wrong track. I'm confusing things. Sometimes I'm completely hopeless when I try to tell a story. Do you ever find that, Tierney? You start on one track and find yourself on quite another entirely. It's infuriating, isn't it? Yes. I was nine. It must have been the end of nineteen sixty-nine. Towards Christmas. That was a real festival for us all, Tierney. One day maybe I'll tell you a story about Christmases, but not today."

He was floundering. He'd lost the focus for his self-pity. Helen inadvertently gave it back to him. She inquired after pudding and Matthew got furious and white-lipped at the interruption. He talked faster. And softer.

"It was often very cold in this house. We didn't have central heating in those days. In the evening sometimes when Mother was at her prayers and D.B. was fast asleep I used to go up and visit Reiko in her room. She'd be mooning over snapshots of home or her so-called husband and we used to cuddle up together. Maybe it was only for warmth. Maybe it was because she was lonely and missed Ivory so much that the son became a barely acceptable substitute for the father. Yes? Did you know about that, Mother? Did you know, did you care? Are you listening? I'm sorry about my mother, Tierney. She's rather decrepit. She's seen better days and the trouble is she remembers what they felt like. Back then she was drunk with religion. A beatific lonely stupor. Saintly. Catatonic even, with such a sweet smile. Reiko still had her room at the top of the house. (Have you seen that room, Tierney? My sister has been known to stay there.) After Reiko became the second Missis Ivory she still spent almost as much time there as before, when she was just our household exotic wearing a headband and bell-bottom jeans doing the cleaning. I went up the stairs to her room. It was dark and it was night and I was ten and I couldn't get to sleep. I think I felt very miserable. You with me? All of you? Even you, Tierney. I even want *you* to listen to me. Are you all listening to me? I want to know you're all listening to me!"

We looked up, all of us, like our faces had been twitched toward him by string.

"You're losing it Mattie," I said.

"Don't you call me that!"

He was panting and his face was awfully pale and there was a bubble of spit trembling at one corner of his mouth, and one day, when he was old, he was going to look more like his mother than his father.

"Reiko's bedroom door was just slightly ajar and I'd always taken that as our signal that she was receiving callers. I was about to go in when I heard the sound of my mother's voice. You were crying, Mother. You often were in those days, but only ever in the kitchen late at night when you thought everyone was asleep, and you never did it in her room. I didn't even know you ever went up there. I looked in through the crack of the door. The two of you were kneeling on the floor, facing one another. Peculiar. Reiko was in her bedtime kimono and you were in your blue dressing gown that you always wore. Your face was red and you'd been crying and it sickened me to see you like that. Reiko was drying off your face with a scarf and talking to you like she always talked, Japanese words mixed in with pidgin English, more Jap than English. But she was speaking softly and calmly and she was calming you down like she used to calm me down and I was jealous of you, jealous she was wiping your face instead of mine."

Your brother gulped for breath and stubbed out his cigar

and took out a handkerchief and wiped it across his forehead as if he'd forgotten that wasn't where he kept his eyes. His expression became soft. He started to look almost sentimental.

"And then came the really curious thing. Reiko got up and pulled something out of a box and picked up a Co-op bag and went back to her position opposite you. And she stood the thing up which she'd taken from the box and it was a little mannequin. I think it was my old Action Man and it had a mustache painted on, I could see that from where I was standing. Then she emptied the Co-op bag onto the floor and out came tumbling all these miniature clothes and the two of you were so delighted and you took it in strict turns to dress the doll."

He looked at us. He paid more attention to you than he did to his mother. Helen was shaking more than I'd ever seen her shake before. Her mouth was still open and I could see her dark tongue trembling in her mouth. Her left hand was in her lap and her right hand kept lifting her water tumbler up to her mouth and placing it on the table again. Over and over like a broken machine. You were turned to your brother. Your chin cupped in your hands as for a formal photo. You were smiling at him. Giving him encouragement.

"You remember this of course, Mother. And we all can imagine how the mannequin was dressed, can't we? Perfect shiny black shoes. A baggy nineteen-forties suit with a perfect razor crease. White shirt. Tie. Borsalino rakish on the head. The complete ensemble. Very correct. It must have taken a lot of love to make the outfit so realistic. Our father who aren't in heaven. One foot high. Plastic and safe.

"And both of you started to laugh when Reiko opened up her needlework kit. I don't think you clapped your hands together when she gave you a long shiny needle to hold just like the one she had, but you might as well have. And you took it in turns to jab the needles in. Fast—voom voom—into the chest, the legs, the feet. Voom voom voom. And then the real places. The mouth. Voom. The groin. Voom voom. The eyes. Voom voom voom. And it got speeded up like film, and the two of you were hysterical now, both of you laughing like billy-o, jabbing in these needles, screaming out nonsense words, such fun you were having. And when you were finished with the needles, Reiko offered the effigy to you and you knew what to do. You lifted it high into the air and you beat it down against the floor and in the air and down to the floor, over and over, the plastic head against the floor, and both of you were mad with this, crazy and screaming, Jap and English mixed all together, her voice shrill above yours (I've always admired your voice, Mother, did I ever say that before?), and then Reiko took out her cigarette lighter and very suddenly you both swallowed your hysterics and very solemnly you stood the Ivory doll back on his feet and pinned them to the carpet and very slowly you watched her set fire to your shared faithless husband.

"The clothes caught quickly. The plastic took a while to burn. Horrible stench. I had to cover my nose and my mouth but neither of you seemed to mind. Laughing and hiccupping and raging again, the two of you, until my father was a blackened pinkish mound oozing and smoldering on the floor which the two of you just watched with quiet satisfaction."

Matthew settled back happily in his chair. He lit another cheroot. You turned to look at your mother. She was crying. Both of you, brother and sister, watched your mother like she was your favorite magical toy. Pudding wasn't going to come. Not this evening. Your mother cried and she shook and cried, and when Matthew got bored watching her he said something about Ginny and how it was time to go home. You looked over at me and held out your hand and I took it even though I knew it wasn't for real, that you were only doing it for your brother. Not for me.

POISON

Do you feel cold? I feel cold. It looks like sunshine outside but it's cold in here. Winter sweaters in fall. The sound of trucks along Holloway Road. Sometimes the house shakes when an eightwheeler rumbles north. I walked up Holloway Road last night. (Did you notice I was gone?) When I got tired of that I walked back down again. Boarded-up clothing stores with circus posters pasted askew across the boards. Takeout kebab joints. A Bruce Lee late-night double bill at the movie house with neighborhood youths practicing their fanciest moves outside. Pubs that sweat the scent of urine. A pawnbroker's establishment conveniently adjacent to a betting parlor. A square patch of grass halfway to Archway on the left-hand side of the road. A parody of a field, what's it doing here? No one sits in it. People will cross over the road to avoid looking at it. We don't trust that kind of nature around here, boy. Nature here is broken sidewalks, smashed pay phones, shivering streetlights. Adam is an Irish drunk weaving his intricate way home. Evie has dyed blond hair and a hard hard face and pushes a pram full of mewling babies into the road, playing her innocent prelapsarian game of not looking to see if the traffic is going to stop for her. It's a subsistence economy around this neck of the woods. We farm doner kebabs around here, and burgers and fish 'n' chips too. Shut your eyes and listen carefully to the struggling engines of stolen cars and you'll hear the lowing of cattle. A ruptured sewage pipe belching shit out into the road, that's our babbling brook. Man gave names to all the animals, then kicked them outside to scavenge in the street. Mongrel dogs with lame legs and hungry worried faces limp around corners and hope for something better.

It's cold in the house. I couldn't figure out the central heating boiler. Maybe the system has been disconnected. The walls covered with lipstick words. POISON. BILL BUCKNER ROTS IN HELL. POOR REIKO. Sometimes I get angry. Sometimes I get mad. I break things sometimes. Look at them and break them. I went past an airline company office on my walk last night. A flyer in the window advertising low-cost trips to the East Coast. New York. Miami. Boston. Boston £250 return ticket. Who needs a return ticket? If I could get away from this place I wouldn't plan on coming back.

Your brother's face when you held out your hand for me to take. (And you were watching for that, weren't you? You were looking at him, not me.) An expression that wasn't arrogance creased his pretty features. It might have been jealousy, maybe even desire. It passed, like it does in your family. The features recomposed, the real feelings were quickly hidden beneath a smooth sexy meaningless surface.

"I'll be off, then. By the way I had a funny little man sneaking round my place the other day. Seemed to think I might have something of Father's. A book. Does that mean anything to you?"

You and your mother both quickly shook your heads. I didn't shake my head, but then he wasn't looking at me.

He gathered his things together. He rolled down his sleeves, slipped on his cuff links, and covered himself again with his nice charcoal jacket. He kissed his mother on her cracked wet cheeks. One kiss for each cheek and the tears transferred to his mouth and made his lips glisten in the candlelight. You let go of my hand to wave goodbye. He nodded at me. Smiled to you. I think it was meant to be a wise smile, superior, knowing, expressing infinite understanding. It came over like the smile of an overgrown boy who was scared of most everything and for the first time I warmed to him. He drove away in his Jaguar.

You let me stay with you that night. Upstairs in your attic flat. I went to the bathroom first while you cleared a few things away in your room. I carried up a bottle of wine left over from

M
A
N

K
I
L
L
S

W
O
M
A
N

•

2
7
1

supper. Kept it in my hand while I took a leak (great care to aim square in the center of the bowl—those are the kinds of things that can ruin a date), set the bottle to rest on the side of the tub while I washed my face and hands. Those ranks of bottles and jars and squeezy tubes of creams, salves, ointments, and paints. I don't have words for all their colors. Blue is easy. Red. Yellow. Quite a few were black. Some of them were white. What do you call the shade of deep dark pink veering to brown? I've seen some of these color-names in fashion magazines in dentists' waiting rooms. Burnt Sienna. Indian Sugar. Ocher. Tuscan Red. Umber. Russet. Never too sure what shades these words represented. You probably had them all. Canisters of lipsticks and mascaras. Sticks of different tones of eyeliner going from brown to kohl. Trays of eye shadows. Jars of foundation creams. After-makeup lotion. Pre-makeup lotion. Perfumes and eaux-de-toilettes with sultry names and corny lettering. Boots, Shiseido, Mary Quant, Cover Girl, Helena Rubinstein, Elizabeth Arden.

I touched your face when I came into the bedroom. Pretended it was a caress when really it was a makeup snoop's fact-finding mission. Nothing came off on my fingertips. It was just flesh I was feeling, yours, soft, resilient, naked, and dodging quickly away from my touch.

POOR REIKO

Reiko. Allergic to butterflies. Dragged unwillingly to that 1973 picnic but your mother insisted. She was under orders. Matthew didn't come, though. He was at school and occasionally, sometimes, there was an authority that was momentarily stronger than your father's. Regent's Park. A cold March day hardly suitable for picnics. You walking in between the two Mrs. Ivorys. Reiko carried the hamper. You were the first to see them and you pointed them out. Your father on a stone bench with a Midnight Blue-lidded woman shivering beside him. The sight of it caused your mother to make a strange noise in her throat. She took you by the hand and the three of you walked quickly on and neither Helen nor Reiko would answer any of your questions. And then Reiko broke out in angry red weals across her face and she complained her tongue was too big for her mouth and you could hear the trouble she was having breathing. The culprit, a red admiral, followed the breeze away from the small party of victims.

Reiko had arrived in London in the spring of '67. Ivory picked her up at the airport in his Jag, brought her back to Tite Street, and you were all out in the front to welcome her. You'd never had a maid before. She was eighteen years old, picture-book pretty, in blue jeans and tie-dyed shirt, her face sweetly smeared with Shiseido powder, her smile hidden behind her hand. She was to be trained a European. The story went that your father had known her family in Kyoto, he'd invited her over as a favor to them. She performed her housework with industry, you and your brother taught her English slang words (and sometimes told her the wrong ones to make her look dumb in the King's Road), and without a friend to introduce her to

Herbert Marcuse or the Small Faces, she accompanied your mother on her visits to church.

"I am child youth rebellion," she told you when her English got a little better. Her mother was a snob, knew the correct Shinto etiquette for every occasion, Reiko wanted out of all of that. She whistled British pop songs while performing the housework. She played *Ogden's Nut Gone Flake* until it was heavily scratched on the dancette in her attic apartment, she pasted the walls with reproductions of Pre-Raphaelite paintings and posters of men she adored, and sang the same song about coffee-colored babies over and over to your brother's weedy guitar accompaniment. When Ivory was staying in the house he didn't let that pass. He had wanted a Japanese woman and he made sure he got one. He discouraged her from learning English. She was to be a decorative household object, and occasionally an instrument of research, no more. When he married her she wore the appropriate kimono at Chelsea Register Office.

Sure, she was in love with him. That was clear to see. Photographs of him taken on her Instamatic replaced the posters of Che Guevara, Steve Marriott, Rod Stewart, Mao Tse-tung. But you never did figure out why he married her. It might have been part of his campaign to see just how low he could push your mother, or it might have been the only way to keep Reiko around. Whatever, her role didn't change. He was in Norfolk and she was with you in London, still cleaning the house, no longer whistling, still preparing the meals, occasionally summoned and then dispatched when he was bored with her again. He hardly ever talked to her when he visited his surgery in the house off Holloway Road.

You heard him once though, a surprising tenderness in his voice. Your mother must have passed on one of his letters, a burgeoning complicity of wasted Mrs. Ivorys. I don't know which one it was, what adventure it related, what sin or cruelty it disclosed. But you heard his voice, a surprising gentleness, and you saw him wipe tears away from her face. "Never cry in front of me," he warned, a gentle warning, a promise of the damage he would do if anyone showed him their weakness.

Later on she went with you sometimes to your punk gigs. Wrapped in PVC, decorative and sad, an unrequired prop waiting for something to happen. You lost sight of her after that when you fell in with your punk drugs crew.

And when he died she disappeared, back to Japan you supposed.

W hat did you do in the years between? Where did you go in those thirteen years before the mailman was due to call? How many countries did you visit? How many jobs did you have? Did you hope his death would be enough to finish him off? Did you forget him? You certainly tried.

Refusals. Deferrals. Sentences that begin with the word "Not," "Not here," "Not now," "Not yet." You stopped shy of saying "Not ever." I didn't go back to the surgery after that first night in your room where the small hours crept past while our bodies lay close together, nearly touching. I worked at the round table by the side of the high window. I slept in your bed. Sometimes you weren't there, but you always came back eventually, the next day or the day after, and you never told me where you had been. We slept together. Not like husband and wife. Not sister and brother. Not lovers. Not friends. Sometimes I'd get a hard-on and you'd usually shift your weight away from it. Sometimes you'd move into it. You did that my third night up there with you.

I was reading letters alone in your bed. You returned sometime after midnight, looking glamorous and tired and worn (you'd been negotiating a book deal, I found that out later). You threw off your clothes and climbed naked into bed. I was pretending still to read but you switched off the light anyway. Neither of us had spoken since your return. You curled up far away from me. I made some objection to the loss of my reading light and you still didn't say anything. I tossed the papers to the floor and curled toward sleep and tried to ignore the undisguised smell of you, a little bitter, a little sweet. I muttered some question about Lizzie Sharp and I shifted toward you and the hard-on was there and I didn't try to disguise it. You drew me into the cleft of your buttocks and rubbed me into coming with your naked ass. I reached for your body with my hands and you wouldn't carry on until I'd let go of you.

And sometimes at night I'd reach for you and occasionally you'd let me. I'd stroke your body with my hands and rub my stubbled face hard against your back. And then I'd jerk you off with my fingers. Not with mouth. Not allowed. And never at the same time as you were paying any attention to my body. Not together. Each of us came alone or not at all.

And I would learn what words to use to push you into the need for it. Talk of your father sometimes did it, sometimes had the reverse effect. Talk of your mother never did it—that meant death to sex. Reiko, often. Your brother, occasionally. Lizzie Sharp, almost always.

We were in your living room. We'd drunk lemonade earlier in the evening with your mother and then drifted upstairs when she fell asleep in front of the TV. You lay down on the sofa, huddled in your leather jacket, and you stared up at the ceiling as if you were about to find secrets there. I went back to what I'd been doing earlier that day, compiling a bibliography of Ivory's publications. A mixed task. Books were easy. Only two of those. Only two published, in any event. But then came the essays and reviews, uncollected, from journals like *The Listener, Encounter, The New Statesman, The Times Literary Supplement, Psychiatry Now*, and on. I'd bought digests of these periodicals from odd men in odd stores and gone through their lists of contributors and found the titles ("The Unfashionable Dog Breeder," "Prince Boothby & The Triumph of Boredom," "Game-Playing with Schizophrenics," "The Uses of Organic Hallucinogens in the Treatment of Neuroses," "Dead Birds in the Work of Henry Green," and so on). Then back to the library, the British Library (watching out for the shade of Miss P——), to read them and xerox them.

"Listen to this one."

You showed no sign of hearing me. I went on.

"You know, I don't think Ivory would have liked me. It's funny, I always kind of assumed he would. But he was really down on Americans. Listen to this. It's from *The New Statesman*. January nineteen seventy. It's a piece called 'The End of America.' He's writing about the Manson-family killings and the Apollo moon landing, are you listening? This is from near the end—'. . . the eschatological'—he liked that word, didn't he?—'the eschatological ecstasy of a junk culture tribe and the fortunes spent in hope to propel two military men on to a dead spinning rock, these are the two most exemplary moments of the modern USA . . .' Then he goes on: 'Take a fool typical of our age. He will be an American whose blood will come from different corners of the globe. He will fancy himself to have a simple relationship with language. He will evince a child's pleasure in the childish play of professional sports. He will believe tirelessly in the future and will be untroubled by the past. What chance is there for him? When the mystery regions have all been charted and his uncomplicated toughness is allowed no new worlds to spoil . . .' You think he's describing me here?"

You half smiled and you shook your head, and that meant there was something in what I was saying. I brushed it away at the time, I went on with my bibliography, but I can figure it out now. That's part of the reason why you chose me, isn't it? You wanted the person who uncovered the truths of Ivory's life and death to be someone your dad would have despised.

And his translations, one Mishima, one Tanizaki, but the rest were hard to find. I wrote to Nipponists at different universities. I asked librarians. I wrote to the cultural attaché at the Japanese Embassy. I called Gibbs and got a brush-off from him. He had nothing new to tell me, but he did say that he was watching my career with interest and I couldn't work that one out at all.

Decadent Pleasures, Thames & Hudson, 1973, 424 pages, £5.95. (Chapter headings include Ecstasy of Fools, War Without Guilt, Watching People Die, The Dream King, The Beast of Extermination, Sex Magick, Waiting for the Barbarians. All these topics were so carefully researched, took years to do; and I'm not just talking book research, and Reiko had her part to play in that.) Published to silence, and then with a little surreptitious publicity work on the part of the author the thing suddenly caught fire, became a best seller. And I suppose that's because there's something in it for everybody. Take it whichever way you like—a fastidious timely chronicle of the end of cultures, or else a naughty thrill dressed up nice in history and art.

Morita, dedicated to Mishima himself, published by Secker & Warburg, 1976, 172 pages, priced at £3.50, and then in

Penguin paperback the next year, 40p. Received with stony disdain. Only Ian Hamilton in *The New Review* praised it. He remarked upon the "grisly coda" and called the novel a "stylish exploration of darkness." The rest of the bunch didn't go for it at all. "Ugly," said *The Daily Telegraph*; "pointlessly extreme," wailed *The Times*; "a self-indulgent wallow in the violence of the decadent mind," said Roland Gibbs in *The Guardian*. And that really got Ivory's goat. Little man Gibbs turning upon him. Ivory was too conscious of dignity to go bleating about it in newspaper print. Instead, in a letter to Helen, Ivory threatened a future mysterious revenge.

"Weird," I said. "Gibbs didn't mention this at all in the obit. He said something nice and polite about the novel. Why do you think he would change his tune? He'd already upset Ivory once and he wasn't going to offend him after he was dead."

You nodded. You didn't care. You were finally ready to do some talking. By now I could recognize the signs. Restlessness. Irritability. You got up from the sofa and you started picking things up and putting them down in the same place again. Making a scrupulous show of avoiding making any sounds to distract me from my work.

I put down my papers, looked over to you. Hair hiding the expression on your face. Words suddenly started to spill out.

"The things that remind me of my father. I dream of him a lot and I see something of him almost every day that brings him near. A banker's hairline on the tube. A picture of Johnny Cash on an album cover. Laurence Harvey in the movie *Darling*. Patrick McGoohan. Tall men with cold eyes. Someone's playing the piano and suddenly he's in the room. Do you play the piano, Tierney?"

"Tell me," I said, "about Lizzie Sharp."

You pushed away your hair like you were contemptuous of it. You smiled and there were unfamiliar creases at the corners of your eyes. You sat down on the sofa with your legs straight in front of you. You kept on your leather jacket. You lighted a cigarette and puffed on it and flicked the ash to the floor.

"Lizzie Sharp was my father's friend. Her father was a poet, Ivory knew him from long ago, Jack Crew, stank of booze. He had long white hair and a big red nose and frightened me like a nightmare clown. Ivory took me sometimes to see him read. Yelling out stanzas in places like the I.C.A. or upstairs at pubs in Hampstead. The poetry was sort of wet, always rhymed, lots of stuff about the ancient wisdom of the working classes, but he was a terrifying ham performer. Thousands of thin veins on his face. Long overcoat and big workman boots. Always looked like a navvy, my father said. A 'thirties affectation, poets of the people, up the Spanish Republic, and knob every rich girl in sight. I don't remember where his wife came from, I don't think I ever met her, I only ever spoke to her on the phone when Lizzie made me answer it and lie for her, she was from Scotland or Canada or South Africa or somewhere but spoke like a member of the Royal Family. Obsessed, mad in love with Jack Crew. They never seemed to spend any time with one another but they had loads of children together. Five, I think. Lizzie was the middle child. You wouldn't believe how beautiful she was. Blond hair. Stocky sexy body. Perfect convent-girl features. I loved the lines in her face when she started to get addled. She looked like a Rolling Stones groupie and she probably had been. Took every drug in sight. Always drunk. Always out of it. Loved to take her clothes off in public—I don't know if she loved to, maybe that's wrong, it never seemed as if it gave her any pleasure, but she'd do it all the same. A compulsion. And photography. She always had a camera with her. Every drawer in her house filled with rolls of fading, undeveloped film. Took photographs of everything and everyone. Would make you take photographs of her. She'd take her clothes off and sit on the sofa and pretend to be making a phone call. And sometimes she'd be bending over, looking at you with fake surprise over her shoulder in a crass saucy pose. But on her even that was innocent. There was nothing dirty about it. It wasn't even seduction. She didn't need to seduce me, I had a crush on her a mile wide and I'd have died for her, I used to dream about her, you know, desire dreams, but she acted as if that was only natural. I don't think we ever touched one another. Even when she gave me my babysitting money she'd leave it on the side for me to pick up, she never handed it to me. I don't think she liked to be touched. I never even saw her holding her children or them giving her a good night kiss. She just needed to be admired.

"There were photos of her taken a long time ago all over the house, blow-ups stuck to the wall like posters, black-and-white shots in silver frames, portfolios of them behind every piece of furniture; she used to be an actress or a model or something but she never talked about it, she wasn't one of those faded types who are always bragging about how beautiful and esteemed and fashionable they used to be, and reel off names of impressive people you've never heard of. It was like everything that happened to her and everything that was going to happen to her and everything that did happen to her were all indistinguishable. She never looked bored or hopeless. Like when she'd take her clothes off, she'd do it as a matter of course, but still—and even though it wasn't sexual, I really don't think it was for her—there was an air of expectancy almost as if she was just getting into the appropriate costume for something amazing which was just about to happen, and the picture she had in her head could easily have been an amazing thing she remembered from twenty years ago but she was remembering it with anticipation instead of nostalgia, does that make sense to you?

"And after she'd got back from a date, it could even have been with my father, she'd come in to the sitting room where I was usually watching the TV, and she'd take off all her clothes in the way that anyone else would take off an overcoat and a scarf, and she'd settle down in the armchair and get out one of those awful Indian silver stash boxes and roll a joint and we'd get stoned together. I hated dope. But I couldn't refuse her anything. So we'd get stoned and the TV would still be on, a test card or just fuzz and snow, and she'd be sitting cross-legged in her chair, and I'd just watch her, watch and watch, and fill my head with nothing but her, and we never used to say much, sometimes it was just completely silent in there, and often she'd put her hands to her tits and inspect them, and her face would suddenly be ugly with a double chin, and she'd stroke herself for so long it seemed like forever as if she was testing for lumps or maybe for wrinkles."

"How did your father know her?"

You didn't like me interrupting. It reminded you that you were talking.

"She was a patient. She'd probably met him when she was a child, with Jack Crew—that's a silly name isn't it? Ivory said he'd changed it from something grand way back in the nineteen thirties—but she came to him years later on her own."

"He gave her a family discount, huh?"

"Never. He never gave anyone a discount. He always charged what he thought would be very slightly more than the patient could afford. He said that otherwise they wouldn't take their therapy seriously enough."

"What was he treating for?"

"I never had the foggiest idea. It could have been anything. She was doomed and beautiful and mad. She was fucked by the 'sixties and took too many drugs and drank far too much, and even though she couldn't bear to be touched she was always off with some man. Only her face aged, you could see that beneath the makeup she always wore, heavy mascara and eyeliner and white powder all over. She'd had three children but her body didn't show it. I don't know what Ivory treated her for. Maybe all of that. Or maybe there was something else that I didn't know. Maybe she thought she was Napoleon, I couldn't say. Maybe she was just tired of taking her clothes off the whole time. Whatever he did for her it didn't work. Although maybe he kept her alive for longer than she would have been able to do by herself, I couldn't tell you."

"What did she die of? When did she die?"

"An overdose, I guess. It would be, wouldn't it? I don't remember quite when she died. Around the time he did, I think. No one ever told me. People thought they ought to protect me from my father's sins."

I brought out the photograph you'd given me way back then. Ivory, aging in the shadows, his bare chest, freckled pate, the flash of the camera, the body of the photographer, a woman, naked.

"Is this her?"

You nodded your head. You didn't need to look at it.

"Does it disturb you?"

You shook your head solemnly, like a child. You jumped up and looked out the window. A streetlight flashed across your white jeans. Then you looked at me, the first time, and smiled. "Cod psychology, Tierney. I'm not—I was never—jealous. That's not it at all. I didn't have a thing for her really. He didn't get in the way of that."

"I was thinking maybe the other way around. Not that you were jealous of him, more that you were jealous of *her*."

You scowled, irritated. You looked back at the window. "Give it up. Don't try to make things straightforward. They're not like that. And you're no good at it anyway."

There was a knock at the apartment door. We both pretended not to hear it. You took your clothes off like you were taking off an overcoat and scarf. Leather jacket to the floor. Shirt over your head. Bra unhitched and dropped. Boots yanked away. White jeans slid out of. You weren't undressing for me, you weren't doing it for yourself. I figured it must be for Lizzie Sharp, whose photograph I fixed into a corner of the dressing-table mirror, clearly visible from the bed. We went to the bed. I sucked at your cunt with my mouth and blew deep long kisses with my tongue and I penetrated you with my nose and investigated the interior of your ass with my fingertips and you lay almost completely still, just arching your back ever so lightly up and then down and then up, with a frosty grin fixed to your face, and you made a series of low-pitched calls to someone who wasn't in the room, who might even have been dead, just before you came.

By the time I woke up you were gone.

Let's hear it for the society ladies, and the supermarket checkout girls. And West Indian Pentecostalist ladies, and Japanese au pairs too, and university girls struggling for money, and ancient dying ladies firm in only one thing, their modern lust for William Ivory. Rutting Ivory, humping Ivory, Ivory tearing hymens with cynical sinister force.

There's a curious book called *Memoirs of a Society Lady* that was published in 1983, a pseudonymous mix of political anecdote, gossipy tittle-tattle, and lists of expensive things that covers the middle half of the century. I found it on a shelf in your mother's bedroom. Our hero has a cameo romeo role.

The society lady wrote: "Some men are good lovers because they're entirely sensitive to a woman's needs; others because they're entirely selfish and know exactly what they want and exactly how to get it. Ivor Y. is both." This was written in 1962 on the terrace of a hotel in Ravello. Her companion, Ivor Y., had left her for a day's expedition to the buried city of Pompeii. He never came back. She waited a week and returned to London, stopping off for a month at a château near Toulouse to grieve over her injured pride. Sensitive Ivor Y., selfish Ivor Y., never attempted to get in touch with her again. She must have bored him. She doesn't mention him again.

The society lady didn't touch "Ivor Y." enough for him to refer to her more than once to Helen. In a note which accompanies a christening present for their second child, a girl, to be named Deborah Stuart Glaven Ivory, he mentions in passing the relief he felt when he was finally free of the company of "your grateful vampiric friend" in southern Italy.

That note was one of a sheaf of different letters from different times clipped together in Helen's black-lacquered Japanese box. There was one thing to connect them—a new Ivory romance each time, sometimes glossed over, sometimes analyzed, duly confessed to his wife, and annotated by her with any information he'd neglected to include. The christening note was sandwiched between Ivory's description on first espying Miss P—— in the British Library and the following "Decadent Day," written on heavy cream paper with yellow lines and margins, the words schoolgirlishly large in light-blue ink with circles used to dot the i's. Helen neatly corrected the spelling mistakes with red ink. Almost as if she was a patient teacher or a proud mother. But she wasn't a teacher and it wasn't written by you and it certainly wasn't written with any thought that she would be sent it the following week. It was written to please her husband.

A Decadent Day

We sat in a line on the sands and took it in turns to play with the gun. There were three of us, the ageing doctor, the Japanese wife, the sad patient. Maybe the doctor would have liked it best for the patient and the Japanese to play with each other but he didn't say so. The doctor went first. He span the chamber and put the gun into his mouth and looked out to sea and clicked the trigger and nothing happened, just a click. The barrel was wet with drizzle and the doctor's saliva but the wife didn't wipe it off because she hadn't been told to. She put the gun into her mouth and her husband had to remind her severely that she hadn't spun the chamber first, so she did. A click. The patient's turn. She put the wet gun into her mouth and loosened her clothing because she was hot. Time might have stopped for her. She thought of many things in the time it took her finger to squeeze the trigger. She was being taught something by this experience but she didn't know what it was nor if she would remember it if she died. She did not want to die. The trigger was harder to move than she would have thought. The gun jolted hard against the top of her mouth as she used her strength to make it go off. Click. An empty chamber.

The sad patient let the gun drop to the sand. The game was over. The wife looked to her husband the doctor and he nodded to her and that meant she was allowed to inspect the weapon. The patient didn't feel sad any longer. She was laughing. She removed her clothes and lay on the sand and she felt the sun touching her flesh. It was a trick, she knew that for certain. There had been no bullet and there had been no chance of death. She felt something hard on her flesh, not a stone, placed there by the light fingers of the Japanese wife. She picked it up with her fingers, held it in the air, and looked at it under the hot sun. It was a bullet, shaped like a penis and shiny like a jewel.

The patient lay back. She waited for the next thing to happen because treatment from this man always came in threes. The doctor asked her what she had learned and she replied that she had learned that she didn't want to die and sadness wasn't fixed after all. But even as she said this she felt the sadness coming back and two more things were going to happen before this day was full.

Later on he hosted a party. He invited the roughest types from the area, boys who worked in petrol stations and gypsies from the carnival, and men who stole cars for a living and broke into people's houses. There was a lot of alcohol and when the guests were all drunk the doctor organized his second game of the day. It was called the Barbarians game. He put his Japanese wife up on a table and he announced an auction and he called for bids. First off there was a lot of joking and drunken boasting and jeering at this hospitable toff. Then when people realized he was being entirely serious the bids started to come. A carriage clock, the keys to a Ford Capri parked outside, a pedigree boxer dog and all her litter comprised. The Japanese wife in tartan trousers and a white T-shirt waited on the table top. The doctor commanded her to open her mouth, to lift her arms in the air. He praised her charms, he bullied the bidders, he sent the sad patient around with more alcohol to top up the glasses. And more bids came in. An oil painting of a horse that had once been kept in the Norwich Castle museum, another Ford Capri, a flat in Spain on the Costa del Sol, a pair of pulling horses, fishing rights for a stretch of bank on the river Ouse. He instructed the patient to remove her clothes and she did, despite the company we were keeping. But they paid no attention to her at all, all eyes were on the Japanese woman up for sale. I was for once invisible.

The party ended in a brawl, as parties like this must. People were fighting and they spilled out on to the lawn and the three of us were left there alone. Failing instruction, your wife went to her bed with a book to read and you played the piano for a while and then you told me to write a phantasy and when I said that was more than I could do, you said to jot down the order of the day's events. Call it "A Decadent Day", you said, and I have.

She wrote this to please him. It did not.

I have Lizzie Sharp's next letter to him. Helen let the spelling mistakes stand this time.

11 February 1980

I am sorry that my discription dissappointed you. I didn't mean for it to be at all amusing and nor did I intend it to be a hidden attack on you but I have to bow to yr better judgement that it is so. I don't know what it is that you want, I did my best. You say that the things we do and the places we go to are more exciting than anything I am able to say out of my head. I have no quarral with the way I think. But then I suppose if that was truely the case then I wouldn't have gone to you in the first place. So you must be right. But still it has gone on too long and I don't see improvement and there are still things I do which make me sad and my feelings which I have which I would much rather had no part of me.

Still I have trouble sitting down because nothing has any substance and when I sit on a chair I have to hold it down to keep it from spilling me on to the floor and when I discovered the rubber band tied around your cock to keep it hard you hurt me. I wrote the russian roulete scene straight as it happened, and I wrote the Barbarians party like that because that's how I saw it. You say that it undervalues your ideas and all you find in it to prase me with is Reiko's passivity. I tell you everything that is true and would alarm anyone but you and I share these things with you and everything with you so why do you require me to make things up? We are not transformed or made into anything better and I am not going to die with you.

Whoa, poor Lizzie. I don't have any more letters from her, cream paper with yellow lines and margins, with that light-blue ink making those full sad shapes. If Ivory kept any more, then up in smoke they went in Helen's jealous grate. Rubber band at the base of his cock? Ivory, sensitive selfish lover, what other tricks did you use when nature started to let you down?

Hey, Deborah, what's up? What's the matter, you don't like to hear these things? A little too close to home? Does it weaken you in your hate? There's more where this came from. Sure, all these women were crazy for your dad. Even your mother kept on coming. But nature has a way of finding out the best of us, and sometimes even the worst.

The Pentecostalist he met on Clapham Common. Outside the wrong church for a Wednesday-night prayer meeting. He spirited her away, a devil man, broke the hymen of this stout middle-aged virgin with a thick rubber band at the base of his cock. Or the university girl in Brighton, a Hindu from Leicester, not long since left home, never fucked a man before. He met her while he was having lunch with you at a café where the waitresses all showed their legs—company policy—he'd come down to the stony seaside to find out what you had decided to turn into, and he took you back to your room and then he returned to the café, took the waitress away to a hotel, paid her to whisper Hindi words, exotic words to keep his penis high. And the supermarket checkout virgin who accused him of pissing inside her—not quite her words, she said he used her for a toilet. (That's kind of horrible, isn't it? But we can figure it out. The cruel wizard lover, praised so highly by the society lady a long time ago just as he was abandoning her. Sensitivity can turn easily to cruelty, can't it?) But he wasn't being cruel when he used the supermarket virgin for a toilet, not that time. He wasn't demonstrating his contempt for her (and his contempt for her you take in your twisted kind of way for contempt for you, don't you, poisoned girl?), all he was doing was trying, simply, to fuck her, and when nature lets you down and you're looking for a little more help from her while trying to defy her at the same time and you decide to pass off a piss-erection as the real thing (aided perhaps by pots of tea and pints of water and maybe some artificial diuretics too, stacked away inside his medicine cabinet, he took them for edema, he wrote about that, pissing away fluid to help his kidneys and his poor damaged heart, I've read the references, I've seen the drugs), then nature has a way of finding you out and making you look a bit silly. Doesn't it?

A tattooed heart dripping faded blood down your shoulder, you stood in your jeans and bra looking into the bathroom mirror. You didn't think I was there. I watched you, your face fixed on your mirror face, your fingers moving like clever independent creatures, running along the shelves at your side, dipping into pots of powder, smearing the stuff across your face, lifting nylon mascara applicators and rubbing them around your eyes, twisting sticks of lipstick and pressing them along your lips pursed into a goodbye kiss. Varnish painted to your fingernails, rouge blushing your cheeks, blue shadow shining nostalgic yearning all across your lids.

And when you were done, when your beautifying voodoo things were covering your face, you clasped yourself in your own arms. I watched your painted fingers claw into that faded tattooed bleeding heart, and I saw you smile at the mirror reflection of all the people you'd become.

W here was I? Put some order into this thing. Man kills woman. Man kills woman. Man drives woman to her death. Forget society lady. Forget Pentecostalist woman. Forget supermarket virgin. Forget Lizzie Sharp even, she's only a distraction at best. I'm trying to explain something. I need it in order. You'd gone away. You'd been gone for days. Maybe three. Maybe more. I didn't keep a diary of your disappearances. I didn't know enough to follow you. I guess I was a little lovesick. Does that surprise you? Does it thrill you? Or just disappoint that I fell for the same sad game? I spent some time with your mother. We drank mugs of herbal tea in the kitchenette. I'd interrupted her drawing jagged charcoal abstract shapes on the back of a 1986 church calendar. I admired her work. She told me it was a function of her disease and then she asked me my opinion of her dead husband.

"I imagine he was a difficult man."

"Difficult. Yes. Hard to understand. But more."

"A powerful man."

"Yes."

"A compelling man."

"Yes. Not enough. More."

"Talented. Gifted. Cruel."

"Yes. Yes. Of course."

"He was a man with ideas. Interesting ideas. I don't know what else you want me to say."

She looked fiercely at me. "You stop short of saying. He was a great man."

"Sure. He was a great man."

"Do you mean that?"

"I guess so. I admire him more than I like to admit."

"Is your book going to admit?"

"In its fashion."

"What kind. Of fashion?"

"I want to write about the whole of the man. The bad as well as good."

"My daughter thinks. He had poison. Inside him. She fears she has inherited. It."

"Where is Deborah? I haven't seen her for a few days."

"She will be in. Norfolk at. His house."

"Doing what?"

"I think she has. It. His final book. She was too quick. For you and too strong for. Me. It arrived. By post yesterday. It was her birthday. Did you know that? She doesn't like. To make a fuss. She is bothered with the thought of him. She. Wants him dead. Again."

"Yes."

"I want him celebrated. I am different from my daughter. The greatest man. Of his. Age."

"I don't know if I can go that far."

A sharp look at the apostate American.

"You are not. The first. Did you believe yourself to be. The. First?"

"The first what?"

"It does not matter sometimes. What one believes. We all must celebrate him. Otherwise we have let him down. Again. I used to call him. Sometimes he would answer. You cannot judge him. By ordinary standards. He proved that."

"I'm sure that's got a lot of truth to it."

"I would not. Have let you. Steal his letters. Unless."

"You let me . . . ?"

"Steal. His letters. I stood at. The door. I encouraged you in my mind. I wanted you to understand. Now I am on the verge. Of regret."

"Can I read the rest of them?"

"That. Depends."

"On. What?"

Your mother smiled. She hugged your father's memory tight to herself. She closed her eyes and admired the greatness of his image. She fell asleep on her stiff-backed kitchen chair.

I went softly upstairs to her bedroom, paused only a moment by the four-poster to inspect the shiny blue garment that Helen chose to wrap herself in at night, and then went over to the vanity table. There was the black-lacquered box. I lifted the lid of the next box along. "Lillibullero" played. I lifted the black-lacquered lid. The box was empty. (As Helen would have said:) Of. Course.

14 February 1980

I look at my fingers, strong fingers but old fingers. Dirt
beneath cracked nails. A signet ring on my left little finger
given by you on our first anniversary, a promise of
(ridiculous word, belongs more to a dog than a man)
faithfulness. My asthma is better because I have switched
back again to cigars but I miss the cigarettes. I am even fond
of them with their ability to dominate me. I yearn for a
cigarette. Control. I know beyond doubt that I will end my
life before it ends me so why do I bother to give something
up that cannot kill me no matter what? Control. Invariably
the answer. A taste in my mouth which is hollow and
slightly bitter like the prelude to a hallucination.

Seneca refused to refer to asthma by its name. He
approvingly cites the doctors who call it "rehearsing death".
Mishima in his commentary on the Hagakure approves the
notion that the samurai should begin each day by
contemplating his own death. Put the two together, and the
asthmatic's first moment of the morning, when he gasps to
exhale the suffocating air, when he reaches for his life-
saving inhaler or syringe, gives him the same steel and
transcendence as the samurai's zen meditation.

As my body crumbles I have bad dreams at night of being
in war in a besieged city.

Received a letter from Mattie today. Shallow protestations
of affection masking a request for money. Shan't get it.

Your loving husband on Valentine's Day,
W.

PS I am nearly done with the final book. Everyone who has ever antagonized me shall fear it. The vultures gather. The beasts will squirm. I have not yet chosen the person who deserves it most nor when he or she shall receive it. Don't fret, dear Helen, if I decide against you.

PPS I enclose a pair of letters which may amuse you. Read the "Decadent Day" first, then the letter. I think you will agree they are a little out of the common run of patient-therapist communication.

When was the last time you saw him? What did you say to each other? Did you try to expose his imagined guilt? Did he then break down in tears and beg your pardon for all he had done? Of course not. You never had the balls and he was never as weak as you would have liked him to be. You let him go through into the surgery where he would pump his lungs full of oxygen and his veins with adrenaline. He turned to you before he shut the door. He told you how pretty you looked. That was at the end of February 1980, three weeks before he died.

Where were you when Ivory died? Who gave you the news? It was the day after when Matthew called you at your flat in Brighton where you were living while you studied at the art school there. You didn't tell your brother that Ivory had called you the previous morning to summon you immediately up to London, a summons you were able to refuse. You didn't come back for the funeral. In your relief you didn't think to ask what he died of. No one showed you the body.

The three of you, Matthew, Helen, and you, went up to Binham to close up his house. A cab took you from Norwich Station out into the flat country, past the ruined priory, through the village, out toward the sea, to the old stone house which was home to some of your worst and loneliest memories. The door was unlocked. The house felt forbiddingly empty. You covered over the grand piano with a tarpaulin. You piled up his favorite black china and stored it away inside wooden cupboards. You were the first to go into the Little Room and you discovered the letter he'd left out for you on his desk, a brief legalistic note announcing the second part of your legacy, to come in thirteen years' time. And for many years you decided you could forget him. You chose lives for yourself like clothes hanging on pegs. Perhaps you were tempted to uncover the truth of his death. And how many times before I stumbled in did you try? But you couldn't do it by yourself and no one else would go the course, so you put it away and you did many things and abandoned many things, until the final thing was still left to do.

Your mother went into a strange butterfly grief. She attended parties for the first time in a generation. She draped her sixty-year-old decaying body in bright silks and tottered out to charity dinners, to society weddings, to midsummer balls, where she would chatter about inconsequential dated things as if the years and Ivory had never happened. And then, just as abruptly, she withdrew.

She accumulated a circle of people from the suburbs who had odd ideas about life and death. You stumbled in on them one night in 1983. You weren't expected, you hardly ever came to call. You let yourself in, went into the kitchenette, the informal sitting room. Nobody there. Something in you wanted to go up to Reiko's apartment in the loft. When you got onto the second-floor landing you heard the sounds from your mother's bedroom. The door was partly open, you pushed it a little wider with your foot. They were there on the bed. A circle of people, exposed by candlelight, all with fingertips pressed tight to an upside-down tumbler that wasn't moving around the ouija board. There were tears on your mother's face, she was weeping out words despite the hushing from the medium beside her, an untidy woman with tits down to her waist. "Please," your mother was saying, trying, with words, to touch, maybe to appease, the spirit of her dead man, "forgive me for letting you down."

I hadn't heard you get in from your birthday vigil up in Norfolk. You were practicing backhand strokes in front of the mirror in your bedroom, tennis racket in hand. Your hair was tied back to keep it away from your eyes. You looked elegant.

"Hi, Tierney. It's a beautiful day, isn't it? It's the summer solstice, did you know that? Why don't we go away for the weekend?"

"Where?"

"Out of London to friends who live near the motorway. They're always having a party this time of year. They said you could come along too."

"Sure. When?"

"As soon as you're ready. Pack a suit. You'll need to dress for dinner."

I rooted around my suitcase for some clean clothes. You moved on to your service stroke.

"You look pretty good. What are you like when you've got a ball to hit?"

"I'll see you downstairs, I want to have a word with Mother."

I'd had my own dream the night before. Bill Buckner was dead. He'd got fat and bald and he'd died, and after I'd packed and before I went downstairs to find you, I wrote BILL BUCKNER ROTS IN HELL on your living-room wall with a silver-cased stick of Indian Sugar lipstick.

I added my clothes to yours and left the bag by the door and found you finally in the formal sitting room. I'd never seen anyone using that room before. Helen was sitting on a footrest in front of the fire. She had a pile of papers in front of her. You were standing behind your mother with your hands on her shoulders jiggling up and down with disease. Helen looked back when I came into the room and announced I was ready. She looked at the fire and looked at the letters and gave me what I took to be a wink. It was as if she was daring me to do something wrong, and then the letters would go. Up in flames.

Your car had a few more marks on it. Long thin scratches along the side. A deep dent at the top of the driver's door and another one at the rear fender and trunk which made it hard to open. We didn't say anything until we'd got into the car and started on our journey.

"Did you see that bus? I don't think you saw it, we almost scraped the fucker. How far are we going? I need to prepare myself. That was the pedestrian's right of way. You scared the shit out of him. How long is this journey going to be? You got any sleeping pills?"

"An hour, a little less. Don't get so nervous on me. I'm a perfectly safe driver. Maybe we should have some music, that might calm you down. Choose a tape."

"Whoo! That was a fucking police car. A lot of people take the left lane if they're planning on turning left. I guess that's a little bourgeois for your taste, huh?"

"Hush, Tierney. You're distracting me."

"Maybe you could take a little distraction. How about this tape?"

"Whatever. Just put it on and stop annoying me."

I was jealous of your car. It took a few dents and scratches but it still gave you everything you asked of it. That little extra acceleration to take us through the tiniest of holes into the fast lane. The sudden braking when you decided not to bust the red light after all and screeched to a stop behind the white line. You patted the dashboard after that. You held the wheel hard in your hands, not sensitive, not passionate, just brutal, and your car did everything you wanted and loved it.

The music started up. A clatter of drums, a guitar thrash, a vocalist's drugged yell. Garage punk. The Seeds' "Pushing Too Hard."

"My brother used to love this number. Did I tell you ever about my brother? He was a mutt. Used to belong to this gang in Boston called the Psyches. A bunch of fourteen-year-olds in cutoff denim jackets and groovy decals and badges. Bell-bottom jeans. Long hair. Dropped acid every day. Listened to West Coast sounds. There was another gang in the neighborhood called the Souls. They were a little older. Leather jackets. Drainpipe jeans. Boots and motorbikes. Duck-ass hairdos. They listened to Stax, Motown, Chess, drank a lot of beer and liquor, and beat the shit out of the Psyches every day outside the record shop in Cambridge or up on the Common, you remember where we were that time? That's where the fights would be. My brother would get home every day strung out and bleeding. Black eyes, got his nose broken once. Even knife wounds sometimes. Still grinning goofily from way up on his astral plane. Just goes to show, I suppose, that hotheads beat hopheads every time. What's the matter? Does it get too much of a bore to stop at every red light?"

"Your brother sounds sweet."

"Sweet? Yeah, you could say that. You'd be wrong but you could say it."

"Where is he now?"

"Ted? Works in computer sales. Still lives in Boston. Got a wife who drinks too much and a dog with skin disease. I don't see him ever. He looks a lot more Mexican than me. Ted Williams was part Mexican. You know how good that made me feel when I found out?"

"What sort of dog does he have?"

"I don't know. It's a little one, sort of a dirty-brown color, but maybe that's because most of its hair has fallen out. It's a crossbreed."

"Maybe I should think about getting a dog. It might be good for me."

"You'd get bored with it. It would get hurt and weak and let you down somehow and you'd end up doing something nasty."

"Do you think so? Maybe you're right, I don't know—don't laugh at me, Tierney, you promise not to laugh?—but dogs can be good. It's the little things. The smells. The mess they make. The simpleness of it all. Food, play, pissing on lampposts. The way they go to sleep and dream of whatever it is they dream about. I can understand those things."

"The little things."

"Yes. Don't laugh at me. Are you laughing at me?"

I wasn't laughing. What you said made my heart tender toward you. Me, I'm different from that. It's the big game I'm after. The mysteries of love and life and death, the shapes they make at night. The big things. But you, I figured, were a little too close to all of those.

"I'm not laughing. I know what you're saying."

"This music's starting to annoy me. Find something else."

I changed the tape to something classical. Turned up the volume but still couldn't hear it too well. We were on the highway now. The M1. The fast lane. Speedometer needle shaking bad as your mother well past the hundred mark. The yell of your engine yelling its speed. The fizzing sound as we zipped past larger cars going the other way on the other side. The wind rushing in between the windows and the soft-top through the gaps made by the dents in the bodywork. Your face was flushed with speed. Your mouth set, grinning. Your eyes delighted, sparkling with the power to make that black road rush so fast beneath your wheels. You shouted out a suggestion that we pull over by the side of the road to take the top down but I managed to persuade you otherwise.

Over all the noise I gave you a shot of my virgin theory. Bawled it out in the fast lane, it was one of the things I'd been figuring out.

"Have you met Martha Brennan? She was the nanny at Hobart Hall, where his cousins lived. When he was a child, Ivory used to go—"

"I know about Hobart Hall," you yelled. "Get to the point."

"Nanny Brennan is a mean vindictive creature. A snob. An evil-minded mean-spirited ugly little ancient virgin Catholic. She was really down on your father." (It was still hard for you to hear that f-word, I almost stuttered over it, and I watched you flinch as I said it.) "She abused him, used him as whipping boy for all the sins of the family flesh. If you ask, if there's anything weird in his virgin thing, it's his revenge against that woman. His way of getting back at this woman who went for him at every—"

You nodded. That meant you disagreed. A signal that someone has just done or said something to confirm your low opinion of him. Or her. You nodded and you slowed the car down,
the better to give me some abuse.

"That is so crass, Tierney. Even for you. Thank god there
won't ever be a book because even Ivory deserves better than
to have you as a biographer. Even with all his faults. He understood what went on inside people and he hated it so he would
damage it—he had a horror of what went on inside people.
He would see inside your heart and twist something inside
there. He did things to people, dangerous mean things, because
he *understood*, and his descriptions were always a lot cleverer
than anything *you* could come up with. He didn't fuck virgins
because he was trying to get back at some old bag who treated
him badly. He fucked virgins because he *liked* to. Because it
made him feel big and strong and manful. Because he liked to
ruin things. Because he had a poison inside him that made him
do the most ruinous things."

You paused for breath. Your face was red with the unaccustomed effort of saying what you meant.

"What do you mean there won't be a book?"

You laughed and that was a relief.

"You're not a publisher?"

"I'm not a publisher. One of his favorite phrases was, 'That'll
teach you never to trust anybody.' "

"You've tried this before, haven't you? I'm not the first."

Silence. You shook your head, abruptly switched lanes, and
swore at a woman in a BMW going a little too slow for your
liking in the fast lane.

"What do you want out of this?"

"You can still do a book if you want. Maybe someone would
want to publish it. I couldn't help you with that. You're really
very gullible. I'll carry on paying you, though."

"Where does your money come from? And your brother's."

"He left it to us. It's all from him. It's the money he left
behind."

"Ivory?"

"Yes. Ivory. His."

I was trying to take it in. I felt like a sap. A very confused sap.

"Do you want to get out? Just say the word. I'll drop you here if you like."

I would have liked to have said the word. It would have given me some comfort. You speeded up the car.

"How much else have you lied to me? You weren't in New York all that time, were you? I did see you on Percy Street. What were you doing there?"

You answered, after a long wait. You said each word so carefully it was as if you were worried what you were saying might hurt you.

"Just tell me how he died. That's all I want to know. Tell me and I'll be glad."

"What were you doing on Percy Street?"

"I've got his last book, you know. Maybe I'll show it to you if you get me what I want. There's others who want it and *they* know. Not Julian Brougham Calder, though. The old scrote didn't have anything to give me in return."

"You didn't need to go to anyone else. I'm getting there. Why didn't you trust me?"

"Don't whine, Tierney. It doesn't become you. I'm sorry if I hurt your feelings. It's not a matter of trust. Just increasing the chances, that's all."

We weren't on the highway for long. Jerked off it onto a tributary road. Left that to go down a narrow country lane lined with overhanging trees above hedgerows, the first I'd seen to match my long-ago anticipation of what British roads would be like. We pulled off that to whiz into a driveway where you sent pebbles of gravel flying into the air as you braked to a halt in front of a large white house with pillars either side of the large wooden Transylvanian-style door.

I t was a party and it was a spectacle. They called it a masque.

Hard to remember the continuity of that moon-heavy night (to borrow a phrase from our man Ivory). Individual moments, tender or jealous, wild flashes of color that an arsonist might love, snatches of conversation that promised meaning but never delivered, grand moonlit gestures made by different people I was never going to know, members all of the same blond tribe, licensed by the dying solstice sun to make crazy shapes and animal sounds. Try. Try and get it in order.

The house appeared empty. You pushed open the door. Into a lobby with a high ceiling and a lighted chandelier, paneled walls dark with the cracked portraits of dead grandees. Do you remember this? It seems to me you're wincing. Forward. Into a kitchen and toward an old woman cloaked in bright fields of silk, whose many chins wobbled as she bustled with cake.

"Deborah?"

"Jane."

"Deborah. You should have let us know you were coming. We'll put you in the Dutch Room. Come here. You look beautiful as ever."

You kissed each other twice, once for each cheek but with lips far far away from skin.

"We're all rather awfully tipsy, you know. It's midsummer—did you remember? You're so clever—and we're performing *The Dream*. Oh, Deborah, we must get out the photographs tomorrow and show your friend the delightful fairy you made—was it that long ago? I'm preparing a cake for tomorrow. I'm rather doubtful of it."

Jane shook her chins a little to show how wonderful it was to see you. Then you said my name, my first name for once, and Jane said Jane and she and I shook each other's hands.

"I've been saddled with Titania again—oh the two of you would have made a delightful Hermia and Lysander—out into the garden, dear, they're starting again."

She waved us through a pantry where dead birds hung on hooks. Out onto the patio, things made weird by the dying sun and giant narrow shadows that wouldn't keep still. Past a long wooden table and a floodlit swimming pool, where a yellow life preserver duck was bobbing against the side. You led me away from a walled garden with an open iron gate. We turned a corner.

Fairy lights on ribbons between the tall trees. Cloth gasoline torches flaming out of the earth. On the lawn, the performers. Shakespeare poetry sung out and murmured and murdered and yelled. *A Midsummer Night's Dream*, you whispered, they do this every year. Three blond English generations painted and costumed and feathered and drunk. Children with pink painted faces and fine blond hair running and squealing and sometimes remembering their lines. The older ones dressed in tunics to flatter their figures and the oldest, swathed in their fields of silk, grand and heavy and sinister and a little foolish. Music sawed on violins and beaten on drums. The solstice sun sinking in the west and the full moon hanging glowing in the sky. Behind the trees, a row of handsome brown heifers had gathered solemnly to watch. And the liquor. Home-made cider in earthenware jugs. Hasty slugs giving instant drunkenness.

"You'll find it here," you said almost regretfully, "what we need to know."

"Who are these people?"

Things misheard and misunderstood. Minced poetry. Elizabethan vaudeville cross-talk. Snatches of Shakespeare—"Be advis'd fair maid. To you, your father should be as a god," the mention of "love juices" to laughter and ribald mock disgust. And everyone was drunk and happy and kind of frisky, drinking and flirting, dogs barking, a few children sleeping by now, and the English at play made a kind of creepy and frightening sight.

You kept your attention on the girl in jerkin and buskins, her blond hair wild in the night, slim gymnast's body, her nose the only thing to poke fun at her beauty, a strange shape that nose, retroussé but long, the sort of nose that if it belonged to anyone American would be immediately replaced by a new one from the cosmetic surgeon's catalogue.

"Who are these people?"

"The enemy."

Her name, Alex, sometimes Allie. Couldn't follow the plot, don't know the play, but I loved the awkward graceful contortions of her body.

"We're not near the sea, I know that. It's weird. I think I can hear the sea."

Instant drunkenness. More cider to see where that would get me. Sprawled on the grass wondering why the clumsy old man who had taken off his donkey mask looked the image of Julian Brougham Calder. Wondering why the oldest grandest man treated him so mean. The old grand man, had to be the loins of this tribe, sat beside his wife, Jane, in companion silks and paint. A magician in silk, his white eyebrows teased into devil's horns, he jumped out of his gold chair and led a dance to the tune of "Jerusalem," and a tall boy, had to be his son (I recognized him under his warpaint and underpants and cardboard crown, the guy you hopped into a taxi with on Percy Street), repeated your favorite line (your body flinching each time you heard it, he might as well have said it for you, like he knew something), "Be advis'd fair maid. To you, your father should be as a god."

"Look at the lights over there."

"Beautiful. Inviolate."

"I can hear the sea. What are those lights?"

The stage more an idea than a place. Toward the end of the show you drifted onto it, lay beside your friend with the strange nose, lay there in the damp grass like emperors separate and apart, leaving me surrounded by children dressed as fairies who tried to tie me up with delicate twine, their faces malicious and swollen with unaccustomed cider.

"Are you an American? Mummy says all Americans are vulgar."

From a cardboard box painted gold they brought out trumpets and pale blond boys blew upon them and Julian Brougham

Calder took pratfalls in his gaudy rags and more pale blond boys labored over poor men's accents that were too obviously phony.

By the time the last words were said and sung, the mad solstice sun had dwindled away. And then, when the masque was done, the torches still flaring but dying, the heifers were scattered by the sudden violence of fireworks. Startling wheels of light. Explosions to threaten the sky. Rockets that shot out of empty cider jars toward the moon hanging pale above us. Bangers that had the smallest children wrenched out of their sleep on the grass and into tears and the large comfort of the oldest woman, the one who had talked about cake when we arrived.

You arrived mysteriously at my side, your eyes reflecting the exploding lights in the sky, your cheeks flushed with something that had nothing to do with me. You took my hand, you whispered that you were tired now, and we went back toward the house. We retrieved our bags from the car and went upstairs, to the Dutch Room.

You lay on the bed. Wide and double, almost indecent in its size. Freshly cut tulips in a vase on the dresser. On the walls framed paintings of botanical specimens and pictures of Netherlandish things like canals and Rembrandt and Anne Frank. Mystery thrillers stacked up on the his and hers bedside tables. The window looked out over the field of timid heifers, a mark of wealth of this fine blond tribe, illuminated by the fairy lights and guttering torches.

I took off most of my clothes with the scrupulous deliberateness of a drunkard and asked why we had come.

"You'll find it here," you said, almost regretfully, "what we need to know."

"In this room?"

"And wouldn't that be cozy? The two of us, nothing else. No. Not here. It's got nothing to do with the two of us. Here, in this house. These people."

"Who are these people?"

"The enemy."

"Who's Alex? I thought I saw Julian Brougham Calder dressed like a donkey."

You opened your mouth and showed me your tongue. You pulled yourself away from your clothes and climbed beneath the covers and kept your arms well hidden because there was light sliding in through the thin Dutch drapes and it made shadows on the walls and around the door to threaten you, and the Death-Breath night monster would be after you here and there was nothing that I was going to be able to do to protect you from that.

"Sometimes, Tierney, you're very dense." The last words I heard before I fell asleep.

I could throw away the fruit, should I do that? Rotting beyond recognition on the table by the door. It's a strange sentimentality to keep it there, watching it decay, remembering the first time I saw it, the first time I saw this apartment of ours, clean, the walls without marks, the floors piled high with boxes for Albania, the bathroom shelves waiting for your cosmetics, the bowl of oranges and apples offered hopefully up to tempt your mother's daughter home. I stuck my finger inside the bowl just now, inside what I think used to be an orange. THROW AWAY THE FRUIT. Retched, nearly puked. An evil acid tang poisoned the air, green juices seeped disgustingly out. I lifted my finger to my nose, lowered it toward your mouth, contemplated pushing it down inside your throat to make you sick and maybe, therefore, well. I shout your name. No response. But I guess that was always going to be so. Before the filth dries on my finger I use it to write your name on the wall. Forgive the stain.

The day after midsummer, a sunshine civilized day. I woke up alone. Waited for you awhile, then went downstairs and took breakfast on the patio with an undersized woman (blonde) who had a baby (blonde or blond) on her lap. We drank coffee and I bolted it down to get away from her conversation. In the shrillest of voices, she was something of an expert on pituitary problems.

The lawn was scarred by fireworks and torches. The fairy lights were still hanging, still glimmering. The heifers were in their field, lying down, peaceably waiting for rain. I saw Jane off in the rose garden pulling up weeds with rubber gloves. Sometimes she'd straighten out and swipe at the sweat on her forehead with her arm, and I didn't like that because it reminded me of my mother.

Noises from the swimming pool. The tribe at play, laughing and splashing. Skirted around it, skulked down through the secret garden, past a greenhouse filled with tropical flowers, and down along a snake path through high grass toward the tennis court.

A few gangs of yellow balls in the corners of the court and on either side of the net. Two rackets propped up against the wire netting at the back. Otherwise, empty. I picked up a racket and sliced a few balls over the net, then hit the rest of them as hard as I could. The sound of the sea lapping around me off in the distance. Still couldn't figure it out—we were inland, surrounded—protected—by fields and woods.

A tremor in the grass. Then stillness. Then another tremor, one spot of grass bending wrong, toward the wind. I lobbed one ball at the tremor, then another. A tanned bare arm threw it back at me over the wire wall of the court. I lobbed another ball and a bare white arm rose from the grass and held it, then dropped it, then retreated back beneath grassy cover.

You and your friend with the gymnast's body and the strange-shaped nose stood up out of the grass like urban nymphs lost in the country. Both of you dressed the same in denim shorts and faded punk-logo T-shirts. You each yawned and stretched, T-shirts lifting to show two navels, Alex's tanned, yours pale and sunless.

"Tierney," you said, "it's you."

Tried a B-movie German accent. "You vehr accepting some-vun else, maybe?" Didn't come off too well, sounded more Israeli than Nazi, and I got a rather evil glance from your grass-stained friend, like maybe I'd been interrupting something. She told you, in an accent that was a mix of upper-class and street, she'd see you back up at the house and she drifted away. You joined me on my side of the wire and picked up a racket and we beat the balls around for a while. You didn't respond to any of my questions (which were planned to sound anything but jealous) and instead set about making me look oafish on the court.

After you grew tired of the sport we walked back to join the rest of them. Roses climbed the walls of the secret garden, and beds of bright-colored things all pointed the same depressing way toward the sun. The greenhouse was filled with tropical fleshy specimens like the sexual parts of sinister animals. You led me into the fields where the herd of brown heifers regarded us from the other side of a ditch. We were on the top of the hill and could see only woods and fields. Shimmering off in the far distance was a ribbon of lights like fairy lights.

"We're not near the sea, I know that. It's weird. I think I can hear the sea."

"Traffic. We're in the middle of the M1 and the M25. You can see the lights over there of the M25. We're only a few minutes away from either motorway. You wouldn't think it. I think Anthony pulled some strings to divert the roads away from here. He wanted it inviolate."

We approached the swimming pool. A few blond adults were in the pool, throwing their blond kids—pink skin scrubbed clean of last night's midsummer paint—screaming splashing into the air. Others lying on sun loungers with wet mystery thrillers open on their bellies. Padding around the pool, the patriarch of the tribe. His dog, some kind of black hunting dog, padding proudly alongside his master. They padded over to us. Anthony didn't possess as many chins as his wife, he had less hair too, but a larger belly, as would befit the head of the tribe.

"Deborah. Good morning."

You kissed him. He kissed you back. Something politely lascivious in the way he kissed you back.

"Lovely to see you here. You caught our entertainment? You haven't been to visit us in such a long time."

You bowed your head in mock shame.

"You know you don't have to wait for an invitation. You're always welcome here."

"I know, Anthony. Thank you."

"And this is your American? I am sorry I didn't have the chance to welcome you last night. We were all too busy with the masque."

"Richard Tierney. Sir Anthony Brougham-Calder. Excuse me. I want to say hello to Alex."

Anthony Brougham-Calder. We turned and watched you go to your friend on the sun lounger. Sir Anthony Brougham-Calder. A large man. Once upon a time the spurned suitor of Helen Newell. And later, the man who had blackballed Ivory from the Reform Club. He hadn't been a Sir back then. I think he'd become larger since then.

"Is Alex your daughter?"

"Alexandra, yes, is my daughter. Friends with Deborah for many years, they had a thoroughly disreputable adolescence together. Then I have five sons—Anthony, Charles, Francis, Edward, Peter. Eight grandchildren at the last count, with two more on the way. No nieces, no nephews. One brother."

"I *thought* I saw him last night . . ."

"A rogue. He says he's resting indoors. Probably at the brandy. Delightful company of course as long as you don't believe a word he says. Full of talk and air, always was. Tell me, what is your interest in my family?"

"Tangential. I'm writing a book. On William Ivory."

Yeah, a book. Remember the plan? The dust covers with William Ivory's grim handsome face superimposed over images of glamorous decadence. The dedication, maybe to you, I never did decide. The witty quotes on the flyleaf: "A father is always your master even when he's gone" from Bukowski; and maybe one from Pavese too, I never was sure about that one—"Women are an enemy race, like the Germans." (Maybe go instead for Wheel's David Cooper line—"There's no such thing as natural death: every death is either murder or suicide.") The photographs, family spreads, Norfolk estates, vacation snapshots, formal groupings in color, in black and white, scattered through the text, not bunched together in the middle, not cheap like that. And at the end, the index, scholarly apparatus for the reader to ape my quest.

I had to repeat what I'd said because Sir Anthony asked me to. I watched his face, boiled a little pink from the sun, watched the muscles flex to keep emotion well down, away from scrutiny. Just a twitch by the side of the mouth, a flicker of the eyes, a blink, and down it went again, like food you have to swallow a second time in order not to vomit.

"Did you ever know him?" I should have opened my eyes round and stuck a finger in my mouth and made with a lisp, I was being so transparent. You don't catch out a high-court judge with tricks learned from Disingenuous 101.

"Of course I knew him. He was a rascal." He dropped his voice to make sure his words didn't carry over to you. You weren't going to hear them even if they did. Sitting hunched laughing on the sun lounger, Alex B.-C. stretched full out, her shorts and shirt removed in favor of a one-piece black swimsuit, laughing along with you, expensive muscles long and hard in her tanned body. An innocent girlish conspiracy, sure.

"Can you tell me why?"

"I would prefer not. And certainly not here."

"It would be an enormous help to me."

A beach ball splashed our way. He kicked it back bouncing into the pool. His dog looked longingly after it.

"If I did I would have to impose one or two conditions."

I encouraged him to name them.

"I should require a written undertaking that any information I gave you would not be ascribed to me. I would not want any member of my family to be mentioned other than my brother. His foolish words are no responsibility of mine."

I agreed happily. I didn't care about the conditions then and I don't care about them now. So, judge, sue me.

"Later then. Not now. In the house. After lunch."

The judge lowered himself into the pool and set off on a leisurely breaststroke. I joined you and your friend. You made no room for me on the sun lounger.

"What were you talking to Anthony about?"

"I'm sworn to secrecy."

"I'm agog," said Alex, and turned her perfect back to me.

I must have registered some disapproval or discontent or maybe it was just the raw smell of jealousy.

"Don't worry," you said, blowing a kiss to me over her perfect shoulder. "It's just an innocent girlish conspiracy."

Patterns repeat. Things become inevitable. And that's what you really hate, isn't it? Like Ivory with his hatred of flowers pointing the same powerless way to the sun. Necessity. Eternal recurrence. I watched you with the girl Alex and I watched her mother and father watching you and there was something like hate on their faces (the same expression that your taxi buddy Charlie, upper-class thin and basketball-player tall in his swimming briefs, was sending my way). Like your father with the Glavens, you with the Brougham-Calders. The same low disapproval from the family, the same kind of secret friendship with a cousin. The same kinds of transgressions, except this time it had been punk and heroin that caused the teenage outrage. I'd say your father coached you into it. You'd say the same thing was inside you. The same hatefulness. The same poison.

I went exploring before lunch. The family were all busy with swimming-pool play, and I didn't enjoy the sight of foolish Charlie failing to persuade you to take a romantic turn around the gardens with him. In the house the only ones were a few sleeping toddlers, and Lady Jane busy with cake icing and stuff she called marchpane, and Julian B.C., still dressed for the masque, slumped in the television room in front of a solitary game of cards with a paper straw from a brandy bottle leading up to his mouth. He raised an invisible hat to me as I looked in through the doorway. I was about to go on when he called out my name. I was surprised to hear him remember it and I told him so.

"That horrible horrible man," he said between deep brandy swallows. Half a century of bitterness and outrage started to well up in his eyes. "He stole my idea for a book. *Essays at Twilight*, he stole it. Everything was going to be perfect but he stole it away from me and after that there was nothing left to do. He told me what he was going to do. In nineteen forty-three."

He started to sob. I left him to it.

I don't know what I was snooping for. Let's dignify it by calling it clues. Making little noise, I slipped around the house, opened doors, lifted things up and put them down again. Didn't find much. I admired the large oil painting of Lady Jane in debutante gear, only one chin then to boast of. I went into the master bedroom, which had a bathroom and dressing room on either side. Sir Tony's bathroom was manly and correct, different-size hairbrushes in a tidy row and a groovy green shaving kit. Lady Jane's, though: sort of messy, sort of higgledy-piggledy, and crammed full of opaque blue bottles of Floris oils and soaps. You've got the same ones, haven't you? In a line on your middle shelf with a hardly used palette of Midnight Blue eye shadow at the end.

After the triumph of Lady Jane's cake, the weather turned ugly on us and we moved inside into the drawing room. A game of bridge was suggested and four of the tribe set up a card table in the corner. Jane brought out an archeology of photograph albums and scrapbooks and sat with you on a green velvet sofa and cooed and pointed and finally found the Kodak snapshots (white borders and crinkled edges, flattering black-and-white prints) of midsummer, 1965, you as First Fairy, smudge-faced adorable and sullen. The rest of us came over to look and poke the expected fun, and you displayed just the combination of embarrassment and pride that was expected of you.

Then the instruments were fetched and the Brougham-Calder string ensemble started to play. Jane on viola, jealous Charlie on angry double bass, sexy Alex on sexy cello, and Tony, the oldest son, an attorney, a less substantial reflection of his father, played a careful violin. After a couple of false starts they launched into a quartet by Schubert, and were doing it rather well.

You sat alone on the sofa, leafing through the illustrated family history. Charlie busted a string on his bass and used the opportunity to come and sit next to you on the arm of your sofa. You banished him quickly back to the music. I sat with Daddy Judge by his desk on the opposite side of the room. We talked softly, and sometimes he broke off to admire a particular musical phrase or nod encouragingly to his wife, the weakest of the players.

We talked generally, of England, and pituitary diseases, and Shakespeare, and progress, all of which the judge seemed to believe in, and then finally, when the second movement was well into swing, I got the subject onto Ivory.

"You called him a rascal."

"Because he was."

"How so?"

"I don't know you from Adam, Richard, and because you are Deborah's friend that can make you any kind of person under the sun, for she was never the most discerning child."

"How well did you know her as a child?"

"Please. Allow me to arrive at the point I was making."

I watched you, bored, smoking a cigarette, slowly turning through pages of photo albums, occasionally looking up to regard me or Alex or Charlie—your three very different suitors—with a disinterested air, as if we were photos too. Sir Judge droned on. He was talking about discretion and the problems of conveying intimate fact to someone he didn't know.

"Please. I'm sorry to interrupt you, sir, but can't we just take that on trust?"

He droned on again. Slowly, like an ancient steamship navigating the approach to a narrow canal, he chugged cautiously toward the subject.

"I was young when I knew Ivory. He was different from the kind of man I was taught to expect from this world. I suppose—and this is the problem of you and I discussing this subject, we have very separate languages, so when I say something that to me is filled with meaning, to you, who are not privy to the associations of my culture, it might easily, naïvely, sound like the baldest of clichés—but nonetheless my first impression of him was, Here is a man who doesn't play by the rules."

"Even when he gambled at cards?"

I was hoping to sway him off balance. It might have worked in my country. Not in his. (Yours.) The English are better at lying than we are.

"You have been talking to my brother. He believes in magic. I do not. Whatever happened that day—when was it? Nineteen fifty-two? 'fifty-one?—had to do with the human spirit, not the supernatural. I can't tell you about his gambling. I expect he followed some rules, perhaps not. I'm talking about the grand picture. He was a user, a corrupter. It may be old-fashioned to think this way, but he was an evil man."

"His wife still cherishes his memory."

A sudden fury, an ancient passion, made him suddenly young. "He ruined her, crushed her, crept like a thief into her life and stole away her spirit. You have met her? How does she look now? Later, I will show you pictures of her. She was the most beautiful one of our generation."

"And one of the richest."

"Indeed yes. And he took it all. She signed away all her money to her fine dashing man, and when he had it all he left. That's all there is to it."

"Surely not. I've read things. Letters. They were in close touch right up to his death."

He shrugged. Drained his glass. Refilled it. "Perhaps so. That would have been because of the children."

"It goes deeper. They loved each other. He told her everything. She loves him still. Protects his memory like he was her child. And she knows how he died, I'm sure of that, just won't say. I'm sure you're right about the fact of the money, but he couldn't have done it without her complicity."

"That's a monstrous thing to say!" His fruity round voice lifted up above the music and the players jumped a beat. They all looked over our way. You didn't look over our way. You'd found something that interested you more.

The music cranked on, a slow third movement. You kept your attention on the same photograph album, I hadn't seen you turn the page in the longest time, nor look up, not at me, not at Alex. Certainly not at Charlie. The judge spoke on, more measured now, controlled.

"Let me put it to you this way. It is fashionable, I believe, in some circles, to decry the state of things, to deny the existence of what we in our time called national values. Caricature me if you like as a dull old justice with outmoded views— what would you call me? A fuddy-duddy?—but I happen to believe in certain things. I happen to believe in democracy. I happen to believe in loyalty to the seasons. One has to ground oneself, in the land, in the law—not blindly, but wisely—and one has to resist the suave persuasions of cosmopolitan types with a blueprint for utopia tucked away in their gun cases. And of course English values have taken a buffeting—I personally believe our immigration policies since the War have resulted in our losing sight of our distinctiveness and worth, but that is a debatable point, I grant you. English values have taken a buffeting from cheap shabby rogues like Ivory with a gift for grandiosity and a con man's way with gestures, but that is all. And let me say this, he was a troublemaker and he timed his trouble well, we all thought he was finished and now here comes his daughter again, and now she's touting her father's trouble around and if you happen to intercept it, Richard, then I will see it goes to your advantage. You, I think I can trust. Deborah is too much her father's daughter . . . But it is cruelly wrong of you to see Helen Newell as anything but a victim —when one starts to dress the victim in her tyrant's clothes, then nothing makes any sense anymore."

"Do things make sense?"

"One hopes they do. Otherwise . . . ?"

We exchanged knowing old-men's clubroom smiles. He re-filled my glass with his dubious Scotch. I asked him something about Norfolk, and while he was brewing up to answer, you screamed.

The music stopped with a whine and a shudder. Lady Jane's chins shook toward you. Sir Anthony smiled, I didn't know why. Alex got up from her seat and her cello clattered on the floor and ugly notes cracked through the air. The bridge play-ers didn't look up. Charlie looked at the floor between his feet. You sneezed once, a loud damaged sneeze, then you pushed away the photo album you were looking at, a green one, gold embossed shapes on the cover. It fell to the floor and you kicked at it and sneezed again, and then ran out of the room, and I jumped up and watched you go through the lobby, and by the time I'd got into the lobby you were opening the front door and letting the rain in, and by the time I got to the door—Alex alongside—you were in your car, and by the time we got onto the drive you were motoring away and Alex got a nasty cut from a pebble churned up at her from beneath one of your wheels, and I gave her my handkerchief to use to dab at the wound. She held it up to her face as we watched you disappear.

We went slowly in. Jane was putting away the photograph albums. It took some arguing to allow me to look through them. Just the green ones, I told her, the ones with the gold designs embossed on the cover.

Alex knew her family history. It was something she was willing to talk to me about. (I remember a letter of Ivory's where he remarks that if you want to break the ice with the English upper classes just ask them for some information about a dead forebear and you're in like Flynn—or words to that effect.) We made a pile of the green albums, Alex and I, and flipped our way through them. The judge took up the cello and the ensemble resumed their music from where they'd left off. The bridge game continued. Julian's snores started to reach us from the next-door room.

Alex talked me through the pictures and gave me the names.

The young bucks who became the great and the good. Lawyers dining in fancy dress in grand rooms. Vacation shots of the family in Tuscany looking around a dusty church. Vacation shots of the family at their second home in the South of France. Oxford undergraduates in 1948 who became members of the government in 1984. Photographs of baby B.-C.s in christening robes lying on antique lace. Graduation shots of the children, pictures of the parents at dinner tables, on shooting parties, in court. The young Julian, in beret and greatcoat, cigarette drooping from mouth, shoulder to shoulder with his more respectable brother. And then, closer to home, Helen Newell as a debutante at the Queen Charlotte's Ball, virginal and sexy, only her wild eyes to give her longing away. Newspaper clippings side by side announcing the marriages of the Hon. Jane Yorke to Mr. Anthony Brougham-Calder and Miss Helen Newell to Mr. William Ivory, clippings reporting Mr. Anthony B.-C. taking silk and becoming a Queen's Counsel. Even a photograph of Ivory, one I hadn't seen before, standing on a white-painted balcony, with the place and date written neatly below in white pencil on the black page, *Ravello, 1962.*

I might have missed the important clipping, the one that made you scream and sneeze, if Alex hadn't gone past it so quick. I returned to the page, to see a shot of the B.-C. hunting dogs in 1980, and there it was, just a headline, alongside Charlie's Cambridge graduation picture:

MAN KILLS WOMAN AND THEN DRIVES INTO LORRY

Nothing else. Nothing to follow. Just that, all alone, separated from the story, the headline, large and brash and sinister and final, with the date written below, 16 March 1980. The next page was filled with a formal portrait of Jane's brother, a Home Secretary, upon his appointment. Nothing more about the man, the woman, or the lorry on any of the other pages.

I flicked through some more albums. Nothing more. And no one was giving anything away. Not Alex, who covered her cut with a band-aid and went to reclaim her cello and make some more music. Not Jane, who briskly cleared away all the albums, asked me if I wanted anything to drink, and before I had time to reply took up her viola again. Not even nice Uncle Julian snoring in a brandy stupor in the next room. And certainly not Sir Anthony. He looked at me with an irritating satisfaction, brushed off all my questions, even the most direct. And when I suggested the reason there was anything in the albums about Ivory at all was because he might once have had a—shall we say?—*friendship* with Lady Jane B.-C., the judge threw me out of the house.

N ivea, Floris, Clinique, Chanel, Body Shop, Annick Goutal, Clarins, Helena Rubinstein, Elizabeth Arden, Revlon, Max Factor, Guerlain, Christian Dior, Boots No. 7, Mary Quant, Bourjois, Yardley, Shiseido, Lancôme, Estée Lauder. Hardly any more than a little used. Some of the lipsticks, yes, their tips worn down with the impression of your mouth in an efficient pout, but the rest, they were never for your innocent use, were they? Ritual magic, that's all, tools of competition. And some of them I can identify now. Floris for Jane Brougham-Calder. Mary Quant for Lizzie Sharp. Yardley, that was Miss P——'s own favorite. Nivea and Helena Rubinstein, they're what your mother uses, decaying faithful Helen. The Pentecostalist had a taste for Estée Lauder. The supermarket girl slapped Boots No. 7 over her flesh to rid it of that urine smell. Body Shop used by the university virgin. Clinique, Lancôme, Clarins, by others who had the luck or misfortune to encounter Mr. William Ivory, monster. The stick of Guerlain, sophisticated and French, he bought for you on your sixteenth birthday. And Shiseido, so prettily wrapped, that was pretty Reiko's choice.

Did you think you could compete with these women by covering yourself up with their beautifying things? You stole them at first, didn't you? Shifty adolescent girl in a big coat sneaking around the cosmetic counters of High Street pharmacies for your makeup voodoo rite. Did it promise power to you? Or was it more desperate than that? Did you lock your bedroom door and smear your face with paint and powder? Did you spray scent on your wrists and behind your ears? Did you then preen in front of the mirror and imagine you were they, and then did you sit downstairs by the telephone and wait for your father to call? Did your father ever call?

Look at me when I'm talking to you. Your father is dead. He's gone. There's no point dressing yourself for him anymore. Your ritual magic never worked, why the fuck do you think it's going to work now? You look like a clown covered in all that goo. Can you hear me? Can you even see me? Can you hear my footsteps now? Can you hear my steps as I go into the bathroom? I'm standing in front of the bathroom shelves. I'm looking at them now, the higgledy-piggledy rows of sweet-smelling stuff. Did you hear that sound? The slap and roll of a plastic jar falling into the bathroom sink, did you hear that? Do you hear this? One vulgar Yankee hand pushing a whole shelf-load of the shit onto the floor. Ooh, some of them roll but some of them break, glass jars cracking open, shards of glass smeared with cream, driblets and droplets of fairy goo running down the side of the bathtub and along the tiles on the floor. Did you hear that? Did you wince? How about this? Another shelf-load crashing and flying and hitting the wall and the tub and the floor, and does that break through to you? The floor is like something out of a New York painting, the smell in here hits you in the head like a hammer wrapped in something poisonously sweet. Poison, yeah poison, I'm on to you, and I'm going to keep on going; there goes another shelf, there goes a vulgar American fist slamming down against a blue Nivea tube and a pulse of the white stuff ejaculates into the tub. There goes another shelf of jars and tubes and prettily packaged things jumping and sliding and rolling and splashing and breaking and yeah I like the sound of this and I like the action of this and even though the air's getting too sickly to breathe, this is giving me some kind of relief.

Back into the room. Go toward you. Stop in the center of the room. There's something too pale and forbidding about you there on the floor beside the sofa. Maybe I should just go back to the story. Calm down. The story. It's almost done. And I'm getting desperate to find out what happens to you when I get to the end.

I recklessly made an insinuation about his wife and it was inspired and it was right and the judge threw me out of the house into the rain. The warning barks of a big black hunting dog were enough to prevent me from heading back inside to try and make a better second impression, and the barks got louder when grim-faced happy Charlie opened the door to toss out our overnight bag.

Walked out onto the tree-lined country lane. Turned up my collar against the summer rain and stuck out my thumb and flattened myself against the hedgerow each time a car drove splashing past. Didn't know too well where I was walking to, just followed the direction we'd taken before and trusted to Irish luck that there'd be a train or a bus or something to rescue me back into London.

It must have been about the eighth car that finally stopped for me. A Mercedes station wagon that skidded a little as it braked. I waited for it to reverse toward me, it waited for me to run up to meet it, and then we did both at the same time and it drove back over my foot.

The door was pushed open by the woman inside and I pulled myself out of the hedge and hobbled aboard, and there was Jane Brougham-Calder in the driver's seat leaning over with a bottle of brandy.

"Here. Drink. You must be soaked."

"Very sensitive. Thank you."

"I'll take you to the station. Are you going back into town? I'm afraid you rather upset my husband."

"I had an idea about something that kind of rubbed him up the wrong way."

She crunched the gears and we lurched away.

"Would you mind telling me what it was?"

"I could have been more diplomatic I suppose. Thank you for the brandy, can I have some more? I think I asked him if you ever had an affair with William Ivory."

She kept her eyes on the road and wobbled her chins.

"Did he answer you?"

"Next thing I knew I was out in the yard and Fido was barking and young Charlie was practicing his cricket with my hand luggage."

I eased the wet straw out of the bottle and put it in the

ashtray and squelched my feet into a slightly more comfortable position.

"I'm sorry and you're probably going to throw me out of the car now but you did have an affair with Ivory, didn't you?"

She smiled in a game kind of way. Made her look almost pretty.

"Ravello. Nineteen sixty-two. Yeah? Later you published a book under the name of Society Lady. Ivor Y. Ivory."

"You're very clever."

"No I'm not at all. That's one of the things I've realized since I came here. I'm not at all clever, just dumb enough not to know when I'm beat. Give an infinite number of Tierneys an infinite amount of time to find stuff out about an infinite number of Ivorys and a few of them will find out something. Eventually."

"My husband will not be glad I came after you."

"Why did you?"

"You're a friend of Deborah's and I feel sorry for her and a little sorry for you. And I owe something to him."

"To Ivory? I thought he was the devil incarnate in your house."

"He wasn't what one would call a nice man but I liked him. We had an adventure together."

I must have registered something that wasn't too flattering. Hard to picture—the glamorous sinner with this large woman with her many chins.

"Yes. I know. You have to remember that we were once more beautiful than today."

I made a wince of apology. We were on the highway now going back into London. I thanked her for taking me so far and she waved my politeness away.

"That newspaper clipping. He died in a car crash?"

"He died in a car crash."

"He killed a woman first? Like the clipping said?"

She smiled at that. Didn't say yes or no.

"Who knows about it?"

"Rather more than you might think. Poor Helen certainly. Deborah, I rather think not. Most of our family, Julian excepted— You must not be too hard on Julian. He has no money of his own and relies entirely on the allowance Anthony gives him. And Anthony, I believe, exerted a little pressure to stop him talking to you. —Some more of the people Will knew know. An awful little man named Dibbs or Bibbs or something."

"Gibbs. Roland Gibbs."

"Exactly. My husband arranged for certain things. The whole thing was kept very quiet."

"Why?"

"Why, to protect his reputation of course. Loyalty to Helen. Does that sound silly?"

That sounded very silly. Silly enough to be English and true. Even if it wasn't. Not entirely.

"Will you tell me about it?"

"I'm afraid I rather gave my word. But you might find it helpful to remember the date and look up the facts in the papers, and also I believe the policeman in charge of the investigation was a sergeant named Brett at Paddington. You might get something out of him."

"I'm very grateful."

"Please don't let on I helped you. I'd come in for some stick if you did. Would it be an awful bore if I dropped you off here? I'd rather not be away from the house for too long. I'm going to say I went out to buy a dozen eggs."

She dropped me outside a subway station. I gave her back the bottle of brandy.

"Please remember," she said through the window as she struggled with the gearbox, "he was evil and he was not. He was the most agreeable interloper into some otherwise ordinary lives."

15 March 1980

Dearest Helen,

Is there any other way? You call me a bully, I am not a bully, an advocate merely of nobility and will. This is not an escape act I'm planning: I am no apocalyptic Houdini wriggling out a dangerous new path away from an insufferable dullness. Mishima not Boothby. Kleist not Pavese. Strike out. Go forward. If you loved me you would not dilly-dally. I have found a new marriage bed for us and I wait for you there.

As always, your husband
W.

Heinrich von Kleist spent ten years trying to argue different women into a lovers' suicide pact. For how many years did Mishima search before he found his clumsy chum Morita? Ivory came close with Lizzie Sharp and even closer with Helen, but then she pulled away. Some things are stronger than poison and stronger than charm. Helen's Catholicism for one. She wouldn't join him in his marital deathbed and he had to find someone else instead.

We had a conversation about this once. Do you remember? In a late-night Italian restaurant speculating about your father's death. We contemplated suicide together and I told you he might have killed himself out of horror at his own decay. You didn't like that at all. You got angry at me, raised your voice at me. "You idiot," you said, "it was a game to please himself with. If he ever killed himself it was because he was *bored*."

This is the final letter I have. Your mother burned the rest.

Y ou were waiting for me upstairs. Using a Scarlet Fire lipstick (whose was that? Supermarket girl's?) to write words on the wall next to my abuse against Bill Buckner. BREAD. COFFEE. CHEESE. You looked a little startled when I came in, like a schoolgirl trapped with an illicit cigarette.

"I'm writing a list."

"Why?"

You went to the window. Looked down at the street. I thought I could see a touch of gray in your hair.

"Have you found it out yet? Mother thinks you have."

"Almost. I'm nearly there."

You didn't move. Suspended animation. Waiting.

It wasn't hard after what Jane Brougham-Calder had told me to find out the facts of his death. From the newspaper report to the policeman in charge of the investigation (now an inspector at Palmers Green) to the eyewitnesses who saw it all. I went to see a man named Gary who sold bunches of cut flowers on a street in Bromley. I even went to see bad brother Matthew. A mews house in Chelsea just round the corner from your old childhood place on Tite Street. Barely furnished, white walls, very clean, and no life inside. He was one of those people whose personalities are too small to fill a place. I caught him at a charming moment, his wife was filing divorce papers against him and that made him feel a little bigger. He didn't know how his father died and I don't think he really cared so we spent a charming afternoon talking family history together. (Genealogy seemed to be his specialty. He had quite a forest of family trees, pasted into scrapbooks. Fastidiously he explained to me how, if twenty-seven people died, he would be the next Earl of Lothian.) The only one who refused to talk was Rolf Karlsen, a retired truck driver with ruined nerves who lived in an industrial suburb of Stockholm.

I also saw Jim Harkin.

Jim Harkin. A white-haired red-faced benevolent man. Tough frame, gentle eyes, a tropics-beaten face that turned a brighter red whenever anything personal was discussed. Shouted when he talked, as if he was accustomed to speaking only to deaf people and foreigners. He was a traveling man, just back from Vietnam, on his way to the Hindu Kush. He was someone whose vocation it was to immerse himself in alien cultures. He'd been friend to a man who did it by stealth, who liked to catch glimpses of things. We took tea at the Overseas Club.

We talked about Vietnam and we talked about Japan, and reluctantly, apologetically, he answered my question about Reiko.

"Ivory knew her parents in Kyoto?"

Harkin sighed. His eyes lowered and his face reddened and his fingers twitched on his belly. "Not Ivory. No. Her father was an academic. Mother bit of a snob actually. The girl wanted to learn English. I knew the father. Worked together at one point. Unesco stuff. Recommended the girl to Ivory. He liked things Japanese you know."

"You sent her over."

Harkin looked abject. And I knew why.

"I'm sorry if you don't like talking about this . . ."

"Honestly. It's all right. Long time ago. Pushed for time though. Off to Hindu Kush shortly. Do you know it?"

I admitted I did not.

"Wonderful place. Very bright."

"Tell me about Mishima. His friendship with Ivory."

Harkin's face blushed redder. His eyes darted about the room. "Introduced them in nineteen fifty-two. Mishima on his European tour. The heliotropic mysteries of Greece. Went to France looking for Baudelaire. Found Marxism only. To his disgust. Known Yukio in Japan. Looked me up when he came into London. He loved the theater, particularly musical shows. Never could sit through them myself. Went to see a production of *Much Ado About Nothing.* Invited Ivory along, thought it would interest him to meet Mishima. Couldn't make it. Came by, though, for a drink at halftime. Not much said. Far as I know, that was the only time they met."

"Not possible, surely?"

"You're probably right. You probably know better than I. Only time I saw them together."

"Not ever in Japan?"

"Ivory never visited Japan."

A city crumbles. A world dissolves. A bashful red-faced man tears it all apart.

"Say that again."

"Ivory never visited Japan. Not to my knowledge. Novel translated over there. Ivory under pressure to publicize the book. Surprised a lot of people when he refused to go. They're still very uneasy about Mishima over there. Tailor-made situation for Ivory you'd have thought."

"Nineteen fifty-five, 'fifty-six, I've got his letters. He was working on a Unesco report, he sent letters to his wife. She wasn't his wife then."

Harkin's face got heavy and luminous with blood. He looked desperately around for escape. "Rather not talk about that if it's all the same to you."

It wasn't all the same to me. I pushed him. He was easy to bully. Too nice a man to resist for long.

"*I* was working on Unesco report. *Ivory* living in South London. Tooting? We communicated. He was fascinated by Japan. Hungry for information. Greedy almost, you might say. Invited him out but he had no interest in seeing it for himself. Said it would get in the way of his imagination. He wanted snippets, glimpses."

"The letters?"

"It's a little shameful," he bellowed, startling men in their chairs. "Didn't inquire into his motives. Didn't know what the letters contained. Sorry if I misled anybody. He sent them to me in sealed envelopes. I posted them back to London. Hope I didn't do anything wrong . . ."

He looked awfully unhappy. A small Asian man under a

funny hat was limping through the clubroom. He passed near our table and smiled to see Harkin there. He asked him a question in English and Harkin replied happily in a quiet foreign tongue. When the Asian limped off, Harkin looked hopefully back at my chair as if I might have taken the opportunity to slip quietly away.

"His translations?"

Harkin sighed in relief. "Those were real enough. Very good. Very very good indeed." Harkin spent a happy while praising Ivory's translations. "Had a real feel for the Japanese temper. They're excellent renditions. Really excellent. Two of them, aren't there? He never went there though. Oh dear. Liked to ask me questions. Used to stop me sometimes when he found my answers too thorough. I'm sure I wasn't his only source."

A bell rang. Things connect. I asked about Roland Gibbs and the story he'd told me. The dinner party at Ivory's house when the generous host had interrupted Harkin's anecdote of Japan and instead decided to humiliate his traveling friend. Harkin nodded. Blood bubbled up into the skin of his face. It was a painful memory.

"Don't know what you've discovered about Ivory. But some people loathed him and others loved him and the rest of us let ourselves be bullied by him because he deserved our loyalty and would always in the end reward it with something. Sometimes forget myself in company and Ivory might have thought I was going to steal his thunder and tell something of myself that he'd already passed off as his, but then again that seemed perfectly right to me. Always made more of things than I ever could. I'd say something and it was what it was. Ivory would say it and he'd find its truth. Even when wasn't telling it.

"Gibbs wrote Ivory's obituary, didn't he? Always many stories going around about Ivory. Encouraged some of them himself. After he died there was talk of a book he was writing and it was meant to take lid off things and a lot of people rather started watching their backs. Remember reading that obituary and remarking how restrained the thing was. Last book never did emerge, did it? Obit must have done the trick. How much more do you need to know?"

"Do you know how he died?"

"Never asked. Wasn't my business. Heard talk of autopsy cover-up but if no one told me then it wasn't for me to know. I'm sorry. Will you excuse me shortly? Running late."

"What color were his eyes?"

"Green. Or blue. Brown? Green? Odd question. Not too good with eye color. Don't remember. Sorry."

He looked at his watch. I thanked him and I excused him and he closed his eyes in his pleasure at not having to do any more talking. I returned to Holloway, hugging to myself the truth about Japan.

When I came back that day after speaking with Harkin, my step was light, my face showed pride. You must have sensed I had it all. You smiled at me. You were made up to look like your mother. You'd even done your hair the same.

"Let's go for a drive," you said.

We went to your car and you gave me the keys and together we drove around Panic Suburbia, a housing estate from the 1930s, you said you wanted to see how the real people live. Semi-detached mock-Tudor fronts, three bedrooms, two gardens, one garage, and on; low rent, brashly colored painted concrete, crazy dents in the railings of the balconies, bright primary colors of metal sheeting, piled together as if someone meant a ziggurat; and on the other side, over the two-lane blacktop, a park with a tennis court, two soccer fields, a children's playground with a slide, a seesaw, a long rocking horse, room enough for six kids on its gently bucking bronco back, a roundabout, colored the same as those metal sheets on the apartment-block project, but older, more dignified; two awkward girls playing tennis, we stood out of the car to watch them for a little while under the nighttime floodlights, both of them benevolently cheating, calling shots in when they were out, each politely making up rules to favor the other as they went along; and we got bored of watching them, and we climbed back into the car and drove on. Panic Suburbia just keeps on going. It spreads like a mass hysteria. We drove through one-street shopping arcades, French restaurants called A Touch of Class, Boots the Chemists, Italian-style delicatessens, supermarkets with post offices, bathroom fittings, betting parlors, banks, and boarded-up stores like missing teeth dotted irregularly in between: and then another bleak stretch of 1930s estates, or 1960s tower blocks or 1980s pastiche reality, and you're looking out of the window the whole time, you only look at me when you think I can't see you, that difficult moment every time I look at the passenger-door wing mirror and you think I'm reaching for your eyes with mine, so I stop using that mirror, it's just too fucking awkward; and you rest your head on your window and blow on it and start to draw a shape in the condensation, then you rub it out before I can work out what it is, and you're muttering something to yourself, a mantra or a lullaby, I don't know which, but then finally you say it, what you've been thinking the whole time.

"I don't want to end up like him."

"You don't have to."

"It's in the blood."

"Your mother has none of it."

"Look at her. Broken and defeated and religious."

"A game old bird."

"You're the only one who thinks so. It's what she tries to pretend. You're the only one who gets taken in by it. But it doesn't matter. I have his blood, too strong for hers, it swamped hers, surrounded it, bubbled up around it. Corrupting or corrupted. What kind of model is that?"

"Tell me about Reiko."

"What do you want to know? She was like a slave to him. Looked after us, bathed us, told us eerie stories at bathtime in broken English. Just another victim—like you, I'm doing the same to you that he did to all his women—you do realize that, don't you?—sucking them in, tossing them aside when the vital thing's been sucked out; I don't know where she is now, sometimes I think I wished she'd kept in touch, we were fond of her, I don't care. Why are we driving here? I'm bored with this. You've got something to tell me. Let's go home."

We drove home. I still had the thing to tell you, but you

would insist on an appropriate ritual first. I watched you as I drove your scarred battered sports car—you were leaning against the window, no longer drawing any shapes on it, just thinking your genotype determinism, contemplating your suicide, as the lanes and roads and streets and villas and gardens and drives and avenues flicked on past us, little cul-de-sacs of life offering you nothing.

A t the end of *Decadent Pleasures*, when Ivory is finished with his stories of magic and beauty and imagination and death, he writes a sad little coda:

> The belief in progress, Baudelaire declared, is the ecstasy of fools. We live in a culturally defeated country. Literary critics analyse the pin-prick embroidery patterns of unambitious novels; in the fine arts, pastiche is all; passion has been replaced by the deathly irony that knowledge of uselessness brings; we are imperfect machines who crank out our spoiled products and die. Progress is no longer possible, even as an idea to gull our children with into hope. We are all decadent Baudelaireans now. The *fin de millénaire* approaches. Let us celebrate it with imagination and at least a little style.

His own spoiled products—*Decadent Pleasures* itself, the sickly *Morita*, and at the end, his *Last Things*. Those mysterious pages he left to you in his will, in trust, that hung after his death over the imperfect lives of his old associates and enemies. Only Julian Brougham Calder appeared indifferent to the book's sinister threat. Maybe that was because he owned nothing to hide, maybe his rebellious disavowal of the family hyphen gave him immunity from that kind of thing, but he even seemed at times to welcome its trickster existence, its legendary stories to cow his brother. Helen wanted it bad, her husband's missing work so long denied her, to be cherished and published and celebrated. And you, you saw it as a tool of barter, to offer to swap for the truth of his death, but no one would go along with that.

And imagination, sure, Ivory had a barrelful of the stuff. Some might call it lying, his patients would call it fantasy or phantasy, he would call it the transforming power of the imagination. Take Japan, the place he wooed Helen from, take Mishima, his own chosen warrior-clown dark double. He never attended Mishima's Wednesday-night parties, he never visited that Western-style house with those low ceilings to make the narcissistic author look taller. Ivory met him only once, briefly introduced by Jim Harkin during the intermission of a production of a Shakespeare play in London in 1952.

Like mad King Ludwig and his nighttime travels around the court riding school, Ivory never went to Japan, he didn't think he needed to. He built his own imaginary Japan, the foundations established in those early days with Mattie conjuring up cruel tales from old wallpaper. He made his own cold place with a perfect surface populated by willing melancholy women and elegant suicides.

But what happened to Ludwig when he got finally bored with riding his horse around the court riding school, when it finally clicked that the thing was a lie, that he wasn't actually going anyplace?

Y ou started getting ready for the bath. You wanted us to be clean for it, you said. You ran the faucets and poured in some perfumed oil and pinned your hair to the top of your head. You didn't hear your mother slip inside the apartment door. The noise of the bathwater covered her soft steps into the living room. She went to the window but she didn't see the street. The graffitied wall didn't force any surprise, her mind was on serious game. She pushed around my papers on the table and her shaking head shook some more. Then she saw it, that innocuous briefcase, monogrammed, brown and battered, in the corner resting against the wall. A thin gurgle of happiness escaped from her throat and that was her first mistake. It coincided with you turning off the hot-water faucet and you caught the huntress's sound and you ran from the bathroom in your blue kimono and you reached the living room in time to see your mother's hands clawing out for the bag.

"Tierney, stop her!"

"It's no business of mine."

Helen lifted the briefcase and clutched it to her body and she saw your expression and she smiled lopsidedly in her triumph and when she spoke the staccato was gone from her voice.

"You have been a very bad girl, Deborah, trying to keep this from me. You had no right." She held the bag hard in both her hands and started toward the door behind you.

"It's mine. He left it to me. He chose me."

"You do not appreciate its importance. It is not a currency to bargain with. It is his work."

"You don't know what's in it." Your face was sullen, your hair had slipped down around your shoulders. Your cheeks looked oddly rounder, more childish.

"It is his. That is the important thing and it must not be lost."

She got to where you were standing and that's when she made her second mistake. Her expression softened to see you looking so sad and she reached out a hand in a way that had become unfamiliar to both of you, to stroke your hair and try to soothe you a little in a way she might last have done when you were a child.

"Don't worry, dear. You have been terribly naughty but it does not matter now. When the book is published it will be dedicated to you. You shan't be forgotten."

You smiled and that alarmed your mother. She moved to walk on but it was already too late. You grabbed for the bag and she tried to hold on to it, but she only had one hand on it, and anyway her dwindling strength was no match for yours. And when it was over you had the briefcase and you were looking almost guilty, and your mother was staring at her empty trembling hands as if she hated them for letting her down.

"I'm sorry, Mother. Go downstairs. You should rest."

"I shall. Not. Rest." Brave hopeless defiance. She walked on past you and out through the doorway and started to go down the stairs before an idea occurred to her and she went back to the door and slammed it as hard as she could, and then we listened to the sound of her footsteps lurching in defeated retreat slowly down the stairs.

You carried the briefcase away to a safer place in the bedroom. When you returned your hair was neatly back in its pile on top of your head.

"That was a little ugly wasn't it? She doesn't realize, but I'm trying to protect her, it's not just selfishness. But we've got things to do. Haven't we? I'm going to take my bath now." You picked up a lipstick and wrote the word MISHIMA on the wall.

MISHIMA

It was like a death rite. You wanted us to be clean for it, you said.

You were in the tub. You sank down below the level of the water when I came in to use the mirror to shave. You'd told me to shave.

"It's funny how your hair always falls into a natural parting," you said.

I drew the razor blade down below my chin and scraped it across my throat. "You've never told me what you did in the years between."

You lifted your shoulders up out of the bathwater, then let them fall again. "I had some adventures, I can't remember them all . . . Did your mother make you wear your hair like that? Is that how you looked when you were a schoolboy?" I pinched my nose to one side and got ready to push the razor up and down between my mouth and nostril. That made you laugh. "You're really very old-fashioned, aren't you? Everyone I know uses an electric razor. My father didn't use one."

"I think I'll leave it," I said. "I think I'm going to grow a mustache."

You lifted up your right arm and swabbed at your underarm with the soap. You examined the wet hairs there.

"Do you like hair on a woman? If I was your girlfriend, is that how you would like me to be?"

I worked at the rest of my face. Shaved fast, but fastidiously.

"Prince Boothby," I said, as I compared the length of my sideburns, "killed himself because it was such a bore getting dressed and undressed every day."

"Pass me a towel. I think I'm ready to get out."

I passed a towel over without looking back. You stood in the tepid water, daring me to notice your body. I dabbed my face with aftershave. Penhaligon's, it had belonged to your father.

"It's good to smell nice. I'm glad you're going to be smelling nice."

I dipped my fingertips in a pot of hair grease, rubbed them together and ran the pomade through my hair, eliminating any hint of a parting. "What are you going to wear?"

"I don't know if I want to wear anything at all. What are you going to wear?"

"My suit. My white linen suit, the one I came to England in."

You stood behind me. You rested your chin on my shoulder. "Couples are meant to look alike. Like owners and their dogs. We don't look alike. Except for the shape of our faces. We've got the same shape face."

"Dry yourself. I'll be in the room."

I left the bathroom. I watched you in the doorway. You thought I'd gone to the bedroom. You went up close to the mirror. Your towel fell half away from your body. The anticipation of your father's death was doing something weird to the color of your skin. I watched you bring your hands up to your face and stroke it as if it was the face of a strange and marvelous lover.

I was waiting for you inside the room. I sat cross-legged on the floor. You were wearing your blue silk kimono. You walked toward me, then abruptly veered away and went over to the window. You sat on the radiator and pulled the curtain back so you could look down at the street. A dying streetlight flickered across your body.

"We should be happy now," you said. "Isn't that what we're meant to feel?"

"I'm happy."

"Are you? I hope so. I was expecting a kind of ecstasy."

"Are you ready?"

"There are people down there. I can see women with shopping trolleys, one of them's wiping the sweat from her brow. Look. Over there the local karate kids doing their best to look threatening and mean. The commuters are crossing the road to avoid them. Are they often there? I don't remember ever seeing them before. And there are a lot of cats, I didn't realize there were so many cats."

"Are you listening? I know it all now. It's time to tell. March sixteenth, nineteen eighty. On the motorway going west—"

"I'm frightened, Tierney. Maybe I don't need it now. Maybe I've got to the point that I needed to get to."

"Heinrich von Kleist killed himself when he was thirty-four. He spent the last ten years of his life looking for the person he could meet death with."

You rubbed the window clear of your breath. "Meet is a silly word. But you're right. This moment would pass and mean nothing if the next thing didn't come. I don't want to put anything else on though. This is how I want to do it. I'm cold."

You let the curtain fall back and walked to where I was sitting. You sat facing me, cross-legged like me.

"I'm ready," you said.

I said nothing. Spun out the silence.

"Tierney. I'm ready."

"The whole thing?"

We looked at each other. Finally connected.

"Your hair is already falling back into its parting. Do you know how much it hurts me to think I'll probably never notice that again?"

"On the motorway," I said.

"On the motorway," you said, repeating what I'd said so sternly in a whisper that was full of tenderness and hope.

You sit on the floor with your head resting against the wall. It's time to talk. Man kills woman.

March 16, 1980. It's late morning. Are you listening? A sunny cold day. Ivory drives down in his Jaguar from Norfolk to London. He deals with some correspondence at his therapy room in West Hampstead, then drives across to Holloway Road. He tries, maybe over a cup of tea, perhaps something stronger, to persuade Helen one final time. No dice. Her Catholic weakness is more powerful than his decadent strength. She hates herself for it, this is the one thing she's never been able to grant him.

He leaves her, probably weeping, in the informal sitting room. He needs company for this, his final endeavor. He makes a failed telephone call, to you. Goes up to the surgery, unlocks the doctor's desk, takes out something wrapped in a white cotton sheath, then goes upstairs to Reiko's apartment. We're going to Japan, he says.

Helen sees them off. She waves as the Jaguar pulls away. She knew where they were going.

Did Reiko recognize that they were on the wrong road for Heathrow? Whatever, she probably didn't make a fuss, she would have just sat there, hands clasped in her lap, waiting so patiently for her husband to tell her what to do. March 16, 1980. On the road going west out of town. Ivory pulls the car over to the side of the road. There's a candy store just there, but that's not why they've stopped. From a cloth sheath by his feet, he withdraws his Mishima sword. Reiko would have seen him do it, she'd have known what he was going to do with it, the final outrage, making her, who so wanted to become a European, die in a comic-book samurai way. Nothing she can do, accept. Ivory swings the sword in the narrow space of the car interior. Reiko lifts her chin. Beside them, on the sidewalk, a family is entering the candy store. The youngest child, a boy named Gary, dressed in a green anorak, looks inside the car. Gary will have a lot of nightmares from that day on. The same image in every nightmare—stern smiling Ivory slashing the sword into his second wife's throat, a bubble of blood, then a rush of the stuff, he lets the sword drop, it hits her knees, cuts into them, falls to rest on her twitching feet. Ivory might then have said something in Japanese, I don't know what, perhaps the words he once claimed Mishima had said to him: "Isshun no seimei no nenshō"—a moment of burning life—or "Tōsui"—rapture—or maybe he was just asking her how she felt, but Gary did see him move his lips. And then he checked his wing mirror before he pulled back onto the road.

On the road going west, the woman's head lolls in the passenger's seat, her throat scythed open with the samurai sword. Ivory drives fast. Past the abandoned Hoover factory. Past the sign to the Polish cemetery. Under the streetlights dwarfishly low because of the road's proximity to the military airport. Past the sign to the airport. Planes angle in low overhead. Ivory switches to the fast lane. The people he overtakes each catch a brief horrible glimpse of the dead woman still bleeding and the mustachioed driver beside her, seat well back, arms almost straight to the wheel, what might be a smile on his face or just the rictus of an asthmatic struggling to exhale air and breathe. Roadworks up ahead. Like a joyrider or a Hollywood stunt ace, he pulls up the handbrake and twists the wheel, and the car, smoking tires, a wail of rubber, shoots through the gap in the median divide and executes a complete turn—the handbrake down again, back through the gap, the car shudders and rolls, then is corrected and speeds back east, speeding on the wrong side of the road, scattering cars ahead like timid metal insects scuttling from danger. He's smiling now for sure, Ivory the crazy driver, a mellow suicide waiting for the impact which takes an age to come. For a while he's untouchable. Cars crash into the central railing or spin out onto the grass verge, roll on two wheels or on their backs, wheels angry spinning, over the fields toward the Polish cemetery. Taxis shunt into taxis, passenger cars twist and spin and make figure of eights in the road, trunks spring open and suitcases lose their clasps and luggage ribbons out, new bathing suits bought by R.A.F. wives for foreign beaches cup the air and drift onto windshields, onto car roofs, hats catch the breeze and lift up, into the air, up toward the planes coming down overhead. Men and women struggle out of the twisted skins of their automobiles, some bleeding, some hurt, some with a hand over the faces of their crying children, or shaking a fist into the air, and Ivory speeds on. On the wrong side of the road, the woman's throat an open ketchup laugh, Ivory shaking now with fear and delight and anticipation, as the truck comes toward him, his immutable opposite, a Swedish truck with a load of pickled herrings, a big Volvo monster, nothing it can do, to take action now would condemn it to a jack-knife roll and ugly smoky death. People shut their eyes, cover their mouths with their hands, a vomit moment that impact. The Jaguar crumples, the truck keeps on, part of the car between its wheels and beneath its chassis, the truck hardly dented, the roar of air brakes can't cover the screech of metal and human sandwiched between the truck and the road. A shuddering awful moment for anyone to see or hear. Smoke rises up from the dead stained road. From the airplanes coming down, the passengers can see people like insects scurrying or still. Cars as if stacked horizontally, higgledy-piggledy, broken hoods kissing broken trunks. The eventual flashing lights of the emergency services. Down on the road, by the Hoover factory, there is blood on the road, there are tears in the air. The smell of death hangs, burning skin and dying automobiles. Dead Ivory. Thoroughly dead wife.

I waited, a long heavy pause. You just shook your head a little, the only reaction.

"And now? Can we see the book now? It's all I need."

"We have to do something first," you said. "Call it a reward."

You got up and went out into your bedroom and I waited for you and when you came back into the living room you were dressed for sex.

With your clothes off you always looked vulnerable. When you'd got out of the bath just before, your hair plastered down to your tattooed shoulder, your pale skin damp with a nicotine tinge, you had looked at me, suddenly startled, and your hand went up to cover your own eyes.

But you're not naked. You're wearing a bodice, laced, that reveals the curling brown hair of your cunt. Your sex corny clothes, as if once you're dressed for it, it would no longer have anything to do with the other parts of you. You approach me, hardly any expression on your face, the gentlest and solemnest of frowns. I move toward you and you stop. A pale muscle twitches at the top of your thigh. You take a step back, you don't want me to come to you, not yet, but I come to you, cut off your retreat, take your shoulders in my hands, your flesh a little oily from the stuff in your bath and painfully smooth against a catcher's hands.

You pull away, back to the edge of the room, nodding your head as you go. You smile at me, and this time I'm allowed to approach you and this time I'm allowed to unlace the top of your bodice, no more, your nipples exposed, cold goose-bumped skin.

Then to the space between the wall and the sofa, where you wait for me to join you. I hold you by your tight drawn waist. I soothe hair away from your forehead. I run my fingers around your wide lips, an ancient crack in the middle not entirely healed over, your tongue dipping out against my fingertips, first licking, then your mouth closes tight against my fingers, and your nostrils flare as you breathe as you suck as your eyes hold mine. Your mouth parts and my fingers withdraw to trace tongue-wet patterns and words on your face, on your throat, over your exposed cold tits, and you shiver and I keep on, words of abuse, of yearning, and names, Mary Tierney-to-be, Lizzie Sharp, poor Reiko, and your father's name written in capitals around your right nipple and in attempted saliva italic around your left.

I hold you there, trying to make you believe with the strength of my touch that there isn't anything else, my left hand hooked into your faded bleeding heart, thumb drawing a circle in the hair of your underarm, my right hand going down, a gentle path along the blue vein in your breast, then bumping down your ribs, slapping against your belly button (and a pause there to trace an imaginary Japanese dragon breathing fire all around it), flattening across the swell of your belly—and you try to pull away but I've got you fixed there, your arms angled in thwarted frozen flight, crazy statue dancer, my fingers now in the cleft of your ass, thumb searching for the vulvic opening while I try to find your mouth with mine but your face keeps dodging mine—cheeks flicking against nose, mouth finding ear, eyelids, strands of hair, never mouth, my fingers tracing now the sides of your cunt, trying to work

out what feeling or what bright image accompanies the answering pulse down the length of your body with every long
silent stroke, my mouth finally finding yours, the salty taste of
your tongue trapped against mine, your mouth opening wider,
stretched into a sudden surprising smile.

Frozen moments of struggle, of arms against arms, foreheads
locking, hands clenching before forced to withdraw, my cock
against your cunt, then pushed away and kissed by your ass,
the room nearly filled with the sound of our breathing, the
clothes I shed, small sacrificial piles of linen and cotton, as our
domestic ceremony takes us to each side and corner and angle
and unoccupied space of the room, our room, which had once
been Reiko's room, the sofa, the window, the floor, against the
table, trying to take it all into my lungs, the increasing smell
of you, bitter and sweet, as you lead me finally back to the
window again as if this always had been the necessary arena.

The side of your head resting against the glass, your only
movement your eyes as they flick to the center of the room
and up, to the ceiling. You lift your ass in the air, hold on to
the window ledge with your hands, small hands. I stand behind
you and you reach between your legs and pull me by my cock
toward you. My chin on your shoulder, my face next to yours,
cheek to cheek, the two of us looking out of the window, an
empty street below.

The two of us, my chest sweating against your arched warm
back, the cold sensation of your bodice cutting straps into my
belly, my hands large across the front of your thighs, mirror
reflection watching mirror reflection, your ass rocking into my
belly, my eyes blinded with your hair and my cock at your
cunt. And you shift away so it's at your ass and then I have it
to your cunt again and I have you now locked between me
and the window and you try to pull away and you call out
your name, and I force my cock up inside you and it takes
some force and this surprises me more than anything.

I thrusting into you. Fast motion, the sounds you make that
don't accord with anything I know about you. You push back
with your thighs and I push forward with mine, a rush and a
shiver that goes on for the longest ghostly time, your forehead

keeps hitting the window, and that's your choice, the growling sounds we make, we keep going, animals of need, your hair in my eyes, in my face, in my mouth, a strand of it between my teeth.

And when I came I came inside you and I made some noise and maybe that was what made you laugh. A brief moment of the two of us together, smiling hip-joined intimates overlooking an empty street; then you pulled away, slipped away, not demure, not denying, not ugly, just slipping back into the person you were most of the time.

I went to find my cigarettes and you stayed by the window, fingers carelessly dabbing at the liquid mix on your thighs, your eyes looking to the ceiling because that's where your father might be. And I didn't care, I could grant you this moment, because I expected it to be the beginning of something, and of course I was wrong.

I don't know what magic I expected. A sudden leap into freedom, perhaps. A happy innocent smile, maybe even a dance to the swirling strings of an invisible orchestra. Maybe this is the wrong way to go about it. Maybe you were right before. Hide from the truth, shirk from it. Pretend the dangerous threatening things don't exist and get on with the rest of it.

"Tierney?"

"Yes?"

"I can smell something burning."

I pulled on my suit, went downstairs to investigate. Into the formal sitting room where your mother crouched in front of the fire. She was heaving letters and Florentine notebooks into the fireplace and stuffing her face with candies from a plastic jar of Quality Street. She gave me a frightened look when I came in, and I flattered myself it was the kind of look she had reserved for her husband.

"I cannot trust you," she said, and I knew what she was burning and it was too late to save them. "The two of you. Have tried to cheat. Me. But his memory. Is safe. With me."

And then she ran. Tottering fast away out into the road, looking awkwardly for a bus to take her to church or Albania or maybe just to Matthew's place. To shake and cherish and love her dead man in the comfort of her son who hated her like he hated himself for being weak.

I followed her out. Caught up to her shivering in the sun at a bus stop on the Holloway Road, clutching a pensioner's travel pass and a few burned scraps of paper to her thin chest. I tried to persuade her back into the house. I tried charm. I pleaded with her and passersby stopped passing by to stare at me like it was a prelude to a rape.

She cursed me quietly. She was mad as hell. She waved me away like a priest would a ghost.

"Once. I let him down. Once Deborah. Let him down. We were not strong enough. To die with. Him. But you cannot beat. Me. I will protect his memory. I," she said grandly, "am prepared to live for ever."

I left her there. Do you understand what I'm saying? She's an old sick lady, she shouldn't be out there by herself. Doesn't that do anything to you? I tried calling Matthew's number but there was just a machine at the end of it. She hasn't come back. She might be out there still.

When I got back upstairs you were standing in the same place, between the sofa and the tall window, looking down at the street. You were dressed in the blue kimono, and you'd painted yourself into an image of horror. Lurid stripes of scarlet slashed across your cheeks. Midnight Blue plastered around your eyes and Indian Sugar smeared over your lips. Your eyelashes weighed down with a load of mascara, your eyebrows heavy with kohl, and your exposed nipples blushing with rouge. Did you look in the mirror while you did that? What are you now? All your father's women?

And then you were gone. Retreated back inside yourself. Standing by the window looking down over the street. Empty in your kimono. Waiting for something more that I couldn't give. Ivory's daughter liked it up the bum, that's what Wheel had told me once, but you didn't especially, did you? Protecting your cunt, it was your good deed to the world. Sex makes babies and Daddy's poison went to you and you don't want to pass it down to any more babies, do you? Or were you just saving yourself for him?

There are people knocking on the door. Do you hear the knocks on the door? If I touched you now would you shout? Whatever, just the slightest flinch from you. No more than that. I can use words to bring you back. Man kills woman. Women kill woman. Man kills man. He made that final telephone call to you the day of his death, his final failed seduction, with Reiko the reliable standby. Tally up the deaths—Miss P——'s mama, poor little Reiko, Silvertown George, maybe Lizzie Sharp, no one knows what happened to her—three and a half, that's all, and at least one is canceled out because Helen, after all, is going to live forever.

Start again. Begin again.

You know how it started, and where. That afternoon on the Common, picnicking on the slope, looking down on Boston.

What? You lift up the lipstick to write. GO HOME YANK. Ignore that. You're making me mad. Continue. MY HEART BE-LONGS TO DADDY.

We'd finished one bottle of wine and were getting to work with another and you still wouldn't tell me why you hated picnics so much and wouldn't allow me that this one was different.

I know why you hate picnics so much. It was a picnic long ago in Regent's Park when you first knew how much you hated your father.

MAN KILLS WOMAN. Yes, man kills woman. That's what it said in the newspaper headline and that's what you believe. Sing along with me. Say this with me. Man kills woman. Man kills woman. Man takes woman for a walk. Man takes woman to the park. Man and woman go to duck pond. Man pushes woman into water. Man watches woman drown. Man smiles to see woman drown. Man kills woman. Man writes letters to woman. Letters make woman cry. Man makes woman cry. Man kills woman. Man takes woman to top of tall building. Observation deck on top of tall building. Man lifts woman by shoulders. Man throws woman off tall building. Man watches woman fall. Woman hits ground. Man takes elevator down. Man whistles song as man walks away. Man kills woman. Man flatters woman. Man has pet names for woman. Man calls woman sweetheart. Man dresses woman in Hollywood clothes. Man pampers beautiful woman. Man ruins woman. Man takes woman's beauty and grinds it away. Man kills woman. Man cuts woman into tiny pieces. Man boils pieces into stew. Man eats woman stew. Man feeds leftovers to his dog. Man kills woman. Man gives woman money. Money makes woman do things. Woman refuses money. Man kills woman. Man meets woman. Man buys chocolates for woman. Man marries woman. Man builds house for woman. Man and woman live in house that man built for woman. Man leaves woman. Woman cries. Woman dies. Man kills woman. Man kills woman. Man kills woman. Man takes woman for spin in car. Man and woman drive out of town. Man slices woman's throat with Japanese sword. Man kills woman. Man loves woman. Man kills woman. Man buys lipstick for woman. Man kills woman.

You like that, don't you? I see you smile through the paint. That's how you think things are. Things don't have to be like that. Despise me if you like, but I think things can be simpler than that. You shake your head, jerky action like your mother.

We're not getting very far. You can make a new start, you can. Build on the little things you say you know. Buy a pooch. Name it Gaspard. Or Reiko or Lizzie. Or something neutral and new. Call it Fido or Rex or Goofy.

You could drive me away, is that what you're doing? You don't look such a catch dressed up like that, you know. The voodoo goo smeared all across your face. Are those tears that are coming down? A trickle of blood from your ruined hymen smeared and cracked along your thigh. Look at me. Come on, look at me. I can deal with things. I found what you wanted. Maybe I can get the book written. Perhaps start at the end, work back from there. Somewhere I've got the beginning of a first draft, little boy Ivory's first few lives. And that means I'm up already on Julian Brougham Calder, my book becomes less imaginary than all of his. All that's left is the *Last Things* and then I'll know it all. Look at me, I'm a Red Sox fan and there's no greater penance than that.

There are too many voices, too many stories. Brougham Calder's tales of wartime treacheries and loves, your childhood stories of hatred and loss, Helen's staccato evasions, your brother's desperate whine. They're all mixed up, the tape transcriptions—Mishima looking for a suicide partner up in Reiko's room, death on a Sussex lawn where the Sniffer plays Norfolk crokey and there are live bloodied bodies beneath the wreckage of the afternoon, a Japanese tour bus taking Miss P—— and her dead picnicking mother out to a Blitz on Hampstead Heath, Nick Wheel and his flipper bully friend play strip chemin de fer with Lizzie Sharp while dutiful Reiko in punk bondage gear dutifully vacuums the hall, and over this, over all of this, look up, look above, see him grinning up above, Ivory somewhere looming, his monster grin, his dark mustache, his eyes glittering with cruelty and the utter absence of hope.

Look out at the street. I think we've got company. There are people on the street. I can see Nick Wheel and I can see Roland Gibbs. What do you think they have to talk about?

Suddenly you stir. A graffiti-daubed statue coming to life. What are you doing? Where are you going? To the kitchenette? Hungry? A post-coital refrigerator raid? Not the kitchenette, you're heading for the bedroom, and I'm with you. Watch you stand certainly at your open wardrobe. Off drops the kimono, and you pull some clothes around you, a slim little white cocktail frock, a string of your mother's pearls around your neck, yes, and then what? Into the bathroom. You can't lose me that easy, you lean blindly against the sink, your face closed-eyed to the mirror. I stand in the doorway, admiring your fingers as they expertly twist off the lid of the jar of cleansing lotion. Cotton wool dabs and off comes the goo. Lotion and cotton and slaps of water and rough work with a reddened face. "Party time, Tierney." Your words hoarse with unaccustomed speech. A smile twists your lips. You lift your arms to inspect the smooth skin yet to spoil. "And I've got something to show you. I'll leave it in the corner. A lot of pages but it won't take time to read."

I follow you into the bedroom, watch you crouch down, watch you reach beneath the bed, watch you poke your hands past the few peahen feathers still fluttering there, and you pull out a brown leather briefcase, battered, *W.I.* monogrammed upon the flap. And out of it, magically, a manuscript, fastened together with thick rubber bands, the top sheet written on in big arrogant scrawl, *William Ivory's Doctrine of Last Things*. Out of the bedroom, into the corridor, into the living room, the manuscript placed so reverently in the corner beneath lipstick words.

I pick it up. I hold it. The final book, the missing thing. I close my eyes and fan the pages and feel the corners bite into my skin.

He left the letter on his desk in the Little Room of his Norfolk house. See the ocean off in the distance. See the ruined priory on the horizon. Feel the wind blustering over the fields. His house, tidy and alone, old Norfolk brick and flint, inside it is empty. Its master died over thirteen years ago, and over thirteen years ago you and your mother and your brother hastily covered the grand piano with a dust sheet. You piled his black china away inside wooden cupboards. The three of you wandered disconsolately, separately about the house, all of you hunched against his presence. You were the first to go into the Little Room, to find the letter on his desk. It was going to be for you, his final book; you took the letter away with you and you didn't say a word about it to the others, and his Norwich lawyer duly sent it by mail at the appointed time, the thirteenth of your birthdays after his death. He wrote your name on a scrap of paper clipped to the top, handwritten sheet. Your legacy.

And you didn't want it, but they all did. And later, when

your infrequent attempts to uncover the truth (how many times did you try? how many came before me?) hit a pretty locked door of silence, then the final book became your pretty opening key.

They all wanted it. Roland Gibbs, the front man (what shabby dull secret is he protecting?), Judge Brougham-Calder, Nick Wheel (your own little secret agent, the one you sent to keep tabs on me, the most dispassionate of these truth seekers, he only wanted to know what was really in the mind of his monster hero), even Nanny Brennan, still out to protect the memories of her dead family. They'd heard about it, he'd alluded to it, in letters, in conversation, in a TV interview. The world according to William Ivory, the secrets of his class. The legend of his final book remained and grew. Like a poker-faced blackmailer who whispers, *I know your guilty secret*, Ivory spread fear after death. Anyone who had ever slighted him was made to squirm. It was reputed to be the ultimate thing, the truth as he saw it through those dangerous eyes that no one will tell me the color of.

What was that sound? The front door slams. Footsteps down below. Music. Where's that music coming from? That slow French melody. Sounds like from the surgery. Do you hear it? Where are you? Your father giving us a slow serenade. Music to remember to. I go downstairs, the manuscript under my arm, pages curling in the fall breeze; not the surgery, farther down below, to the first floor, the grand piano suddenly back in tune in the formal drawing room. Nick Wheel at the keyboard playing some airy *fin-de-siècle* stuff, sweet sad melodies on the point of exhaustion. You leaning against the piano, white cocktail flapper, inexpertly smoking a cigarette that's flattened on one side. Wheel gives me a gentle nod of the head, in time to the rhythm of his playing.

The song slowly ends. You clap your appreciation, you call out my name.

"Tierney. So glad you could make it."

Wheel starts another tune, head close down to the keys, shoulders swaying. You look about the room, disappointed, one hand sadly in the air as if it's your birthday party and you're holding a solitary balloon and no one has come to celebrate with you.

Your mother loved him and feared him. She tried to protect his memory. You, you wanted to destroy it. But at least you had the guts to remove the top page of his *Last Things* and you steeled yourself to read it. As, finally, do I. With Wheel beside me, the piano abandoned, you turning alone in the center of the room, Wheel's desire for knowledge tainted now by greed, that's what he was talking to Gibbs about, dollar cash-register signs in his eyes as he imagines the lucre these fancy secrets will bring. I fight back the fear, the worry of what I will find there, the truth it will shine on my own poor task. There it sits. Approach it. Own it.

I remove the rubber bands. Ignore the sound of Wheel's avaricious breath panting in my ear. Won't let him rush me. These pages are too precious to be treated with anything but care. The top page with your name written on it in your father's hand. I put it aside and square off the remainder. Remove the title page. *William Ivory's Doctrine of Last Things.* Reveal the first page. Blank. And the second. Blank. Nothing written upon it at all. Just the page number, 2. Flip through them all. Throw them around. Watch a teary Wheel make paper boats and paper airplanes and paper hats. And there is nothing written on any of them at all. Just six hundred and sixty scrupulously numbered blank pages. Twelve blank pages for each year of Ivory's life.

Decadent Pleasures was really his final word, and after that there was nothing more to be done. The sickly will to death of *Morita*, and then the picking at neurotic secrets offered by patients who paid him more than they could afford. *Last Things* was his final joke and his final lesson and I admire him all the more for it. To show there was nothing worth waiting for, it's almost an expression of hope.

Nick Wheel goes out onto the street with a paper hat on his head and a paper airplane in his hand. Let's go upstairs, take my hand, let's go back to our room and watch him from our window.

There he is, you see him? He pushes past Roland Gibbs (whatever secret he's been guarding it's safely hidden now, he can alert the others: for them at least Ivory is finally truly dead— Is it anything to do with you, the trite Gibbs secret? You studied in Brighton once. I've seen the way he looks at co-eds) and watch him, watch Wheel as he throws the airplane into the air and runs after it; it catches the breeze and he runs beneath it, and don't you want to applaud as he finally catches it in his left hand so stylishly behind his back?

William Ivory comes calling at night. The grinning mustachioed shade, the man with the power. He fills this house with his pride, fills our identical dreams with cruelty. I see him in the surgery, in the formal sitting room, preparing something grand in the kitchen, driving away from the house in his crumpled Jaguar.

And during the day we watch his image on the VCR. Over and over. Ivory on a black-and-white interview show in the early 1970s. Let's watch the TV, baby.

Ooh, Daddy looks grand in close-up. He's a natural for the screen, flirtatious and pugnacious, handsome and anachronistic and bold. His sharp eyes in his muscled face glinting with the pleasure of his inevitable triumph at the end of this duel. The visual conceit of the show is the shadow world around the highlighted face, the darkness that surrounds, so the face is everything, the key, the window, the wall, the soul. His eyes are like holes cut in the centers of mirrors, his voice is like James Mason's, smooth and damp around a hidden phallic sword. Sometimes he lifts a cigarette to his mouth and the program's directors like what happens then, the smoke clouding out from his mouth and dispersing around his head in a disappointed halo. And sometimes he lifts his hands when he wants to make a point or just when he wants to deflect the attention of his interrogator, and while he talks about decadence and the fleeting chance at perfection his hands chop down against the air by the side of his face, and then his fingers form a ruined cathedral in front of his mouth and his voice slides through it like a particularly sinister god's.

———

You're puking. Well, that's a start. Freeze the frame. Hold his face there hiding behind the ruined cathedral of his fingers. Come on. Move. Feel some more. Puke some more. I will feed you and stick my fingers down your throat. I will stay with you. I will clean up your shit and your puke. I will tell stories to you. You held yourself so close in your blue summer dress. Remember? Out in Boston. On the Common.

Where are you now? Don't look to the street. There's nothing in the street. Gibbs and Wheel flitter and die in the shadows. Do you want to go to Sweden now? To the outskirts of Stockholm to find a retired truck driver with ruined nerves? Look at me. Don't think to escape. I can bring you back. Prove your existence with my story. Again and again if necessary. All the truth is contained in there. You held yourself so close in your blue summer dress. You brushed a wasp away from the curling slices of Italian meat and you looked at me solemnly. You hadn't been looking at me for a while. Then you took that envelope out of your bag. A silver stick of French lipstick had snuck inside and you lifted it out and you looked at it as if you didn't know what it was for a moment—